For William and Rosalind
—with love

To Execute an Executioner

The executioner checked in his side mirror, and he saw that the motorcyclist had pulled out from behind his car, and was now poised to come alongside. He saw that the young man on the motorcycle had reached inside his bag that hung across his chest, that he steered the motorcycle only with his right hand.

The executioner was aware of the shape beside him, looming close to his wound-down window.

He saw that the motorcycle was virtually against the side of his car.

He saw the grin on the face of the rider, and the rider's arm was outstretched above the roof of his car.

He heard the thump of an impact on the roof of his car.

Cold sweat, sweat racing on his chest, in his groin. He could not stop. He could not pull over. He was reaching for his pistol, and he was watching the motorcycle power away ahead of him, but what could he do? He couldn't fire through the windshield.

The rider turned one last time to wave, and to see that the box was held to the roof of the executioner's low-slung car. The metal box contained two pounds' weight of commercial explosive, a detonator, and a stopwatch wired to explode the detonator and the polar-amon gelignite in forty-five seconds. . . .

GERALD SEYMOUR

SEYMOUR

THE RUNNING TARGET

HarperPaperbacks
A Division of HarperCollinsPublishers

This is a work of fiction. The characters, incidents, and dialogues are products of the author's imagination and are not to be construed as real. Any resemblance to actual events or persons, living or dead, is entirely coincidental.

HarperPaperbacks   *A Division of* HarperCollins*Publishers*
10 East 53rd Street, New York, N.Y. 10022

This book is published by arrangement with William Morrow and Company.

Cover photo by Herman Estevez

First HarperPaperbacks printing: February 1991

Printed in the United States of America

HarperPaperbacks and colophon are trademarks of HarperCollins*Publishers*

10 9 8 7 6 5 4 3 2 1

Prologue ✣

June 25, 1982

She was led down the iron steps and across the hallway and out into the chill of the morning. She would have gone on her toes to protect the rawness of the wounded flesh on the soles of her feet, but the guards on either side of her held her firmly above her elbows and she was hurried across a chip-stone yard. She did not cry out. She did not flinch from the pain that burst into her body from her feet.

There was a jeep parked on the far side of the yard. Beyond it four posts in front of a sandbagged wall. There were two groups of soldiers lounging on the ice wet grass between the jeep and the stakes and some were cleaning their rifles. She saw the ropes that were knotted to the posts. They

✣ 1 ✣

were waiting to do their work, but she was not a part of that work.

At the back of the jeep she was handcuffed, then lifted roughly inside under the loose canvas. Her escorts climbed in after her. She was pushed to the floor where the fuel fumes merged with the sweat stench of the black and hooded *chador*. The jeep lurched forward. She heard the exchange between the driver and the sentries at the gate, and then she heard the early morning choking whine of the street traffic. She closed her eyes. There was nothing to see. She had learned when she was taken to the jail, three months before, that her ears were to be her eyes.

It was an hour's journey to the airfield.

The canvas at the back of the jeep was raised, the tail dropped. She was levered out of the jeep. For a moment she was slumped on the tarmac, before the guards hoisted her to her feet. She saw no pity in their faces, she thought that they hated her as their enemy. She knew where she was. As a child she had many times been brought here by her mother to welcome home her father from field exercises away from the capital. She could remember soldiers and junior officers, all polished and creased and snapping to attention to salute her father as he passed them. She could remember the disciplined laughter all around her as she had broken free from her mother's hand and raced forward to jump at her father's chest. Precious memories now. She was shepherded by her guards up the rear ramp of the aircraft.

As she was taken forward in the closed cave of the aircraft the light of the morning died and the soldiers tucked in their boots and shifted their rucksacks and their weapons to allow her and her escorts to pass. They took her to the front of the aircraft to where some seats had been curtained off with sacking. The guard who fastened the seatbelt across her waist leered into her face, and his breath was heavy with chilies. The engine pitch rose, the aircraft stumbled forward.

The flight from Tehran to Tabriz, a distance of 350 miles, took seventy-five minutes. She did not turn her head. She did not try to look out of the small porthole window behind her left ear. She did not need to see the gold sun streaming from behind the great mountain of Damavand. She sat still, unmoving, unspeaking. She found a place on the cabin floor in front of her, a place among the ammunition boxes and the ration crates. She stared down at the place.

It was an old aircraft. She heard the rumble of the engines and sometimes the cough of a missed stroke, she heard these sounds above and dominating the reading of the Koran from beyond the sacking screen. Her guards talked quietly and kept their eyes from her, as if contact with her could contaminate them, taint their souls. She tried not to think. Was her short life an achievement, was it wasted? Better to shut her mind to thoughts.

The pitch of the aircraft changed. She closed her eyes. She had no God, she willed courage into her body.

The transporter rattled down onto the long strip of the Tabriz field and the interior was flooded with light and the squeal of the tail ramp going down. After the pilot had braked and the aircraft had stopped, she was kept in her seat until the last of the soldiers on the far side of the sacking screen had gone with their kit and weapons and ammunition and food. Their voices trailed away from her. She wanted so much to be brave. She wanted so much to be worthy of her father. The guards unfastened the safety belt. They made her stand. From a plastic bag one of the guards took a loose white robe, with open seams and tapes under the armpits. The white robe was lifted over her head, and the tapes were tied at the sides. She was alone. In four days she would have been eighteen. She had been brought to the second city of her native country for public execution.

They led her down the echoing interior of the

aircraft, out into the bold crisp sunlight of the morning. She was a small, waif figure among the men. She wanted to think of her father, and she could not because the pain of her body had crept through to her mind. She wondered if her father, at his same moment, at the moment when he was lashed to the post in the garden of the Evin jail, had thought of her, his daughter. A short and hazed thought, and then gone. The lorry waiting a few feet from the aircraft ramp spilled out its exhaust fumes over them. A guard on each elbow, half walked her, half carried her to the back of the lorry, and a small knot of men waited there for her arrival. The young Mullah was there. She had stood in front of him in the courtroom high in Block One of the Evin jail in the late afternoon, only yesterday. Perhaps he had traveled from Tehran to Tabriz last night, after he had heard the case against her, weighed it, passed judgment, announced sentence. Perhaps he had boarded the aircraft after her and sat away from her and among the soldiers. It was of little matter. The Mullah stared into her face. She tried to stare back at him, but her guards pulled her forward to the back of the lorry and lifted her bodily up and inside. The Mullah had taken a very few minutes to hear her case. She had not spoken in her defense. She wanted it over. She did not know how long she could stay brave.

The lorry drove into Tabriz. She was not innocent of the crime of which she had been convicted. Yes, she had thrown the grenade. And yes, her regret was very keen that it had not killed more of the pigs. She knew why she had been brought to Tabriz, she knew it was the custom of the regime to exact retribution and punishment at the scene of the crime.

Sometimes the lorry was held up in traffic that not even the bellow of a siren could clear. Slow, jerking progress. She pictured in her mind the road they were taking. It was the same route that she had traveled with the two boys into the city, the heart of the city and the offices of the *pasdaran*. To her mind, the *pasdaran* were the symbol of slavery, repression, bigotry. The Islamic Revolutionary Guards were the embodiment of an evil that had consumed her nation . . .

The lorry stopped. The hands of the guards rested on her arms. She saw that they watched her, eager to see how she would be, in the last minutes. They lifted her from the wooden seat of the lorry, propelled her toward the open end of the lorry. Numbness in her mind, a quivering weakness at her knees. She heard the bellowing of a loudspeaker, and realized that it was the same voice, hushed and musical then, that had sentenced her to death late yesterday. She stood at the edge of the lorry's floor. There were people as far as she could see. A roar greeted the sight of her. The sound of the voices came at her as waves across shingle, repeated and again. Impossible to make out what was shouted because her ears were still confused by the pressure drop of the aircraft. The faces told her. The faces were shouting their hatred, their pleasure at what was to happen to her. As far as she could see, faces of hate and faces of pleasure. She could not see the Mullah but she heard the excitement in the shrillness of his voice.

Hands reached up for her. She was lifted down from the lorry. No pain in the soles of her feet now. Her guards dragged her forward, and men in uniform forced a passage clear ahead of them.

She saw the crane.

The crane was on a platform behind the cab of a flatbed truck. The truck was outside the front gate of the offices of the *pasdaran*. The truck was parked where she had thrown the grenade, where the two boys who had been with her were shot down, where she had been captured. There was a table of heavy wood under the lowered arm of the crane. There was a noosed rope hanging from the crane, and beside it a man in the combat uniform of the *pasdaran*. He was stout, heavily bearded. At the side of his leg he held a long strip of leather.

The guards lifted her very easily onto the table. She gazed around her. She was aware that the executioner now crouched beside her and she felt the tightness of the leather strip at her ankles. So ridiculous. So ridiculous that so many had come to watch the putting to death of so small a person, so young a person. So ridiculous, all of those people in front of her, below her. So ridiculous that she smiled. Her face broke into a smile. The smile of her youth. The smile of her puzzlement. She heard the Mullah's voice above all the thousand other voices in unison. And then suddenly the shouting had gone.

A great booming quiet around them as the executioner draped round her neck the string that carried the white cardboard sheet on which was spelled out in large characters her crime. His fingers fumbled with the noose of the rope. He pulled the noose over her head, tightened it under her chin.

He had never known such quiet.

They would all remember her, all of those who watched the handcuffed girl in the white robe, standing alone on the table as the executioner jumped down.

The arm of the crane surged upward.

She died painfully, struggling, but quickly.

For two hours, high above the street, her body hung from the arm of the crane.

The old man made his way along the corridor.

He was an institution in the building, a throwback really to the days before the Service had been equipped with consoles, software and instant communications. In his own way the messenger as something of a celebrity at Century House because of the time he had been with the Service. almost alone, had known intimately the warren of the former offices that spanned Queen Anne's Gate and Broadway; he had been on the payroll under seven Directors General, and it had become difficult for any of the older people at Century to imagine being able to cope without him. His approach was slow. He had never quite mastered the artificial limb fitted below the right kneecap. He had been a young man when he had lost his leg, a corporal of infantry on Garrison duty in Palestine when he had stepped on a crude antipersonnel mine. He was paid for a thirty-eight-hour week, and not a week went by when he was inside Century for less than sixty hours.

Across the Thames, muffled by the sealed windows of the tower block, Big Ben struck nine-thirty. The steel toe and heel caps of the messenger's shoes scraped along the composite tiles. There was silence around him. Office doors locked, rooms darkened. But he could see the light at the distant finishing post of the corridor. This evening, every weekday evening, the messenger performed a personal service for Mr. Matthew Furniss. He carried by hand the transcript of the main evening news bulletin on the Home Service of Tehran Radio, monitored and translated at th BBC premises at Caversham, relayed by telex Foreign and Commonwealth Office, and thence Century.

He paused at the door. The transcript was gripped between his thumb and a nicotined finger. He looked through the dusk of the open plan area and toward the light shaft that was the door into the inner office of Mr. Furniss. He knocked.

"Come."

The messenger thought that Mr. Furniss had a lovely voice, the sort of voice that would have sounded lovely on the wireless. He thought Mr. Furniss with his lovely voice was also a lovely man. He thought Mr. Matthew Furniss was the best of the Old Guard at Century, and a proper gentleman.

"You're so kind, Harry. . . . Bless you, and you should have been home hours ago."

It was a sort of a ritual, because the messenger brought the transcript every weekday evening, and every weekday evening Mr. Furniss seemed so pleasantly surprised and grateful, and he thought that evening that Mr. Furniss looked rotten, like the world was on top of him. The messenger knew enough about the man, plenty, as much as anybody at Century, because the messenger's wife in the years gone by had baby-sat, minded the girls, for Mr. and Mrs. Furniss. The room stank of pipe tobacco and the ash bowl was brimming. That was not usual, nor was the bottle of Grant's that was on the desk and had taken a beating.

"No problem, sir . . ." The messenger handed over the transcript.

Twenty-four hours earlier, to the minute, the messenger had delivered the previous monitored and translated news bulletin from the Home Service of Tehran radio. It was all very clear in the messenger's memory. Mr. Matthew Furniss had given him his chirpy and conspiratorial smile and eased back in his chair to gut the résumé, and the chair had snapped forward, and the paperwork had flaked down from his hands onto the desk top, and he'd looked as if he'd been hit. That had been last night. . . . The messenger watched. He peered through the smoke haze. The evening's transcript was on the desk and Mr. Matthew Furniss was scanning it, taking it line by line. He stopped, he looked as if he was unwilling to believe what he read.

The messenger stood by the door. He saw the fist over the transcript clench, saw the knuckles whiten.

"The bastards . . . the filthy, vicious bastards . . ."

"That's not like you, Mr. Furniss."

"The wicked, fucking bastards . . ."

"Not at all like you, sir."

"They hanged her."

"Hanged who, sir?"

The messenger had seen the moment of weakness, but it was gone. Furniss poured a generous measure of the whiskey into a fresh glass and offered it to the messenger, and the small glass already on the desk was filled, splashed to the top. The position of the messenger at Century was indeed unique, no other uniformed servant of the Service would have been offered hospitality in the office of the senior Desk man. The messenger bent and scratched at his knee where the strapping chafed.

"The daughter of a friend of mine, Harry . . . What you brought me last night told me that it was on their radio that she'd been tried, found guilty, sentenced, probably a short ten minutes of playacting at justice. And tonight it says that she's been executed. Same age as our girls, roughly . . . a sweet kid . . ."

"If anyone harmed your girls, Mr. Furniss, I'd want to kill them."

"Yes, Harry . . . I'll drive you home. Be a good chap, find yourself a chair outside, just one phone."

The messenger sat himself down in the outer office. He could not help but hear. Carrying papers, post, internal memoranda around the corridors of Century he knew so much, eavesdropped so often. He heard Mr. Furniss place, through the operator, a call to California. He heard the calm voice on the far side of the partition wall. "Kate, that's you, Kate? It's Mattie. I'm very sorry, Kate, but I've awful news. It's Juliette, she died this morning in Tabriz. Put to death. I'm terribly, terribly sorry, Kate, and our love to you and Charlie. . . . You're still going to send him? Of course, we'll look after Charlie, whenever you think he's ready to come. . . . Kate, our very sincere sympathy." He heard the telephone placed down gently. That was awful, hanging a girl, that was diabolical. There was no call for hanging seventeen-year-old girls, not in Harry's book. Mr. Furniss was in the doorway, coat over his arm.

"Time we were going home, Harry."

Chapter ❖ 1

 ahmood Shabro always invited Charlie Eshraq when he threw a thrash in his office. Shabro had known his father, and his sister and his uncle. The wide windows looked out onto the busy east end of Kensington High Street. There was a teak veneer desk and shelves and cabinets. There was a computer console in the corner, a pile carpet on the floor with a centerpiece of a good rug brought many years before from home. The easy chairs were pushed against the walls that were covered with photographs of a far away country—mosques, landscapes, a bazaar scene, a portrait of an officer in full dress uniform and two rows of medals. Mahmood Shabro was somewhat rare among the London exile community, he had done well. And when he did better, when he had clinched a deal, he celebrated, and he asked the less fortunate of his community to push out the boat with him.

Mahmood Shabro was a conduit for electrical goods going down to the Gulf. Not your low-life stuff from Taiwan and Korea, but high quality from Finland and West Germany and Italy. He didn't do badly. He liked to say that the oil rich buggers down in the Emirates were putty to him.

Charlie could put up with the cant and boasting of the Shabro husband and wife, and he could put up with the caviar and the canapés, and the champagne. A thousand top of the range Zanussi washing machines were going down to Dubai, and some cretin who was happier on a camel was paying the earth for the privilege of doing business with Mahmood Shabro. Good enough reason for a party. He stood by the window. He watched, he was amused. He was not a part of the cheerful talk that was fake, the tinkling laughter that was fraud. He knew them all, except for the new secretary. One man had been a minister in the penultimate government appointed by Shah Reza Pahlavi as the roof was caving in over the Peacock Throne. One was once a paratroop major who now drove a minicab, nights, and he was on orange juice, which meant he couldn't afford one evening

off to get pissed. One was a former judge from Esfahan who now collected Social Security pay-
ments and who went to the Oxfam shop for shoes.
One had been a policeman and now went every
two weeks to the offices of the Anti-Terrorist
branch at New Scotland Yard to complain that he
was not given adequate protection for someone so
obviously at risk.

They had all run away. They weren't the ones
who had ripped off the system and come out with
their dollars folded in their wife's underwear, if
they weren't farsighted enough to collect them
from banks in Switzerland. They were all pleased
to be asked to Mahmood Shabro's parties, and
they would eat everything within reach, they
would drain every bottle.

Charlie always had a good laugh out of Mahmood Shabro. Mahmood Shabro was a rogue and
proud of it. Charlie liked that. The rest of them
were pretense, talking of home as if they were off
to Heathrow next week for the flight back, talking
about the regime as if it were a brief aberration,
talking about their new world as if they had conquered it. They had conquered nothing, the regime was in place, and they weren't going home
next week, next year. Mahmood Shabro had put
the old world behind him, and that was what

Charlie Eshraq liked. He liked people who faced facts.

Charlie was good on facts. Good enough on facts last month to have killed two men and made it clear away.

The talk flowed around him. It was all talk of home. They had exhausted their congratulation of Mahmood Shabro. Home talk, all of it. The economy in chaos, unemployment rising, the Mullahs and Ayatollahs at each other's throats, the war weariness growing. They would have gagged if they had known that Charlie Eshraq had been home last month, and killed two men. Their contact with home was long range, a drink in a hotel bar with the captain of an IranAir jumbo who was overnighting in London and who was prepared to gossip out of earshot of his minders. A talk on the direct-dial phone with a relative who had stayed inside, petty talk because if politics were debated then the line would be cut. A meeting with a businessman who had traveled out with foreign currency bankers' orders to purchase items of importance to the war effort. Charlie thought they knew nothing.

He reckoned Mahmood Shabro's new secretary looked good. Charlie and the girl were younger by twenty-five years than anyone else at the party. He thought she looked bored out of her mind.

"I rang you a few weeks back—good party, isn't it? I rang you twice but you weren't there." Mahmood Shabro at his shoulder.

He had been watching the girl's backside, when her skirt was tight as she had bent down to pick up a vol-au-vent that had been dropped on the carpet and that was steadily being stamped in. The carpet, he supposed, was worth fifteen thousand.

"I was away."

"You traveling much, Charlie?"

"Yes, I'm traveling."

"Still the . . . ?"

"Travel courier," Charlie said easily. He looked across at the secretary. "That's a pretty girl. Can she type?"

"Who knows what talent is concealed?"

Charlie saw the watchful eyes of Mrs. Shabro across the room.

"You all right, Charlie?"

"Never better."

"Anything you want?"

"If there's anything I can't get by myself, I'll come to you."

Mahmood Shabro let go of Charlie's arm. "Save me the taxi fare, take her home."

He liked Mahmood Shabro. Since cutting loose from his mother and pitching up in London without a family, Mahmood Shabro had been a friend, a sort of uncle. He knew why he was Mahmood Shabro's friend. He never asked the man for anything.

The secretary had come to his corner of the room, taking her boss's place. She had a bottle of champagne in her hand. He thought it must have been the last bottle, and she had come to him first to fill his glass almost to the lip before moving on and pouring out a few drops for everyone else. She came back, bearing the empty bottle. She said that Mahmood Shabro had told her to put a bottle aside for herself. She said with those eyes that had been worked with such care that she would not object to sharing the bottle. She told him that she would have to clear up. He told her his address and gave her a key and a note to cover the cab, and he said that he had to meet a man on his way home, that she was please to wait for him.

He went out into the early summer night. It was already dark. The headlights of the traffic flow scratched across his features. He walked briskly. He preferred to walk. He could check for a tail. He just did the usual things, nothing flash. Round the corner and waiting. Stopping on a pavement, spinning, walking back, checking the faces. Just being sensible.

He went to his meeting. He had put out of his

mind the gathering of no-hopers, losers, dreamers, in Mahmood Shabro's office.

She was nineteen.

She was a mainliner.

The middle of the evening, and the darkness spreading. She stood in shadow at the side of the toilets in the small park area off the main shopping street. She was a mainliner because dragon chasing and mouth organ playing were no longer sufficient to her.

Lucy Barnes was a tiny elf girl. She felt the cold. She had been waiting for two hours, and when she had left the squat the sun was still hovering among the chimneys of the small terraced homes. The sleeves of her blouse were fastened at her wrists. The light above the toilet block had been smashed and she was in a black hidden space, but she wore a pair of wide dark glasses.

Two weeks ago she had sold the remote control color sixteen-channel portable television set that had been her parents' birthday present to her. She had spent the money, she had used up the grams of scag the sale had bought. There was more money in her pocket, more notes crumpled into the hip pocket of her trousers. That afternoon she had sold a teapot from home. Georgian silver, good price. She needed a good price.

The bastard was bloody late, and her legs ached in cramp, and she was cold and she was sweating. Her eyes were watering, as if she were crying for him to come.

Mattie Furniss would not have shared the conviction with even his closest colleagues, but the last fourteen weeks had convinced him that the Director General was just not up to the mark. And here they were again. The meeting of Heads of Desks, Middle East/West Asia, had kicked off an hour behind schedule, it had dragged on for close to three hours, and they were bogged down a third of the way down the agenda. Nothing personal, of course, simply the gut feeling that the Director General should have been left to vegetate in mainstream diplomacy at Foreign and Commonwealth, and not been inflicted on the Service in the first place. Mattie Furniss was a professional, and the new Director General was most certainly not. And it was equally certain that the Secret Intelligence Service of Century House could not be run as if it were merely an offshoot of FCO.

Worst of all was the inescapable conclusion that the Director General, wet behind the ears in intelligence tradition, was gunning for Iran Desk. Israel Desk, Mideast Desk, Gulf Desk and Subcontinent (Pakistan) Desk, were all in his sights, but Iran Desk was taking the bulk of the flak.

"That's the long and the short of it, gentlemen, we are simply not producing top-quality intelligence material. I go to JIC each week, and they say to me, 'What is actually *happening* in Iran?' Perfectly fair question for Joint Intelligence Committee to be asking me. I tell them what you gentlemen have provided me with. You know what they say? They say to me, and I cannot disagree, that what they are getting from us is in no way different from what is served up by the usual channels along the Gulf . . ."

"Director General, if I may . . ."

"Allow me, please, to finish. I'd appreciate that . . ."

Mattie sagged back in his chair. He was the only smoker round the mahogany table that the Director General had imported upon arrival. He had his matches out. Every other DG he had worked for had stuck to one-on-one meetings where a bit of concentration could be applied, where speeches would seem inelegant. He smoke-screened himself.

"I won't be able to defend my budget proposals for the coming year if the Service is producing, in such a critical international theater, the sort of analysis that is going into FCO day in and day out. That's the crux of it, Mattie."

It was the fourth time Mattie had listened to this monologue. The three previous sessions he had stood his corner and justified his position. He sensed the others round the table praying he wouldn't bite. On three previous occasions he had delivered his answer. No embassy in Tehran as cover for a resident Station Officer. Not a hope in hell of recruiting anyone close to the real power bases inside Iran. Less and less chance of persuading British technicians to do any more than decently keep their eyes open while setting up a refinery or whatever. Three times he had come up with the more significant data that his agents in place had been able to provide . . . all water off a duck's backside . . . including the best stuff he had had last time from the boy, and unless they finished soon he would be too late to pay for it.

"I hear you, Director General."

The Director General hacked a cough through the wreaths of smoke drifting past him. "What are you going to do about it?"

"Endeavor to provide material that will give greater satisfaction than the hard-won information my Desk is currently supplying."

The Director General flapped in front of his face

with his agenda paper. "You should go out there, Mattie."

"Tehran, Director General. First-class idea," Mattie said. Israel Desk was the youngest in the room, high-flier and still irreverent, too long in the field, and having to bite on the heel of his hand to stop himself laughing out loud.

"I cannot abide facetiousness."

"Where would you suggest I travel to, Director General?"

"The fringes."

Mattie asked quietly, "To what purpose?"

"Pretty obvious, surely. To brief your people on what is now required of them. To take the opportunity to get your agents in place out from inside so that they can be advised, in exact terms, of our needs."

He bit at his pipe stem. "You are forgetting, Director General, that Desk Heads do not travel."

"Who says so?"

"Since ever, Desk Heads do not travel because of the security implications."

"Do not travel, wrong. Do not usually travel, right."

If he bit through the stem of his pipe he would at the same time break his teeth. "Is that final?"

"Yes, it is. And I think we'll pause there."

There was a rapid gathering of papers. Israel

Desk was already out of the door when the Director General said, "Goodnight gentlemen, and thank you for your patience. What's worth doing is worth doing right."

Mattie Furniss didn't wait for the lift to get up to the nineteenth floor. He ducked away from his colleagues for the fire escape stairway. He went down nine flights at two steps at a time, praying that the boy would still be waiting for him and for his present.

It had been a short road for Lucy Barnes from home in a mews house in London's Belgravia to the attic of a terraced house in the West Country town. On this cool and early summer evening she was at the end of her financial resources. She had gone to London that week, she had broken into the family home through a kitchen window, she had taken the teapot. They would change the locks after that. Probably they had already changed the locks. She couldn't remember now why she had only taken the teapot. She had no idea where she would go for more money, for more scag, after the doses that were on the floor beside her were exhausted.

A short road. Cannabis smoking behind the school's sports pavilion, an act of adolescent defiance and experimentation. She had been through dragon chasing, heating the scag powder through tinfoil and inhaling the fumes through a soft drinks tube. She had tried mouth organ playing, dragging the same heated fumes into her lungs through the cover of a matchbox. One and a half years after her expulsion—and pretty goddamn embarrassing that had been because darling Daddy was already signed up to hand over the prizes at next term's Speech Day—she was a mainliner and needing a grand a month to stay with it.

The pusher had said this was new stuff, purer than he had ever had through his hands before, the best stuff he had ever been sold. None of the usual dilution shit in the cut, no talcum or chalk dust or fine sugar. Real stuff, like it had been before the dealers got to be so bloody greedy.

She loaded the hypodermic. She could estimate the dose, didn't use fragile weighing scales. She sat cross-legged on a square of threadbare carpet. The attic was lit by the beam from a streetlight that pierced the dirty glass of the skylight window. She could see what she was doing. The arm veins were no longer any good to her, the leg veins were failing on her. She kicked off her shoes. She wore no tights, nor socks. Her feet were dark-stained, she had not had a bath in more than a month, but she knew where the veins ran on the underside of her feet.

She gritted her teeth as she inserted the needle behind the ball of her right foot. She drew back the arm of the hypodermic, sucking blood into the container, allowing the blood to mix inside the syringe with the scag powder. Slowly, trying to control the trembling of her thumb, she pressed down on the syringe.

She lay back on the bare mattress. She anticipated the peace and the dream.

The boy was where he had said he would be.

Old habits would die hard for Mattie Furniss. The old way of doing things was to meet in a park's open spaces where it was comparatively easy to guard against surveillance and eavesdropping. The boy was a shadow under a sycamore tree close to the lake. Mattie was almost trotting, and the supermarket bag flapped against his trouser leg. Out in the road that fringed the park a van did a U-turn, and its headlights played across the open ground with the maneuver and the boy was lit. Tall, bearded, a fine-looking boy. Mattie had known young Eshraq so long that he would always regard him as a boy. But Charlie did not seem to Mattie like any other twenty-two-year-old that he knew, not in build and stature, not in temperament or attitude. A hell of a fine young man, but then so had his father been. . . . He reached the tree. He drew at his breath. He had run all the way from Century on the other side of the river, over the Bridge and across Whitehall to the park. He would have to put in some extra training if he were to finish the half marathon this summer.

"Tied up, dear boy. Apologies."

"No problem, sir."

Mattie liked the way that Charlie addressed him. That was his father's stamp on the young man, and his mother's too, in fairness to her.

"Long time, dear boy."

"It's a new skill for me, learning to write reports, sir. I hope it will be of use to you." Charlie reached into his blazer pocket, took out a thick envelope, handed it to Mattie. Mattie didn't examine it, just slid it down into an inner pocket of his suit then drew across a zip fastener at the top of the pocket, another old habit. Wouldn't do for a Desk Head to get his pocket picked in the underground.

"I'm looking forward to it. . . . Heard from your mother?"

"No." Charlie said it as if it didn't matter to him that his mother never wrote nor telephoned from California. As if it was nothing to him that the golf course and the bridge club and the riding school filled his mother's days and evenings, that she regarded him as a relic of a former life in Iran that was best forgotten, that was pain to remember.

"I read about your escapade, the good old *Tehran Times*. Carried on the radio as well."

A slow smile on Charlie's face.

". . . You weren't compromised?"

"There was a search afterward, plenty of roadblocks. No, they didn't know what they were looking for. They put it down to the 'hypocrites.' It went quite well."

Mattie could almost have recited the text of the IRNA communiqué reproduced in the *Tehran Times*. In separate incidents in south Tehran two Islamic Revolutionary Guards martyred in broad daylight by MKO (*Mojahedin-e Khalq* Organization) counterrevolutionary *mustaqafin* (hypocrites) working in conjunction with American mercenary agents. Now that Harry had retired, gone more than four years, the IRNA communiqués reached him ahead of the BBC's transcripts. He missed the messenger's service.

"We came up with a nice one for the next run," Mattie said. He offered the supermarket bag that was taut from the weight of its contents. "Instructions inside."

"Thank you."

"I'll want another report."

"Of course, sir. Mrs. Furniss is well?"

"Grand form, and the girls. You'll come down to the country when you're back? We'll round up the girls. Make a weekend of it."

"I'd like that."

"You all right for money? I could scrape the bucket a bit for you."

A present in a plastic bag he could manage with ease. Money was harder. Money had to go through Audit. The present in the plastic bag was by his own arrangement with Resources/Equipment, on the ninth floor.

"I'm fine for money, sir."

"Glad to hear that."

He saw the boy hesitate. The boy looked as though he were framing his request and not certain as to the best face to put on it. He felt the first drops of rain, and he was sweating now from his run.

"Cough it out."

"The target that I want most has an escort and his car is armored."

"Meaning?"

"It would be difficult to get close enough."

"And . . ." Mattie wasn't going to help.

"I need what they call stand-off capability. Do you understand that, sir?"

"I understand." Mattie gazed into the boy's

eyes. The hesitation was gone, the request had been made. There was cool and attractive certainty in the boy's eyes. "You would have to go for longer, your reports would have to be regular."

"Why not," Charlie said, as if it were a small matter.

Mattie thought of the boy's father, a generous host, a true friend. He thought of the boy's uncle, a mountain of a man, a superb stalker of boar and a brilliant shot. He thought of the boy's sister, delicate and winning her arguments with the brilliance of her smile, and kissing him when he brought gifts to the villa. He thought of Charlie's mother, brittle because she was uncertain, brave because she had tried to blend and assimilate her foreignness into that society of the wide and prosperous avenues of north Tehran. It was a family that had been dismembered.

"That would be very expensive indeed." A sharpness in Mattie's voice. Yes, he was a stickler for protocol and procedure. No, he should never have allowed his Service life to meld with the crusade that was the boy's.

"I could pay for it."

Mattie Furniss was off on his travels, and that was no business of the boy's. And he didn't know his schedule yet. He did not know when he would return, when they could next meet. So much to talk about. They should have been talking in comfort of gentler matters, relaxed, they should have been gossiping—not prattling around the subject of stand-off capability and armor-piercing weapons under a tree in St. James's Park for God's sake, with the rain beginning to come down in earnest. He took out his pen and a sheet of paper from a leather-backed pad. He wrote briefly on it. A name, an address.

"Thank you, sir," Charlie said.

The keen statement. "In for longer, the reports more regular."

"Please give my best regards to Mrs. Furniss, and to the girls."

"Of course I will. They'll be glad to know I've seen you." He wondered whether the boy had been more than a friend to his daughters, either of them. They'd been very close, down in the country, and when his brood were all in London and the boy was their guest. It had been in London, three years before, in their little drawing room, the boy on his first trip from California and away from his mother, that Mattie had told Charlie Eshraq, as straight and as baldly as he could, what had happened to his sister and his father and his uncle. He had never seen the boy cry since then. Bottled it all up, of course. "When do you go, dear boy?"

"Pretty soon."

"You'll telephone me, at home, before you go?"

"Yes."

"You'll go steadily?"

"Yes."

The rain dribbled over Mattie's face, and caught at his trimmed and silver moustache and darkened the front of his shirt. The boy's face was a blur in front of him and masked by the fullness of his beard.

"If anything happened to you, while you're away, Harriet and I, and the girls, we'd be . . ." Mattie squeezed the boy's shoulders.

"Why should it, sir?"

They parted.

He walked home. Mattie felt dirtied because he encouraged the folly of the boy, and yet he did not know how he could have dissuaded him. And he had the thick bulk of the envelope in his pocket, and the boy had said that he would be going in for longer, and that the reports would be more regular. He thought that in a decent world Matthew Cedric Furniss would deserve to be flailed alive.

He fervently hoped that Harriet would still be up and waiting for him. He needed to talk to her, play a record, and be warmed and wanted. He had never in three years seen the boy cry, and the boy had murdered two Revolutionary Guards and planned to go back in again with his present in a plastic bag. The boy was talking about stand-off and armor-piercing. He was talking about war, dammit, and the boy was no less than a son to him.

Mattie said an abbreviated prayer for Charlie Eshraq as he crossed at the traffic lights outside his London flat. And if the boy had bedded his daughters then good luck to him.

He was soaked. His face ran with water. His sodden trousers were clinging to his shins and his shoes squelched. When he looked up he saw the light behind the curtain welcoming him.

There could be as many as fifty thousand persons addicted to heroin inside the United Kingdom.

On that night one of them, Lucy Barnes, had failed to compensate for the increased purity of the dose with which she injected herself. Alone, in a coma and on a stinking mattress, she choked to death on her own vomit.

Chapter ✤ 2

$\mathcal{T}$he detective had led the way up to the attic. During that day he had become familiar enough, as familiar as he wanted to be, with the cramped space under the slope of the roof. He eased back against a wall, brushing against the peeling paper. Below him the stairway protested at the weight of the two that followed him. The local detective thought it understandable that the Secretary of State would have his own man from Protection with him. The bodyguard would have lived long enough in the Secretary of State's pocket to have become a part of the retinue, almost family. He understood that the Secretary of State needed a face to trust. The Secretary of State emerged into the attic, white dust

and cobwebs on the collar of his black overcoat.
The detective had taken to the farthest corner, he
left the center ground to the Secretary of State
and his bodyguard. He had seen them all. The
ones on the breadline, and the most powerful in
the land. They all came bowed and subdued to witness the place, the stinking corner, where their
child had died. Usually the mothers came too. He
knew that some would be aggressive, some would
be broken, some crippled with shame. Their child,
their future, blown away by a hypodermic syringe. The room was pitifully bare, and even more
confused than when the police had first been
alerted by the ambulance team because his squad
had turned the place over and ransacked every
inch of it. The mattress had been taken apart. The
girl's clothes had been put into a black plastic
sack after examination. Her papers were collected
into a cellophane bag which would go to his office
for further examination.

The bodyguard stood at the top of the stairway.
He gave the sign with his eyes, he told the local
man to get on with his talk. The Secretary of State
was known to the policeman only through the
television in his living room and the photographs
in the newspapers that he never seemed to find
time to read but which were kept for lighting the
fire before he went to work. The Secretary of State

was not a pretty sight, looked like a man who had been kicked hard in the testicles an hour before. He could stand, but the color was gone from his face. He'd done well, the local man, he had had the name, alerted the Metropolitan, and now had the parent where the parent wanted to be, and all this before the rat-pack had wind of the excitement. Drily he thought to himself, if nothing else went right on this one then getting the Secretary of State into and out of this crap heap before the photographers pitched up was good going. He took the lead from the bodyguard.

"Lucy had been living here for several weeks, sir, at least she was here for a month. Only known means of support, the Social Security. Preliminary postmortem indicates that she was a serious victim of addiction—we don't regard users as criminals, sir, we tend to refer to them as victims. Her wrist veins have been used, no good anymore, and her thigh and shin veins have also been used. She had taken to using the smaller veins in her feet as an injection route. I am assuming that you were aware that she was addicted, sir—I mean, it must have been pretty obvious, obvious that is if you were still in touch with your daughter . . ."

The Secretary of State had his head down, made no response. Just like all the rest of them, feeling it a duty to get some feel of where their child had died. Christ, the room stank.

". . . We cannot yet be certain of the cause of death, not in exact terms, that will come later when Pathology have had their full whack, but the first indicators are, sir, that she took a rather pure dose. What she took was just too much for her system. That causes a coma, and then vomiting. Blocked windpipe does the rest—I'm sorry, sir."

The Secretary of State's voice was a flat monotone. "I've an old chum, medic in London. I talked to him right at the beginning. I said, 'Whose child becomes an addict?' He said, 'Your kid.' He said, 'No one worries when the addict is that nice kiddie from next door, but by Heavens they worry when it's the nice kiddie upstairs.' We thought that we had done everything for her. She went to the best schools, when she went onto heroin we sent her to the best withdrawal clinic. Just a waste of money. We cut her allowance, so she sold everything we'd ever given her. She moved out, then came back and stole from us. Can you imagine that, Officer, stealing from her own parents . . . of course, you can imagine it, you are accustomed to the misery caused by this addiction. The last thing we did was have the Ministry's own security system in our own house changed. I mean that's coming to something, isn't it, when the Secretary of State for Defense has to have his own alarm system changed because his own daughter might want to break in. . . . Her mother will want to know, can't hide much from her mother, would she have been in pain?"

"Coma first, sir. No pain." The detective was past shock, past sympathy, and way past apportioning blame. He could be matter of fact. "She had the stuff. It's if she hadn't had the stuff that she would have been in pain."

"How much would it have been costing her?"

"From what we've seen, anything between a hundred and two hundred a week—when it's got that bad."

The local detective wondered how the politician would survive it. He wondered whether he would shut himself away from public life once the storm blew, the headlines tomorrow and the coroner's court reporting. Whether he would carry on as if his public and private lives were separate compartments. He wondered if the pursuit of his public life could have so damaged a private life that a lone, lost child took to a syringe for companionship, for love.

The Secretary of State had a good grip on himself, his voice was clear. Nothing staccato, nothing choked. "A colleague of mine said recently, 'This abuse brings hardened criminals and indulgent users together in a combination that is potentially lethal for good order and civilized values—the price of ultimate failure is unthinkable.' That was before Lucy had her problem, I didn't take much notice of it then. What are you doing about it, Officer, this lethal combination?"

The local detective swallowed his first thoughts. Not the moment to spit out his gripes about resources and priorities, and bans on overtime payment which meant that most of his squad clocked off on the dot of office hours. He said, "Gather what evidence we can, sir, try and move our investigation on from there."

"Do you have children, Officer?"

"Yes, sir."

"What age?"

"About half your Lucy's age, sir."

"Could it happen to them, what happened to her?"

"As long as the stuff's coming in, sir, flooding in like it is—yes, sir."

"What would you want done, Officer, if she had been yours?"

"I'd want to get to the fuckers . . . excuse me, sir . . . to the people who made the stuff available to your Lucy."

"You'll do what you can?"

"Bluntly, sir, that's not a lot. Yes, we will."

The bodyguard had flicked his fingers, a small gesture close to the seam of his trousers. The local man had the message. He moved around and behind the Secretary of State, to the head of the staircase. The bodyguard was already warily descending. There was music playing on a lower floor. The detective had had one session with the other residents of this terraced house, and he would have another later that afternoon when he had got himself shot of the big man. He hadn't been heavy with them, the others in the squat, not once he had discovered who Lucy Barnes's father was. Counterproductive, he would have said, to have leaned too hard on them right now. He wanted their help, he needed all they could give him. From the top of the staircase he looked back. The Secretary of State was staring down at the mattress, and the bag of clothes, and the junk litter that might the previous week have been important to a nineteen-year-old girl.

He paused at the bottom of the stairs.

"What does he think I'm going to do about it?"

The bodyguard shrugged.

Two, three minutes later, they heard the creaking of the stairs. The detective thought he saw a redness at the eyes that were distorted by the Secretary of State's rimless spectacles.

On the pavement the Secretary of State paused beside his car. The chauffeur was holding open the back door. "Thank you again, Officer. I am not a complete fool, by the way. I understand the very real difficulties that you face in your work. I can promise you one thing. I will, quite shamelessly, use every vestige of my authority and influence to ensure the apprehension and prosecution of those responsible for Lucy's death. Good day to you."

He ducked down into the car. The bodyguard closed the door on him, and slipped into the front passenger seat. The detective saw the Secretary of State lift from a briefcase a portable telephone, and the car was gone, heading away fast.

He went back upstairs. In a confined space he preferred to work alone. Half an hour later, under newspapers, under a loosened floorboard, a long way back in a cavity, he found Lucy's diary.

"This is a great deal better, Mattie. Much more what I've been looking for."

"I'm gratified."

"I'll explain to you my assessment of Iran theater . . ."

Mattie studied the ceiling light. It was not so

much an impertinence, more an attempt to avert his eyes so that the impatience could be better disguised.

". . . We are talking about the region's principal geopolitical and military power, sitting astride the most important petroleum trade routes in the world. We are talking about the country with the potential for regaining its position as thirteenth in Gross National Product, with the largest army in Western Asia, with no foreign debt, with the capacity to blow over every other regime in the area . . ."

"I have specialized, Director General, in Iranian matters since 1968—I have actually lived there."

"Yes, yes, Mattie. I know you are close to Iran. Short service commission in the Coldstream liaising with the Imperial army, '65 to '67; Station Officer '75 to '78; Bahrain and Ankara after the Revolution. Give me the credit, Mattie, for being able to read a personal file. I know you were familiar with Iran before your entry to the Service, and that since entry you have specialized in that country. I know your file backward and I'll tell you what I think: you're probably too close to your subject. My training is as a Kremlinologist, I'm a cold war freak, and I should think you have a clearer view of how we should be targeting the Soviet Union and its satellites than I have. Just as I believe I have a clear idea of what's required from Iran. It's time we understood each other, Mattie . . ."

Mattie no longer stared at the ceiling. He looked straight ahead of him. He hadn't his pipe out of his pocket, he hadn't his matches on the mahogany table. He had his fists clenched. He could not remember when he had last felt such anger.

"You're in a rut. That's why I've been brought in to run Century. There are too many of you in a rut, going through the motions, never questioning the value of material. I won't accept paper pushing. . . . This is the best material you have supplied me with."

Mattie squinted his gaze across the table, across to his rewrite of Charlie Eshraq's report. Good, but not that good. A useful start for something that would get better.

". . . It's crude, but it's factual. In short it is the sort of material that crosses my desk all too infrequently. There are five valuable pieces of information. One, the movement of the 8th and 120th Battalions of the IRG 28th Sanandaj Division from Ahvaz to Saqqez, movement by night indicating that this was not simply a tactical readjustment, but more the reinforcing of a particular sector prior to using those Guards in a new push. The Iraqis would like to know that . . ."

"You'd pass that on to the Iraqis?" A hiss of surprise.

"I might. Good material earns favors. . . . Two, the German engineer on his way to Hamadan, and at Hamadan is a missile development factory. Good stuff, stuff we can confront our friends in Bonn with, make them quite uncomfortable. . . . I've marked up all of what I consider to be relevant, five points in all. The training camp at Saleh-Abad north of Qom, that's useful. Fine stuff."

The Director General had carefully placed his pencil on the table. He upturned a glass and filled it with water from a crystal jug.

"And who is going to emerge as the power among the clerics, and how long the war is going on, and what is the state of disaffection among the population, am I to presume that is unimportant?"

"No, Mattie. Not unimportant, simply outside your brief. Analysis is for diplomatic missions, and they're good at it. I trust there will be more of this."

"Yes."

"Who is the source?"

"I think I've got your drift, Director General."

"I asked you, who is the source?"

"I will make sure that a greater flow of similar material reaches you."

The Director General smiled. The first time that Mattie had seen the flicker of the lines at the side of his mouth.

"Please yourself, Mattie, and have a good trip."

Charlie Eshraq was personal to Mattie, and would not be shared with anyone. He stood, turned and left the room.

Going down in the lift he wondered what the boy was making of his present. It was personal and private to Mattie that on his last journey inside Charlie had killed two men, and equally personal and private that on this journey he would kill another.

They had been colleagues since University, since the youth section of the Party, since sharing an office in the Research Division headquarters in Smith Square. They had entered Parliament at the same election, and the Cabinet in the same reshuffle. When their leader finally determined on retirement they would probably compete in the same dogfight for the top job. That time had not yet come, they were close friends.

"I'm dreadfully sorry, George."

Once the Home Secretary's assistant had brought in the coffee, placed it on the desk and left, they were alone. It was rare for two such men to meet without a phalanx of notetakers and agenda minders and appointment keepers. The Secretary of State sat exhausted in an easy chair, the plaster dust and the cobwebs still on his overcoat. "I want something done about this stinking trade."

"Of course you do, George."

The Secretary of State looked hard into the Home Secretary's face. "I know what you are up against, but I want them found and tried and I shall pray you get them convicted and sentenced to very long terms, every last one of the bastards that killed Lucy."

"Very understandable."

"My detective told me that we are stopping one kilo out of ten that comes in . . ."

"We have stepped up recruitment of both police drugs officers and Customs. We've put a huge resource at the disposal . . ."

The Secretary of State shook his head. "Please, not a Party Political, not between us. I've got to go back to Libby tonight, I've to tell her where her—our—daughter died, and then I shall have to leave her and put on a cheerful face for dinner, ironically enough with some bigwigs from Pakistan, from the heart of what I expect you know is the Golden Crescent. I don't think, and I mean this, I don't think Libby will survive tonight if I cannot give her your solemn promise that Lucy's killers will be found and brought to book."

"I'll do what I can, George."

"She was a lovely girl, Lucy, before all this . . ."

"Everything we can do, that is a promise. You'll give my love to Libby. I'm so very sorry."

"Oh, you'd by God be sorry if you had seen how Lucy died, how she was—dead—and where she died. Libby will need the strength of twenty to survive this. In my heart of hearts I have known, for almost a year, how it might end but I couldn't imagine the depths of it, George. You must see it day in and day out, but this time the minuscule statistic on your desk is my dead daughter and I am going to hold you to your promise."

The detective worked his way steadily through the diary. He found an asterisk in red Biro on every third or fourth day of the last few weeks, the last against the date on which the girl had taken her overdose. There were also telephone numbers. There was a string of seven-figure numbers, almost certainly London numbers, which for the moment he discarded. He had wrung from the others in the squat that Lucy Barnes had not been away from the town in the last days of her life. The local numbers were five-figure numbers. There was one number underlined in the same red Biro. The local detective worked to a formula. He would work into the early evening, and then lock away the papers on his desk, put on his coat and drive home. What other way? If he and his two juniors worked twenty-five hours in the twenty-four they would still make no noticeable dent on the narcotics problems that had spread even to this country town. Where did the bloody stuff stop? The detective went to the area seminars, he had heard endlessly of the big city problems. And their problems, the problems of the major city forces, were his. If he hadn't shut it away, locked it into the drawer of his desk each evening, then the scag and coke would do for him too.

Before he put the key back into his pocket, he told the better of the two juniors to get onto the telephone exchange and cut all incoming and outgoing calls from the underlined number.

He wished them well, bade them a "Good evening," and left for home.

"The gloves off, is that what you're asking for?"

He was a former Chief Constable. He had seen it all and heard it all. He wanted the guidelines crystal clear, and from the horse's mouth. He headed the National Drugs Intelligence Unit, based on New Scotland Yard, with responsibility for coordinating efforts to stem the flow of narcotics into the country.

"Yes, I suppose that's it. Yes, that is what I am asking for." The Home Secretary shifted in his seat. His own Private Secretary was busy at his notepad, and at the back of the room the policeman's aide was scribbling fast, then looking up to see whether there was more. The Home Secretary wondered how similar their two notes would be.

"What I could say to you, Home Secretary, is that I might be just a little concerned at hardpressed and limited resources being diverted onto one case, however tragic, merely because the victim happened to be well connected. You would understand that I could say that, would be entitled to say that."

"It's no doubt a straightforward case. It's nothing that hasn't been successfully dealt with countless times. I just want it solved, and fast," the Home Secretary said.

"Then I'll tell you, sir, what's landed on our desks over the last few days. . . . Four Blacks bullock their way into a house and shoot the mother and her schoolboy son, the boy's dead. That's drug related. A blind widow is beaten up in the West Country, for a hundred pounds in her pension book, that's to pay for drugs. Twenty-eight police-men injured in two months in West London in one street, in one hundred fifty yards of one street, be-cause we're trying to put a stop to trafficking in that street. What we call designer drugs, cocktail amphetamines, there are at least two new labora-tories in East London which we haven't found. A six-year-old kiddie who's hooked on reefers, and his Mum's come in to tell us that he pinched one hundred fifty pounds out of her handbag to pay for them. . . . That's what's hitting our desks at the moment. Now, do I hear you rightly, sir? Do I correctly hear you say that that type of investi-gation, pretty important to the men and women involved, goes on the back burner?"

"Yes."

". . . Because the daughter of a Cabinet Minister is dumb enough to squirt herself an overdose?"

"Don't let's play silly buggers."

"Thank you, sir, I'll attend to it."

"And be damn certain you get a result."

There was a wintry smile on the policeman's face, a smile that sliced the Home Secretary's de-fenses. He looked away, he didn't want to see the man's eyes, the message of contempt that a man in his position could break the civilized order of priorities because he had given his word to a col-league.

"You'll keep me informed," the Home Secretary told his Private Secretary. "And you can ring down for my car."

"Charlie Eshraq rang," Harriet Furniss said.

Mattie was heaving out of his overcoat. "Did he, now?" Reaching to hook it tidily behind the front door. "And what did he have to say for himself?"

It was Mattie's way that he did not bring his office home. He had told his wife nothing of his dealings with the boy, nor that Charlie, whom Harriet Furniss treated as a son, had killed two men on his last journey home. They had been married for twenty-eight years, and he had spent twenty-one of them as a member of the Secret Intelligence Service and he had stuck to his rule book, and the rule book said that wives were no part of the Service.

"He said that he was sorry that he had missed you. He was off tonight . . ."

"Was he, now?" Mattie made a poor fist of unconcern.

Harriet would have noticed, but she would not have commented. Harriet never attempted to draw him out.

"He said that he had a rather good job for a few weeks, something about playing courier to tourists in the Aegean."

"That'll be nice for him."

"He said thank you for the present."

"Ah, yes. Just a little something that I saw, and posted to him," he said, too fast. He could lie with the best of them at Century, and was a miserable failure at home.

"He said it would be very useful."

"That's excellent. The country this weekend, I think, Harriet. Some reading to be done."

He kissed her on the cheek, like it was something that he should have done earlier. In all his married life Mattie had never looked at another woman. Perhaps he was old fashioned. He thought a little more each day of his advancing years—his next birthday would be his fifty-third—and happily acknowledged that he was just damned lucky to have met and married Harriet (née Owens) Furniss.

He opened his briefcase, took out the black cloth-bound book that was all of its contents. He went to work each morning with a briefcase, as if it were a part of his uniform, but he never brought it home filled with office papers. He showed her the elegant lettering on the spine, *The Urartian Civilization of Near Asia—an Appraisal*. She grimaced. He opened the book and showed her the receipt from the antiquarian bookseller.

"It had better be your birthday present."

His birthday was not for another nine weeks. She would pay for the book as she paid for most of the extras in their lives, as she had paid the girls' school fees, as she had paid the airfare for Charlie Eshraq to come over from California to London years before. Mattie had no money, no inherited wealth, only his salary from Century, which looked after essentials—rates, mortage, housekeeping. Their way of life would have been a good deal less comfortable without Harriet's contributions.

"How did Charlie sound?"

"Sounded pretty good. Very buoyant, actually. . . . Supper'll be frizzled."

They went down the hallway toward the kitchen. He was holding his wife's hand. He did it more often now that the girls had left home.

"You'll have something to get your teeth into for the weekend?"

"Indeed I will. . . . That wretched man who's bought the Manor Farm, he's plowed up the footpath across Ten Acre. I'll have plenty to keep me busy."

God help the poor bastard, Mattie thought, the newcomer from the big city if he had come down to the countryside and plowed up a right-of-way and made an enemy of Harriet Furniss.

She looked into his face. "The Urartians, aren't they Eastern Turkey?" She saw him nod. "Is that where you're going?"

"Gulf first, but I might get up there." There were times when he wanted nothing more than to talk through his days, to share the frustrations and to celebrate the triumphs. But he had never done it and he never would.

In the kitchen he made himself a weak gin and tonic, and gave Harriet her schooner of Cyprus dry sherry. Supermarket gin and cheap imported sherry, because drinks came out of the housekeeping. He was quiet that evening. While she washed up the pots and loaded the dishwasher, Mattie sat in a chair by the window, and saw nothing through the opened curtains, and wondered how far on his journey Charlie Eshraq had traveled.

"Come on, Keeper, for Christ's sake . . . get a wiggle on."

The pub was full, getting near to closing time, and the swill under way before "Time" was called.

David Park was away from the bar, outside the group. He stared back at them.

"Bloody hell, Keeper, are you in this round or are you not?" There were six of them up at the bar, and some had shed their jackets, and all had loosened their ties, and their faces were flushed.

A hell of a good evening for all concerned, except for David Park. He hadn't made his excuses and gone home to Ann, but he hadn't played much of a part in the piss-up that had been inevitable after Mr. Justice Kennedy's remarks following the sentencing.

"Keeper, it is your round."

True, it was David Park's round. He drained his bitter lemon. He made his way to the bar. In a quiet voice, and the barmaid had to heave most of her bosom onto the beer mats to hear him, he ordered six pints of Yorkshire bitter, and a bitter lemon with ice. He passed the beers from the bar to the eager waiting hands.

"Bloody good, Keeper. . . . Cheers, old mate. . . . 'Bout bloody time too. . . . Keeper, my old love, you are something of a wet towel tonight . . ."

He grinned, fast, as if that were a weakness. He did not like to acknowledge weakness.

"I'm driving," he said calmly. He slid away from the heart of the group, back to the fringe. His radio call sign was Keeper, had been ever since he had been accepted into the Investigation Division. He was Park, and so some bright creature had labeled him Keeper. Mucking in, getting pissed-up, falling around, they weren't Park's talents. He had other talents, and Mr. Justice Kennedy had remarked on them and commended the

April team's dedicated work, and to everyone else in April that was reason enough to be on their seventh pint with a cab home at the end of it. Mr. Justice Kennedy had handed down, late that afternoon, a Fourteen, two Twelves, and a Nine. Mr. Justice Kennedy had called for Bill Parrish, Senior Investigating Officer and in charge of April team, to step up into the witness box so that the thanks of "a society under threat from these hellish traffickers who deal in wickedness" could be expressed. Bill Parrish in a clean white shirt then had looked decently embarrassed at the fulsome praise set out by the old cove. Parrish earned, basic, 16,000 pounds a year. David Park earned, basic, 12,500 pounds a year. The bastards who had gone down, for Fourteen and Twelve and Nine, were looking at a couple of million hidden away in the Caymans, and not touchable. It would take Park forty years to earn what the bastards had waiting for them after their time, less remission, and by then he would be retired with his index-linked pension to cuddle. He liked the chase, cared little about the kill, couldn't care less once the cuffs went on. Parrish would get a great welcome from his wife when he made it home after closing, and she'd pour him another jug full and sit him down on the settee and roll the video so that he could belch his way through the recordings of the two main news bulletins of the evening and hear the message to the nation that Customs and Excise was super bloody marvelous, and keeping the nation safe, etc., etc. Park hoped Ann would be asleep.

April team was Iranian heroin. Park had been four years with April and had an encyclopedic knowledge of Iranian heroin. He had been the front man in this investigation, deep inside the guts of the organization that was doing the running of the scag; he had even driven for them. Ann knew sweet nothing about what he had been at. Best if she were asleep when he reached home.

He watched the group. He thought they looked stupid and very drunk. He couldn't remember when he had last been the worse for wear in public. One of the reasons he had been selected, that he could be relied upon invariably to stay the right side of the bottle. To be less than 1,000 percent clear-headed on a covert operation would be real bad news, like a shotgun barrel in the back of the neck. He didn't tell Ann what he did. He told her the generalities, never the details. He couldn't have told her that he was insinuated into a gang, that if his cover were blown he'd be facedown in the Thames with the back of his skull a bloody remnant. He thought one of the guys was going to fall over.

Bill Parrish had detached himself from the group at the bar session, made his way stiffly to Park. An arm looped around his shoulders. He took the weight.

"Mind if I say it . . . ? When you want, you can be awesomely priggish, David."

"You can say it."

"April's a team, a shit hot team. A shit hot team stands or falls on being together. Being together doesn't match with one bugger on the edge and looking down his nose."

Park disentangled the arm, propped it onto the mantelpiece of the bar's fireplace. "Meaning what?"

"Meaning that this has been a great scene, worth celebrating . . ."

Park dragged the breath down into his lungs. Parrish had asked for it. He'd get it.

"Did you see them in there? Did you see them when they were being sent down? They were laughing at us, Bill. One Fourteen, two Twelves and a Nine, and they were looking across at us like it was some sort of crack. Did you see their women in the gallery? Deep tans from the Costa. And that wasn't paste on their fingers, ears, throats. . . . Hear me, Bill. What we are at is a confidence trick. We aren't even scratching at these pigs, and here we are pretending we're winning.

It's a confidence trick the Judge plays too, and that way the British masses go to their beds tonight thinking everything is hunky-dory. We're kidding ourselves, Bill. We're not winning, we're not even doing well. We're drowning in the bloody stuff. . . ."

"That's daft talk, David."

"How's this for daft talk? Heroin's an explosion, cocaine's gone through the roof, 'phets are up, with cannabis we're talking tonnage not kilos. We're deluding ourselves if we pretend we're on top of it. We're down on the floor, Bill. Yes or no, Bill?"

"I've drink taken, I'm not answering."

"Sorry, out of order. You know what I think . . . ?"

He saw Parrish roll his eyes. Wouldn't be the first time that Keeper had spouted his view of salvation.

"Give it me."

"We're too defensive, Bill. We should be a more aggressive force. We should be abroad more, we should be ferreting down the source. We shouldn't just be a line of last resort with our backs against the wall. We should be out there and after them."

Parrish gazed into the young face in front of him, into the coolness of the eyes that were not misted with drink, at the determined set of the youngster's chin. He swayed. "And where's out there? 'Out there' is the arse end of Afghanistan, it's the happy little villages of Iran. My darling, you go there on your own. You don't go there with your old uncle Bill."

"Then we might just as well give up—legalize the stuff."

"For a joker who's going to get a Commendation, who's just had the Judge's praises sung up his bum, you are mightily hard to please, Keeper. . . . You should go home. In the morning, a good shit and a good shower and a good shave and you'll feel no end better."

Parrish had given up on him, headed back for the group.

He stood a few more minutes on his own. The rest had now forgotten him. He could not help himself. He could not turn it off, like they could. He was right, he knew he was right, but none of them came over to join him, to hear how right he was. He called across to say that he was on his way. None of them turned, none of them heard him.

He drove home. He observed the speed limit. He was stone cold sober. It meant nothing to him that the Judge had singled him out for praise. It only mattered that there was a war, and it was not being won.

Home was a two-bedroom flat in the southwest suburbs of the city. He could afford to live in the flat because of his overtime and Ann's work in a local architect's office. He garaged his Escort at the back of the block. He felt half dead with tiredness. He was a long time selecting the right key. What made him tired, what made him want to throw up, had been their looks from the dock as they had heard sentence. The bastards had laughed at April's best effort.

Inside there was a note on the narrow hall table.

"D. I've gone to Mum's for the night. Might see you tomorrow if you've the time, A."

The detective, bright and early, thanked the supervisor at the exchange. A small country town, of course there were easy and unofficially good relations between the exchange and the police. The number that had been disconnected last evening had been reported out of order three times during the night. One caller had left his name and telephone number. And not a name that surprised him. Young Darren was quite well known to the local detective. He suggested to the supervisor that it would be quite in order for the telephone to be reconnected.

In his office he told his subordinates when they

came in not to take their coats off, and he handed them the address, and told them to bring in Darren Cole for a chat.

He was whistling to himself, Gilbert and Sullivan. He would enjoy talking old times to young Master Cole, and talking about Lucy Barnes's purchases. A fine start to the day until his clerical assistant informed him that he was required in the Chief Superintendent's office, and that two big shots were down from Constabulary Headquarters.

Chapter ✤ 3

$\mathcal{H}$e was dressed as a *pasdar* in the loose-fitting dun khaki uniform of the Revolutionary Guards, and he walked with a limp that would be noticed but which was not ostentatious.

He had left his motorcycle a hundred yards behind where the man that he followed had parked his paint-scraped Hillman Hunter. He had trailed the man through the alleyways of the closed bazaar, past the steel-shuttered doors, and toward the Masjid-i-Jomeh. He walked on, ignoring the pain of the pebble taped under the ball of his right foot. He watched as the man passed the guards at the outer doorway of the mosque, entering the dark shadow beneath the linked domes. When the man was lost to him, Charlie veered away, and crossed between the sparse traffic to the far side of the street. For years now there had been heightened security at Friday prayers, all across the country, ever since the bomb hidden beneath a prayer mat had exploded at Friday prayers at Tehran University. Charlie watched and waited. The Guards at the entrance to the mosque had seen the young man who now sat on the cracked pavement across the street from them. They had seen his limp, and they waved to him, and smiled a comrade's greeting. A veteran, they would have supposed, of the great marshland battles on the perimeter of Basra far to the south, maybe a casualty of the fierce fighting around Halabja on the mountain road to Baghdad. Charlie knew that men in uniform, and with guns in their hands, and who were stationed far behind the lines, always had respect for a wounded veteran. He would cross the street and listen to the Mullah's words from the loudspeakers high on the domes of the Masjid-i-Jomeh, and he would talk to the Guards.

Charlie had not been brought up to respect the faith of modern Iran. It had been his father's concession to his American-born wife. His mother had had no religion. Charlie had been raised without the teachings of the Ayatollahs, and without the teachings of the Christian priests who had served the expatriate community in Iran. The children he had played with, been taught with before he went to the American school, they had taught Charlie enough of the Moslem faith for him to be able to pass as a believer. He would want to talk with the Guards. Talking was what Charlie did well, and he was better at listening.

He listened to the Guards. He let them talk. Duty rosters, "hypocrite" outrages, troop movements. To questions about himself he was modestly reticent, his wound was a small thing, he hoped that soon he would be fit to return to the service of the Imam.

Charlie saw the man come out of the mosque. At one moment he was listening attentively to their talk, at the next he had made his farewells, pleading weariness, he must rest, and he had drifted away.

He had known the name of the man for two years, and he had known his address for seven weeks, since he was last home. He knew the age of the man and the name of his wife, and the number of his children, and he knew the man's work. He knew by heart the case histories of at least a dozen of those executed by this man since the Revolution. He knew that, depending upon the order of the Islamic Revolutionary Courts, sometimes the man made his executions by hanging and sometimes by shooting.

The man was at peace, safe after communication with his God, safe in his home city, safe in the service of his Imam. The man had hanged a teenager of the Baha'i faith who had refused after torture to recant his heresy. He had shot the ninety-four-year-old former Captain Iraj Matbu'i, who had been helped to the execution post, sentenced for leading the Gendarmes against the Mullahs in the Mashad revolt of 1935. In public, he had hanged Juliette Eshraq.

Charlie had known the man's name for two years, since he had first returned to Iran, since he had scraped away at the story of his sister's death. It had taken longer to find the names of the two Guards who had lifted her onto the table, beneath the crane, in front of the Guards' barracks in Tabriz. These two he had now hunted and killed. He knew the name of the investigator who had tortured his sister. He knew the name of the Mullah who had tried and sentenced his sister.

He saw the man climb into his old car. He rode behind him across the bridge, over the broad river that was swollen by the melting mountain snows from the north, along the straight road beside the cemetery and the gardens that once had been the city's pride. The midday heat, trapped in the valley, blistered the squat concrete buildings. Charlie felt the warmth of the air on his face as he rattled in the wake of the Hillman Hunter, bouncing over the coarse paving of the old road.

The car ahead of him pulled off the road, no signal, wound up a dry dust lane. Charlie braked, cut his engine, dismounted and seemed to be adjusting his chain. He watched the children stream out of the house, and the man laugh with them, reach for them, and lift them.

He had seen enough. Charlie remounted and powered the motorcycle away.

Young Darren had been left to sit in an interview room, watched over by an expressionless policewoman, and sweat.

His two juniors reported to the local detective, and in the Chief Superintendent's office, sitting back easily, feigning the indifference of rank, were the big shots from Constabulary Headquarters. The local detective liked what he heard. Young Darren had been lifted outside his address, taken on the pavement as his hands were busy with the keys and door handle of his car. Two arresting officers approaching from different directions, and the suspect taken unawares, and without the chance to dispose of the evidence.

The detective heard them out, then muttered a

lukewarm congratulations. He could play politics with the best of them. Nothing too fulsome, because that way he gave the impression that it wasn't a miracle that they had done it right. When they had finished, and bowed their way out of the presence, the detective addressed himself to his seniors. He had the file. He glossed through the prime detail. Cole, Darren Victor. Age, twenty-four years. Address . . . Previous: Possession (fined), Possession (fined), Possession (6 months). Common-law wife, two babies. Income: No visible means. Upsum: Hick, seocnd-rate villain, pusher and user. . . . Young Cole was what would be expected in a country town. Small time, small beer, not the sort of chummy who would ever expect to be confronted in the interview room by big shots from headquarters.

They left the local detective with no doubts. He was working to them, they were in charge, they had taken over. He would do as he was told and be thankful for it. He didn't complain, had never in his police career tried to buck the system. He was to go back to Darren Cole's address with his two juniors and a dog, relieve the uniformed constable who had been left to watch over the woman and her brats, and take the place apart. He would not be required for the interview with chummy, and God help him if he came out of that house with at least one evidence bag not filled.

In the interview room they dismissed the police-woman. They introduced themselves, a Superintendent and a Chief Inspector. They sat and tilted their chairs back as if that were more comfortable. They looked at Darren Cole like he was filth, like they'd want a good wash after being in the same room with him. Their chummy's eyes flickered, hovered from one to the other. They let him soak it in, they wanted him soft.

"It's Darren, right? Darren Cole, is that right?" The Chief Inspector said softly.

Their chummy pursed his lips, stayed quiet.

The Superintendent said, "I am going to assume, Darren, that you are not wholly retarded. I'm going to give you the benefit that you are not completely dumb. Now, it's not every day that the likes of my colleague and I miss our breakfast to get down here to talk with a shit bag such as yourself, Darren. Have you got me?"

Young Darren nodded, nervous and showing it.

"Can we start again, Darren?" The Chief Inspector passed his pack of cigarettes across the table, and Darren Cole fished one clear and his hand was shaking as he held the cigarette to his mouth. It was lit for him. Neither of the big shots took a cigarette. "You are Darren Cole, is that right?"

A feeble reed reply. "Yes."

"Good boy, Darren . . . I said to my colleagues that Darren Cole was cute enough to know what's good for him. I said that Darren Cole would know how to behave. You push scag, chummy."

"Might have done . . ."

"You push it regular."

"Maybe."

The Chief Inspector's voice hardened. "Regular."

"So, I do."

"You pushed to Lucy Barnes."

"I don't know the names."

"To Lucy Barnes."

"Perhaps."

"Getting silly again, Darren . . . To Lucy Barnes."

"Yes."

"You gave Lucy Barnes her scag."

Darren shrugged.

The Superintendent said, "Lucy Barnes is dead, chummy. On the slab. Don't tell me that you didn't know. Christ, is this bloody cow town so bloody slow . . . ?"

There was a quiet knock at the door. A uniformed policeman came in and handed the Superintendent a folded message sheet. He read it slowly, he smiled slowly, then he handed the message sheet to the Chief Inspector. Another smile and then the fast look of satisfaction between the two of them. Darren Cole saw the signs. He was shriveling in his chair.

"The dog's been down at your place, Darren. I tell you what, when you get through this, when you've done whatever's coming your way, then I'd learn to hide things a little better. I mean that approximately four hundred grams of what we are presuming to be a prohibited substance, namely heroin, could be better hidden than under the bloody mattress. That's making it easy for the dog, Darren, oh dear, oh dear me . . ."

"That's not very clever, chummy," the Superintendent shook his head.

They had the well-oiled routine, they had been working in tandem for more than a decade. Straightforward, this one, a roll over.

"You are looking at a bad scene, Darren," the Chief Inspector said as if it hurt him.

"I didn't know she was dead."

"You've only done an open prison, Darren. Closed prison isn't the same. The Scrubs, Pentonville, Winson Green, Long Larton, Parkhurst, they're not the same as where you were. They are nasty news, Darren. Do you know what you're looking at, Darren?"

Cole did not reply. His head was sinking.

"You could be looking at a tenner, Darren, because of who and what Miss Lucy Barnes was. God's truth, Darren, a tenner. A very hard time in those places, Darren, if we weren't speaking up for you."

The voice was muffled through the hands, pathetic. "What do you want?"

"We don't want *you,* chummy, that's for sure, we want up the chain from you. We'd speak up for you, if you gave us the name of the dealer."

A long silence in the interview room.

The Superintendent said easily, "Just the name of your dealer, chummy."

Cole's head burst upward. He was actually laughing. His shoulders and upper body were convulsed, like it was the funniest thing he'd ever heard. His mouth was frothing.

"You trying to get me blown away? I don't get less than a tenner, if I grass I get stiffed. You get a name and they don't ever forget. Shove it, mister."

For the next hour Darren Cole stared fixedly ahead of him. His mouth never opened.

The big shots from Constabulary Headquarters seethed, shouted, bribed, and won nothing. The local detective had a quiet chuckle around lunchtime when he heard how well they had done.

In cumbersome longhand, using a thick-nibbed pen, in handwriting that only Miss Duggan could decipher, Mattie wrote out the signals. There were those to the Station Chiefs around the Iranian frontiers and sea boundaries, where the watchers of events inside that closed country operated, and there were those that would be received inside Iran. The Station Chiefs in Dubai, Bahrain and Ankara were informed by coded teleprinter messages beamed by the aerials on the roof of Century House to a radio farm in Shropshire and then on to a booster clinging to the summit point of the Troodos mountains in Cyprus, that Codeword Dolphin was coming. Signals to inside Iran were drafted for transmission on the evening Farsi language commentary as broadcast by the World Service of the BBC from Bush House. Those signals would be received by a man who worked in the harbormaster's office at the newly developed port of Bandar Abbas, by a man who had a carpet business in the close and covered alleyways of Tehran's bazaar, and by a man who repaired heavy goods vehicles in a yard behind the old railway station at Tabriz.

When she had sent down the messages and signals to the basement, his PA reverted to form. She began to fuss him with detail. Were Mr. Furniss's inoculations up to date? When could he manage an appointment with the medical staff for malaria pills, stomach pills, sleeping pills for the aircraft? She would go to the third floor for his travelers' checks, but would he sign this authorization? And for his tickets. Please sign here, here and here. And would he be wanting the car to collect him for the airport directly from home, or from Century? Should a final appointment be arranged with the Director General? And inside the passport was a folded slip of paper as a reminder not to forget the girls, nor Mrs. Furniss, of course. "I don't suppose she was taken in for one moment by that cardigan I found in the Strand the last time you came back."

The routine of travel was no longer second nature to him. He gave way before the organizational blizzard that was Miss Duggan. He sat on the two-seater sofa in the partitioned office, he had the ripple of her keyboard in his ears. Quietly he read his book. He was stocking his mind with detail. Wonderful people, the Urartians, an extraordinary and flourishing civilization of three hundred years, and then gone. A thousand years before Christ's birth, this stocky people had made their mark across the wedge that was now divided among Turkey, Iraq and northeastern Iran. He was already an authority of some stature concerning their artifacts, their belts and earrings and bracelets, their cuneiform script that he had seen gouged out on the walls of ruins and caves. Most certainly he would get to the Van Kalesi. The Urartian fortress at Van, safely inside Turkey, was earmarked as the next stop after Tabriz. Very much indeed he would look forward to being there. He summoned up the memory of Van Kalesi, built of dressed stone blocks that weighed up to twenty-five tons apiece, the canal that brought water to Van from forty miles away. A civilization reduced by the Assyrians to bronze trifles and pottery shards, and amusement for men such as Mattie Furniss. The books he now read described the excavation in 1936 of a Urartian fortress town in present-day Soviet Armenia, the first time that he had come across a readable and unabridged translation of the report. The purpose of his reading was cover. Whenever Mattie traveled in the Gulf and Near Asia it was as an archaeologist. One day he would write his own book on the Urartians. Damned if he knew how he would get it published commercially, but if all else failed Harriet would probably pay for a private printing of his view of Urartian culture.

Miss Duggan was locking her papers into the

wall safe. Time for lunch. Time for the canteen queue. He seldom took lunch in his office, he enjoyed the chance to spend the time with colleagues at the Formica-topped tables of the canteen. The food was edible, the view across the river was always interesting. He put a marker in his book and followed her out.

Mattie was a popular figure at Century. Not just because of the long time that he had been with the Service, but because no man, young or old, senior or junior, could remember the least discourtesy or pomposity from the Head of Iran Desk. He had not reached his rank by treading on the prospects of anyone else on the staff. He was generous to any colleague in difficulty, or who sought his advice. Many did. He would never have claimed to be popular, was not even aware of it.

He went down in the lift with Israel Desk.

"Sorry about what happened the other day up there, Mattie. The DG's no right to speak like that in front of colleagues, nor privately. I didn't reckon at the time it would have helped you had I stood your corner, if it happens again I will. Chin up, eh, Mattie . . ."

Mattie could summon his fluent smile, as if little things like that didn't annoy him.

At the counter he took a full lunch onto his tray because Harriet was out that night, a committee on something or other, and at home he'd be doing for himself. Percy Martins was behind him. Percy Martins ran Jordan, Syria and Iraq. He had done something worthwhile, and quite insane, a couple of years back and had himself promoted a light-year beyond his ability, and the new DG hadn't yet got round to sorting it out.

"Thanks for that about the Sanandaj units, Mattie. We slid it down to the Baghdad chappies, by now it'll be into the Iraqi system. Very grateful. . . . Sorry about your run-in with the bossman. My own view is that he's no background and shouldn't have been let past the front desk. If there's any time you need speaking for then I'm your man . . ."

A tiny, warm smile, which said, "Wouldn't be necessary, old fellow, but thanks all the same."

He found himself a table. He needed to be alone. He had his knife into the liver when the seat opposite was taken. Old Henry Carter . . . Good God, thought he'd gone in the first reshuffle. Henry Carter, bachelor, prissy old thing, but sharp, had been in place when Mattie was joining. He couldn't imagine what Henry Carter did round the place these days. Used to be something about safe houses and debriefs, never quite certain, and it was the way of the Service now that work was specialized that officers were not encouraged to gossip with men and women from unrelated sections. Such a hell of a quiet voice, and it was rude not to listen, but so damned hard to hear what the man was trying to say.

"I can see it in your face, you thought I'd gone. Should have done, I was supposed to have been pensioned off last year, but I managed twelve months' extension. They all think I'm a lunatic, still being here, but what does a retired spookie get up to? I dread retirement, it's the only thing in my life I'm actually frightened of, handing my ID in and walking out of Century for the last time. Sorry about your problems, that man needs a brain scan. . . ."

It must be all round the building, Mattie concluded, and that was extremely unprofessional. . . . Two others came over and muttered at him, as if to a bereaved husband, before he had finished his treacle tart and custard. He felt that he was being set up as a faction leader. He would not tolerate that. He would refuse most categorically to become a center of resentment against new management.

Carter asked, "What are you going to do, Mattie, when you retire?"

"Write a book. The tale of a lost civilization."

"That's very good. Subtitle, *A History of the Secret Intelligence Service.*"

The news from the National Drugs Intelligence Unit was spring-water clear.

"Listen, my friend, I have a powerful breath on my collar. If you can't get a dealer's name off a pusher in the backwoods, just let me know, one hour from now, and I'll send down one of my graduate trainees. Do I make myself plain, old friend? The name of the dealer or you're off the case."

The telephone purred into the ear of the Superintendent. He was flushed. His Chief Inspector was head down into his notes and not wishing to witness the discomfort.

"Our local hero, where is he?"

"Still down at the Cole residence."

"Get him here."

The Chief Inspector gagged. "You're not going to hand it over to him?"

"Right now, if it would concentrate that little bastard's mind, I'd hand it over to the dog."

The radio transmitters and the teleprinters were in the guts of the building, and that was where the decipher clerks worked, in a constant air-conditioned breeze. The signal from London was passed to the junior spook.

The junior spook had now to walk up two flights of stairs, and down a corridor that was shared with the Military Attaché's office before getting to the secure area from which the Service worked. The original embassy planners had made no allowances for the fall of the Shah of Iran and the consequent upgrading of the mission. That Bahrain would become a listening post, a base for watchers, and analysts of events in the country across the Gulf waters, had not been foreseen. To rebuild the embassy to satisfy the needs of the Service was out of the question. To have moved the Service personnel out of the embassy and into quarters of their own would have increased their running costs, and denied them the embassy security umbrella.

The teaboy had carried cups of tea and soft drinks up the embassy stairs, down the embassy corridors for twenty-five years. He had access to any part of the building with his thirst-quenching tray except the secure upper corridor beyond the Military Attaché's office. The teaboy saw the Station Officer going down on the second flight of concrete stairs, his lightweight jacket slung on his shoulders, making for the golf course before the light went. He recognized the voice of the junior spook. He heard him say, halfway down the first flight of stairs, "Just through, 'Dolphin' is on his way. Here next week."

"What the hell for?"

"Something about reassessment of aims and means."

"That's bloody inconvenient. . . ."

The junior spook hurried on up, past the first floor corridor and toward the secure upper story.

An hour later, his cups, saucers and glasses washed and laid out on a draining board with a tea towel covering them from flies, the teaboy left his place of work, and walked out into the dry glare heat of the late afternoon.

The local detective lit a cigarette. As an afterthought he tossed one to Darren across the width of the cell. They were alone. The smoke curled between them. There was the smell of damp and vomit from last night's drunks.

"Let's understand each other, Darren, so that no mistakes are made which might later be regretted. We've got you for a tenner because you have volunteered the information that you pushed to Lucy Barnes. That and possession of four hundred twenty-eight grams of scag. That's all wrapped up. Trouble is that it's gone beyond that. You see, Darren, and you have to look at these things from our point of view, we find four hundred twenty-eight grams of scag under the mattress of the bed that you share with your lady love. I don't think I'd find it difficult to persuade any dozen good men and true, women would be easier, mind you, that your lady knew the stuff was there. I'm marching on, Darren, and you must stop me if you're not following me: so now we have an accomplice in your trading. That's not going to be nice for her, Darren. I'll put it another way: that's going to be very unpleasant for her. I reckon we do her for a fiver. . . . See it from our point of view, Darren—you haven't helped us, and we're getting you a tenner. You haven't helped us, and we're getting your lady a fiver. So, what happens to your kids, Darren? They get care. They get care orders. They get to be scooped up into council care. By the time your lady comes out they'll be fostered off, nice couple of kids, and God knows, it's not always a disaster, fostering. But she won't get them back, you won't get them back. That's looking at it from the bad side, Darren. Look at it from the good side. You know me, you trust me. You know I'm straight. What I say I'll do, I bloody well do. Straight swap, as far as I'm concerned. I get the dealer's name and detail. You get a great write-up from us for the judge and no charge against your lady, and no council care order for the kids. I'm leaving you a piece of paper, Darren, and a pencil, that's the brown item here with the lead in it, and I want you to write that name down, and every last thing you know about that man.

Don't think you'll be helping me, Darren, think that you'll be helping yourself. . . ."

Half an hour later the detective carried upstairs four sheets of paper covered by a sprawling hard-worked handwriting, and a name.

"Bloody well done," the Chief Inspector said hoarsely.

"Won't be forgotten," the Superintendent said.

"If you don't mind, sir, I'll be off. Bit past the time I usually get home."

He started out of his sleep.

He heard the latch door close. He was awake, but there was a long moment when he could not gather where he was, when his own sitting room seemed a stranger. He heard the footfall beyond the door. It was all there in front of him, there was the vase on the mantelpiece that his parents had given them for Christmas two years back, there on the sideboard was the photograph of himself and Ann, marrying. There was her sewing basket beside the fire grate . . .

Park called out, "Is that you?"

He could hear her shrugging off her coat. He heard her voice. "Who else would it be?"

He had his mind clear. The wall clock told him it was seven. Seven what? Which seven? He shook his head. Christ, and he had been so tired. The plate on which he had taken his lunch was on the arm of the chair, bucking as he moved. It must be evening. He must have been asleep six hours. All of April had a day off, courtesy of William Parrish, and none of the hours lost going through the civil service time sheets. He hadn't changed two bulbs, he hadn't fixed the washer on the kitchen sink tap, he hadn't tacked down the carpet in the hall, he hadn't even made their bed.

She came into the sitting room.

"What are you doing here?" As if she were astonished. "I didn't think you'd be here. . . ."

"We were given a day off." He stood, he felt ashamed that she should see the plate on the arm of the new chair. She had bought the chair. He had said they couldn't afford it, she had said that she refused to live in a slum and that while she was working she would bloody well spend her money how she pleased.

"Why, why did you have a day off?"

"There was a trial finished yesterday. We had a good result. We were given a day off."

She picked up the plate. There was no mark on the chair's arm but she flicked it with her fingers anyway. "There was a trial yesterday that ended at early afternoon, I know that because I heard it on the car radio coming home. I sat here until past nine. . . . I am a dim little thing, aren't I, but

I didn't understand how it would take you more than five hours to get from the Old Bailey, Central London, to here."

"We had a celebration."

"Nice for you." She headed for the kitchen. He followed. She spat over her shoulder, "A pity about the tap."

"I'm sorry."

"David, if there is a choice between April, the Lane, or your home, me, I know where the apple falls. Please, don't tell me you're sorry."

She was a great-looking girl. She had been a great looker when they had first met, when he was on uniform duty at Heathrow, and a great-looking girl in white at their wedding day, and a great-looking girl when he had come home to tell her, all excitement, that he had been accepted into the Investigation Division. She was still a great-looking girl, shoveling his dirty plate into the dishwasher. Ann had bought the dishwasher. David had said they didn't need a dishwasher, Ann had just gone out and bought it in the sales. She was as tall as him in her heels, and she had flaxen blond hair that she drew up into a pony, and she had fine bones at her cheeks and a mouth that he thought was perfect. She worked in the outer office of a prosperous architect, and she dressed to impress the clients.

"So, you all went off to the pub, where there was, of course, no telephone . . . and I presume you took the opportunity to tell them how they were getting it all wrong."

"I told Bill what I thought we should be doing. . . ."

"Great way to celebrate."

He flared, "I said that I thought we weren't winning. I said that we should be more aggressive, work overseas more, I said that the men we put away yesterday were laughing at us when they were sent down. . . ."

"God, they must think you're a bore."

"Do you know that last year our cocaine seizures were up by three hundred fifty percent? Do you know that means that three and a half times as much stuff came in last year as the year before . . . ?"

"What I care about is that my husband works seventy hours a week, that he's paid what a probationer constable in the Met gets. I care, used to care, that my husband is never at home when I want him, and when I am privileged to see him all he wants to talk about is filthy, sleazy, nasty drugs."

His breakfast plate and his breakfast mug followed his lunch plate into the dishwasher.

"It's a disease that'll kill this country—AIDS,

that's nothing in comparison. Ann, there's a billion pounds spent on drugs in this country each year. It's the principal reason for mugging, burglary, assault, fraud . . ."

"I don't know anyone, David, who is a junkie. No one in our block is, that I know of. No one in my office. I don't see junkies when I'm shopping. Drug addiction is not a part of my life, except when you bring it into our home."

"It's not something you can just turn your back on," he said flatly. "Whether it's me you're married to or anyone else."

She turned. She came toward him. She put out her arms and looped them around his neck. Her mother had told her to come back, and not just to collect her suitcases, her mother had told her to try again. One last bloody time, she had told her mother, she would try again. "Are they all like you, in April?"

"Yes."

"All on seventy hours a week, seven days a week?"

"When it's hot, yes."

"Do all their wives bitch?"

"Those that have stayed, yes."

"I bought some steak, and a bottle."

She kissed him. He couldn't remember when she had last kissed him. He held on to her, and the telephone rang. He picked the telephone off the wall bracket.

"Yes, it is, hello Bill . . ."

He felt her arms coming away from his neck. He saw the sadness flood her face. He was listening. He saw her grab inside her bag, and slap the meat down onto the kitchen table.

"The Lane tomorrow. Eight sharp. Look forward to it. . . . Ann, she's great, she's in great form. Thanks, Bill, see you in the morning."

He could see that she was not crying. Park did not know how to stop his wife's tears. He did not know how to tell her of his excitement because the April leader had called him for a meeting, eight o'clock in the morning, at Investigation Bureau's offices on New Fetter Lane, and promised a good one.

The teaboy's message was carried by a passenger from Bahrain to Abu Dhabi on the Gulf, and then flown on, having been passed to a member of an Iran Air cabin crew, to Tehran.

The message reached the desk of a countersubversion investigator in an office on the fourth floor of a small office block, close to Bobby Sands Street, once Churchill Street. The block was not identified in any way, but was a part of the Ministry of Information and Intelligence. To the investigator the transcript of a briefly heard conversation was a source of amazement.

The investigator had read the message several times. He knew "Dolphin." There would have been a dozen men in the section who knew the codename of Matthew Cedric Furniss. He had known the codename from far back, from times that were not referred to when he had worked for a different master, before the Revolution. He was astonished that the same codename was still maintained over so many years. In the Islamic Republic of Iran the British Secret Intelligence Service was hated with a loathing second only to that reserved for the Central Intelligence Agency, the Spies for the Great Satan. The investigator was not a man to initiate action, too great a survivor for that. To have survived a career with the *Saxman-e Amniyat Va Attilaat-e Keshvar,* the Organization of National Security and Intelligence, to have found a safe haven in an organization dedicated to rooting out all traces of SAVAK, that was survival indeed. His way was to assemble information and present it to those few people in the regime who had the power to act. To many, the investigator was a valued tool.

On his computer, IBM state-of-the-art, he punched up the entry on Matthew Cedric Furniss, and composed a brief note on the information that the British head of Iran Desk was traveling in the region to pass on a reassessment of intelligence aims and means.

The investigator always worked late in his office. He liked the cool and calm of the evening, the silent shadows in the corridors. He made his decision, he lifted his telephone. When he talked it was against the distant thunder of an air raid striking the west of the city.

He traveled on a false passport in his wife's maiden name, and with the occupation of "Academic."

Harriet had seen him off, which was unusual, but then it was wholly unusual for a Desk Head to journey abroad. They had had their little nuzzles at each other's cheeks, and he had told her to get back to the Bibury cottage and keep on giving that city farmer hell, double time, over the rape of the footpath.

Actually Mattie was rather pleased to be airborne, in harness again, but he hadn't said that to Harriet. Good to be on the road, not pushing paper.

Chapter ❖ 4

$\mathcal{T}$he car had coughed to life, and thick fumes poured from the exhaust. He let the engine run while he thanked his neighbor for the loan of the charged battery that had been attached to the leads. He could ask any small favor of his neighbor and it would be granted. His neighbor knew his work. Most men, in fact, who knew his work, treated him with respect. No man in his company offered him offense or cursed him. Perhaps no man in Tabriz could feel with certainty that he would never look across the space of a cell at the deep brown eyes that would peep from the slits of the tight-fitting black mask that he had taken to wearing when he performed his work. The highest in the land, and the lowest, would all walk in the fear that they might, one day, feel the grip of his thick-fingered fist upon their arm. It had not been done by himself, but he knew the man who had carried out the sentence of the Special Court of the Clergy on Mehdi Hashemi, and Hashemi had been the protégé of the man named by the Imam as his successor. Likewise, he knew the man who had put Sadeq Ghotbzadeh to death, and Ghotbzadeh had been the Foreign Minister of the nation and the favorite of the Imam. No man in Tabriz trifled with the executioner. He was adept in hanging and shooting and lashing and organizing the casting of stones at women taken in adultery, and in the handling of the newly arrived machine that was powered by electricity and that could slice with a guillotine knife through the fingers of a thief. He would use it this day: a thief who had stolen from a vegetable grower. And three executions, all in the city: a trafficker in narcotics, a Kurd who had aided the "hypocrites," a rapist of small children.

His wife was scrubbing shirts in the yard behind the house. She hardly acknowledged his shouted farewell from the back door. His children, all four of them, were playing with a deflated ball around their mother's legs, too intent on their game to hear him. Inside the house, from a cupboard beside the bed in the room he shared with his wife, he took a 9mm Browning pistol—old, well cared for, accurate. He heard the car engine running sweetly beyond the open door.

He walked out into the morning. He tiptoed between the rain puddles because he had earlier shined his shoes. He climbed into his car, and laid the Browning, that was loaded but not cocked, on the seat beside him, and he covered the pistol with yesterday's *Ettelaat*.

As he drove away he hooted his horn. He smiled briefly, he did not think that the sound of the horn would interrupt the game of football.

He tacked up the lane, avoiding the deeper holes, going slowly so as not to damage the suspension of the old Hillman Hunter. He rolled to a halt at the junction with the main road. There was a flow of lorry traffic heading toward the center of the city. He waited for the gap.

He saw a young man a little down the far side of the main road, facing toward the city center, astride his motorcycle. The young man was stopped at the side of the road. The young man wore a blue tracksuit, and was well bearded and bare headed, and he carried a satchel bag slung around his neck.

He saw the gap open for him, a small space, and he lurched the Hillman Hunter forward, seized his opportunity. He heard the high long blast of a horn behind him, but the Hillman Hunter had little acceleration and the lorry's brakes seemed to punch the air as the huge grille closed on his rearview mirror. Another howling blast on the lorry's horn and then he was under way. It was always a difficult maneuver, getting out of the lane in which he lived, and joining the highway into Tabriz.

He was boxed in. There was a central reservation to his left. There was a Dodge pickup to his right, filled with construction laborers. There was a cattle lorry to his front, there was a lorry with refrigerated cargo behind him. He could not go slower, he could not go faster. No matter that he could not pass the livestock lorry. He was not late for his work.

When he looked into his rearview mirror, he saw the motorcyclist. That was an excellent way to travel. The motorcycle was exactly the right transport for going into the city in the early morning's heavy traffic.

It was the motorcycle that had been parked on the side of the highway. The executioner looked ahead, then checked in his side mirror, and he saw that the motorcyclist had pulled out from behind him, and was now poised to come alongside him, and to pass him, coming through the narrow gap between the Hillman Hunter and the Dodge pickup. That was freedom, to be able to weave in and out of the heavy trucks. . . . He saw that the young man on the motorcycle had reached inside his bag that hung across his chest, that he steered the motorcycle only with his right hand.

He was aware of the shape beside him, looming close to his wound-down window.

He saw that the motorcycle was virtually against the side of his car.

He saw the grin on the face of the rider, the rider grinning at him, and the rider's arm was outstretched above the roof of his car.

He heard the thump of an impact on the roof of his car.

His window was filled by the grinning face of the rider.

Cold sweat, sweat racing on his chest, in his groin. He could not stop. He could not pull over. If he braked hard he would be swept away by the refrigeration lorry behind him, sixty kilometers an hour and constant.

It never crossed the executioner's mind that he might be the victim of an innocent joke. He was reaching for his pistol, and he was watching the motorcycle power away ahead of him, he flicked off the safety, but what could he do? He couldn't fire through the windshield. There was a moment when the motorcycle rider, the young man in the blue tracksuit, seemed to swivel in his seat and wave back at the old Hillman Hunter, and then was gone. He no longer saw the motorcyclist, only the lorry tail. He did not know what to do . . . Where to turn to . . .

He was staring into the mirror above him, and he saw the image of his own eyes. So many times he had seen staring, jolted, fear-filled eyes.

Charlie had had to turn one last time to wave, and to see that the box was held to the roof of the low-slung yellow car. The metal box contained two pounds' weight of commercial explosive, a detonator, and a stopwatch athletics clock wired to explode the detonator and the polar-amon gel-ignite forty-five seconds after the control switch had been pulled. A nine-pound strain magnet locked the tool box to the roof of the Hillman Hunter.

He waved, he saw the tool box stuck like a carbuncle on the car's roof.

He twisted the accelerator handle, then stamped up through the gears. Great thrust from the motorcycle, taking him speeding past a cattle lorry.

Charlie, in those stampeding moments, could imagine the stench of fear inside the car, the same fear smell as the man would have known when he

took the arms of those who had been brought to
him. He swerved in front of the cattle lorry.

The explosion blew in from behind him, buffeted him.

The thunder was in his ears.

The hot wind rushing over his back.

And the motorcycle speeding forward.

He took a right turning, he was off the main
highway. He accelerated along a lane and scattered some grazing goats that were feeding on the
verge. He took another right. He careered forward, full throttle. He was on a track parallel to
the main highway, two hundred yards from it. He
glanced to his right and could see above the low
flat-roofed homes the climbing pall of smoke.

He went fast, and he was whistling at the wind
on his face, and he was blessing the present that
had been given him by Mr. Matthew Furniss, who
was his friend.

"So why hasn't it been given straight to us, why
are the 'plods' involved?"

There was a sort of democracy inside the Investigation Division. A military type of rank structure had never been part of the Lane's style.

The Assistant Chief Investigating Officer
showed his patience. He did not object to the di-
rectness of the challenge, that was the way of the

ID. "The police are involved, David, because at this stage of the investigation the death of Lucy Barnes is still a police matter."

"They'll cock it up," Park said. There was quiet laughter in the room, even a wisp of a smile from Parrish, who sat beside the ACIO. The whole of April team was in the room, and they didn't mind the interruptions from Keeper. When he wasn't hanging round the edges in the pub, when he was at work, Keeper could be good value, and he was good at his job.

The ACIO rolled his eyes. "Then we will have to sort out what you regard as an inevitable cock-up, if and when we gain control of our friend."

It was one of the working assumptions of the Investigation Division that its members were superior creatures to policemen. The senior officers did little to suppress the boast. Morale was critical to the *espirit de corps* for the war against the fat cats and the traffickers and the money bags. Most men in the ID would have put their hands on their hearts and sworn that a policeman just wasn't good enough to be recruited into one of their teams. Unspoken, but at the depths of the resentment of policemen was the pay differential. The guys on April and the other teams were civil servants, and paid at civil servant rates. True, there were allowances to boost their take-home, but they were poor relations. There were plenty of stories of the bungling of the plods. Customs had targeted the Czech-born importer and overseen his arrest following a nine-million-pound seizure, the plods had been guarding him when he had escaped out of a police cell. Customs sitting at Heathrow and waiting for a courier to come through with all the surveillance teams ready and poised to follow the trail to lead to the real nasties, except that the plods had flown over to Paris and picked up the creep there and blown all chances of the arrests that mattered. Near open warfare. The police had suggested they should form an elite squad to tackle drugs; Customs said the elite squad was already in place, the Investigation Division, a squad in which no man had a price, which is more than you could say of . . . and so on and so on.

"For us to gain control, what has to happen?"

They were on the upper floor of the building. No self-respecting policeman would have tolerated such premises. There were cracks in the plaster of the walls, there were no decorations other than annual leave charts and duty rosters. The lukewarm green carpet was scarred from where it had been heaved up for the new wiring, and from the latest shift round of the desk complexes. They were all on top of each other, the desks, and half large enough once the terminals and keyboards had been shoved onto them. It was home for the April team, and at the end tucked away behind a plywood and glass screen was Parrish's corner. The ACIO and Parrish sat on a table and shared it with a coffee percolator, and dangled their legs.

"Right, if the whining's over . . . Lucy Barnes was supplied by Darren Cole, same town, small time. Darren Cole names as his dealer a Mr. Leroy Winston Manvers, about whom the courts have not yet been told, about whom CEDRIC is a mine of happy information. . . ."

For effect that wasn't needed, he held up the printout from the Customs and Excise Reference and Information Computer. A good deep shaft of a mine with a quarter of a million names, and room for half a million more, CEDRIC was their pride. They didn't reckon the plods could hold a prayer to it, and bitched every time Central Drugs Intelligence Unit at the Yard wanted a peep at their material.

". . . Leroy Winston Manvers, aged thirty-seven, Afro-Caribbean origin, no legit means of support, Notting Hill Gate address, a real bastard. I am not going to read the form to you, try and manage that for yourselves. . . . What had been agreed by CDIU is that we shall mount a surveillance on the address we hold for Manvers, while our colleagues of the police will be investigating all background leads, associates, etc. It is, however, important, gentlemen, that one point remains high in your minds. We will be happy to put Manvers inside, happier still if we can get a conviction which permits seizure of assets, but the principal reason for our involvement at this early stage of an investigation is to move beyond Manvers, the dealer, and into the area of the distributor. The identity of the distributor is our headache. We want the body who is providing heroin to Leroy Winston Manvers. Do not doubt that this investigation has a high priority. . . . Questions?"

"Why?" Park asked.

"Goddammit, Keeper, wash your head out," Parrish snapped.

"Facts of life, young man," the ACIO said sharply. "And don't give me shit about it. The facts of life are that the only child of the Secretary of State for Defense dies from a heroin overdose. That Secretary of State has a good cry on the Home Secretary's shoulder. That Home Secretary pulls a load of rank and calls the shots. That's why. . . . More questions? No? Bill will give you all the details. . . . Last point, I have laid down for you the priority, adhere to that priority. Thank you, gentlemen."

After the ACIO had left, Parrish sorted out the

initial details of the surveillance that would be mounted from late that morning on a third floor council flat in Notting Hill Gate.

Because he had opened his mouth, because he had had too much to say, and because he never seemed to care what hours he worked, it was pretty well inevitable that Park would start the surveillance duty. He wasn't complaining. And he didn't ring Ann to tell her that he didn't know when he'd be home.

He did not ring her because he was not thinking of her. He was studying a photograph, covertly taken, and recent, of Leroy Winston Manvers. Just staring at the photograph and absorbing the features.

". . . Our entire land is now engulfed with the bereavement, separation, death, destruction, homelessness, corruption and despair brought about by the clerics' antihuman rule and catastrophic war. The clerics have brought ruination on our people. Do you know, ladies, gentlemen, that because of the chronic economic situation more than eight thousand factories in Iran have had to shut. Our oil revenues were the envy of the world, but we now find that production is down by more than one half, because of the war. . . . Perhaps you are less interested in the cold figures of economics, perhaps you are more interested in the fate of human beings. I tell you, nevertheless, that economics have brought poverty, unemployment and starvation to millions of our people. But I will tell you about the effect on human beings of this cruel war, fought with the cynicism of those clerics while they themselves are safe behind the lines. Do you know that to continue this thirst for blood the clerics now send children to that front line? Don't take my word, take the word of a newspaper. A newspaper wrote: 'Sometimes the children wrapped themselves in blankets, rolling themselves across the minefield, so that fragments of their bodies would not scatter so they could be gathered and taken behind the lines, to be raised over heads in coffins.' Ladies and gentlemen, have you ever heard anything more obscene? That is the regime of the clerics, a regime of bankruptcy, a regime of blood, a regime of callousness . . ."

When he paused, when he mopped perspiration from his forehead, he was loudly applauded. It surprised him that so many had come to listen to him during a lunchtime in the City of London. It saddened him that he did not see his brother in that audience. He had urged his brother at least marginally to involve himself in the political world of the exiles. He could not see his brother, he accepted that failure.

He sipped at a beaker of water.

At the back of the hall was an Iranian student, enrolled at a Bayswater college, and taking a detailed note of all that Jamil Shabro said in his vilification of the reign of clerics.

Jamil Shabro spoke on for twenty minutes. When finally he sat down he was warmly applauded, and his hand was pumped by well-wishers, and he was congratulated for his courage for speaking out against tyranny.

And that afternoon the student in the English language took his written notes to a mosque in West London in which hung a photograph portrait of the Imam, and upon production of his Islamic Republic of Iran passport was admitted to an inner office.

In the outer corridor to the Cabinet room, after the meeting had broken up, the Secretary of State for Defense made the opportunity for a private word in the Home Secretary's ear.

"I'm in Washington for a week, won't be back until the day before the funeral. I'm going home now, pick up my bag, then the airport . . . what can I tell Libby? I have to tell her something."

"It is a police investigation, George. They've got it going."

"What do I tell Libby?"

The Home Secretary said softly, "You can tell her that we have the pusher, that we have a good line into the dealer. You can tell her that the Yard, the National Drugs Intelligence Unit, and Regional Crime Squads are all involved. You may also tell her that one of Customs and Excise's rather useful heroin teams is watching developments in the hope that the dealer will lead us on toward the distributor. If one word of this got out, George, one word, I would be severely embarrassed . . ."

"That will be a great comfort to her . . . we cannot shake it off, the guilt. Why didn't we notice things at the start? It's as if the disintegration of a happy child just passed us by, Libby's taken it all fearfully . . ."

"I hope to have more positive news by the time you come back."

The conversation was ended. The Chancellor and Energy and Education were spilling from the Cabinet room, full of good humor at the latest opinion poll, which gave government a six-point lead, and in mid-term.

Another meeting finishing, another conference table in Whitehall left with empty cups and filled ashtrays, the weekly session of the Joint Intelligence Committee had broken. There had been no politicians present. The Committee was the purlieu of civil servants and permanent officals. Had a politician been present then the meeting would have been severely constrained. Among these men there was a feeling that those who were reliant on the voters' whim were not altogether to be trusted with the nation's fortunes. Present had been the Directors General of the Secret Intelligence Service, the Security Service, Military Intelligence and Government Communications Headquarters, Foreign and Commonwealth officials, and in the chair had been a Deputy Under Secretary with the formal title of Coordinator of Intelligence and Security. This Committee decided what the politicians should see, what they should not.

The Coordinator had waved back into his chair the Director General from Century, a barely observable gesture to indicate that he should stay behind after the others had gone to their cars and their bodyguards.

"Between ourselves, and I didn't want to express this thought in front of the others, I had no wish to embarrass you, I think you've done rather well," the Coordinator beamed. "You were put in to do a job of work at Century, and I'd like to say that I reckon you're at grips with the problems there. From the Prime Minister downward, we wanted that place shaken out of its complacency, and you are achieving that."

"It would be easier to manipulate a brick wall, but we're getting there," the Director General said grimly.

"It was time for fundamental changes in attitude and direction. We have agreed to get away from the dinosaur belief that the cold war is still the focus. Agreed?"

"I'm shifting resources from the East European Desks and into all Mideast areas. There's a measure of resistance. . . . Do you know Furniss?"

"Doesn't everybody know Mattie Furniss, good fellow."

The Director General was hunched over the table. "He's a very good man, and he's seeing the light."

"Iran is critical to our interests."

"That's why I've packed Mattie off down to the Gulf. I've told him what I want."

"Have you now . . . ?" The Coordinator rolled back in his chair. "You brought some good stuff to the meeting. Is that Mattie's stuff?"

"He's running a new agent. Keeping the fellow tight under his wing." The Director General chuckled. "Typical of Mattie. I tell you what, I gave him a good kick up the arse, and he's been good as gold since. He's running a new agent, and he's gone down to the Gulf to sort out those that he had in place inside, and to breathe some fire into our watchers on the perimeter."

"Excellent. The Iranians believe, quite literally, they can get away with murder these days. I think the Pentagon taught the Libyans a lesson, and we have done the same to the Syrians. They're both better-mannered now. In my opinion, it's time the Iranians were given a short sharp shock of their own. . . . Why don't you stay and have a bite of lunch here?"

In Bahrain, Mattie had met the carpet merchant from Tehran. The man brought in foreign exchange, and his family was left behind, and he had two sons conscripted, so he could usually get a visa to fly out and back. And in Bahrain he had talked with his Station Officer. And he had picked up a tail.

Mattie had flown from Bahrain to Dubai to see the junior in place there, and he had been watched onto the aircraft and watched off it. He had dealt with the junior in a bit over four hours, given him the pep talk, told him to chuck out his university essay style, and to get himself down to the docks more often, to ingratiate himself more with the shipping fraternity.

Had he taken the road from Dubai to Abu

Dhabi, had he been driven the hundred miles from Dubai to Abu Dhabi, past the cars left to rust in the desert because the oil rich could not be bothered to fix another starter motor or whatever, then he might have noticed the tail. Traveling by air, watched through an airport, watched out of an airport, he did not see the tails.

And little opportunity here in the Gulf for him to lay a trail as an archaeologist. He found these communities with their air-conditioned Hiltons, their chilled ice rinks that were proofed against the 100 degree outside temperature, their communities of tax-avoiding British engineers, rather tedious. Van would be different, the Urartian ruins would be blissful.

He lost the trail that he did not know he had picked up in Abu Dhabi. He employed his standard procedures. He had checked into the hotel, been given a room on the twentieth floor of an architectural monstrosity, and then slipped down the fire escape service staircase and out through the work-force entrance. He had entered the hotel wearing his dun-colored linen suit, left it in jeans and a sweat shirt. And he sweated hugely as he walked the few hundred paces through the city to the small office that was nominally base for a firm of international marine surveyors. In a first-floor room, the venetian blinds down, he met the man who worked in the harbormaster's office in the Iranian port of Bandar Abbas.

Mattie had to hug the man. That, also, was standard procedure. He was not fond of overt displays of affection, but it was the way of these things that a man who had come secretly by dhow across the waters of the Gulf must be hugged like a prodigal returned. The man kissed him on both cheeks, and Mattie could smell the man's last meal. It must not concern Mattie Furniss, head of the Iran Desk, that the man had perspired his fear of discovery while lying among the nets and hawsers of a dhow that had ferried him from Bandar Abbas to the wharfs of Abu Dhabi. If the dhow had been boarded, if the man had been discovered by the Guards, if the man had been taken before a Revolutionary Court, then the man would have been tortured, would have screamed for the release of execution. And yet Mattie must, as a professional, keep himself emotionally aloof.

They sat down. They sipped tea. The man listened, and Mattie gave him the prepared lecture.

"It is detail that we want. Hard facts . . . I don't just want to know that a Portuguese or Swedish or Cypriot registered ship is coming in to Bandar Abbas with containers on the deck, I can get all that from satellite photography. I want the contents of the containers. I want the markings on the containers . . ."

He watched the man, saw that his fingers were twitching at the string of beads that he held over his lap. If over the years he had become emotionally involved with the man then he would have found these demands well nigh impossible to make.

". . . There is an international arms embargo on Iran. No weapons of war are supposed to be shipped into Bandar Abbas or any other port of entry, yet we understand that the Iranians are spending two hundred fifty million dollars a month on hardware. We want your country, your regime, strangled of arms supplies. Without the arms supplies the war effort will fail, and if the war effort fails then the clerics are gone. That's the incentive for you."

Not, of course, for Mattie Furniss to share with an agent Century's exasperation at the government of the United States of America who had dispatched 2,086 tube-launched optically tracked wire-guided missiles to the clerics along with a plane-load of spares for their old F-4 Phantoms. He could have reeled off the roll of honor of countries shipping arms to Iran: USSR, China, UK (anything from antiaircraft radar to military explosives), Italy, Spain, Greece, North and South

Korea, Taiwan, Pakistan, Syria, Libya, the Czechs, the East Germans, the Japanese, Brazil, Argentina, the Netherlands, Israel, Portugal, Belgium, even the Saudis. . . . Where a buck was to be made . . .

". . . Fine, we know that they are steadily turning to home-produced weaponry, but for the moment it is not sophisticated enough for modern warfare, and must be backed up by essential spares for items such as strike aircraft—that's what we have to know about. Don't shake your head, you can walk on water when you set your mind to it. Any arms shipment is going to be met with security, with military vehicles, it's going straight through the Customs checks, no formalities. Those are the ones that we have to know about . . ."

Those who knew Mattie Furniss down in the Cotswolds, the other weekender in Bibury, the cocktail set of Saturday evenings, would have described him as a very straight sort of cove, a pretty gentle sort of fellow. Those who talked to him about footpaths, and milk yields, and the stock market, would have been upended to have known that he would drive a volunteer, a very brave spy, to suicidal risks, and seem to think nothing of it. He was a hard man. He was a Desk Head in Century.

The following morning, while the official from the harbormaster's office was returning to Bandar Abbas, once more secreted in a dhow, Mattie was watched as he boarded the flight to Ankara, the capital city of Turkey.

He was missing four front teeth, and the rest were yellowed stumps. The old man's hair was tangled, uncared-for. His lined face was the color of a walnut. It was a tough life that he lived on the lower slopes of the mountain. He ran some hardy goats and some thick-coated sheep on the side of the Iri Dagh mountain and in the shadow of the summit, always snow-capped, that rose to eighty-eight hundred feet above the level of the distant sea. On a clear day, and in the early morning when the sun was rising behind the mountain, it was possible for the old man to look down on the metropolis of Tabriz. His glance would be cursory. He had no interest in that city.

He was steeled by the roughness of the ground on which his livestock grazed, on which he grew vegetables close to his stone-walled, tin-roofed home, and he was tempered by the sadness of his old age.

Majid Nazeri closed the wooden plank door and walked toward the building where the animals wintered and where he stored their fodder. He walked like an old soldier. He had no part of the present world, which was why he was happy to live in this isolation, alone with his dogs on the slopes of Iri Dagh, away from Tabriz, which the regime had made their own.

He inserted into the padlock the key that hung from a leather thong around his neck. There was a cut of pain on his face, because the new shoes that he had been bought would take weeks to mold their soles around the misshapen outlines of his feet. He was not ungrateful for having been bought the shoes, but it would be the next winter before they were comfortable for him. The nearest habitation was the village of Elehred, away over the mountain to the north, toward the Soviet border. He had chosen to spend his last days in a wilderness that housed the free soaring eagles, and the ravaging wolf packs, and the leopard if he was lucky enough to see it and his body smell were not carried on the stiff winds that never forsook the slopes of Iri Dagh.

He had not always been a recluse. He had once known how to polish boots. He had known how to pour and serve a pink gin with the right measure of bitters, and he had been familiar with the formation of a platoon-sized unit in attack, and he had once stood at attention an arm's length from the Shah of Shahs. Majid Nazeri had risen to sergeant in Charlie Eshraq's grandfather's regiment, and he had been batman to Charlie's father. The day that Charlie's father had been arrested, he had started the journey from Tehran to Tabriz, and then traveled on, northward, in search of a place where he could shut out the abomination of what happened on the lower ground beneath him.

It was two years since the young Eshraq, the quiet man replacing his memory of a noisy boy, had reached his home on Iri Dagh, found him.

Always, when Charlie came to him and then left him, he wondered whether he would see the young man again. Always when Charlie left him, after they had exchanged their gruff farewells, there was a wet rheum in his old eyes. It was of small concern to him that his once keen sight was sliding from him. His dogs were his sight, and as his eyes faded so also disappeared the hazed outline of the city of Tabriz. Charlie had told him that it was in the city of Tabriz, in front of the headquarters of the Revolutionary Guards, that Miss Juliette had been hanged. He had no more wish to see the gray outline of the minaret towers of Tabriz.

To Majid Nazeri, his life winnowing away, Charlie was an angel of revenge. To the old soldier, loyal servant and batman, Charlie was the last of a line he had worshiped.

He pulled open the door of the shed. He had old rags in his hand, the remnant of an army shirt that had rotted on his back.

He spent all of that afternoon polishing the petrol tank, and the wheel spokes, and the engine work of the Japanese motorcycle that was Charlie's. The motorcycle did not need cleaning, and by the time that Charlie had next taken it down the stone track to the road running from Ahar into Tabriz it would be filthy. And after he had cleaned the motorcycle he checked that the blocks on which it was raised to protect the tires were firmly in position. He never knew, never asked, when Charlie would next be hammering at his door, shouting for admission, squeezing the breath out of his old body.

He picked up the discarded two parts of a blue tracksuit, and he took them to the stream beside his house for washing.

The dusk was closing in. He did not have to go to his bed of rugs and furs as soon as the darkness came. Charlie had brought him kerosene for the lamp hanging off the central beam of his main room. He could sit on his wooden chair, and long after the night had come to the slopes of Iri Dagh, and the dogs outside had started their chorus to keep away the wolves from the animals' stockade, he would gaze at his most prized possession. He would stare at the gilt-framed photograph of the army officer and his foreign wife and their two children.

The joy of Majid Nazeri's life was Charlie Eshraq's coming, his despair was Charlie Eshraq's going.

He had reverted to the clothes of a *pasdar*.

He was sleeping toward the back of the Mercedes bus. Several times he was jolted awake by the man sitting next to him, because the Guards had stopped the bus at a block and were checking papers. His own papers were in order. Like every Iranian he carried with him at all times his Shenass-Nameh, his recognition papers. The recognition papers listed a false name, a false date of birth, a false record of military service in the Guards. The papers aroused no suspicion. He was unarmed, he had nothing to fear from a search of his one small bag. He had been wounded in the service of his country, he had been home on convalescent leave to the home of his parents in the fine city of Tabriz, he was returning to Tehran where his unit was to be re-formed. He was greeted with friendship by the Guards who searched the bus.

The bus stopped at a café. Charlie dozed on. He had no wish to queue for food. He had eaten well at the home of Majid Nazeri early in the morning.

To be hungry was to be alert, and it was sensible of him to sleep because in the morning the bus would arrive in Tehran.

He had the signature of the Mullah on his proposals for action. The investigator only proposed. The Mullah, whose signature and office stamp were on the document, had been chosen with care by the investigator. He knew his man, he knew which cleric could be trusted to rise, a trout in a waterway in the Elborz hills.

It was late in the night. The room in which the investigator worked was without decoration, save for the portrait of the Imam. So different from the office he had occupied when he had been the trusted servant of a plucked Peacock. No carpet now, no drinks cabinet, no easy chairs, no color television. In the struggles waged among the Ayatollahs and the Mullahs in the twilight months of the Imam's life the investigator did not believe the dice would fall for those who were described as the Pragmatists, the Realists, the Moderates. He believed that the victors would be men such as the Mullah, whose signature he had on the two proposals.

The city was quiet below him. He telephoned to the Manzarieh camp on the northern outskirts of the capital. He waited for the telephone to be answered in the building that was once the hostel of the Empress Farah University of Girls and was now the Revolutionary Center of the Volunteers for Martyrdom.

Chapter ❖ 5

$\mathcal{S}$he was different, but she was the only girl among them. He had been given short shrift by the boys. She wore no makeup, and her dark hair was combed away from a center parting, and she had discarded the headscarf that would have been obligatory out on the street, and she wore the jeans and the blouse that would have to be covered by a *chador*.

"I might have been away, OK I've been away, but that wasn't my decision. I was taken away. Now I am able to make my own choice, and that choice is to come back and live my life inside Iran."

They had all been his friends, the boys and the girl, at the American School. The name of the girl was La'ayya. Charlie sat on a straight-backed chair and the girl lounged on the wide sofa. This was the reception room of the villa of her parents. Before the Revolution there would have been framed photographs of La'ayya's father, about his official business, and with minor members of the First Family. The images of the other life were gone, along with the servants and gardeners. Her parents were taking the last of the snow on the ski slopes above the Caspian Sea. The girl was alone in the villa that was set back from the wide street, where the cherry blossom was starting to bloom, and she was amused, and not frightened as the boys had been.

"I went with my mother to California. I loathed it. I was sent to London, where we have friends. I live there, but I hate that city too. I am Iranian and I want to make my life in the country that is my home."

He had said the same to the boys. None of them had wanted to hear him out. He had been given little chance to talk in any one of the boys' homes before being shown the door, but the girl was in no hurry to expel him. She had always had more guts than any of the boys in his class. Now she smiled frankly at him.

"You don't believe me?"

"I'm not a fanatic, Charlie. I don't pray for the

eternal life of Khomeini. I just exist here. If anyone tells me that they want to live here when they have the chance to live in California or London then I think that either they are addled in the head, or they are lying."

"But you haven't thrown me out, the madman or the liar. The others were fast enough."

"Your father was killed, and your sister, and you talk about coming back as if it were the matter of crossing a street. . . . Let me tell you why the boys are frightened of you. When you left there were twenty-two of us in the fourth grade. The boys that you have been to see and me, we are the only ones still living in Tehran. There are eight in exile, and eight have been killed."

"A war doesn't last forever, not forever, a war finishes. The Imam finishes. There is a new country to be built. There will be a new Iran, and that will be my country. . . ."

Her eyebrows flickered. "You believe that?"

"It is why I am coming home."

And then the keenness of the girl. "And what part in your new order would I play, or the boys who rejected you?"

He was thinking that he needed a place to store the weapons that he would carry back on his next journey, which would be the last journey, that he might need a driver or a minder at his back.

He said, "I would want someone who will share my vision."

She laughed. She sounded as though she mocked him. "You know nothing of Iran . . ."

"I know that I want to live out my life in my own country."

She stood. She played the hostess. She walked toward the door. "I am in love with life, Charlie. I too have friends, relations, who were taken to the Evin jail, and to the Qezel Hesar jail and to the Gohar Dasht jail, and I don't wish to follow them. Nor, Charlie, do I believe a single word, not one, that you have told me."

She had been leggy and spindly when he had last seen her. He thought that now she was beautiful.

"When I come back I will come here, to see you, to show you my truth."

She grimaced. "And we could go for a drink in the cocktail lounge of the Hilton. . . . Trouble is, Charlie, that the Hilton is now the Independence Hotel, Oppressed Area Base Three of the Mobilization Volunteers of Beitolmoqaddar, it is now the property of the Deprived People's Organization. Goodbye, Charlie. It was amusing to see you, but not sensible."

"I did not believe you would be afraid."

There was the first moment of bitterness in her

tongue. Her voice was sharp. "That's California talk, or London talk. You insult me. You know nothing of my Iran, you know nothing of my life. You come here and you tease me, you laugh at me, and for whatever reason you also lie to me."

"What would you like me to bring you?"

"If you contact me then you put me at risk."

"Just tell me what you would like."

"Soap," she said simply.

She let him out of the house.

He thought she was very pretty, very sad. She closed the door before he had reached the pavement. He walked away down the street, and his feet trampled the early fall of the cherry blossom.

The first time he had come to the Manzarieh camp in Niavaran the statue of Lord Baden Powell, Chief Scout, had been at the gate and he had been employed in the secret police of the former monarchy. He had been sent to the Empress Farah University for Girls to arrest a student who was believed to be a member of a Tudeh cell. The hostel for the college girls was now sealed from the outside by heavy coils of barbed wire, guarded by troops of the Mobilization of the Deprived Volunteers, separated from the main expanse of open ground by electrified fences. And much was different in the appearance of the investigator and his transport. The dark gray suit and the BMW coupé had given way to plain gray trousers, and sandals on his feet, and a long shirt outside his waist band; his cheeks were laced in stubble, and he drove a humble Renault 4. It was not quite necessary for him to have renounced all of his previous life, the SAVAK trappings, but the investigator was a cautious man.

In what had once been the Dean of Studies' office, the investigator was made welcome and given tea. Each time that he came to this room it was to seek advice on the suitability of a candidate for operations overseas. It was the responsibility of the Director of the Revolutionary Center to consider the target, the location, the method of attack, and then to recommend a volunteer. The investigator had been many times to Manzarieh because the regime was often anxious to exercise the long arm of its discipline against traitors in exile.

The students at Manzarieh were trained in the teachings of the Koran, the ideology of the Imam, and close quarters killing. Prayers at dawn, noon and dusk, learning the trade of killing for the rest of the day. To brief the Director he took from his attaché case his notebook. The Imam glowered down from the wall at him. He tried never to think about it, but he had been at the meeting where the assassination of the Imam in exile had been discussed. If the investigator had a nightmare in his life it was that a minute of that meeting should have survived, a minute with a list of those attending.

His voice was a forgettable monotone.

"The exile is Jamil Shabro. In spite of warnings telephoned to his home in London he has continued to vilify the Imam and the Islamic government of Iran. I will leave with you a résumé of his most recent speech. It is our suggestion that explosives be used. One restive tongue is cut out, but a hundred others are silenced by fear."

The Director gazed down at the photograph of Jamil Shabro. "London . . . London is so very open to us."

"There is another matter . . ."

The investigator reached again into his attaché case. He produced a second file. On the outside, written large in the investigator's hand in the Farsi language, was a single word that if translated back to the English would have been written as Dolphin.

He saw the high steel gates open, and he saw the car's bonnet pushing into the narrow space, and he saw the Guard who had opened the gate duck his head in respect.

The width of the street was forty paces. The traffic was solid. The Mercedes could not nudge into the flow. It was as it had been the last time that he had stood on that pavement. The building behind him was abandoned, its garden was overgrown and the oleander bushes had been allowed to grow wild and provide a screen of evergreen cover. He had been in the garden, and he had seen the place where he could stand on the wall of the old and demolished conservatory and see over the outer wall of the derelict building. The driver of the Mercedes hammered at his horn, and made space.

He saw the Mullah. He saw a man who was still young. The face of an academic. Charlie saw the thin glasses, and the sallow face, the clean turban, and the shoulders of his camel-hair cape. The Mullah sat alone in the back of the long Mercedes, and Charlie noted once more that the car windows distorted the width of the face inside. He noted also that the carriage of the Mercedes was low over its tires. The Mercedes was armor-plated along its sides and its windows were of reinforced glass.

The gates creaked shut. The Guard was again positioned outside them, his rifle slung on his shoulder. The Mercedes had moved on.

Charlie drifted away.

He walked for a long time. He liked to walk because when he walked he could rehearse what he had learned in the previous hours.

He had that morning found the investigator. He had not seen him, but he had discovered his place of work.

Charlie was staying in a small hotel. In London it would have been a guesthouse behind Paddington Station. In Tehran it was down an alleyway crowded from dawn and beyond dusk with food stalls and metal craftsmen. A well-scrubbed little establishment, and cheap. There was a telephone in the hallway of the hotel. All morning he had telephoned different numbers at the Ministry of Information and Intelligence. He had been passed from one number to another. Fifteen calls, and always the same question. He had asked to be put through to the man. Fourteen times he had been denied. The fifteenth time, he had been told to hold. He had heard the extension ringing out. He had been told that the man was not in his office . . . and he had rung off. An hour later, more depth disguising his voice, he rang again. He had said that he had an appointment at the building, but had lost the address. Now he knew.

The procession passed him.

Students marching, goosestepping.

Boy children striding and overstepping, uniforms too large.

Women shuffling their feet under the full flow of their *chadors,* the widows of the war.

Men carrying buckets, and money being thrown from the pavement into the buckets, screwed-up bank notes.

Portraits of the Imam carried high, the streets filled with the shouting of the slogans.

Charlie put some notes into the bucket when it reached him. Not to have contributed would have attracted attention.

He found a taxi.

An age it took, to wind through the clogged streets, through the drab and smog-blanketed mass of the city. He would never be at ease in the south of Tehran. It was the shrine of the Imam, the working-class ghetto of those who shouted loudest for the war, for the death of their enemies. South Tehran was the bedrock of the Revolution. He kept his peace in the taxi until he was dropped.

He stood outside the main entrance to the Behesht-i-Zahra cemetery. It was a pilgrimage for Charlie Eshraq. Each time he came to Tehran he came to the cemetery. He had to wait at the gate as a line of taxis drove through. There was a coffin on the roof of each taxi, martyrs were being brought back from the front line, with a horde of family mourners alongside them for an escort. He followed. For hundreds of yards Charlie walked among the graves. A rippling sea of flags. Small wooden and glass-fronted box shapes, on stilts, in which were placed photographs of the dead. He saw a bulldozer excavating the yellow earth from a pit the size of a swimming pool, waiting for the dead from the next battle. He saw the raven women and old men and small children threading between the death markers.

He hurried on. His country's youth was laid to rest here amid the keening cries of women, the drone of the bulldozer, and the coughing of old taxi engines. The Gateway to Heaven Cemetery, and there was a queue to get there. Deep inside the Gateway was the Fountain of Blood. The water spouting from the fountain ran red. Charlie thought that was sick. He thought it was as sick to color the cemetery fountain water as it was to issue young soldiers going to the front with plastic keys, made in Taiwan, so that if they were killed in battle they could get through the Gates, make it to Paradise. On his first journey here he had given a bribe to a clerk in the Administration Office. A hundred dollars in small notes, and that had produced the burial charts, the names against the numbers.

He could not forget the way to this outer plot . . . far beyond the flags and the stilted boxes and their photographs were the bare concrete slabs on which, while they were still wet, a number had been scratched. He would not forget the number of his father's grave.

His father had said that a professional soldier, a soldier who forswore politics, had nothing to fear from the Revolution and his father lay in a grave marked only by a scratched number.

He had no idea where his sister was buried, or his uncle who had been clubbed, butchered, shot on the roof of the Refah school where the Imam had made his first headquarters after his return from exile. This was the only grave that he knew of, and each time in Tehran he was drawn to it.

Mattie Furniss could not abide sloppiness. It bred complacency, and complacency was fatal to field operatives.

He was not good at delivering an old-fashioned dressing down, but he felt it time to let the Ankara Station Officer know that he was quite dissatisfied with what he had seen.

The Ankara station was not located in the embassy building. The Service had several years before taken a long lease on the third floor of an office building in the government sector of the Turkish capital, where the high-rise blocks seem to stretch without end. The cover of the office was that the Service staff working there were employees of a British firm of structural engineers.

They had an hour before an appointment at the Turkish National Intelligence Agency, the only occasion on this trip when Mattie went official. An hour, and he intended to use it well.

"Don't interrupt me, Terence, that's a good fellow, and do not imagine for a single moment that I get pleasure from what I am about to tell you. . . . It's the oldest scenario in the book. A chap gets abroad, and all that he's absorbed when he was on courses at home goes out of the window. We'll start at the beginning, the car that picked me up and brought me here. The driver, he was not alert. We were cut off by a car full of men, and your driver just sat there, never considered the prospect of kidnapping, of having to take evasive action, your driver was dead from the neck up. It is the third time I have been to this office, and each time your driver has taken the same route. Your car is not fitted with a rear-seat passenger mirror as it should be. Your driver came into the hotel this morning to wait at Reception for me, and when he had met me, taken me out to the vehicle, he made no effort to check for an IED . . ."

"Mr. Furniss, this is Turkey, not Beirut. We don't have improvised explosive devices on every street corner."

"Hear me out, Terrence. . . . Your car is not armor-plated, your tires are not run flats, and I would hazard a guess that the petrol tank is not self-sealing . . ."

The Station Officer said, "Run flat tires cost three thousand pounds each, Mr. Furniss. I don't have a budget for that sort of carry on."

"I will take it up with London. . . . This room has been furnished by someone who has ignored every precaution in the book. Windows without the blinds drawn, anyone from that building, that one over there, can see you inside, could shoot you. That painting, is that shatter-proof glass? An elegant cocktail cabinet, but glass-fronted. Has no one told you that glass splinters and flies when explosives are detonated?"

"This is not a high-risk posting, Mr. Furniss."

"Neither is Athens, nor is Brussels. We were scraping chaps off the walls there who a few moments before would have happily said those cities were not high-risk."

"I'll get them fixed, sir."

"Very wise . . . Now I'd like to turn to matters Iranian . . ."

Mattie Furniss set out in detail the kind of information he would be requiring in the future from the Station Officer on the Iranian theater. He painted a picture that filled the young and fast-promoted Terence Snow with bleak despair. He required minutely recorded and frequent debriefs of Iranian refugees who had successfully legged it through the mountains and the river gorges, past the patrols, and into northeast Turkey. He had no use for the opiate dreaming of the exiles in Istanbul, he wanted fresh, raw intelligence.

They walked down the staircase together. Mattie said that the next morning he planned to head off toward the World War One battlefield at Gallipoli. He said that his father had been there, a gunner, never talked much about it. And then his voice lit up, and he said that they would follow that visit with a couple of days pottering among the excavated ruins of Troy. Did Terence know that all of the finest examples of Trojan jewelry had been lodged in the Berlin museum, and then pillaged by the Soviets in 1945? No, he did not.

"And then I think we'll go up to Van together."

Good grief. Three days nonstop tutorial. Terence's spirits sank. "I'll enjoy that, Mr. Furniss."

The council flat was home to Leroy Winston Manvers and his wife and his four children. The door was sledgehammered, off its hinges, and the wind brought the rain in from the walkway outside. It was three in the morning and the dog had failed.

The dog was a decent-enough-looking spaniel, and the handler was quite a good-looking girl, a bit butch in her dark slacks and the tightness of her navy regulation sweater. Park hadn't noticed her. Great while the dog was still searching, the dog had kept the adrenaline moving for them all. But the dog had failed and was sitting quietly at the feet of the handler, and all the rest of the team were looking at Park, because he was the case officer, and the decisions were his. Couldn't talk in the living room. Leroy had the sofa with the children in blankets beside him, and his wife hugging her knees in the only other easy chair. Park was in the corridor, standing over the dog, and the team was milling around him, still hanging on to the pickax handles and the sledgehammers that had taken the door off, what they called the keys. Pretty calm Leroy looked to Park. Vest and underpants, hair dreadlocked, and the composure that Keeper could best have wiped with a pickax handle.

Parrish was there, but out on the walkway. April's team leader was taking a side seat, leaving the tactics to the case officer.

Keeper did not believe that the stuff was not there.

The flat had been under twenty-four-hour surveillance for a full week. The flat had had the works—check on all movements and photographic record. Each pusher visit logged. Each movement out by Leroy tailed. Each meeting listed. Eighteen hours a bloody day, Keeper had done in one or other of the surveillance vans. He could have kicked the tail off the dog, because the stuff had to be there.

"Are you *sure*?" A venom when he spoke to the handler, like it was her fault.

"Not me, dearie, *I'm* not sure," the handler said. "And she's not saying there's nothing there, she's just saying she can't find anything. That's different to being sure it's clean."

The straight search had already been done. Leroy and family in the main bedroom while the living room and the kitchen and the kids' rooms were gone over. Leroy and family in living room while the bathroom and the main bedroom were gone over. All the beds stripped, drawers out, cupboards opened, everything gone through, but that shouldn't have been necessary because the dog should have led them to it.

What to do? To start again? To begin from the front door again?

The two constables were watching him. Customs had their own Search Warrants, and their Writs of Assistance that meant they could do just about anything short of shoving a broom handle up Leroy's backside, but they were obliged to take the constables with them. Supercilious creatures, both of them. They were armed, the April team was not. The constables were there to see there was no Breach of the Peace, that April didn't get shot up.

He could pack it in. He could take Parrish into the kitchen, and he could tell him that in his humble opinion Leroy Winston Manvers just happened to be clean, and they could all go home to bed. It didn't cross David's mind that he should do any such thing.

Back at the Lane they had a photographic record of the nine known small-time pushers visiting Manvers within the last seven days. No way the place was clean . . .

"Take the place apart," he said.

He showed them how. Down on his hands and knees in the hall, both hands on the carpet, and the carpet ripping off the holding tacks. Crowbar between the floorboards, and the scream of the nails being prized up and the boards splintering. Parrish in the doorway looked away, like he was contemplating a cash register of claims for compensation if the search didn't turn something up. Plus racial harassment, and the rest of the book, all coming his way. But he didn't intervene.

The sounds of a demolition job inside the flat.

One of the team watched Leroy every moment,
watched his face, tried to read apprehension, tried
to find a clue from his face as to whether the
search was warming, and not just lifting boards.

There was the shout, a coarse whoop of celebration, and Duggie Williams, codename Harlech,
was lifting out from under the kitchen floor an insulated picnic box. The top came off. There were
at least a dozen cold bags, and there were the
packets at the bottom.

The dog handler said, "It's not her fault, dearie,
don't go blaming her. I've always told you that she
can't cope with frozen stuff."

By the time they had finished, and sealed the
flat, and taken Leroy off down to the Lane, and
dumped his wife and kids on the council's night
duty housing officer, going home didn't seem
worth it to Park. The last two nights she'd left the
spare bed made up for him.

Not worth going home anyway, because he
wanted to be up early and talking with Leroy Winston Manvers.

Chapter 6

Bill Parrish always went home. Whatever time he finished, whatever time he had to start again, he went home for a snuggle with his wife, a clean shirt, and a cooked breakfast. Park reckoned he couldn't have been in his house above an hour. He would have taken the early train from Charing Cross down into Kent, walked from the station to his modern estate semi-detached, had his snuggle and his shirt change and his shave and his breakfast, and walked back to the station to be among the first of the morning's commuters back to Charing Cross.

David had changed his shirt in the Gents, and he had shaved, he had gone without breakfast, and he hadn't thought about Ann, and he hadn't slept. He lolled back in his chair, he didn't stand when Parrish came in reeking of aftershave lotion. The clerical assistants wouldn't be in for another half an hour, and the rest of April would come straggling back to the Lane over the next two hours. Parrish wasn't fussed that his Keeper didn't stand for him. Customs and Excise had their own *esprit de corps* and it wasn't based on a military or a police force discipline.

He saw that the coffee percolator was bubbling gently, and he rinsed out his own mug that was still on the tray beside the coffee machine, tidelined, from the briefing before they had gone out to bust Leroy Winston Manvers.

"Been to see Leroy?"

"No."

"What's in the other cells?"

"Nothing, empty."

"Better not let him sleep too long."

Wouldn't have been worth coming in early if he had not been able to guarantee that Keeper would be sitting back in his chair at his desk in the April office.

"You've told the ACIO we've got him?"

"Certainly. He's impatient."

"A result is what matters?"

"Very much David, a result matters. He's got

the CIO on his back. The CIO had CDIU standing over his shoulder. The CDIU is under pressure from the politician. They want to hear what Leroy has to say and they want it in a hurry."

"And I'm covered?" Keeper asked.

"Like it never happened."

It went against Parrish's grain. To Parrish, thirty years in Customs and Excise, twenty-six years in the Investigation Division, it was out of order for an investigation to take priority because of connections. But he was a part of a system, he was a cog, he didn't argue.

"Then we'd better get on with it."

Keeper led him down the stairs, didn't use the lift, because the lift would be getting busy with the early risers coming to work. All the squeamish ones would be in early—the secretaries and the accountants, and those from the Value Added Tax sinecures, and the computer boffins. Didn't want to see them. Down the stairs to the basement of the New Fetter Lane building.

They came to the reinforced door of the Lane's cell block. Park pressed the bell, and stood aside for Parrish to come forward.

A short chat. Parrish would be taking charge of the prisoner. The guard could go and take a cup of tea and some pieces of toast in the canteen, and have a cigarette, and chat up the girls there, and not hurry himself. The guard looked from Parrish to Park, and saw the expression on Park's face, and said that he would be pretty happy to have a cup of tea and some toast.

Park went inside the cell. Parrish leaned against the wall in the corridor, and thought that he might throw up his cooked breakfast.

The dealer wasn't that often on his feet before midday and he had made the mistake of sleeping naked. He came warily off the cell bed when Park tore the blankets away from him.

"My lawyer . . ." the man said.

"We'll deal with him next. You first."

With a short left arm punch, Park hit Leroy Winston Manvers in the pit of his stomach. The man's body bent, and as it uncoiled, the man gasping for breath, Park's knee jerked into Leroy Winston Manvers's groin. The man collapsed, folding himself into and over the pain. Park pulled him upright by his hair. One violent heave. And then, very calmly punched him. Again and again.

All the blows were to the body, those parts of the body that were hard to bruise, except for the testicles.

The punches belted into the flab body of the big man. When he was on the tiled cell floor, when he was whimpering, when he thought his body would break in the pain, then the questions came . . .

Through the running pain, Leroy Winston Manvers could hear the question.

"Who is the chummy?"

He could hear the question, but before he could focus on it he was once more flung upright, crashed into the corner, bent, protecting his groin.

"You supplied Darren Cole, what is the name of the chummy who supplied you?"

And his eyes were filled with streaming tears and he could hardly breathe and he thought that if he didn't kill this fucker then he was going to be dead, and he threw a flailing blind hook with his right fist, and a huge explosion of pain landed and blossomed in his guts and his head struck the floor, and the voice came to him again the same as before, "The chummy that supplies you, who is he?"

"He's Charlie . . ."

Park stood back. He was sweating. He stared down at the demolished man on the cell floor.

"I'm listening, Leroy."

The voice was whispered, wheezed. "I know him as Charlie . . . Charlie Persia. The stuff is from Iran . . ."

"Keep rolling, Leroy."

"He's from London, Charlie Persia, but he goes to get it himself."

"And he is Iranian?"

"But he lives here."

"What age?"

"Your age . . . less maybe . . . ah Jesus, man."

It was a minute since he had been hit. Another fear winnowing in the mind of Leroy Winston Manvers. "You get me killed."

"That's OK, Leroy. You're quite safe here. Charlie'll be dead long before you get out of here."

"Don't you tell that I grassed."

The dealer crawled to the bunk against the cell wall, and he lifted himself onto it, and his back was to Park. He said nothing more.

The guard was hovering by the door to the cell block corridor. Park told him that the prisoner was tired and should be allowed a good sleep.

Park took the lift up to the April office with Parrish white-faced beside him, his fist locked on the notebook.

The lights were on. The girls were at the keyboards and answering telephones, and Harlech, in his shirtsleeves, was massaging the shoulders of the redhead as she worked.

"Go home now, Keeper, just go off home," Parrish said.

His *pasdar* uniform was folded into Charlie's rucksack.

He had traveled by bus from Tehran to Qazvin. From Qazvin, after a long wait under the plane trees of the Sabz-i-Meidan, he had joined another bus heading for Resht on the Caspian Sea. He got off by the river near Manjil, and had hitched his way along the track beside the fiercely running water. He had no fear. His papers were good, as they ought to have been at the price he had paid for them in Istanbul. He had a ride from a local official on the pillion of an ancient BSA for fifteen painful miles, and he had been thankful to have been able to spend two hours mostly asleep in a donkey cart.

He had reached the village shortly before noon.

The stone dwellings, too few, too insignificant to be marked on any map of the region, nestled at the base of hills and alongside the river. Once every decade on average, when the spring came following a particularly heavy snowfall in the mountains, the river would overspill and leave a deposit of loam soil across the washed-down fields. The plain beside the village was an excellent area for all crops.

Because of its isolation, and because of the quality of the fields beside it, the village was a place of quite startling prosperity. There was no out-

ward sign of that wealth. The American dollars
and the Iranian rials that the headman had accu-
mulated he kept buried. It was his persistent fear
that the village would one day attract attention,
that the wealth of his community would be discovered and that he would be taken by the Guards
to Qazvin and put to death in the yard of the Ali
Qapu. Charlie had never been able to prise from
the headman how he planned to use the cash that
he risked his life to amass.

He had eaten with the headman, and the headman's sons and brothers. They had slaughtered
and roasted a goat in his honor. He sat now on the
carpet that covered the dirt floor of the principal
room of the headman's house. They would be good
Shi'a Moslems in the village, they would follow
the teaching of the Koran. He looked for the fault
in the pattern, the mistake of the craftsman wea-
ver. There was always a mistake in even the most
precious carpet. Only God could make what was
perfect. For a human creature to attempt perfec-
tion, to try to imitate God, was heresy. He could
see no flaw. . . . He had eaten too much, he had
allowed the rich meat of the goat to blunt his wits.
In the evening he would need to be at his sharpest.
He would negotiate with the headman then.

The village was condemned to sleep for the afternoon. The sun belted into the tin roofs of the

houses, and scorched the alleys between. There was a corner of the room where he had been told to leave his rucksack and where blankets had been laid out.

He stood in the doorway of the headman's house and gazed out toward the gray brown of the flowing river, across the rich fields, over the shimmering scarlet of the poppies in flower.

The packets taken from the picnic cold box in Leroy Winston Manvers's council flat had been sent to the Scotland Yard forensic laboratory in Lambeth for analysis. And with the packets had gone the instruction of the ACIO that absolute priority was to be attached to the first, if superficial, study. There were only twenty-four scientists at Lambeth who specialized in drug-related investigations, and their backlog was soaring. A cocaine possession charge had just a month earlier been thrown out by an inner-city magistrate after he had been told at five remand hearings that forensic had not yet come through with its results. Simple analysis was now subject to a nine-week delay. So the ACIO had demanded that all else be dropped, this was a matter for the best and the brightest. He could do that once in a while, heaven help him if he made a habit of it. When he was bawling down a phone line, when he was trying

to extract blood from men and women already
drained dry, it was inevitable that the ACIO
would ask himself whether they were all, all of
them at the Lane, wasting their bloody time. Was
government, parliament, authority, really serious
when they confronted the drugs epidemic with
just twenty-four scientists? Buggered if he knew
whether they were serious, buggered if he cared.
He was long enough in Customs and Excise to realize the absurdity of getting steamed under the
collar about resources. In the last week he had
been up before the National Audit Office to justify
the way he ran the drugs teams, and the week before that he had had to defend a paper to the Staff
Inspection and Evaluation Board. He had talked
to Bill Parrish. He knew what had happened in
the cell early in the morning after the door had
closed behind his case officer. Typical of Parrish,
that he had gone straight into the ACIO's office
and shared the dirt, spread the load up the ladder,
so that if the shit was flying then it would be the
ACIO fielding it and not dear old Bill.

When he was alone in his office, when he was
not spitting about the delays in forensic analysis
and the scrutiny of the National Audit Office and
the nit-pick ways of the Staff Inspection and Evaluation Board, the ACIO could understand the way
the system worked. The system was pretty bloody

rotten. The system said that if a Cabinet Minister's daughter took an overdose because she didn't know that the heroin was of a purer quality than she was used to, then her disgusting self-inflicted death took priority over the very similar deaths of the ordinary and the humble. It was a surprise to him that young men like Park ever chose to get themselves involved or stay involved, and he thanked the good Lord that they did.

The ACIO had his preliminary report brought over the river by courier just as his secretary was bringing him his afternoon pot of tea and a buttered scone.

He read.

Initial study showed that the probable origin of the thirty-four packets, total weight at 2 kilos and 742 grams, was northern Iran. Attention was drawn to a stenciled marking on each plastic packet, a small symbol of a dagger. The symbol had been observed on other hauls over the past six years. The quality of heroin in packets stamped with the symbol of the curved blade dagger was invariably high.

He rang Parrish's office on the floor below.

"Don't you worry, love . . . Just leave him to me."

Park pushed himself up from his chair. The front door was already open, Ann was putting the key back into her handbag, her head was down, and his father was standing behind her. He was all puffed up, chest out, back straight, as if he were going on duty. Maybe he was, because he wore his navy blue trousers, and a white shirt and black tie, and his old anorak in which he was always dressed when he was either on his way to the station or when he had just clocked off. His father was a big man, and Park reckoned that because he sat all day either in a Panda or in the station canteen, he had a gut on him. Since his father was a policeman David had gone into Customs and Excise, a sort of bloody-mindedness, and he had had a bellyful as a kid of hearing his father moaning about the force.

He led them into the living room and closed the file that he had been reading.

Inside the room he could see clearly into Ann's face. She was red-eyed. His lip pursed. She had no business taking their marriage into his parents' home, and crying in front of them.

"Very nice to see you, Dad . . . Mum well, is she? . . . I was catching up on a bit of reading. We had a late night up in town and they sent us all back with a day off . . ."

"It's freezing in here . . ." Ann strode forward, snapped on both bars of the electric fire.

He paid the electricity bill. The last bill had

been 148.74 pounds. He remembered that. He had had to pay the electricity in the same week as the telephone that had been 74.98 pounds, and the car service that had been 101.22 pounds. He had gone overdrawn.

He looked steadily at his father. "As I said, I was catching up on a bit of reading. I'm doing a paper for the ACIO. What I really want is to get out of heroin and join a team who do cocaine. This paper is to persuade the ACIO to put a man into Bogotá . . ."

He wondered if his father knew where Bogotá was.

". . . Bogotá is the capital of Colombia, Dad. We've got a Drugs Liaison Officer in Caracas, which is the capital of Venezuela . . . but I reckon that Caracas is too far from the action. We need much more hard intelligence on the ground. Colombia exports eighty percent of the world's cocaine. I rate heroin as peaked, but cocaine is really growing up. I mean, last year's heroin figures were just about the same as the previous year, but cocaine was going through the roof. There could have been half a billion pounds' worth going through the UK system last year. Do you know, there's a place called Medellin in Colombia where the big traffickers live quite openly? We've got to get in there after them. Having a DLO in Caracas means that too much of our intelligence is second-hand. Do you know, Dad, that last year the Drugs Enforcement Agency made a seizure in Florida of ten tons of coke? That's worth fifty million dollars on the street. That's where the action is. What do you think, Dad?"

"What I think is that you're getting to be the biggest bore I've ever met."

"That's not called for."

"And the biggest prick."

"Then get out of my house."

"I'm here at Ann's invitation and I'm staying until I've done some talking." A flush was in his father's face, big veins leaping in his neck and his forehead. "Is that all you do when you get home, bore on about drugs?"

"It matters."

"Do you think Ann cares two pins about drugs?"

"She's made her feelings plain."

"There's nothing else in your life, it's getting to be an obsession."

"What do you want me to do, chat up bloody geraniums in a bloody greenhouse?"

"Look after your wife—try that for a change."

"Don't lecture me on how to look after Ann."

"If someone doesn't have a go at you, you won't

have a marriage to worry about. You don't deserve Ann."

"You're out of order."

"Not as out of order as the way you treat your wife."

He exploded. "Something you never learned, Dad, but if you don't do a job with commitment then it's not worth doing at all. In ID we don't just clock watch, we're in the front line. We're not just handing out parking tickets and checking shotgun licenses, and taking down the details of people's bloody cats that have got lost—we're in the front fucking line. If we all go home when the bell rings then there's no line left, and all that filth is swimming in here. Got me? Have you the wit to comprehend that? You know what I did this morning when you were watering your bloody geraniums before another second-rate day, what I did while she was painting her face before getting into her posh little office, you know what I did...? I beat shit out of a man. I hit Leroy Winston Manvers every place where the bruises don't show. I kicked him, punched him, till I was fucking tired ... until he gave me a name. Isn't that what you 'old-fashioned coppers' used to do? Hand out a bit of a belting, in the good old days. I smashed up Leroy Winston Manvers because he's a heroin dealer, and he fixed up the pusher, and the pusher sold to some government crap artist's daughter. I hit shit out of Leroy Winston Manvers because I hated him. I hated him as much as I wanted the name of his distributor.... That's what it does to you, that's the fucking filth you get into when you're hunting the distributors. You don't have an idea, do you? Not a fucking idea. I could go to jail for five years for what I did this morning.... I tell you, I enjoyed hitting the black bastard. I loved hitting him. You know what? He gave me the name. He was such filth. He's a pig. He makes more money in one month, probably, than I can make in ten years. He's a rat from a sewer.... They don't ask you to do that, do they, Dad? They don't ask an old-fashioned constable to be case officer when we're talking heroin, do they, Dad?"

"Like you said, David, out of order." His father stood.

Ann said, "I'm sorry, Pop, for asking you."

"I can't walk away from it," David said. "You can follow me if you want to. If you don't want to then I go on by myself. That's fair warning. You do what you like, I'm not quitting."

"Do you want to come with me, love?"

David saw his wife shake her head. She was muttering on about getting some supper, and she was gone out of the room and heading for the kitchen.

"We love that girl, David, your mother and I. We love her like she's ours."

"I don't hold that against you, Dad. I'm glad of it. But don't turn her against me. There's enough to contend with without that. It's a war we're in, do you see that, goddammit, a war."

But his father's face was set, astonishment, fear, disgust. And then he was gone.

It was a game to them. He thought at the end he would get what he wanted and they would concede. He played the game. He even rose off the carpet and walked out of the house and into the dirt street, stood in the moonlight and listened to the dogs yelping and the distant wolf howl. All part of a game because they were all tired and looking for sleep, then they would give him the whole of the seventh kilo.

They could have taken Charlie's money and put him down an old well or dug him into a field.

The thought was in Charlie's mind, but not uppermost. He reckoned on their greed. He believed the squirrel mentality of the headman preserved him. They would want him back. It was his protection that the headman had no notion that this was Charlie's last shipment.

Late in the evening the headman's hand snaked out, grasped Charlie's hand. Charlie reckoned that the headman was tired, or that he wanted his wife and bed. The strong dry hand caught Charlie's, held it, shook it, sealed the bargain. A game was at an end.

The cash was in wads of fifty notes, fastened with elastic bands. Charlie fetched the rucksack and put the ten bundles carefully onto the carpet in front of him. He sat cross-legged. That was awkward to him, and his back ached from the stretching of muscles that were unused. When his hand was shaken then he knew that his safety was guaranteed. Never in much doubt, but that was certainty.

Charlie left the village before dawn. In his rucksack were seven kilos' weight of pure heroin powder in sealed plastic bags, and on the bags was the stamp of the drugs' pedigree. He had watched them stencil onto the plastic the symbol of the curved dagger. That early in the morning there was no cart to carry him alongside the river. He strode out on the dirt trail.

This was the currency that would buy him armor-piercing missiles. He was in a hell of a good humor, and whistling to himself, and he was alone in the mountains of his homeland.

Keeper, restless, fretting, pacing the ragged and worn carpet in April's office. He was a bloody pain, and even Parrish didn't have the spirit to tell him that to his face, and Harlech, who was the nearest that Park had to a friend, just cursed him and stayed quiet.

Charlie Persia. The great silent stomach of the computer had no entry on Charlie Persia. Nothing under the name, and nothing like it from the scores, hundreds, of cross-referenced Suspicious Movements Reports that were daily fed into CEDRIC's system.

It was Keeper's opinion that Leroy Winston Manvers had come clean in his pain, had told all. Charlie Persia was the name that the distributor traded under. He believed that. The face and the gasping admissions of Leroy Winston Manvers had a truth about them. He knew from forensic's analysis that the packets found in the Notting Hill council flat were of Iranian origin. He took as his base position that Charlie Persia was Iranian, had carried the good, hard stuff to London. He waited on a phone call to take him forward now that the computer had come up blank. He needed a break. He needed luck. And he was pacing because his phone call had not been returned, and because he did not know where else the break would come from.

It had been luck that had heaved Park out of uniform at Heathrow Airport and into the ID on the Lane. He would never have argued with that. He had spotted the girl coming off the Varig from Rio, and she looked like a towrope, and her accent was an East London slur, and her clothes weren't good enough for a return ticket to Rio, and she had been the only passenger he had stopped all that morning off the overnight intercontinentals. She had had an airline ticket and 500 pounds for couriering a kilo of cocaine, fastened in a sanitary towel between her legs. That was a break, that was noticed. Luck was different, luck could only be taken advantage of. A slack half hour between the clearing of the Customs hall and the arrival of the next jumbo and he had gone out into the concourse to get himself an afternoon paper, and he had seen the man waiting at the barrier, in position to meet a passenger off the incoming flight. At Heathrow they had the police mugshots of all convicted pushers and dealers. Not everyone looked at them, but the young David Park had made a point of studying them every week. He recognized the face, eighteen months at Isleworth Court and he could only have been out a few weeks. That was luck, recognizing the chummy. He had tipped off the local ID based at the airport. The "greeter" had been watched, the meeting had been observed, the passenger had been challenged and asked to return to the Customs area . . . a few grams more than a kilo stuffed into the cavities in a pair of platform shoes, and back to Isleworth Court for the "greeter," and seven years for the courier. Luck, but there were those in the ID command who said that a man earned his luck, and his luck had been noticed, noticed enough for his application to join the Investigation Division to be processed at speed.

When the telephone on his desk rang out Park was at the far end of the room and he charged for it. God, and he needed the break and the luck when CEDRIC had gone down on him.

Ann . . . would he be in for supper? He didn't know. . . . Should she cook for two? Probably best not. . . . Did he know what time he would be home? Could she clear the line, he was waiting on a call.

He pounded on over the carpet. The carpet was a disgrace, and so were the blinds that sagged unevenly across the windows, and so was the crack on the upper wall behind his desk that had been there for a year and not repaired. Without luck he was going to stay grounded.

The telephone call, when it came, left him flattened. The Anti-Terrorist branch at Scotland Yard had the most complete records on Iranians living in London. A Chief Inspector told him that they had no record of any exile who went under the name of Charlie Persia . . . sorry not to be of help.

The folder on his desk contained a single typed sheet, which was the preliminary report from forensic. Another sheet was his own handwritten record of the interview with Leroy Winston Manvers. He was certain that his man took the name of Charlie. He thought the man was most probably an Iranian. He had written Tango One on the outside of the folder. Tango was ID's word for a targeted suspect.

For the moment, he was damned if he knew how he would put a face into the Tango One folder.

The investigator worked late into the evening. He had no family, he had no call to go back to the cramped one-bedroom flat that had been his home since his former life. Beneath his window the Tehran streets had emptied. The recruit from Manzarieh Park would be flying out in the morning, that part was simple, but the arrangement of the detail of the collections that he would make upon his arrival, and the backup that he would receive on the ground, all of that required care. It was, of course, his intention that no "smoking pistol" would remain behind. He was working at long range, and great distances always posed problems. When he had finished with the matter of Jamil Shabro, traitor and collaborationist, he switched his attention to the business of the British intelligence officer, Dolphin/Matthew Furniss, in the city of Van.

He had on his desk all the sightings marking Furniss's progress across Turkey, just as he had them for his journey around the Gulf. The man came like a lamb to him, to within reach.

As the crow flies, the ebony scavenging crow, the city of Van was sixty miles from the nearest crossing point into Iranian territory.

The watch on Furniss had been kept to a bare minimum. He had been shadowed from airport to hotel, from hotel to airport. Away from his hotel, in between his flights, he had been free of his tail. That was of no matter to the investigator, not at this moment.

He worked late because, early in the morning, he would fly to Tabriz to put in place the final pieces of a mosaic of which he was proud.

Chapter ❖ 7

"*T*he fascinating thing about this region, Terence, is that it was never touched by the European civilizations. Here what you have are the unadulterated remnants of the Hittites and the Urartians and the Armenians."

As far as the Station Officer from Ankara was concerned, Van was one of the most forgettable cities it had been his misfortune to visit. His eyes streamed and he had an aggravating catarrh from the street dust thrown up by the traffic. To Terrence Snow, Van was quite stunningly ordinary.

"It's all lying around here to be picked up. Get a spade, dig in the right place, and you'll find the artifacts of old Sarduri, king here in ninth century B.C. Fascinating . . ."

The Station Officer's chief preoccupation was how to attract the attention of a taxi that would stop where they stood a hundred yards down the street from the hotel where the orderly tourists waited in line, and his second anxiety was how he was going to extricate himself altogether from this cultural excursion and get back to Ankara.

"Do you know, Terence, that within half an hour's drive of here there are cave paintings made fifteen thousand years ago? I cherish that sort of knowledge. I believe it gives a man a sense of his own mortality, which is absolutely healthy."

"Yes, sir . . ."

The morale of the Station Officer had been on the wane almost since their flight out of Ankara had been airborne. They had flown over the huge, bleak wilderness of the interior. Never mind the history, he reckoned that Van was a quarter of an hour beyond the outside rim of civilization, ancient or modern. No car at the airport, though it had been booked from Ankara. No rooms for them at the Akdamar hotel, booked and confirmed by telephone. True, he had the car now, and he had two singles in the Akdamar, but they had taken sweat and fury and the last iota of his patience. When he was back in Ankara he'd dine out on the baroque excrescence where they had laid their heads on their first night in the city. Warmly com-

mended by the hall porter in the Akdamar but un-
listed by any of the guidebooks. No hot water, no
breakfast, no toilet paper . . . And these people
thought they were ready to sign on for the European Economic Community.

What really pissed him off was the certainty
that his Desk Head was completely at ease in this
godforsaken town.

He was angry just being there. He was frustrated by his inability to wave down a taxi. He was
careless. He was playing host to the man from
London and he was not running his checks. He
had not seen the man who had followed them from
the hotel steps, and who now lounged against a
wall behind them.

"Have you ever bought jet here, Terence? It's
really quite excellent. You can alter the stones,
make a very pleasant necklace with the local
stuff."

The Station Officer's wife might well have
thrown him out of their flat if he had come home
to her with a peace offering of Van jet. He smiled.
He couldn't help liking Mattie, everyone in the
Service liked the man, but, Christ, you had to wonder whether he wasn't just a wee bit soft in the
head.

"No, sir, I never have."

They had spent two days talking to refugees

from Iran. The Station Officer would have had to hand it to Mattie, that the old blighter was ever so casual, ever so easy in his approaches, and he had them eating from his hand as he milked them. The Station Officer appreciated that the talk was for his benefit, that he was being shown what was expected of him in the future. The Desk Head had been talking about him coming up to Van or Hakkari or Dogubeyezit at least once a month henceforward, to where the refugees crossed. The Station Officer wasn't good with the refugees. Frankly, they embarrassed him. They were young, they were still in shock, they were exhausted from their hike across the mountains and from the long nights of fear from the Iranian and the Turkish military patrols. Bloody unpleasant as it was, the Station Officer would have to admit that the Turkish authorities had no choice but to police their frontier and turn back those trying to cross out of Iran. They had three quarters of a million Iranians, draft dodgers and riffraff, settled in their country. They had problems of gang crime and heroin trafficking from the refugees. They had every right to turn the refugees around and send them back whence they came. Bit bloody stark though, when he thought of the young, exhausted faces he had seen these past two days . . .

"That's our boy, Mattie."

The taxi had swerved over to them. From afar there was a chorus of protest reaching out from in front of the hotel. Mattie didn't seem to hear.

They went fast.

The Station Officer damn near cracked his head open on the taxi's roof when they flew over the potholes. They skirted the huge inland sea of Lake Van, azure blue, with a ferry boat on it making a postcard, and they rattled north. Through Caldiran and on to the Dogubeyezit road, and the surface worse, and the driver not attempting evasive action. The Station Officer was rubbing his forehead, and saw that Mattie had his eyes closed, as if he were catnapping. He lit a cigarette. He thought he understood why Mattie Furniss was a Desk Head, and why he had no enemies in Century. They were on their way to meet a field agent, a man from inside, a guy who was taking one hell of a risk to travel outside, and Mattie had his eyes closed and was beginning to snore. The Station Officer reckoned that was true class. He had been fussing about a taxi, and Mattie hadn't given a damn, because he would have believed that a field agent who had crossed out of Iran wasn't going to be going home when his contact was a quarter of an hour late. He was being given a lesson in how to soak up the punishment of getting to the sharp end and meeting up with agents whose necks were on the line. Sit back and let it happen, and don't bother if you start to snore, well done, Mattie. . . . He checked behind. No tail. Should have done it earlier, should have checked when he was still hot from not being able to find a taxi. He could see a long way back down the road, and the road was clear. After two days with his Desk Head he could have drafted a tourist pamphlet on Van's history. He knew that Xenophon had led his Ten Thousand in battle at Van, that Alexander had been there, and Pompey, and the Mongols of Tamerlane; that Van had not come into the Ottoman empire until Sultan Selim the Grim had done the necessary butchering in A.D. 1514. He wondered if, in twenty-five years' time, he would be able to sleep in the back of a taxi on the way to brief a field agent, and seem as antediluvian to a young Station Officer.

When Mattie started awake, and looked around him and had his bearings, and had apologized with a shrug as if it were rude to sleep, then the Station Officer invented an important meeting in Ankara the next day and asked whether it would be all right for him to catch the morning flight. No problem. He hadn't the spunk to tell Mattie outright that it was his wife's birthday, and that they were throwing a thrash for her at his flat.

They stopped the taxi at the front of the coffee

shop. There was a repair yard at the back, and a shed of rusted corrugated iron. The yard was a cemetery for disabled vehicles, some cannibalized, all defunct. The Station Officer saw the lorry with Iranian registration plates.

It was a good place for a meeting. Any long-distance Iranian driver might have cause to stop at the yard.

He thought the agent must be an old friend of Mattie's. The Station Officer stood back and watched the beaming welcome of the man who pumped Mattie's hand, and then held his arm. The Station Officer had joined the Service straight from Cambridge, he was well thought of and young for the Ankara post, but by now he thought that he knew nothing. . . . He saw a field man take hold of a Desk Head's arm and cling to it as if Mattie's arm were a talisman of safety. He saw the controlled affection in the way Mattie tapped with the palm of his hand at the knuckle of his agent, the close gesture of warmth. He could not have told his wife, but the Station Officer fancied that if he ever faced a crisis of his own, then he could be certain of Mattie Furniss's support. He had no agents of his own behind lines, he was an analyst. He had men in place, inherited, of course, in the Ministry of the Interior and the Army and the Jandarma and the Ministry of Foreign Affairs, but that was in Ankara, not behind the lines and in Iran. Mattie had his arm around the agent's shoulder and he was walking him round the lorry, out of sight from the road, and from the mechanics who labored in the shed with their oxyacetylene cutters. . . . He knew nothing. . . . He would not have known of the perpetual, gray fog fear that blanketed a field agent, and he would not have known of the kind strength that was given the field agent by his controller.

He was not included. He was left for an hour to kick his heels.

He was sitting on an old upturned oil drum when Mattie came back to him.

"Did you get all you wanted, sir?"

"Stiffened his backbone, told him what we need. Usual carrot and stick job. . . . Your meeting in Ankara tomorrow, won't go on too long I hope."

"Shouldn't think so, sir."

"Don't want it to interfere with your party."

Mattie was walking away, and the Station Officer had seen the dry vestige of the smile.

The bus churned through the miles as the road climbed toward Zanjan. Through the dusted window Charlie could see the small oases, surrounded by poplar trees, and the mud brick villages on either side of the route. It had been night when he had traveled from Tabriz to Tehran, but high sunshine now and he could see into the spreading distance. There was no heat haze, the altitude of the road was too great for mists. He was looking south of the road, he wanted to see the ruins that when he was still a child Mr. Furniss had first told him about. The Mausoleum of Sultan Oljaitu-Khocabandeh in the sprawl of ruins near Soltanieh. Charlie, eight years old, and meeting the friend of his father at their villa. Mr. Furniss always had good stories to tell the boy. The Mausoleum of Sultan Oljaitu-Khocabandeh had stayed in Charlie's mind. A man, a Sultan of the Mongols, had died 550 years before, and he had sought immortality, and his resting place was a monument that reached 170 feet above the ground. That was the ultimate folly. There would be no photographs of Charlie Eshraq ever raised on a wall. None of his sayings ever daubed on high banners. When he died . . . whenever . . . Charlie wanted a grave like his father's. A corner of a cemetery with a number scratched into the wet cement slab, and weeds at the edge. He thought that made him his own man.

When they passed it, the Mausoleum was clear from the windows of the coach, and Charlie wiped hard at the window although most of the dirt was on the outside of the tinted glass. He saw the great octagon shape of the building and the cupola dome. He saw the goats grazing at its base.

The sight of the Mausoleum was only of a few seconds. No other passenger on the bus bothered to look at it. He thought that he hated men who built mausoleums to their memory, and who had their photographs overlooking public squares, and who demanded that their sayings be scrawled on banners. The hate was active in his heart, but did not show on his face. He appeared relaxed, dozing. He was leaning on his rucksack on the seat next to him. He had no fear that the rucksack of a *pasdar* would be searched at a road block. He had the correct papers. The Guards would be friendly to a *pasdar* returning to Tabriz, they would not search him.

He hated the men who built mausoleums, and despised them.

He remembered what Mr. Furniss had said to him, when he was eight years old.

"A man who is afraid of death, dear boy, does not have the courage to live."

In the car taking him from the airport to the Guards Corps headquarters in Tabriz, the investigator listened to the radio. The *pasdaran* operating from speedboats had rocketed a Singapore-flagged tanker en route to Kuwait, and crippled it. Many soldiers had been martyred after the Iraqi enemy had once again dropped mustard gas on their trenches, and of course there had been no condemnation from the United Nations Security Council that was in the pocket of the Great Satan. Spies, belonging to the Zionist regime of Baghdad, had been arrested in Tehran. *Mojahedin-e Khalq* counterrevolutionaries had been captured at the western borders carrying 250 kilos of explosive. The Islamic Revolution Committees' Guards had carried out exercises in Zahedan and displayed their ever-increasing readiness to destroy outlaws and smugglers. A bomb had exploded in Tehran's Safariyeh Bazaar, no casualties reported. A grenade and machine gun attack on the Guards corps headquarters in Resselat Square in Tehran had been repulsed. The Speaker of the Majlis had spoken at a military meeting of the success of the Republic's home-produced ground-to-air missile in bringing down an enemy MIG-25 over Esfahan. Thirteen foreign cargo ships inspected at sea, and allowed to continue . . .

The war was endless. He had been at war all of his adult life, he had worked ten years for the SAVAK, and ten years for the Ministry of Information and Intelligence. All his time at the SAVAK, reading the files, assessing the statistics of opposition, he had known the certainty of ultimate defeat, so he had built the bridges, covertly prepared for the transfer of power, avoided the firing squads that had been the fate of most of his colleagues. He had changed sides, and he could not now predict the shape of things after this next defeat. Military defeat seemed to him most probable, but would it alter the power structure in Tehran, and if so, how? The investigator could read between the lines of a news bulletin. Ever-increasing references to battles, losses, insurrections, threats from outside the country, they were all to prepare a crushed people for even greater sacrifices. To himself, he would wonder how many more sacrifices the people, however willing, could sustain. . . . There had been a time when he had believed in the ultimate victory. When the MKO had shown their naïveté and attacked in force, and been thwarted, beetles under hobnails, then he had thought that victory was close. But the war went on, and the bombs went on . . .

He had chosen the radicals. He had banked on their success over the moderates.

The man from Manzarieh Park who flew to London that morning, IranAir, he would strengthen the hand of the radicals, and the matter of the Englishman, Furniss, if that were successfully accomplished, that would be muscle in their arm.

Coming into the city of Tabriz, the driver had slapped a police light on the roof of the car, and had hammered the vehicle's siren.

They came to the square outside the Guards Corps headquarters. There was heavy security at the gate, even the instructor traveling in an official car was asked to produce identification. There had always been security at this building, since a bitch girl had thrown a grenade at the gate and the Guards. An office had been prepared for the investigator, direct telephone lines had been installed, and a telex link with Tehran. He at once examined again the arrangements for the movement of the transport, and he summoned the men who would travel for their final briefing. Later he would oversee the preparations at the villa.

"You'll be all right, sir?"

"Of course I'll be all right, Terence, and do stop nannying me. I will not drink the water, I will eat only in the restaurant, I forswear salads, and yes, thank you; before you ask, I do have ample loo paper. All in all, even without you as nanny, guardian or devoted student, I shall be in bliss. I will be pottering on the battlements of the Van Kalesi. I will be climbing the stone steps on which the feet of Sardur the Second stood. I will stand in the rooms that were his home seven hundred and fifty years before the birth of Christ. I don't know when I shall have that chance again. Not now that you are trained to undreamed-of heights, Terence. I fancy I am redundant here. What do you say?"

The Station Officer smiled wanly and slapped the inside pocket of his jacket. "I'll get your report off as soon as I'm in the office."

"Yes. It will give them something to chew on. It is a perpetual source of amazement to me how much a field man can provide if he is directed in the right way. I mean, you might not suppose that running a repair depot in Tabriz gives you the chance to observe much that is important to us, and you would be wrong. They'll be pleased with that."

They would be pleased with what they had because they were now beggars searching for crumbs. Sad but true, that the Desk Head, Iran, had been able to sprint round the Gulf and up to northeastern Turkey and brief his three field men without the anxiety of knowing that he had missed an opportunity of meeting other operatives working inside. Iran Desk had access to the reports of only three agents in place. Not the sort of thing he would have discussed with Master Snow, of course, and the young man was left, most probably, in cheerful ignorance of the poverty of information from Iran. Mattie knew. He knew that Iran Desk was damn near dead. Eight years after the Revolution, eight years after the purges had started, Mattie Furniss was wafer thin on the ground. No question, not in the land of the Mullahs, of volunteers queueing up to offer their services to the Secret Intelligence Service of the United Kingdom. Looked at logically, he was rather lucky to have had a single agent remaining. The Americans never told him much about their operations inside Iran, and what they did tell him he took with a fistful of skepticism. For all the money they had to spend, which he did not himself have, he doubted they had many more agents than he. The wear and tear of terror, of arrests, firing squads, had left him shorthanded. He was down to three agents . . . and to Charlie Eshraq. Thank the good Lord for Charlie Eshraq.

"I'll meet you off your plane, sir."

"That's kind of you, Terence. Run along now, and give your lovely wife the excellent evening she deserves."

Mattie watched the Station Officer slip away into his taxi. He thought Terence Snow had much to learn, but at least he was capable of learning it. More than could be said for the buffoons in Bahrain. . . . His report was gone, a weight off his mind. He would write a fuller report when he was back at Century. He had sat up half the night writing it, and sipping sweetened yoghurt, alternately with water, bottled, and the substance of the report pleased him. In Mattie's experience the preliminary report was the one that would do the business. His longer paper would circulate wonderfully swiftly and be back in the files within forty-eight hours.

At the reception desk he ordered a hire car.

In the lounge he introduced himself to a group of tourists, and chatted easily with them to pass the time before the car arrived. Americans, of course. Such stamina for travel, it always impressed him. From Milwaukee and Boise, Idaho, and Nashville. They were going to Lake Van in the afternoon in the hope of seeing pelican and flamingo and they told Mattie that if they were lucky, and if their tour literature was to be believed, then they might also see greater reed warblers and redshanks and potchards. He was mightily impressed with the power of their field glasses and camera lenses, and humbly suggested that it would be prudent not to point these implements at anything military. In the morning they would be heading on for Ararat. They gave Mattie a catalog of their expectations and he did not disabuse them. It seemed only too possible that they would indeed light upon Noah's Ark. Such very pleasant people. It was the pity of Mattie's life that he so rarely mixed with the likes of them. And it was an immediate pity that they would be off to capture Mount Ararat first thing in the morning, and would not be able to share with Mattie the glory of the Van Kalesi, fortress of Sardur the Second.

In good humor, and thinking well of Terence, Mattie Furniss bought a card to post home.

George's wife was out of earshot, being wonderfully brave as they would afterward say, a thoroughbred performance, shaking hands and thanking other mourners for coming.

Four of the Secretary of State's staff had come to the service, showed support, and a pretty impressive turnout altogether. The photographers and reporters were kept back from the porch of the building by police and a crash barrier. George walked away with the Home Secretary at his side.

"Are you backing off?"

"Most certainly not."

"I expected results by now."

"We're working very hard."

The Secretary of State snorted. "There have been no charges."

"There will be, very soon."

"She was just a child, destroyed by scum . . ."

Typical of the man, the Home Secretary thought, that he should pick a fight outside the chapel in which his only child had just been cremated. The Home Secretary would not tell him what he deserved to be told, not at this moment. Nobody had made little Lucy take the damn stuff, she was a volunteer, she hadn't had to be press-ganged. If that pompous sod had spent less of his time working the constituencies, burnishing his image, if he had spent a little more time at home. If that poor suffering mother hadn't been so mountainously self-obsessed they certainly wouldn't be here now.

"I can tell you, George, that in addition to the pusher of the heroin your daughter used, we now also have in custody the dealer, that's the next step up in the chain, and we have the beginnings of a line to the distributor. The distributor . . ."

"I know what a distributor is, for heaven's sake."

"No, I'll tell you, George, what the distributor is. The distributor is bringing into the United Kingdom anything upward of half a million sterling, street value, of heroin. He is a practiced criminal with too much to lose to make the sort of mistakes that enable us to pick him up the instant you flick your fingers and call for action. Are you with me, George?"

"But you're going to get to him? If you wouldn't do it, make it happen as a simple duty, you will by God surely do it, whatever it costs your vast empire, as an act of friendship."

"It will be done."

"I will hold you to that."

The Secretary of State turned and stalked back to his wife's side, seeming impatient now to be away. The Home Secretary was breathing hard. God, and he'd been very close to losing his temper. He thought that if that man ever became Prime Minister then he might just as well pack up the black car and return to his farm. He thought that mucking with pigs would be preferable to sitting in Cabinet with an elevated Secretary of State for Defense. He watched them go, sitting back in the limousine with their faces lit by flashbulbs.

The border was a small stream, knee-deep and a body's length across and cutting through a gully of smoothed rocks. The water was ice cold, biting at his feet, sloshing in his boots. The crossing point was at the apex of a salient of Iran territory to the west of the village of Lura Shirin. Each time he had taken this route he had traveled alone. He was north of the sector through which the refugees usually tried to escape, with the help of Kurdish villagers who would lead them to the frontier if the money were right. With his life, Charlie Eshraq trusted no other person. He had heard from the exile community in Istanbul many stories about the crossing of the frontier. In the cafés, in the bars, he had spoken with those who had come through, stripped of their money by the guides, their nerves shredded by the patrols on either side. He knew that the Guards Corps regularly patrolled the Iranian side and were committed to hunting down those they hated most, the draft dodgers. He knew that Turkish paratroopers were set out in strength on the west of the border with night vision equipment and with helicopter gunships. He knew that a boy, running from conscription, running from a place in the trenches outside Basra, could evade the Guards Corps patrols only to be caught by the Turks and handed back. The first time he had crossed he had chosen a route that was well away from the paths used by the Kurdish guides.

When he had forded the stream, he felt a small sense of sadness. He remembered the wetness in Majid Nazeri's eyes, and he thought of him polishing the motorcycle. He thought of the girl. He knew he would not be happy until he was back.

He moved forward as quickly as he dared. It was a steep rock climb up a feeder gully, the rucksack was heavy on his back. His hands were cold and slippery and he worked hard to get away, up out of the streambed. He wanted to be over the line of the ridge before the sun had risen behind him, before he could be silhouetted on its back.

Araqi flew to London on a jumbo of IranAir. During the flight and on disembarkation he wore the blue livery of a cabin steward. By chance he was known to one of the Guards Corps who traveled the route as a sky marshal. They silently acknowledged each other and made no occasion to exchange greeting. Araqi knew the sky marshal, one of four on the aircraft, because they had been together at Manzarieh Park.

He would not see the sky marshal after the crew had left the aircraft because it was the job of the guards to stay with their charge at all times. The sky marshal would sleep onboard, while Araqi traveled with the incoming and outgoing crews to the hotel in West London where there was a permanent block booking for IranAir personnel.

Araqi rode in the airline bus to the hotel. Whereas many of the crew, excepting the Captain and Second Officer, would double up, he had been allocated a room to himself. It was a small point, but it should have been noted by the Anti-Terrorist squad personnel that watched over matters Iranian in the British capital. A number of factors led to this oversight: there was intelligence on the movement of an Active Service Unit from West Belfast; there had been a diversion of manpower following the planting of incendiary devices in two Oxford Street department stores by the Animal Liberation Front; the squad's guard was perhaps a degree down since there had been no Iranian terrorist action in the United Kingdom for eleven months; and to cap it there were casualties from the virulent influenza sweeping the city. Later there would be an inquiry as to how that small point had been missed, but that would be the familiar if painstaking slamming of the stable door.

The materials would be delivered to Araqi; he would manufacture the bomb, he would put it in the killing place, and then he would get himself back to the hotel and leave the country in the same way as he had arrived. Those were his concerns. The provision of the explosives and the reconnaissance of the target would be handled by others, they were not his concern.

Araqi was a dedicated man. He had brought with him the map of the world from the aircraft's inflight magazine, and he had in his case a small compass. So when he knelt in prayer he could be certain that he faced the shrine of the black Kaaba building at Mecca.

After his prayers, behind his locked door, waiting to be contacted, he read verses from the Koran.

He recognized the wide sweep of the shoulders, and the wisping hair that ranged over the collar of the old linen jacket. And the voice was unmistakable. Ancient Britons nearly always shouted when they spoke to a person whose native tongue was other than English. The whole of the reception area was aware that Mr. Furniss was visiting one more fortress, would be handing over the car at noon the next day, and would then be checking out.

To Charlie Eshraq, tired and dirty himself, it was quite wonderful to have walked into the Akdamar, in search of a hot bath, and found Mr. Furniss.

He stood back. There were mud stains on the trousers of Mr. Matthew Furniss, as if he had been kneeling in the earth, and his shoes were mud-caked. He waited until Mr. Furniss had finished at his desk, and slung his camera bag on his shoulder, and had headed for the staircase. He thought that he knew which camera would be in the bag. It would be the old Pentax, everything manual, that had photographed him on the grass lawn behind the cottage. His mother, in California, had a picture of her son taken on the lawn at Bibury with that camera. He followed his father's friend up the stairs and on to the first floor.

When Mr. Furniss had stopped outside a door, when he was scrabbling in his pocket for his room key, Charlie spoke.

"Hello, Mr. Furniss."

He saw the man swivel. "I'm Dr. Owens," he said. Charlie saw the astonishment and the recognition. "Good God . . ."

"It is a real surprise."

"Fantastic, dear boy. Quite amazing. What on earth are you doing here?"

"Looking for a bath, Mr. Furniss."

"You'll be extraordinarily lucky to find some hot water, but you're very welcome to the bath."

"And you, Mr. Furniss, what are you doing here?"

He should not have asked that question. The question was cheek. He saw the fun streak in Mr. Furniss's eyes. Mr. Furniss had long ago told Charlie that he could make an old man feel young.

"Turning over some old stones, what else?"

So natural . . . the door was opened. Charlie was hugged, like a son, and his back was slapped as if he were a large dog. The room was chaos. The only patch of order was the bed which had been made. No one had tidied the clothes, clean or dirty, and the guidebooks, and the handwritten notes, and the drawings of sections of the Van Kalesi lay scattered on and about the dressing table.

"An extreme form of liberation, dear boy, a man staying in a hotel on his own. . . . Good heavens, Charlie, you've just walked out today? Forgive me meandering on. You must be done in. Can I send for something for you to eat and drink? Meantime, run a bath. What would you like most?"

After a stone-cold bath and a trolley of food, Charlie set out to tell Mr. Furniss all that he was clearly impatient to hear. Charlie told him first of his crossing of the frontier. The bus ride from Tabriz around the shores of Lake Urmia to Rezaiyeh. Moving at night, on foot, into the hills and then on into the mountains. Crossing . . . Slipping the Turkish army patrols, getting to the main road. Hitching to Van.

And then he talked of unit movements between Tehran and Tabriz. He talked of a meeting on the bus with a sergeant in artillery who complained that on the front-line Dezful sector the 105mm howitzers were restricted to seven shells a day. He talked of the Mullah that he had shadowed, and how the bazaar gossip had told him that the Mullah was climbing high in the faction that was radical. He talked of a mechanic in the Engineers who had told him in a café that an armored regiment positioned at Susangerd was about to be moth-balled because every one of the seventy-two British-built Chieftain tanks had a mechanical failure and the unit was without spare parts. He talked of the feelings that had been expressed to him about the *Mojahedin-e Khalq* and their oper-ations into Iran from behind the shelter of the enemy Iraqi army. "... They're dead. They cannot exist inside the country. They do nothing outside the border areas, believe me. There is no resist-ance inside the country. The resistance has been crushed . . ."

For two and a half hours Charlie talked and Mr. Furniss covered every sheet of the hotel note-paper that was left in the room. The interruptions were few. When they came they were nudgings of Charlie's memory, prompting him to recall fur-ther what he had seen, what he had heard.

"First class, dear boy . . ."

"What are your own movements now, Mr. Furniss?"

"Tragic but true, business has overtaken recre-ation. I've fixed myself a military pass into the To-prakkale army zone. Quite pleased about that. It's a closed area, but there's a fort inside the perime-ter. I meant to go this afternoon, but it'll have to wait until tomorrow. Always work first, eh?"

"Is that why you are in Van, to visit ruins?"

Charlie smiled at Mr. Furniss's frown. Then the grin, as if the mischief were shared. He believed he could see a glow of happiness in the older man's face.

"Did you use my little cracker?"

"I did it just as the instructions told me."

"Tell me, Charlie."

"The motorcycle, the drawing up alongside, slamming it on the roof. I saw his face before I drew away from him. He didn't know what it was, but he had fear. There was nothing he could do because he was boxed around by lorries. He couldn't stop, he couldn't get out. He had nowhere to go."

"Well, just remember what a fine girl Juliette was. Put the rest of it out of your mind. You've done enough."

"With armor-piercing weapons I can take out the Mullah who sentenced her, and I think that I can get also to the investigator who tortured her. I have identified both of them."

He saw that Mr. Furniss was staring out of the window. He thought he understood why Mr. Furniss had turned his head away. The view from the hotel room window was nothing more than a mass of different, improvised rooftops. It had been Mr. Furniss who had told him the details of his father's execution and the hanging of his sister. Each time, then, Mr. Furniss had turned away his face.

"But if I don't have the armor-piercing it would be much harder. In fact, I don't know how it could be done."

"I think it would be better, Charlie, if you didn't come down to Bibury again . . . more professional that way."

"Is that going to be a problem, that sort of weapon?"

"Dear boy, I've told you where to go. You can buy anything if you have the money. Do you have the money?"

"The money is no problem, Mr. Furniss."

Parrish wasn't surprised to find that Keeper had beaten him into the Lane.

He poured himself coffee from the percolator.

"Nothing . . . ?"

Park shook his head.

". . . What have we got?"

"Surveillance on Manvers's place. The name and type at ports, airports . . . nothing's showing."

"Something'll show, it always does."

"Well, not yet it hasn't."

"What I always say . . . fortune favors the patient."

"It's bloody hard," Park snapped. "I don't think I was cut out for Fortune."

Mattie was tired. He had slept badly because the young man with a blanket bed on the floor had tossed, rolled, right through the night, and then been gone at first light.

He was elated. This visit to the ruins in Toprak-kale military was the zenith of his whole journey. But he was running late. That was inevitable, given the fascination of the ruins, and he had to get the car back to Van, pack up his bags, settle his hotel bill, and catch the flight to Ankara.

Because he was exhausted, excited and in a hurry, he was not aware of the Dodge pickup closing on him from behind. He had not thought twice about the tractor hauling a trailer from a sheep pen by the roadside ahead of him. He had not planned his route from Van to Toprakkale, merely followed the map. He did not react well. . . . The tutors at Portsmouth would have been disgusted. All those hours teaching him AOPR: Awareness, Observation, Planning, Reaction. If it had been Mattie's class and a youngster had let himself into that mess at the training center, Mattie would have roasted him in front of all the others.

A straight stretch of road was all he saw. The

road ahead empty except for the tractor and its long trailer stacked high with bales of fodder. It was empty behind him, and he wasn't checking, except for the pickup.

Mattie should have been in a performance car. He should have been using a professional drive. He should have seen the block ahead, and the block behind.

The tractor stopped.

And that should have triggered the alarm bell for Mattie. He should have gone off the road, risked a soft verge. He should have tried the "bootlegger turn," hand brake on and wheel spin to throw him around.

He was like a lamb to the slaughter. He pumped the brake gently, he brought the Fiat 127 to a stop. He pressed the horn, once, politely.

There was a violent shuddering crash as the Dodge pickup smashed against the trunk of the Fiat. Mattie was flung back, skull against the headrest. He twisted, heart racing, sickening fright welling into him, to look behind.

Men running from the pickup toward him, one from either side, and a man coming at him in front, charging toward the car. He saw the handguns and the machine pistol. Three men coming at him, all armed. His engine had cut when he had been rammed.

The door beside him surged open. Christ, and he hadn't even locked his door . . .

He shouted loudly, in English, "I haven't got much money, I'll give you . . ."

He was pulled out, thrown onto the road surface, a boot went into his face, his wrists were heaved to the small of his back and he felt plastic ties going sharply into his flesh. He was dragged toward the rear door of the pickup.

Mattie understood. He would have been a bloody fool not to have understood.

He was lifted and thrown hard into the back of the truck. The doors slammed. Light died.

The immigration officer gazed from the young man standing in front of his desk back down to the travel document.

"Stateless Person . . . ?"

"The government of Iran does not recognize my old passport. I hope soon to have British citizenship, and a British passport."

The immigration officer squinted down at the writing. "And you are . . . ?"

"Charles Eshraq."

The eyeline, at measured speed, moved again from the travel document to the young man who wore a smart navy blazer with a travel company's logo over the breast pocket.

"Sorry . . ."

"I am Charles E . . . S . . . H . . . R . . . A . . . Q."

When he worked fast at the desk top that was out of sight of the man standing in front of him, the immigration officer could still maintain an air of impenetrable boredom. His fingers were flicking at the pages of the book with the printout of entries. It was sharp in his mind. He and the rest of his shift had had the briefing when they had come on duty in the late afternoon. The queue was stretching out behind the man. That was all right, too, they could all wait. He had the Iranian, he had Charles/Charlie, born August 5, 1965, and he had a Customs ID call. The name in the Suspects' Index was Charlie Persia, probably a nickname, followed by the reference letter "o." "o" was Customs referral. The immigration officer pressed the hidden button on his desk top.

The supervisor hovered behind him. The immigration officer pointed to the travel document, Charles Eshraq. Place of Birth: Tehran. His finger slid across to the Suspects' Index, Charlie Persia, assumed Iranian. Date of Birth: early, middle 1960s.

"Would you mind stepping this way, sir?" The

supervisor asked, and his hand rested easily on Charlie's sleeve.

"Is there a problem?"

"Shouldn't think so, sir. Just routine. This way, please, sir."

Chapter ✣ 8

"**W**e put the dog onto his bag—hung on like it was marrowbone."

The room was crowded.

There were men from the Immigration Control, and from the uniformed Customs strength, and Park stood dead center. Parrish and Harlech were hanging back by the door. Park listened carefully. He had learned long before that the initial brief was the important one, and he would make his case officer decisions from that first information.

"We've him sat in a room now. He thinks there's something wrong with his documentation. I tell you what, he doesn't look fussed, not like I'd be if I had the sort of quantity in my case to make the dog go clean off its whistle. OK, your airport

✤ 196 ✤

dog will get a good sniff every so often, so they're not as you might say blasé, but, Jesus, I've seen nothing like it."

Parrish had not yet recovered his sanity from the style of the journey down from the Lane to Heathrow. He still looked like a man clutching a spar in a high sea. Harlech was pale from sitting in the passenger seat where he could not escape from the swerving and the overtaking and the raw speed; Harlech would tell the rest of them later that Keeper's drive down was the worst experience in his life. Harlech had been the late duty, Parrish had been clearing his desk and checking the overtime sheets, and Keeper had just been using up time, polishing his shoes for the third time that day, when the telephone call had come through from the airport.

"We got his ticket off him, and the baggage tag was stapled. We collected the bag off the trailer and let the dog close. Damn near pulled the handler off his feet." The senior uniformed officer had been Park's governor at the airport. He didn't like the boy, but he'd seen his quality and he had written a fulsome recommendation for transfer to ID. ". . . The bag is a rucksack, the ticket is from Istanbul. Listen, the dog tells you a fair amount when it gets going. The way that dog went then, our chummy is carrying one hell of a load. We haven't

opened anything up, we haven't touched anything. So, it's your baby."

Parrish wasn't saying anything, still shaking
his head like he were trying to get rid of the bad
dream of the Escort's wheel caps touching the
wheel caps of a taxi. Park would not have been
able to remember when he had last been so elated
at the contact with a suspect. He was the case officer. Like the man said, his baby.

"I'd let him run." He knew that there were two
other cars on the way to Heathrow, April team
members summoned without apology from home.
"Just as soon as we've the backup."

The lift of Bill Parrish's eyebrows told him of
the concern. Normal practice would have been to
bust the chummy, and if the chummy wasn't to
be busted, then the second most obvious procedure
would have been to open the rucksack, empty the
contents and substitute dross for the real thing.
Parrish's raised eyebrows were a warning to him.

"Sorry, Bill, but what I'm saying is to let him
run."

It was Parrish's style to trust to the flair of the
young men in the ID. If he had a deep disliking
inside the civil service office where he worked it
was for those of his contemporaries, the old lags,
who believed that only age and experience
counted when decisions were taken. Parrish

❖ **198** ❖

backed his youngsters, he gave them their heads, and he sweated blood over it. He went to a telephone. He leafed through his diary. He dialed the home number of the ACIO. He was brief. He didn't tell the ACIO that the dog had gone berserk when confronted with the rucksack, that they were sitting on a major haul. He reported that there were thought to be traces of narcotics in the suspect's baggage. He said that a man of Iranian birth, and traveling on a UK-issued Stateless Person's document, the right sort of age, would not be carrying the April team's tag of Tango One. He said that Tango One would be released from the airport as soon as he was satisfied that a sufficient number of personnel had gathered for effective surveillance. Perspiration on his forehead, not blood . . . by Christ, there would be blood if Keeper fouled up. Nothing in this world surprised him, not since an archbishop had been stopped by his Customs colleagues at Rome and waved his arms about in protest and thereby dislodged three packets of heroin that had been stuck in his belt under his cassock. Nothing surprised him, not even that a young man should try to walk through Heathrow with a heavy load of stuff in a rucksack. Most of them tried the clever way. Most of them used carefully hollowed out Samsonite cases, or chess pieces fashioned from solidified cocaine, or they stuffed it up their backsides, or they swallowed it in cellophane packets. They'd try any bloody thing. It did not surprise Parrish that Tango One had it loaded in a rucksack where even the most casual search would have found it. And yet, what did they stop? They stopped one PAX in a hundred, or one in two hundred. A fair risk, a chance worth taking . . .

"It's okayed, David. You can let him run . . ."

He took Keeper out into the corridor, out of range of the men in the room.

Only Harlech heard the ferocity of his whisper into Park's ear. "If you screw up, David, I'm gone, and the ACIO who has backed you will be gone with me, and we'll bloody well hang on to your legs to make sure, damned sure, that you go down with us."

"I hear you, Bill."

"Too right, you'd better hear me."

The telephone rang, and it was passed to Parrish, and he listened and then told Park that the two other April cars had arrived, were outside Terminal 3, waiting for instructions.

They set off down the corridor. The man from Immigration, and Parrish and Keeper and Harlech, and a uniformed Customs man caught them up carrying a khaki rucksack. Parrish would have sworn that he could see flecks of the dog's saliva

on the rucksack's flap. The rucksack was grimed
with dried mud. They didn't open it. That sort of
bag was much harder to unpack and repack than
a suitcase. No need, really, because the dog had
told them what they would find. They transferred
from Customs and Excise territory to Immigration. A new set of corridors, another set of duty
rosters pinned to notice boards.

In the door of the room where Tango One had
been sat, and where he was watched, there was
a one-way window. Keeper went close to it, nose
against it, stared through the glass. There was the
slightest quickening of his breath. He had the
break and he had the luck, and he had not really
believed in either. He looked through the window
at Charlie Persia. Charles Eshraq, now Tango
One. He saw a well-built young man with a strong
head of dark hair, and a beard of a couple of
months, and he saw that the man sat quietly and
flicked ash from his cigarette into the tinfoil ashtray. He saw that the man was calm. He wouldn't
go in himself. He motioned Harlech to the window. Wrong for either of them to show their faces.
He gave a wry smile to Parrish.

"Better we hang together than hang separately,
Bill."

Parrish wasn't in the mood for banter. He
shouldered past Harlech, opened the door.

Park stood close to the door. He could hear everything. Something massively reassuring about old Parrish's competence when it came to keeping the suspect at ease.

"I am really sorry about the delay, Mr. Eshraq."

"What was the difficulty?"

"No real difficulty other than you happened to hit a desk man who was less than knowledgeable about Stateless Persons documentation."

"Is that all?"

"They're changing the form of the documentation and that young fellow had it in his head that the change had already taken place.... You know what it is, late at night, no one to set him right until they called me."

"It's taken a long time."

"I'm very sorry if you've been inconvenienced . . . can I just have the details, Mr. Eshraq? Everything that happens in Civil Service work, there has to be a report. Name . . . ?"

"Charles Eshraq."

"Date of birth, and place of birth . . . ?"

"August 5, 1965, Tehran. It is in the document."

"Never mind. . . . Address in the UK . . . ?"

"Flat 6, 24, Beaufort Street, SW3."

"Very nice, too. . . . Occupation, Mr. Eshraq?"

"Freelance travel courier."

"Get all the sunshine, do you?"

"Eastern Mediterranean mostly, yes."

"We've delayed you horribly, were you being met?"

"No, I have my wheels in Long Stay parking."

"Christ, I wouldn't leave anything decent in there, I hope it's all right."

"It's only a little Suzuki jeep."

"Can we give you a lift over?"

"Thanks, but I'll take the bus. I'm not in a hurry."

"Well, it's quite a fine night. Again, my apologies. I suppose you've some luggage?"

"Just a rucksack."

"Let's go back to baggage reclaim then, Mr. Eshraq."

Harlech and Park ducked away and into an empty office. Through the door he saw Parrish leading the Tango One out into the corridor. He told Harlech for Christ's sake not to let himself be seen but to watch chummy onto the bus and then wait to be collected by Corinthian by the bus stop. Then he sprinted to get to the Escort in the Customs parking lot. Keeper found the others, detailed Corinthian to collect Harlech and then join Statesman at the gates of the Long Stay parking lot, one a hundred yards to the west and the other a hundred yards to the east. "Target in a Suzuki jeep, Keeper's Escort not far behind. Take nothing

for granted. He says he lives in Beaufort Street
in Chelsea, but he's so fucking cool this one he
may just fancy his chances at Windsor Castle. As
soon as the line of flight is established, usual procedures to apply."

Then he hammered under the tunnel to get to
Long Stay parking to give himself time to locate
the Suzuki before his Tango One.

He had been held up at Immigration before, but
never for so long.

It was not a surprise to him. The Immigration
men always took a hard look at Stateless Persons'
documentation. He had learned in Britain that
foreigners were always given a hard time at the
airport, almost part of an immigration policy.
What had been a surprise was the courtesy of the
senior man who cleared the matter up. That man
was one in a thousand, and not a well man by the
look of him. Wouldn't last, that was certain. He
checked his mirror and saw that a dark-colored
Ford, possibly a new Escort, was immediately behind him.

He had lived in London for four years, but it had
never felt like home to him. He did not think that
any of the exiles who had come first to London
would have thought of the city as anything other
than a temporary refuge. But it had effectively

swallowed them all. They would still all dream of going home. They would dream, but Charlie was going, and he realized that this was his last journey back from the airport. "Get all the sunshine, do you?" Oh yes, he would be getting all the sunshine. He was off the motorway, and heading past the old Lucozade building. Temperature 5. He looked up into his mirror and saw that he was followed by a Vauxhall, almost certainly a Vauxhall.

There was no tension in his driving. He was controlled, at ease. It had not crossed his mind that he could be busted at Heathrow. He was Charles Eshraq, Stateless Person, but he would not be stateless for long. . . . Charlie Eshraq had taken out two Guards with a handgun. He had blown away the executioner of Tabriz. He was the friend of Mr. Matthew Furniss. He was going home with just two more items of business to deal with. And then . . . then he would be Charles Eshraq, Iranian citizen. Probably no longer the friend of Mr. Furniss, certainly no longer the very close friend of the Misses Furniss. He thought of La'ayya and he patted the rucksack and made a wild calculation of what in perfumes and soap seven kilos of first-grade heroin would buy. After the small matter of the armor-piercing missiles, of course. He was on the King's Road. He looked up into the mirror as he changed through his gears, as his foot eased on the brake. There was a Maestro behind him.

If he was quick with a shower, he would be in time to get to the pub before closing. Charlie Eshraq would get a great welcome before "last orders." He would tell some good stories about dumb tourists losing passports or knickers in the Turkish resorts, and he'd get a good laugh and a good welcome.

He parked.

He didn't look at the car on the other side of the road. He didn't see the couple clinching. He didn't hear Amanda, codename Token and the only woman of April's team, bitching that codename Corinthian, who this year had failed to complete the eighth mile of the London Marathon, could keep his bloody hand out from under her blouse. And he didn't hear Token issue a violent warning when Corinthian whispered that it was just playacting in a good cause.

Charlie humped his rucksack up the stairs to his flat. He threw, street value, more than a million pounds of sterling of heroin down onto the floor.

He went to the window and looked out onto the street below. A girl got out of a car opposite, slammed the door furiously and then got into the backseat. Charlie smiled to himself. He thought that La'ayya would have liked the King's Road, and he didn't suppose she'd ever see it.

He ran his shower.

Mattie was trussed tight.

He had lost the feeling below the ankles, and the pain was cutting at his wrists.

He was very alert now. Old training was surfacing, things that he had been taught ten years before, and twenty years. For Christ's sake, he had even lectured on it, back at the fort at Portsmouth. He had been a student more than once on the Escape and Evasion courses, and he had been the instructor. He knew it all. He was lying on the hard and hurting steel ribbing floor of the pickup. His captors had put a gag of thick leather in his mouth and lashed the thongs at the ends of the gag behind his neck.

The training had told him that the optimum escape moment was at the very moment of capture. That's what he had told his students. Right, he had been looking for the optimum moment, been looking at it from the start, right into the barrel of an automatic pistol. The optimum moment was also the time of the maximum danger—that, also he had told his students. The time of the lift was the time that the hit squad were most highly stressed, most irrational. He had looked up the barrel of the automatic pistol and been kicked in the head. His ear had bled, was now congealed. He rationalized that his bleeding ear would have been shot off, with half his head, if he had struggled at the roadside. He was an old man, and there were four of them and none of them looked half his age.

Two of them were in the back section with him, and both now wore cotton hoods with eye slits, and both kept handguns trained on him, and neither had spoken.

He was aware that, at first, the truck had traveled several miles, and that then the engine had been stopped for what might have been three hours. He knew that when they had stopped they had been in a garage or a farm shed because he had heard the doors being shut, and he had heard the echo as the engine was cut, and later restarted, which told him that the vehicle was in a confined space. He lay alone. The pain had come and gone and reached point after point that he thought would be unendurable. He weighed pain against anxiety. He worked to restore the circulation in his hands and feet, told himself over and over that another opportunity to escape would present itself.

The truck doors opened, his bonds were examined by torchlight, and then the outer doors were opened and the truck headed off again, a long drive, over those awful bloody roads. It was part of his training to remember everything possible about his journey after capture, basic stuff that. Easy enough in the New Forest, or the back terrace streets of Portsmouth, damn sight harder after the shock of capture, after being kicked in the head, and when there were two handguns a couple of feet from his ear. A weekly game of squash did not leave a fifty-two-year-old in ideal shape for kidnapping, but he understood that they had driven a good distance.

He had been aware first that the pace of the truck had slowed, and he could hear other vehicle engines around him. He heard voices, Turkish spoken, and then the truck was accelerating. He thought they were back on a decent road surface. The truck lurched to a stop, Mattie slid forward and into the bulkhead and scraped his scalp.

He heard the driver shout, *"Asalaam Aleikum."*

He heard a voice outside, *"Aleikum Asalaam."*

The truck gathered speed. The words were revolving in his mind.

"Peace be on you."

"On you be peace."

Mattie had lived in Iran as a military liaison officer, and he had lived there as the Station Officer.

Second nature to Mattie to recognize the greeting and the response.

He was sagged on the floor of the truck. He was inside Iran, beyond the reach of help.

From the Customs post a telephone call was routed through the office that had been made available in Tabriz to the investigator. The message was terse. The investigator was told that a Dodge pickup had just passed through the frontier and had begun the 150-mile journey to Tabriz.

In his former life, the news would have been cause enough to break out a bottle of French champagne . . . much that was missed from the former life. The investigator instead, in his turn, made a telephone call, to the Tehran office of the Mullah who was his protector, to the man who had authorized the kidnapping. Unable to celebrate with champagne, the investigator curled up on his camp bed, tried to catch a few hours of sleep.

No, Dr. Owens had not checked out, and that was an embarrassment to reception because they had been promised he was going and they had a client for the room, and it was still occupied with Dr. Owens's possessions.

No, Dr. Owens had not brought back his car,

and the hall porter had twice been phoned by the rental company.

From the airport, after the Van flight arrived without Mr. Furniss, it had taken the Station Officer a full hour to get through on a pay phone from Ankara to Van. It took him another hour to reach the embassy's Air Attaché.

No, of course he had confirmed there were no flights to Van that night.

No, for crying out loud, this was not a trivial matter. He wanted a light aircraft, and he wanted the Air Attaché to pilot it, soon as possible, like an hour ago.

"I was half into bed, Terence. This is on the level?"

"Sadly, yes . . . right on the level."

It had been a ghastly flight in a light Cessna across a great expanse of raw countryside, buffeted by gale-force winds. The Station Officer was a poor air traveler at the best of times, but now he noticed not at all the yawing progress of the aircraft. The Air Attaché didn't speak to him, had his hands full. He took his cue from the furrowed anxiety of the young man strapped in beside him.

When they'd landed, the Station Officer asked the Air Attaché to go directly to the Akdamar, to make sure that the room in the name of Dr. Owens stayed sealed.

He went to the local offices of the *jandarma*. He
said that he was from the British embassy. He
knew the registration number of the hired Fiat.
It was close to dawn when the report came in, car
discovered abandoned, indications of an accident.
He was taken to the scene. He said that Dr.
Owens, the driver of the damaged car, was a distinguished archaeologist and the guest of the ambassador. He tried to minimize the concern that
had brought him at night across the country, and
a poor job he made of it. The headlights of the jeep
had picked out the Fiat's rear reflectors. It was on
the verge, off-balance, it seemed, both right-hand
wheels sunk into the soft mud. They gave him a
flashlight and let him make his own examination.
To them it was a small matter. No big deal, death
on the roads, not in eastern Turkey, and this
wasn't death, this was just a missing person. True,
there was nothing inside the car to suggest that
Mr. Furniss was hurt, no blood stain that he could
see, no broken glass. But outside he saw the Fiat's
skid tracks on the tarmacadam and he saw the
dirt trail across what would have been the path
of the Fiat. He saw the broken shields of the brake
lights and the indicators and the stoved-in
bumper. Pretty straightforward . . . A vehicle coming off the open fields in front—wide tracks, probably a tractor or farm lorry—a vehicle ramming

from behind . . . and the unaccompanied Desk Head in between.

The *jandarma* officer said, "It is possible that he has been concussed, that he has wandered off the road. . . ."

No chance.

". . . There is no other explanation."

The officer drove him to the Akdamar.

He gutted the room. Clothes everywhere, books and papers too, and many pages of scribbled notes, not in English certainly, must be some sort of code. He looked carefully at the disorder and decided that it was as Mr. Furniss had left it, that it had not been searched. He packed everything into Mr. Furniss's suitcase.

The Station Officer paid Dr. Owens's bill. He woke the Air Attaché from a deep sleep in an unlit corner of the lobby.

"Sorted out your little problem, Terence? Knickers all untwisted, eh?"

"No, I am afraid the news is all bad."

"Anything I can do?"

"Just fly us home. No jokes. No japes. No funny faces. Just don't say anything at all. Please."

Standing on the hotel steps, waiting once more for a taxi, the Station Officer felt an aching anxiety. Whatever else, Mattie Furniss was not gone walkabout in eastern Turkey nursing a concussion. He had been thinking, how would it have been if he had been there too? Would he be alive now? Where would he be? Come what may, he'd be crucified, he knew that, for leaving a Desk Head alone. Probably finished altogether.

They took off, with the dawn rising behind them.

A blustering wet early summer morning in London. The traffic clogged the Thames bridges. The commuters below the high windows of Century House swarmed in ant columns along the pavements.

The first report from the Ankara Station Officer was deciphered then passed, marked URGENT, to the desk of the night-duty officer. The night-duty officer was ready to clock off, and he was enjoying his last cup of coffee when the message reached him. He signed for it, he read it, and he spluttered coffee over the morning newspapers. There was a procedure for catastrophe. Telephone the Director General's PA. The PA would alert the Director General wherever he was. The night-duty officer would then ring the Director General on a scrambled line.

The night-duty officer read over the message in a clear and firm voice. That was a sham. His throat had dried, his fingers drummed on his desk.

He knew Mattie, everyone at Century knew Mattie Furniss. He listened to the silence at the other end of the distorted connection.

"Did you get that, sir?"

A clipped voice. "Yes, I did."

"What can I do, sir?"

A longer silence. What could anyone do? And what the hell was old Mattie, a Desk Head, doing in Turkey? Last he'd heard of him he was in Bahrain and God knows what he was doing there. Not the night-duty officer's place to question. . . . The night-duty officer had cause to think well of Mattie Furniss. His son had had pretty serious problems with his teeth, came up one day at lunch in the canteen, and Mattie had taken a note, and a week later he had the name of a specialist in Wimpole Street, and the specialist had sorted out the problem over the following nine months, and the bills hadn't been bad. The night-duty officer's wife always spoke well of Mr. Furniss, and when the night-duty officer went home that morning he would not be able to tell her that Mattie Furniss was posted missing, and in a country he'd no business being in.

The voice jolted him.

"All the West Asia Desk Heads, and the DDG, in my office at nine—inform Downing Street that

I'll be there in half an hour. I shall require to see the PM."

The telephone clicked, went dead.

The truck had slowed, and there were the sounds of a city's traffic flow around him. He thought that they were close to a commercial area. He could hear the hawkers' shouts, and whenever the truck stopped he could smell the pavement food stalls. They had come down a fast road for two or more hours that could only be the Tehran road from the border. If they were now in a city then they had reached Tabriz. A lifetime ago since he had been in Tabriz. That was wrong. . . . A lifetime ago was being trapped and kidnapped on the road from To-prakkale. That was more than a lifetime ago.

In the hours that he had lain in the truck no word had been spoken to him. His head, where he had been kicked, was not hurting any longer. His gag was constantly painful. His mouth was parched. His feet were dead below the binding.

The truck stopped, lurched forward and then swung to the right, revving in low gears, stopped again. The engine was cut. He heard everything. The click of the door, the squeaking of the driver's seat as the driver left it, and then it slammed shut. The same at the passenger side. He heard a low conversation beside the driver's cab, but too quiet for him to understand what was said. He saw his captors in the back of the truck move toward him. He didn't flinch. He was not afraid, not yet. Their hands came at his face. He could smell their breath through the masks they wore. He did not try to wriggle away from them, because he thought that would have invited a beating. They fastened a strip of cloth around his eyes.

Mattie was lifted down from the truck. He felt a warm wind on his cheeks. The binding on his ankles was freed. The blood was pounding at the base of his shins, and squeezing down again into his feet. Hands held him upright. He could not have walked by himself, and he was half carried, half dragged up some steps and then maneuvered into a doorway. They went up a full flight of stairs, and they crossed a small landing, and a door was opened. The strip of cloth was removed from his eyes.

He stood in the center of the room.

The gag was taken from his mouth. The strap was released from his wrists.

The door closed behind him. He heard a key turn.

He stared around him.

The window was barred on the inside, had no glass, and beyond the bars the space had been boarded up with plywood. There was an iron bed frame, like the ones used by the junior boys in the dormitories of his old school. There was a flush lavatory in one corner and beside it a table on which was a plain ceramic water pitcher and a steel bowl. There was no other furniture in the room. He turned. The door was heavy wood, there was a peephole at eye level. The walls were freshly white-washed over plaster. The floor was tiled.

If he had been planning a custody cell for a prisoner such as himself he would have created a very similar room. The kidnapping, the lack of any form of communication, the cell, they were all much as he would have planned them himself. Mattie Furniss, Desk Head at Century, long-time officer of the Service, was a professional, and he could recognize the professionalism of his captors.

He sat on the bed. He massaged his ankles and his wrists. He forced his mind to work at the details of his cover. His cover was his only protection.

The Prime Minister sat rigid at the edge of the sitting room chair. The coffee was untouched, the toast had cooled.

"And he's just disappeared off the face of the earth?"

"Not disappeared, Prime Minister. The signs all point to his having been kidnapped."

"But to have been there at all, that tells me he's not very important . . ."

"In that theater of operations, Furniss is of the utmost importance."

"Then you had better tell me what he was doing all by himself—I suppose he was all by himself? You haven't lost a whole department, have you?—in such an obviously risky enterprise?"

"In my opinion, Prime Minister, the performance of the Service on Iran had been second-rate. Upon taking up my position at Century I determined to get that Desk back on course. I told Mattie Furniss, who is incidentally a quite outstanding servant of his country, what I wanted. Obviously affairs inside Iran are at a crucial point. We need to know, very precisely, who is going to come out as top dog in the new Iran. We are talking about a sophisticated and very capable regional superpower, one that controls huge resources of oil inside its own borders and one which has the capacity to destabilize every smaller state on its frontiers, possibly excepting Iraq. We earn very considerable sums of monies from the Gulf states, from the Kuwaitis, from the Saudis. All of those earnings are potentially at risk in the barely disguised warfare between moderate and radical factions for ultimate power in Tehran. The American government has wished to put its markers down in that battle, we more prudently want only to have a better perspective on the end result. For the time being at any rate. Obviously if the radical faction wins out we may have to kiss good-bye billions invested in that region, billions of future sales. We are talking about the possible perversion of one of the great economic markets currently open to us, along with the loss of great numbers of jobs, if the radicals win and continue to export revolution and Islamic fundamentalism."

"I don't need a Foreign Office tract, Director General. I just want to know what the devil this obviously senior man is doing all by himself in a very dangerous part of the world."

"It was I who made the decision that Furniss should travel to the Gulf and Turkey . . ."

"*You* made that decision?"

". . . to the Gulf and Turkey to visit our watchers and also to hold meetings with some of our principal operatives inside Iran."

"I suppose this decision flies in the face of long-established practice at Century. This is symptomatic of your new broom, is it, Director General?"

". . . in order that those with day-to-day responsibility for Iranian intelligence should know more fully what was required of them."

"Day-to-day Iranian intelligence. Yes, well, you haven't said so in so many words but I take it we may assume that Iranian intelligence will be exactly what Mr. Furniss will be dealing with, even now."

"It hardly bears thinking about, Prime Minister."

"You sent him, you'd better think about it. You're running a tight ship, Director General. Do all your people go overseas with a Union Jack sewn on the breast pocket? Does his passport say 'Iran Desk, Century'?"

The Director General said, and his eyes gazed back into the Prime Minister's sarcasm, "Naturally he is traveling under a well-established alias. He is an archaeologist, rather a distinguished one, I gather. A specialist on an early Turkish civilization, I believe."

"I dare say he is, but archaeologists do not ordinarily disappear an hour's driving time from the Iranian border. Or do they, Director General? I have very little information on archaeologists. It sounds to me as though Furniss's cover was blown, as I think you put it, long before he got anywhere near Turkey. You wouldn't have to be terribly bright to wonder what a specialist in an early

Turkish civilization was doing hopping round the Gulf in his Olympic blazer. And if he is inside Iran, if he is identified, then he is going to have a difficult time?"

"Yes, Prime Minister."

"Well, thank you, Director General. I think that's enough excitement for this morning. Keep me posted, please, and kindly resist the temptation to send in a team of Israeli snipers to see if they can find him. I think you have enough of a mess on your hands as it is."

He let himself out of the room. He took the small lift to the ground floor. On the pavement between the front door and the car, he gulped for air. Furniss must be an imbecile. And now, by God, he'd be paying for it. And so would a great many others.

The car drove away down the lane. Harriet Furniss watched it go. The wind was up, and a gale was forecast, and she thought that the blossom would not be much longer on the trees. He had been very nice to her, the young man, and he had emphasized at least three times that it was the Director General who had personally sent him. Not that it mattered, whether the young man was pleasant or unpleasant, the message would have been the same.

Mattie was missing. It was believed that Mattie had been kidnapped. Mattie was an archaeologist . . . so pathetic. A woman could have run Century better, and still had time for the housework. She was very deliberate in her movements, she bent down to her garden kneeler and went on with the weeding of the border that she had been at when the young man had arrived. There was a surprising amount of groundsel in the border this year. . . . She was numbed. Cleaning the groundsel out of the bed was her safety. . . . She was crying softly. She loved that man. She loved the calmness and the kindness and the patience of Mattie, and she loved his gentleness. No, he was not as clever as she was. No, he could not paint as she could. He did not enjoy the theater or music as she and the girls did, but she loved that massive and reassuring strength. He was the man she had depended on throughout her adult life. She could not remember the last time that he had raised his voice to her. . . . Those fools in London, fools for what they had done to her Mattie.

She spent the whole morning on the border. She filled a wheelbarrow with weeds. She cried her heart out for the whole morning.

Khalil Araqi walked two hundred yards from the hotel's rank, flagged down a taxi and asked for the

McDonalds in the Strand. He then walked back up the Haymarket, and all along the length of Regent Street, and to any casual observer he would have been seen to spend a long time looking in shop windows. The stops in the windows and doorways of the stores enabled him to check frequently that he was not tailed. He followed exactly the instructions that he had been given in Tehran. He did not expect to be followed, and he could detect no one following him. On the corner of Brook Street and Bond Street, after he had waited at the curbside for three, four minutes, he was picked up by car. He was taken by the student of the English language south and west across the city. Araqi had been to London before, but that was many years earlier. He gazed around him. He was at ease. His confidence in the planning behind his mission was complete.

They parked five hundred yards beyond the mews.

The student followed Araqi back up the road, well behind him. There was a narrow entrance to the mews cul-de-sac, and Araqi's eyes roved to find the lighting above so that he could estimate the fall of shadows at night inside the cobbled entry. Briskly, Araqi walked the length of the cul-de-sac, keeping to the right-hand side, keeping away from the 5 series BMW. There were cars parked outside each of the brightly painted front doors.

He was satisfied.

When he had driven back to within ten minutes' walk of the hotel, the student gave Araqi a brown paper package. The student did not know what was in the package, nor that it had been brought by a courier from West Germany, passing the previous evening through the port of Felixstowe.

The student was told at what time, outside the garage on Park Lane, he should collect Araqi that night. For the rest of the day, Araqi worked on the assembly of an explosive device by which a mercury tilt system would detonate one kilo weight of military explosive.

The PA stood in front of the desk.

"You won't shoot the messenger, sir?"

The Director General winced, his head dropped. "Tell me."

"We've got Mr. Furniss's bag back from Turkey. All his kit that the Station Officer, Ankara, collected from his hotel. There's a report which I couldn't make head or tail of but which Miss Duggan has typed up for you. You'd better read it. . . . Sadly, it gets worse. Mr. Furniss's passport was with his things. That's the passport in his wife's maiden name. What it would appear is that Mr. Furniss does not have supporting documentation of his cover."

"That just about caps it."

The Director General had served half a lifetime in the Foreign and Commonwealth with Benjamin Houghton's father. He and Houghton's father were golfing partners of old and they had once courted the same girl, she'd turned them both down. He had made certain when he came to Century that young Benjamin would be his personal assistant. The boy was cheeky and casual and very good. He would go a long way, if he cared to stay the course.

"Just thought you should know, sir."

And Houghton was gone, almost indecent haste. Just the same at the meeting with the Deputy Director General and the Desk Heads. They'd all been exasperatingly aloof, distinctly themselves. Bastards.

The Director General began to read Furniss's report, apparently based on the observations of an agent traveling quite widely inside Iran. Very recently, too. Not world shaking, but good, incisive stuff. His PA came through on the internal phone. A meeting with the Permanent Under Secretary, Foreign and Commonwealth, at two. A meeting with the Joint Intelligence Committee at three. A meeting of the Service's Crisis Management Committee at four, with the possibility of a teleprinter link to Ankara. The Prime Minister at six.

"Would you like me to raffle the ballet tickets, sir?"

"No, dammit. Call Angela and ask her to take one of the children. And you, too, can cancel anything you had planned for this evening."

He didn't notice the builders' van parked opposite the block of flats, across the playground from the concrete entranceway. He stared up at the side windows of the flat. There were no lights on, and it was a damp clouded morning. There should have been lights on in the flat. He knew the children did not go to a preschool, and he knew that the flat should have been occupied at that time in the morning.

He did not hear the click of the camera shutter, and he did not hear the suppressed whisper of Harlech as he reported Tango One's arrival into a lip microphone. To have heard the camera noise and the voice whisper Charlie would have to have been hard up against the grubby side of the builders' van. Charlie stood in the center of the playground. Kids played on the swings and larked in the sandpit, their mothers sitting and nudging their pushchairs and pulling on their cigarettes, huddled in conversation. There was a Corporation cleaner out with a broom and a bin on wheels rounding up the swirl of crisp packets and fag wrappers and Coke tins. There was a soccer kick-about and the goal posts were snapped-off young trees.

He climbed three flights of concrete stairs. Charlie saw the plywood hammered across the door of the flat. He ran down the stairs, fighting a fierce anxiety. All around him was the normality of the estate. The young mothers heaving their lung smoke into their kiddies' faces, the cleaner whose work would never be completed, the kids who played their eternal soccer. The flat of Leroy Winston Manvers seemed to Charlie as dead as the broken goal-post trees. He was irresolute. Inside Iran, inside his own country, closing with the silenced pistol on two Guards, riding behind the executioner of Tabriz, he would not have known the feeling of sudden apprehension. That was his own ground, the estate in Notting Hill in West London was a foreign country to him.

He looked around him. There were the parked cars, and the builders' van, and the people . . . there was a stunning ordinariness about the estate on a gray morning.

He snapped his back straight. He walked for-

ward. He went to a group of young mothers. He
pointed up to the flat with no lights.

A snort of rich laughter. They were the women
who would have been at the front for a public
hanging in Tabriz, they would have thought that
a good show. Bright laughter, enough to make
them choke on their fags. A cigarette was thrown
down, not stamped out.

"Got busted, didn't he. Old Bill took away
plenty. He won't be back."

Charlie felt winded, the control ripped from
him. He took off, and he had the hoots of their
mirth behind him.

Half an hour later, when the mothers had retrieved their young and scattered, the builders'
van pulled lethargically away from the estate.

"What he is not going to do is dig a hole in the
ground and bury his stuff. He is going to find another dealer. He's sitting on a pile. He's got to find
somewhere else to drop it."

Parrish thought he agreed. He thought Keeper
had taken a good attitude.

"Where is he now?" he asked quietly.

"Top end of Kensington High Street, his
motor's on double yellows. Harlech says he's looking pretty pissed off. The sign on the door where

he's gone says it's an import-export company.
Haven't any more yet."

"Tally ho, Keeper."

Park grinned. "For the moment it's fine, but it's
just a beginning."

"Home Office files, a stateless person has to
have a guarantor."

"Nice one, Bill."

"What would not be nice would be for you to
lose track of a load of stuff. Got me? That would
not be nice."

The load of stuff was still in the flat in Beaufort
Street, Park would have sworn to that. The
Suzuki had the canvas back off, and the stuff
wasn't in the cab. There was a watch on the front
and back of the flat, twenty-four hours, and the
tail was solid on the jeep when it went out, just
as it had been solid when Tango One had come out
earlier in the morning and gone down to the deli-
catessen for a pastry and a coffee.

Park would be going down to the Home Office.
Parrish would be linking the radios. That was the
way Parrish liked it best, left in the Lane with just
the typists and clerical assistants to spoil him and
share their lunches with him, and keep him fu-
eled up with coffee. The youngsters all out, raring
to go and gone. It took a fair amount to wind up

old Parrish, it took the whole of his team out and hunting to wind him right up.

He was in one hell of a great mood that morning, and thumping out on two fingers his progress report for the ACIO. Of course he was excited, of course it had been one hell of a risk to let Eshraq and the stuff loose.

"You're very kind. I thank you."

"For nothing."

Mahmood Shabro walked through the outer office with Charlie. He was no fool, he saw the way his new secretary glanced up from her desk at the boy. He saw the trace of the smile at Charlie's lips. He took Charlie to the outer door.

"You pass to Jamil my best wishes."

"I will, Mr. Shabro. I will see him tomorrow, if he can manage that."

He had not asked why Charlie should wish an introduction to his brother, the renegade and the fly one from whom he kept a secure distance.

"Look after yourself, my boy."

The outer door closed on Charlie's back. He stood in the center of the outer office for a moment.

"I think Charlie has disappointed you, my dear."

She shrugged. "He might have rung."

"He should have rung."

"I mean . . . I don't just go, go out, with anyone. I'm not that type . . ."

She was efficient, she had his outer office organized, she was starting to learn the detail of his work. He wanted to keep Polly Venables. It was a peculiar request that Charlie had made to him that morning for an introduction to his brother. His brother was involved in politics, and his brother had no visible means of financial support. Nevertheless, he had arranged the meeting.

"It would not be wise for you, Polly, to concern yourself too greatly with Charlie."

Park strode out of the Home Office building.

It had taken only an hour. He had in his briefcase a photocopy of the paperwork completed at the time of issue of a Stateless Person's travel document to Charles Eshraq, refugee from Iran.

The name of the guarantor was Matthew Furniss, Foreign and Commonwealth Office.

Chapter ✣ 9

"**G**ood morning, Mr. Furniss." The voice was a wind whisper in trees.

Mattie started up from the tiled floor. He had been doing his push-ups.

"It is excellent to stay in good health, Mr. Furniss."

His jacket and his shirt were on the bed, his shoes were placed neatly under the bed. He was sweating under his vest and his hair was disheveled. Of course they had watched him through the peephole in the door. They would have waited until he was stripped down for his exercises before making the entry. The fitting of the plywood screen on the window had tiny gaps in it, and he had known hours before that it was daylight. He

did not know how many hours because his watch
had been taken from his wrist when he was still
semiconcussed in the truck. He had sat for what he
reckoned had been hours on his bed, sometimes he
lay and tried to sleep, waiting for them to come,
and when the hours had drifted away he had decided to do his exercises. Of course they had
watched him.

"It is my great pleasure to meet you, Mr.
Furniss."

Mattie spoke fluent Farsi, but the man spoke almost unaccented English. It was another tiny
shaft into the shell of his spirit.

He was stumbling to his feet, and breathing
hard. He would have liked to have stood his
ground in the center of the room, but his muscles
were blood alive and his lungs heaved. He sat
down heavily on the bed, and he started to pull
his shirt over his shoulders.

"You are . . . ?"

"I am the investigator in your case, Mr.
Furniss."

"Do you have a name? A name would be a small
courtesy. And let me tell you my name. I am not
your Mr. Furniss. I don't need an investigator,
thank you. I am Dr. Owens, University of London,
and I insist on being released immediately and on

transport, at once, to my hotel. This has gone on long enough."

"Excuse me."

The man glided across the room and bent down close to Mattie and with sure movements he threaded the laces from Mattie's shoes and pocketed them, and then his hands came to Mattie's waist and he unbuckled the belt from the trousers and pulled it clear. There was a small expression of regret in the hazel eyes. Mattie read him. Not regret that he had to take away his prisoner's laces and belt, but irritation that it had not already been done.

It was the first time that he had been spoken to since his capture. The tray on which food had been brought to his room was on the floor beside his shoes. Neither of the men had spoken when the food was brought. The door unlocked, the tray put down just inside the door, a second man standing behind the one who had carried the tray.

It was as Mattie would have done it himself.

He had his shirt buttoned. He had his shoes loose over his socks. He smoothed down his hair.

He supposed that he was surprised that the investigator was not wearing a suit and tie. He noted the American jeans, faded, and the long-tailed shirt, out of the trouser waist, and the sandals, no socks. He saw the harsh, short cut of the man's hair. He thought the man was a little younger than himself, he had spotted the gray pepper-pot flecks over the temples of his head, and care lines below his eyes. Pretty horrible eyes. Eyes without life.

"I should explain. You are in the Islamic Republic of Iran, Mr. Furniss. You are of interest to the struggling masses of our people in their fight to rid themselves of American and Zionist and British domination. That is why you are here."

He straightened his back, he drew the deep breath down. "I am an archaeologist, I am not very interesting to anybody and I am no part of what you call British domination."

The words hung, fell. Mattie saw the smile curl at the mouth of the investigator, but no humor in those awful eyes. He said nothing.

"I can only suggest that you have made, whoever employs you has made, a mistake of which I am the victim. If a scholar cannot go about his work then the world has come to a pretty pass. I have devoted my adult life to the study of the Urartians, to their culture, to their architecture, to their disappearance. You have people in London, I presume. You can check what I say with the Curator of Near Eastern Antiquities at the British Museum."

"No doubt, Mr. Furniss."

The smile had gone from the investigator's face.

"I would be most grateful if you could make such checks as speedily as possible so that this ridiculous business can be concluded. I have no quarrel with the people of Iran, with their Revolution. I am not a politician, I am a scholar. I am engaged on work that is purely historical in its nature, and before I lose my patience will you kindly get it into your head that my name is O-W-E-N-S, Owens. I am not, quite obviously, who you think I am."

"Mr. Furniss, I came this morning to see you to establish that you were well, that you had not been injured. I did not come to discuss the cover story that you have manufactured for yourself."

"Cover . . . this is preposterous. Go away, now. I have had enough of this. Go away and check before you get yourself into serious trouble."

"Mr. Furniss, later today you will be brought some sheets of paper and a pencil. You may begin to write down your reasons for traveling to that area of Turkey which has a common border with our country. You should write of your activities most fully."

"I will, most gladly. You'll have a full account, and by the time I am finished I shall expect you back with a handsome apology. But I must warn you, I shall take this matter up at the British embassy in Ankara, apology or no apology."

The hazel eyes hovered over Mattie's body, seemed to weigh him, explore him. The voice was softer than before.

"Mr. Furniss, let me remind you: between 1975 and 1978 you were the Station Officer in Tehran representing the British Secret Intelligence Service. There was a day in February 1976, a morning as I remember, when you came to the headquarters of the SAVAK. I remember it clearly because it was I who brought in the coffee for you and the officers with whom you met. Myself, Mr. Furniss, I handed you the coffee . . . I do not recall a discussion of Urartian fortifications."

Like a punch to the stomach. "I'm afraid you have a case of mistaken identity."

"When the paper comes, Mr. Furniss, it is advisable that you fill it."

Mattie's head dropped. He heard the shuffle of the sandals on the tiles, and the door opening on oiled hinges, and the turning of a key.

A pale body, sinew under the skin. Park never wore a vest. In his chest of drawers at home he had vests that Ann had bought him the first January sales after they were married, and they had never been worn. The girls in the April office didn't look up because none of them was that interested in Park, a cold creature, and anyway they were pretty used to seeing men with their shirts off, strapping on the canvas harnesses for radio transmitter/receivers. It was a harness that could support a Smith and Wesson .38, but the ID never carried "pumps." If the guns were thought necessary, then the marksmen were supplied by the police. Park had the microphone on a cord around his neck, and he shrugged back into his shirt, and put the clear plastic earpiece in place.

There would be two cars and a van in place that morning. They could follow Tango One wherever he cared to lead them. The van had a miserable clutch and wouldn't be able to keep up with the cars, but it would get there eventually. Corinthian would be on the Pentax with the 500mm lens, Keeper would be telling him what was wanted on the celluloid, what wasn't worth it.

Parrish had wandered out of his office.

"Still in his pit, is he?"

"He came out for his bun and coffee, went back in . . . we'll be there in half an hour."

"Anything on his phone?"

"He hasn't used it."

"What about the profile?"

"I'm going to do half day in the van, then have

Harlech take over. Then I'm going down to shake up the FCO chappies a bit."

"Ah yes, the best and the brightest," said Parrish.

Park grinned. The military and the Foreign Office were the officers, the police and the ID were the poor bloody infantry, that was Parrish's unchangeable view. Parrish would never take a six-bedroom farmhouse in Tuscany for his holidays, he was in a caravan at Salcombe . . . for that matter Park didn't take any holidays at all.

"I was actually quite polite last night. I asked for their personnel officer, I explained that I needed to talk to a Mr. Matthew Furniss, and the guy went off, bloody supercilious but perfectly nice, and came back twenty minutes later and just shut a real heavy door in my face. Didn't say he was abroad, nor on holiday, just that he wasn't available. I sprang about a bit, got absolutely nowhere. He looked at me like I'd come in with the cat. Upshot is, I'm back there at four. I promise you, Bill, I'll have an answer then."

"I'll come down with you," Parrish said.

"Frightened I might thump someone?"

"To hold your delicate hand, Keeper—now get yourself moving."

Parrish thought his squad were the pick of the world, and he was buggered if he was going to

have them messed around by some creep in the
Foreign and Commonwealth. He'd be an interesting fellow, Mr. Matthew Furniss, guarantor of a
big-time heroin distributor.

The Director General showed himself that morning. He saw himself as the captain of a storm-
shaken ship, not that he would have cared to voice
that feeling. He believed passionately in the re-
sponsibilities of leadership, and so he wandered
the corridors and rode the lifts, he even took his
coffee in the canteen. He took Houghton with him,
the only fairly anonymous courtier, to whisper
the name of any officer he didn't know and his job
in the Service.

Century was compartmentalized. The North
American Desk was not supposed to know of the
day-to-day successes or failures of East European
Desk. East European Desk was supposed to be insulated from Far East Desk. No other Desk would
know of the abduction of Mattie Furniss. That was
the system, and it was bust wide open. The Director General found his whole building riddled with
rumor and anxiety. He was asked to his face if
there was any news of Mattie Furniss, whether it
was true about Mattie Furniss. He sought to de-
flect all but the most persistent, to reassure them,
and to switch talk whenever possible to other mat-

ters—the new computer, the cricket match against the Security Service on Gordon Street's ground, the rewiring of the building that was scheduled to begin in the autumn. He decided to call it a day long before he reached Iran Desk's office.

Back in his office he sent for his Deputy Director General. The man was just back from three weeks in Bermuda and paid for, no doubt, with family money. The sun had tanned the Deputy's face, darkened it to the roots of his full head of blond hair and accentuated his youth. The Director General would finish his career in public service when he left Century, and it was assumed throughout the nineteen floors that the Deputy would follow him into the DG's job. Their relationship, twenty years apart as they were, had been at best strained since the arrival of the Director General from Foreign and Commonwealth, because the Deputy had narrowly missed the nod for the job himself, said to be too young and to have time in the bank. The DDG regarded himself as the expert and the DG as the amateur. They worked best when they had clearly distinct spheres within which to operate. But on that morning the Director General was not in any way combative. He needed movement, he would have to suffer a third meeting in two days with the Prime Minister in the late afternoon.

It was agreed that field agents inside Iran should be warned of a possible compromising of their security, but not at this moment advised to flee the country. It was agreed that the World Service of the BBC, English Language, should report, and without comment, that a Dr. Matthew Owens, an English archaeologist, was reported missing while on an expedition to northeastern Turkey. Little thing, but could be a boost to Mattie's cover. It was agreed the Turkish authorities should not for the time being be informed of Mattie's true identity; they might, in limited circles, know from his meetings in Ankara, but it would not go at a government-to-government level; Station Officer, Ankara, to hack that into place. It was agreed that Central Intelligence Agency should not be informed at this stage. It was agreed that the Crisis Management Committee should be kept in session for the duration. Iran Desk to report directly to the DDG until further notice. The DDG to select a senior officer to go to Ankara and work with the Station Officer to prepare a minutely detailed report on Furniss's time in Turkey. Precious little to take to the Prime Minister, but until they had some indication of who had abducted Furniss—and God alone knew where that

was going to come from—there was nothing else
that could sensibly be done.

The Director General ticked off the points
agreed.

"Did you know that Furniss was running a new
agent? Some very useful material. I had Library
run through a check on him this morning. Nothing there. No case history, no biography. That is
most peculiar. I mean, Furniss is steeped in
procedure . . ."

"Furniss can't even type," the Deputy Director
General said coldly. "That woman, his PA, is like
a mother hen to him. Flossie Duggan. She types
everything for him, she'll have the case and biography on the floppies. She'll have them in Mattie's
safe. DG, you'll have to fight your way past her.
But that's hardly top concern now. That's just one
agent that's now vulnerable, one of several . . ."

The Director General cut in. He was hunched
forward over his table.

"What's the scuttlebutt downstairs, I mean, on
this news? It's clearly not a secret."

"You want to know?"

"Of course I want to know."

"They're saying that Mattie warned against it,
that he was pressured into going. That the security of a senior member of the Service was put in
jeopardy."

"Perhaps that's the black side."

An explosion across the table. "For Christ's sake, with what he knows, they're going to torture it out of him. They may already have started. And we stand to lose the whole of our Iran network, because it's all in Mattie's head. They'll torture him for those names. Do you know about torture, DG?"

The DG leaned back and swiveled his chair to face the gray morning beyond the windows. "Is he a brave man?"

"It's nothing to do with being brave. Don't you understand that? It's about torture."

There was a light knock at the door. The Director General swung to face it. Bloody little Houghton, and not waiting to be called in.

"I don't know why you bother to knock, Ben. What the hell is it?"

"Sorry to interrupt, sir. Something rather puzzling has come up. Personnel are asking for guidance. FCO's been on. They've had a little cretin from the Customs round asking to see Matthew Furniss."

"*Customs?* I don't believe it. . . . What in heaven's name for?"

"It's someone from the Investigation Division, sir. Quite a serious outfit, I gather. They have es-

tablished that Mattie was guarantor to a young
Iranian exile now resident in the UK . . ."

"So, what is he, out of date with his renewal?"

There was a blandness about Benjamin Houghton that could infuriate the most high and the
most mighty. "Not as serious as that, sir. Just that
he's been trafficking in heroin, quite a lot of heroin by the sound of it."

Parrish's voice crackled into Park's ear.

"April One for April Five, April One for April
Five."

"April Five to April One, come in. April Five to
April One, come in."

"What's moving, April Five?"

"April Five to April One, be busier in Highgate
bone yard. Tango One is still inside the location.
We've done well. We're just inside the mews
entry. We've got a great lens view on the front
door. Harlech is in the street, he's squared the
meter maid. There's a back entrance to the house,
just an alley, Token's on that. Tango One's jeep
is in the alley."

"Sounds fine. You ready for the goodies?"

"Ready, April One."

"OK, April Five . . . The five series is registered
in the name of Jamil Shabro, Iranian born, age
fifty-seven, address as per your location. But he's

choice. Vehicle registration has a cut out on that number. We had to go through the Met. Got the bum's rush from the plods, referred to Anti-Terrorist. Tango Four is on their list for security guidance."

"What does that mean?"

"It means that Tango Four has got up the Ayatollah's nose. Getting interesting, eh? Tango Four has security briefings from the Anti-Terrorist mob, varying his routes, that sort of chat. They say Tango Four is a devious crap artist, but he's got guts because he stands up at the drop of a hat and pitches the old aggro back at the Ayatollah."

"So we just sit tight."

"You just sit tight, April Five."

It took more than one hour for the news to seep from Heathrow Airport to the offices of the Anti-Terrorist squad on the fifth floor of New Scotland Yard.

The IranAir flight, nonstop from London to Tehran, had taken off more than forty minutes ahead of schedule, at twenty minutes before noon. The news came via the British Airports Authority to the armed police officers stationed at the airport and who watched over all incoming and outgoing flights of that airline. From them, the information was passed to the Special Branch officers on duty at Heathrow, and they in turn filed their report, which was, after processing, sent on the internal fax to the Anti-Terrorist squad.

The fax finally landed on the desk of a detective sergeant. It was bald, factual, related to nothing else. He thought of an aircraft taking to the skies, leaving behind more than a handful, he supposed, of furious passengers. Still, they'd mostly be Iranians. No one else would be fool enough to fly IranAir. That made him smile. But he was a thorough man. He rang through to the Authority and asked if they had been given a reason for the new flight plan.

Operational reasons . . . what else? He asked if the plane were now actually airborne.

The detective sergeant hurried down the corridor to the office of his superior.

"The bloody thing's in French airspace now. I'd have ordered it held if it were still on the ground. If they're going early for 'operational reasons,' then that says to me that they're carrying someone out, someone who's got to get clear. We're sitting on a bang, sir."

There were the usual photographs, silver-framed, of the old soldiers with their Shah of Shahs. There were gold-embossed invitation cards to functions, all exile binges, most of them on which the hosts requiring the pleasure listed all their decorations and titles. There were volumes of Persian poetry, bound in calves' leather on a walnut side table. The interior could have been lifted straight from north Tehran, save for the picture window from knee height to the ceiling looking down onto the mews.

The daughter was upstairs and Charlie could hear the rattle of her cassette music from the floor above, and the wife was out shopping. Charlie was alone in the living room with Jamil Shabro.

"What's it for, Charlie?"

"Does it matter?"

"Too double damned right. You ask for a contact, you tell me why."

"Pretty obvious. I have stuff, I want to dump it."

"Don't be insolent, boy. Why?"

"What anyone trades for, money."

"What do you want the money for?"

"I think that's my business, Mr. Shabro."

"Wrong. My business. You come to me, you want me involved, and I am involved if I send you to a dealer. I don't fuck about, Charlie. You give me some answers, or you go away empty."

"I hear you."

"Charlie . . . You're a nice boy, and I knew your father. I would have bet good money that you would not have begun to think about running heroin, and you end up at an old fucker like me. This old fucker wants to know why you want the money."

Charlie said, "I want the money to buy armor-piercing missiles . . ."

He saw Jamil Shabro's jaw fall.

"That way I can destroy those who murdered my family."

He saw the widening of the man's eyes.

"When I was in Iran last week and the week before, I killed the executioner of Tabriz. On my previous visit I killed two Guards. There is still unfinished business."

He saw the blood run from Jamil Shabro's face.

"When I have the money, when I have the armor-piercing missiles, I will go back inside Iran, and I will dedicate my life to the future of our country."

"Charlie, you must be in love with death."

"I love my country, Mr. Shabro."

Jamil Shabro's hands flexed together. There was the sweet smile of reason. "I know about your family, Charlie, your father and your sister and your uncle, we all know about that. We understand your outrage . . . but you are talking like a fool . . ."

"It's you who talk, Mr. Shabro, and it's you who left. The Communists and the Democrats and the

Monarchy party, they all fucked up. They don't have the right to demand another chance. I do, my generation does."

"I risk my life for what I believe, I have been told that by the police."

"While I am inside Iran, Mr. Shabro."

Jamil Shabro walked the length of his living room. He disliked the boy for his arrogance, he admired the boy for his guts. For the first time in many years Jamil Shabro felt a small sense of humility, humility before the courage of Charlie Eshraq.

"I help you, you have my name, you go back inside, you are taken. When they interrogate you they will have my name. What happens to me?"

"You're in London, Mr. Shabro. And I have many names that are more precious to the Mullahs than yours."

He went to his desk. He flipped open the notepad beside the telephone. He wrote a name and a London telephone number. He tore the sheet of paper from the pad. He held it, tantalizingly, in front of him.

"I get ten percent."

"That's fair."

There was no handshake, just the passing of the paper, and the sound below of the front door opening.

Jamil Shabro went to the doorway, and he shouted into the music upstairs that he was going out, and that her mother was home. She had struggled up the stairs, cloaked in a fur coat and weighed down by two plastic Harrods bags and a third from Harvey Nichols. Perfunctorily, as if he did it because there was a stranger watching, he kissed his wife.

"This is Colonel Eshraq's boy, Charlie, dear. He needs a drink . . . Charlie, my wife."

"Very pleased to meet you, Mrs. Shabro."

"I don't know when I'll be back."

The bags were dumped onto the carpet, the fur coat draped over them.

"What would you like, Mr. Eshraq?"

"Scotch would be excellent, a weak one, please."

He heard the front door shut. He thought that Jamil Shabro hadn't been able to get out of the house fast enough, not once his wife had returned. It amused Charlie, the way she punished him, spending his money. She brought him the drink in a crystal tumbler, and there wasn't much water, and then she was back to the sideboard, lacing vodka with tonic. He sipped his whiskey. From the window he could see Jamil Shabro bending to unlock the door of his car. The door was pulled open and he saw the man's glance flash up to the window, and his wife waved vaguely to him.

"Cheers."

"Cheers, Mrs. Shabro."

She stood beside him. He wondered how much money she spent on clothes each month.

"I'm exhausted—shopping is so tiring in London."

Charlie watched the three-point turn. He heard the scratch of the gears. He saw a battered van parked at the top end of the mews. The turn was complete.

"I'm sorry, she's rather a noisy child, my daughter."

The car burst forward.

He saw the light.

The light came first.

The light was orange fire.

The 5 series BMW was moving, lifting. The passenger door separating from the body, and the boot hatch rising.

The windshield blowing out. The van alongside rocking.

The body emerging, a rising puppet, through the windshield hole.

He felt the blast. Charlie cringing away, and trying to shelter Mrs. Shabro. The full-length window cracking, slowly splintering into the half-drawn curtains, and the hot air blast on his face, on his chest. The same hot air blast as had hammered his back on the wide road leading into Tabriz.

He heard the thunder. The thrashing of an empty oil drum. The dead hammer blow of military explosive detonating.

He was on the carpet. There were the first small blood dribbles on his face, in his beard, and his hands were resting on glass shards, and the woman was behind him.

Charlie crawled on his knees to the open window, to beside the ripped curtain shrouds. The sound had gone. The 5 series BMW no longer moved. There was the first mushroom of the smoke pall. The body of Jamil Shabro was on the cobbles of the mews, his right leg was severed above the knee and the front of his face was gone. His trousers seemed scissored at his groin. Charlie saw the back doors of the van opening.

A man spilling out, with a camera and a long lens hanging from his neck, and the man was reeling drunk. A second man coming. The second man clutched, like it was for his life, a pair of binoculars. Two drunks, neither able to stand without the other, holding each other up, pulling each other down. Two men, and they had a camera with a long lens and binoculars.

Charlie heard the shout.

The shouting was above the screaming of the

woman on the carpet behind him. The woman was nothing to Charlie, the shout was everything.

"April Five to April One, April Five to April One . . . for fuck's sake come in. . . . This is April Five, Police, Fire, Ambulance, immediately to April Five location. . . . Bill, there's a bloody bomb gone off."

Charlie understood.

"There are casualties, Bill. Tango Four's been taken out by an explosion. . . . Just get the fuckers here, Bill."

There was a girl running into the mews. Running for dear life toward the two men, and she had a personal radio in her hand.

Surveillance. His meeting with Jamil Shabro had been under surveillance.

He went fast.

He went down the stairs. He went out through the garage door at the back into a small garden, and he went over the high trellis wood fence at the back because he could see that the gate was bolted. He sprinted the length of the alleyway to the jeep.

The body had not been moved, but it was covered now with a groundsheet. The leg was in a plastic bag, holding down a corner of the groundsheet. Harlech's traffic warden, hardly a stitch of clothing left on her, had been tenderly loaded into the first ambulance and driven slowly out of the mews. Too slowly, Park thought, for survival. The scene-of-crime photographer went about his work. The mews was sealed off but there was a great melee of men round the car. There were men from the local force, uniformed and plainclothes, there were Special Branch, there were Anti-Terrorist squad, and two who stood right back and didn't seem to Park to know quite what they were doing there. He had those two as Security Service. There were a couple of WPCs in the house, and all of them out in the street could hear the crying. There were ambulance crews still in four other houses in the mews. Two cars close to the blast had been wrecked.

Corinthian had gone to the hospital. He'd been taking a photograph of Tango Four as the BMW had driven toward them, he'd had the body of the camera heaved into his nose, cheekbone and eyebrow. He'd have some stitches and a Technicolor eye.

He had seen quite a deal in his time, but he had never seen anything remotely like the havoc in the mews. He was on the outside, so was Token. They were the ID and they had strayed into police territory. Of course, the local force had not been informed that April were on their patch. Of

course, the Anti-Terrorist squad had not been informed that an Iranian exile, on their files as "at
risk," was being targeted. So naturally Keeper
and Token were getting the cold shoulder. They'd
be caught up with, later. They'd be interviewed
when the mess was cleared. Park was still dazed.
He had the noise in his ears. He had the ache in
his shoulder from when he had been pitched
across the dark interior of the van. He was lucky
to be alive.

Parrish arrived. He strode past the constable,
who held out an ineffectual hand to stop him, and
into the mews. He walked straight to Park.

No rubbernecking, no preamble.

"Where did he go, Tango One?"

"He's not in the house now," Park said.

"You were round the back, Amanda. Did he
come out of the back?"

She was looking at the cobbles. She had her
handkerchief tight in her hand. "I heard the bang,
I came running. They could have been killed."

Parrish snarled. "Next time you want to play
Lady with the Lamp, for Christ's sake get a relief
first."

Parrish had his personal radio in his hand.
There was a tight anger in his snapped words.
"Alpha Control, this is April One. If any of April
team are not doing good works could they be got

soonest, if it does not interfere with visiting hours, to Tango One's home location, and report back on whether Tango One is in residence. Out."

They walked out of the mews. Park thought half the plods were looking at him like it was his fault, like it had happened because the ID had nosed in. The muzzy haze in his ears was clearing. He hadn't done it before, but he took Amanda's hand in his and gave it a squeeze.

The message came back into Parrish's earphone when they were close to the Lane. He heard it. He didn't take his eyes away from the traffic in front. He turned to Park, all phlegmatic.

"Tango One's done a bunk. He went off in a hell of a hurry, didn't even close his front door. Well done, Florence Nightingale, we've lost the bastard. That hurts. It hurts rather more that we've lost a heap of scag."

"Leave off it, Bill. She did what anyone would have done. That wasn't a firework. Another thirty paces and we'd have been gone."

"Rotten old world, Keeper, you can quote me. . . . You going to be fit for the Foreign Office?"

"Yes," Park said.

When the body had been moved, when the widow had left with her daughter to go to the home of the dead man's brother, a team of detectives went inside the mews house. There was no point at that time in trying to interview the widow and her daughter, both hysterical and about to be tranquilized.

"I regret, Mr. Parrish, that Mr. Furniss will simply not be able to contribute to your investigation."

"We would like to establish that for ourselves."

"You misunderstand me . . . there is no question of Mr. Furniss being able to talk to you."

Park thought that if he had been a yobbo and lost his passport in Benidorm, then they'd have treated him better. He and Parrish were in iron-framed chairs in a Foreign and Commonwealth Office interview room. There were two men on the other side of the polished table, one of whom didn't speak. The one who spoke wore a three-piece suit, a stiff collar in this day and age, would you believe it, and a Brigade of Guards tie puffed out, and his voice was a drawl as if it were almost as much as he could manage, having to speak to the likes of Park and Parrish. Park felt a pillock anyway, because at the Lane the duty nurse had put an Elastoplast over a dressing soaked in witch hazel across a ridge of bruise on his forehead.

"We usually find that we are the best judges of

who can, and who cannot, help us with our inquiries."

"Let me try it out on you, Mr. Parrish, with words of one syllable. . . . You will not see him."

"I am a senior investigation officer in the Investigation Division of Customs and Excise. I am working on a case involving the importation from Iran of several hundred thousand pounds' worth, street value, of heroin. My principal suspect, the importer, was issued with a Stateless Person's travel papers naming Matthew Furniss as a guarantor. . . . I hope I haven't gone too fast for you. . . . that makes Mr. Furniss necessary to my investigation as I build up a profile of a resourceful and dangerous criminal."

"You should exclude Mr. Furniss from your investigations, Mr. Parrish."

"We are getting dangerously close, I must warn you, to obstruction. Obstruction is a criminal offense."

"I doubt it, in this case."

"In some quarters the importation of heroin is regarded as a very serious matter."

"Quite rightly, but Mr. Furniss will not be able to help you."

"I'll go over your head."

"That's your privilege, but you will be wasting

your time. My advice would be to stay with the essentials."

"You'll eat those words."

"We'll see. Good luck with your investigation, gentlemen."

They drove back to the Lane. Marooned in traffic, Parrish turned on Park.

"You were a lot of help."

"Stood out a mile."

"Tell me, clever clogs, what stood out a mile?"

"He's a spook."

"Enlighten me."

"Secret Intelligence Service, the jokers over the Thames in the tower block. He was telling you to piss off, Bill. If a spook is sent over to tell us to go away, then it stands to reason that Matthew Furniss is an intelligence wallah, presumably pretty big. Otherwise they wouldn't try that sort of high and mighty shit."

"Sickening, but you're probably right."

"I want a promise, Bill."

"Shoot."

"They're going to try and block us, I bet you. Right now the phones are purring. We've got Iranian heroin, Iranian exiles, we've got car bombs, and we've got a big boy spook. They don't want grubby little Customs sniffing into that."

"What's the promise?"

"That we don't back off, Bill, just because a stiff white collar tells us to."

"Promise."

"Screw them, Bill."

"Too right, young Keeper, screw them."

He started to sing "Jerusalem." Parrish was in full flood by the time they made it back to the Lane.

In the evening, when his food was brought to the door, Mattie gave his guard three sheets of paper filled with his handwriting. The text detailed his study over many years of the Urartian civilization that had been based around the present-day Turkish city of Van.

Guards, and brought up to the same standards. Perhaps he had rebelled against those standards, his father's rigid code, perhaps that was why he had left the military and gone to Century, and yet the standards and the code remained his bedrock. The pure soldiering had appealed to him less and less. He had spent too much time as a young officer as liaison in Iran, wearing his own clothes and mixing with civilians, but the deep base of disciplines had stayed with him. He had been lectured, and he had himself lectured on personal standards as a weapon against the despair that came after the shame of the "emotional rape."

Had it been possible to speak with his guards, then he would have spoken with courtesy, but hard to be courteous to a pair of sods who never caught his eye, never acknowledged his thanks. He had already done his exercises, and that was important, always important to stay mentally and physically fit. He went to the wash basin beside the lavatory. There was no brush to clean the pan of the lavatory, and that was a small wound to him because he thought he would have benefited from being able to set a standard of a clean lavatory. There was no cloth to wipe clean the basin, but he could make something of that with his fingers. Only one tap. He was denied hot water. Well, Mattie Furniss could live without hot water. He turned the tap. A few moments of pressure and then the spurt was reduced to a dribble. The water ran ochre brown. God alone knew what filth was in the water, but the rules demanded that he wash. His hands were cupped to take the soiled water, and he closed his eyes tight, and splashed the water on his face. He took off his shirt, cupped his hands again, and washed underneath his arms. He could not shave, of course, and the growth on his cheeks was an irritation. When he had finished washing he began to wipe the basin clean, to peel away the grime.

Tomorrow, if there was a tomorrow, he would wash his shirt. Today he rinsed his socks. He could wear his shoes without socks. Christ, Harriet, how do I dry my bloody socks? . . . Harriet . . . who would have been to see her? He had once been to visit a Century wife in crisis. Just her own crisis, not the Service's crisis, just that the lady's husband had piled in with his car on a road out of Sharjah. He hadn't made much of a job of telling her the news, but he and Harriet still received a Christmas card from her every year. He wondered how they would be with Harriet. . . . Harriet always washed his socks at home, and she knew how to dry them, even when it was too wet for them to go outside, and in the days before they had a proper heating system in the cottage at Bibury.

The poor darling who washed his socks, and knew how to dry them, he had never, ever talked to her about the risk . . . never. Not when he was Station Officer in Tehran, not when he was running the show down in the Gulf, not when he was packing the clothes as she passed them to him from the wardrobe for this trip. If Harriet had ever said to him that, God's truth, old boy, this life really pisses me off, this life is for kiddies, this life is not for us, old boy, then Mattie would have been shaken to the roots, but he would have packed it in. He hoped they would have sent a good man to see her.

After he had hung his socks on the bed frame, he had cleaned the basin again. Good lord, made in the UK. He could see the manufacturer's emblem, and the symbol of the Queen's award to industry. Must have been a good little export order. Purveyors of bathroom ceramics to His Magnificence.

"Christ, Harriet . . . I am so afraid . . ." His lips mouthed the words. "These charming domestic scenes will surely end, my darling."

"Survive, old boy." That's what she would say and that was the name of the game, survival. Survival was going back to Harriet, one day, going home. And the price of going home, at any rate going home in a skin she would recognize, well, that price was unthinkable. "Don't think it, old boy. You can't afford to think it because you know so much. So many lives depend on your silence."

"You'll tell the girls, won't you? Get them to come and take care of you until this is all over. Oh yes, it will be over. Sooner or later, most probably later, it will be over. I rather fancy there'll be a debriefing of sorts and then they'll drive me to Bibury and you will be at the door. It will be summer still, oh yes." He wiped the underside of the basin with his hands and saw the beetles. Small black beetles on the floor. They had an entry point where the tiles were poorly fitted against the wall.

He started to count the beetles. They were difficult to count, because the little blighters were meandering all over the floor under the basin.

He had not heard the footfall, nor the bolt being drawn back, nor the key being turned.

He was counting beetles, and there were three men in the room. There was a moment of annoyance when he lost his place among the beetles. The men came fast. He was dragged upright. His arms were twisted behind his back. One of the men buried a fist in Mattie's hair and pulled him across the room. Pain on his scalp, and pain at his shoulders from his bent back arms, and his shoes flapping loose and his trousers dribbling down over his hips.

He was trying to remember the rules. At all times courtesy and good manners. Bloody important. Bad-mouth them back and he'd get a kicking. Fight them and he'd get a beating. That's what he used to tell his students at the fort. "No future in getting a good hammering if the only witnesses to your pride are a gang of low-life thugs."

The one who had hold of Mattie's hair kept his head bowed.

He could only see the floor. He could only see the steps down. He was propelled forward.

They were going fast down the stairs and then across the entrance hall of the building, and toward the back of the hall, and into a narrow doorway. Down a flight of breeze block steps, into the cellar.

A room of white, bright light. He saw the zinc bathtub. He saw the hose pipe that was attached to a wall tap. He saw the heavy hooks protruding at different heights from the wall. He saw the plant bed with the leather thongs fastened at each end. He saw the lengths of insulated cable lying casually on the floor.

He saw the table and the two chairs, and the white, bright light was facing one of the chairs. That chair was empty. In the other, his back to the light, was the investigator.

He was put down onto the empty chair. He wriggled on the hard seat to get the waist of his trousers back up from his hips. The men who had brought him down the two flights of steps were all behind him. He could hear their breathing, but he could not see them. He could only see the face of the investigator, and if he looked past the face of the investigator then there was only the ferocity of the white, bright light. He could feel the tremble in his thighs, and in his fingers. He could feel the sinking of his stomach and the looseness.

He heard the creaking turn of a tape recorder's spools. He thought the machine was on the floor beside the feet of the investigator. He could not see the microphone. The investigator put a small attaché case on the table and opened it. He took out the sheets of paper Mattie had written, and a single cardboard file holder. He closed the attaché case, put it back on the floor.

The investigator pushed the file halfway across the table. The light fell on it. The title of the file was DOLPHIN. The investigator took the handwritten sheets of paper and held them in front of Mattie's face and tore them into small pieces.

He saw them flake to the floor.

"I am not stupid, Mr. Furniss, and I had not expected that you would be stupid either."

As soon as he was out from under the railway bridge, the rain streamed down over his face.

He turned, but no one stirred or watched him go.

Because Charlie had brought a bottle of sherry he was good news among the dossers who used the pavement under the bridge. He hadn't had more than one swig himself. The bottle had passed from hand to hand, and he had even been lent a sheet of cardboard packing to use as a blanket. Good guys. Didn't bother with questions. Guys who had accepted him because he'd passed around the bottle.

The rain was dribbling off his nose. He might be back, and he might not. He was another of the city's flotsam, footloose for the day and congregating for the night where there was shelter from the rain. He could have gone to a hotel, or to a boardinghouse, but Charlie had reckoned that was risk. He had felt safer in the dossers' sleeping place. He had been aware of the light of a policeman's torch on his face, past three in the morning. They wouldn't be looking for him among the dossers, no way.

At the underground entrance he ducked out of the rain. He bought a newspaper; scanned it fast. He saw the photograph of the burned-out, blown-up car, and he saw a picture of Jamil Shabro, and the caption "dedicated monarchist." Three dead. Shabro, the traffic warden, DOA, and an old lady who lived right above the blast. Five seriously injured, the old lady's sister among them, blinded in both eyes. No mention of a surveillance operation. He had not dreamed it, and he had no means, even now, of gauging what was the scale of the hunt. They'd pick him up, sure as hell, because they'd mounted surveillance on his meeting, they'd have him held at the airport whenever he flew back.

And then the jigsaw pieces started tumbling. They had spotted him at Heathrow on the way in. That was what the performance at the airport was all about. He'd been under surveillance ever since. They could have lifted him and the rucksack at any time. Why had they not? What were they waiting for? Maybe they would think Jamil Shabro was his dealer. If so, that gave him a tiny breathing space. One less hand at his throat.

Inside the ticket hall he dialed the number that Mr. Furniss had given him in St. James's Park.

He was answered by a secretary. He asked for Mr. Stone. He said he wouldn't give his own name.

"Yes?"

"Who is speaking?"

"I am a friend of Mr. Matthew Furniss."

"Of Mattie's?"

"He said I should call you."

"Did he, now—in what connection?"

"To discuss business with you."

He heard the hesitation. "Mattie said that?"

"He told me to come to you."

"What's the name? No name, no meeting."

"Charlie."

"Hang on. Shan't be a second."

Flossie Duggan responded to the winking light, lifted her telephone. Neither of her telephones had a bell. Mr. Furniss did not like telephones ringing all day around him. She was still red-eyed and her wastepaper basket was a quarter filled with screwed-up Kleenex.

"He's not here at the moment, Mr. Stone. . . . Yes, he knows Charlie. Old friend of Mr. Furniss's family. Is there anything else, Mr. Stone? . . . And best wishes to you, too."

He fed more coins into the machine. He wrote down the address and the time of his appointment, then rang off.

Inside the station he paid for a key to a left luggage box, and at the box, and masked by its open door, he lifted a Sainsbury's bag from his rucksack, before squeezing it into the locker. He

wound the top of the plastic bag round his wrist.
He went back to the telephones.

Another call, another meeting set up.

Charlie carried away from the underground station one packet containing a full kilo of pure and uncut heroin.

"Good God . . . What are you doing here?"

Park didn't think, too tired to think, just opened his mouth. "Bill told me to get home."

She had a super mouth, except when it was twisted, when she was bloody furious.

"Marvelous, you came home because the philanthropic Mr. Parrish said it was all right, remind me to grovel to him. . . . What's that on your head?"

His hand went up. He felt the Elastoplast, and it was curling at the edges. "There was a car bomb . . ."

"The Iranian?"

She must have just come back from work. She had an apron over her work dress, and the vacuum cleaner was out of the cupboard and plugged in.

He said, "We were on a surveillance, the car went up about thirty yards away. We got chucked about a bit."

"It's today, afternoon. That was yesterday, morning."

He hadn't kissed her yet. He was still in the doorway. And so hellishly tired, and it was an old script.

"We had a panic on."

"All the telephones down, were they?"

He didn't know whether she was picking an argument, or whether she was concerned that he had been close to a car bomb. Her cheeks were flushed. He reckoned she wanted the fight. He could remember holding Token's hand the previous day—never understood why Token didn't have a steady fellow—he just wanted cocoa hot in his throat, and his head cool on the pillow.

"I said a panic. We picked up a target the other night at the airport. I don't know how much, but he's got a substantial amount of stuff. Yesterday morning he visited Shabro, the Iranian who died. The target got away. We don't know where he's gone. It was my decision to let him run, and we've lost him, plus a hell of a load. . . . That's what I mean by a panic. That's why I didn't think of ringing you . . ."

"David, what the hell is happening to us?"

"I'm just pretty tired."

"When are we going to talk about it, when?"

"Right now, I want to go to sleep."

She flounced aside, made a way for him. She snapped the switch on the vacuum cleaner and he had to step over the cable to get to the bedroom. At least the suitcase was back on top of the wardrobe.

He didn't register that the vacuum cleaner had gone off.

She came into the room. She sat on the bed beside him.

"Is it really bad for you?"

"If I foul up? Yes."

"How bad?"

"Kiss good-bye to a Liaison Officer posting . . ."

"In Bogotá?"

"Yes."

"Well, that's the best news I've had all week. It sounds like hell on earth, does Bogotá."

"It just seems important to me."

"More important than *anything*?"

"I'm very tired, Ann. . . . I'm sorry I didn't ring."

She went to the dressing table. She took off it an opened envelope, and picked an invitation card out from the envelope.

"What is it?" His eyes were hardly open.

"Invitation . . ." She laughed, a brittle ring. "The ID Midsummer Ball . . . are we going, David?"

"It'll be awful."

"I want to meet all of those wonderful people who are so important in your life. I am going to talk to all those fantastic people who have the power to send us to Bogotá . . ."

"We'll go."

"You stand me up . . ."

"I said that we'll go."

". . . and we're dead."

"I'm just so tired. . . . Ann, I don't want us to be dead."

"Then do something about it."

She had the apron off and her shoes and her dress, was half undressed, when she saw that he was asleep.

At the airport he had worn a blazer with the badge of a travel company sewn onto his breast pocket. The travel company knew nothing of a Charlie Eshraq, had employed no courier in Turkey during the period of Charlie's last trip out of the United Kingdom.

In his flat they found a receipt from a bucket shop—followed up, blood out of a stone and the threat of a VAT inquiry before the blood started to trickle. Three return tickets to Istanbul.

No address book. No check stubs. The place was eerily clean. Fingerprints, yes they had all that. But that wasn't going anywhere. Not a single pho-

tograph to build on. Nothing to say whether Eshraq was his real name. The coffee shop and the
laundromat knew him, had never seen him *with*
anyone, if you know what I mean. The owner of
the flat had never met him and an estate agent,
who blushed rather prettily Statesman thought,
said he paid always in cash, always on the nail.
There were three possible leads. Manvers, who
may have known nothing about him at all. The
man in the import-export business in Kensington,
who turned out to be the brother, wouldn't you
just have guessed it, of the Iranian in the car, so
his office was shut very tight and the family scar-
pered and the Anti-Terrorist people were taking
the line that if the ID were going into the film
business and if Mr. Park thought he was Mr.
David Puttnam that was all very well, thanks for
the tip-off, and do us a favor, son, don't ask us to
tell you where Mr. Shabro's brother is, because
you people are bad news and anyway you're so
clever that you can surely find him without assistance from Anti-Terrorist Branch. Mr. Corinthian's film? No, it was still being examined. No, the
Met would probably want it for a couple of days.
Expect it in a week or so.

And there was Furniss of the FCO, as Harlech
called him.

The ACIO said that Leroy Winston Manvers

was now on remand at Brixton prison and out of reach, and that they'd had their chance with him, and no way were they going back there now that the dealer was in the hands of a Legal Aid solicitor.

So Parrish had said to the ACIO that this Matthew Furniss was the key, and the ACIO had not been able to contradict him.

Three of them went to the Home Office. The ACIO had roped in the head of the National Drugs Intelligence Unit, they'd gone round to New Scotland Yard and picked him up. They'd leaned on him, so that he couldn't excuse himself.

Into the Home Secretary's office.

The ACIO did the talking. Bill Parrish did the prompting. The head of the NDIU was the weight behind them.

"What it comes down to, Home Secretary, is that we are being denied access to this Matthew Furniss. Now, we've played this very straight. We have not, I repeat not, chased this man and sought him out. We accept that he may be a sensitively placed government servant, and we have gone through the correct channels, and we've been blown off. . . . Let's not beat about the bush. We were instructed to carry out an investigation into the supply of the heroin that ultimately killed Lucy Barnes. Quite disproportionate resources have been deployed . . . and we're being blocked. It's right that we should be frank with each other, Home Secretary. You wanted a priority made of this case."

"You've lost this man Eshraq, and you've lost his heroin?"

"Correct, Home Secretary. We lost him in freak circumstances, you will agree. If we are to get him back, and get his stuff back, without wasting an immense amount of time, then we have to have Matthew Furniss."

"I'll look into it."

"Either that or the investigation has to go into the trash can, sir."

"I said that I would look into it, Mr. Parrish. Thank you, gentlemen. Good day to you."

Parrish, not a vindictive man, thought that the Home Secretary looked like a cornered rabbit. Not his to reason why, but he didn't mind taking a small jolt of consolation from the man's discomfiture.

It was a well-arranged meeting. No chances taken. Charlie liked that. He had been under surveillance, and he was pretty sure that he had busted the surveillance, but he liked the style of the Greek and the meeting. He had been picked up in Chiswick in West London by an anonymous little bastard with a sallow face and bad eyes. That had been arranged on the telephone. He was pretty sure that the rendezvous was checked out, that they were watched by the Greek's payroll. He was told to take the underground to the end of the district line in Wimbledon. His description must have been telephoned on, because after he had kicked his heels and had a couple of coffees at the station cafeteria, he was met again. They put him in the back of a van and they drove him round for an hour and a half, and when the van stopped, and he hadn't an idea where he was, then the back doors had opened, and the Greek had climbed in beside him.

The Greek was thorough. He had Charlie stripped down in the van to his underpants. No way he was going to be stung, that Charlie was going to get away with a microphone in his clothes. That was the preamble, then there was the business. A quarter of a kilo of pure heroin on display. The Greek was no baby in the game, and the Greek knew the stamp on the wrapping. Enough of the stuff to have covered a teaspoon was taken out of the packet, and was passed in a small see-through sachet through the slightly opened back of the van. Going for analysis, running a fast check. Good style, Charlie liked it, more thorough than Manvers had ever been. The check came back. The sachet was passed again into the interior of the van, there was an anonymous raised thumb. They'd talked business while the analysis was being done.

"Cash is hard."

"Cash, or no deal."

"You brought it in yourself?"

"From the Qazvin district. I collected it myself."

"And there's going to be more?"

Charlie lied. "Yes, it'll be regular, and top grade."

"And you're looking for . . .?"

"A quarter of a million, for seven kilos."

"Two hundred."

"Two fifty."

"If it's tomorrow, in cash, two hundred thousand is top whack for seven kilos."

"I'll call tomorrow for a meeting."

They shook hands. There was a clinging oiled sweat on the Greek's hands. Charlie thought it was a good deal. The Greek would get double what he was paying Charlie, but Charlie didn't cough at that.

"What's it for?"

"What the hell does that mean?"

The Greek smiled. A twisted smile. He had a deep scar at the side of his chin from far back, from a school playground fight with Stanley knives. "Just that this isn't your scene—so, what's it for?"

"Something you won't ever hear about."

"What on earth does he want?"

Benjamin Houghton could see the nervousness in Miss Duggan's face. The likes of Flossie Duggan were never called to the nineteenth floor. She was a few years short of retirement, less than Mr. Furniss has left to him, but she had had his promise that he would get an extension for her, she would go when he went. It was her whole life, being the personal assistant to Mr. Furniss. More than anything else she dreaded the day when she must hand in her Polaroid cards and try and pick up old age away from Century. She had joined the Service in 1950 after she had read an advertisement in a smart magazine in an optician's waiting room that called for applications from "Girls of good education for position in London with good prospects and possibility of service abroad—aged 18 to 30." She would be going, when she handed in her Polaroid card, to Weston-super-Mare where her sister kept a guesthouse, open only in the summer season. She would have her debrief, a day or two of counseling, and she would be out on her neck with her memories. To Flossie Duggan, genteel and poor and loyal, Mr. Furniss was the finest gentleman that it had been her privilege to work for.

"He just wants a little talk with you."

"He's already stolen Mr. Furniss's floppies."

"That's not fair, Flossie . . ."

"Miss Duggan." The boy would never have been so impertinent if Mr. Furniss had been there.

"The Director General is entitled to see the computer records of a Desk Head even when those records are stored in the Desk Head's personal safe and not where they belong, in Library. So can we go, please."

He saw the neatness of Mattie's desk, his ashtray had been cleaned ready for his return. His pencils were in a holder, sharpened. His In tray and Out tray were empty. He thought that the photograph on the shelf behind the desk, Mrs. Furniss, had been polished. There were some late daffodils in a vase beside the photograph. She was registering her defiance, taking her time to cover up her keyboard with its plastic shroud, and then she was riffling in her handbag for her lipstick. Again, he could see her nervousness, because the effect of the vivid lipstick against her pale and puffed skin was appalling.

"I hold him responsible."

"Tell the Director General that, Miss Duggan,

and he might just chuck you down the lift shaft."
He held the door open for her.

She gripped the handrail in the lift.

He led her down the corridor, and made way for
her so that she could go first into the outer office.
He knocked.

"Miss Duggan, sir."

She walked in. She hesitated. She heard the
door shut behind her.

She hated the tall and thin-boned man who rose
from his chair, a leather-backed chair, and
beamed at her, and waved her to a sofa. He was
certainly responsible.

"Good of you to call by, Miss Duggan . . . dis-
tressing times for all of us. Would you like
sherry?"

She shook her head.

"I am sure that even with Mr. Furniss away you
are extremely busy, Miss Duggan. I'll come
straight to the point."

The Director General had come in front of his
desk and he perched himself on the edge of it.

"Presumably, Miss Duggan, you are pretty well
up in Mr. Furniss's activities for the Service?"

She nodded her head emphatically. That was
one of Mr. Furniss's little jokes. The worst time
of the year was when she took her holiday at

Weston-super-Mare, just one week, and she wasn't there to run his office.

"First of all, Miss Duggan, we are all, every one of us, doing our best to get Mr. Furniss back, that goes without saying . . ."

She glowered at him. He should never have been sent. Desk Heads were never sent abroad.

". . . All of the very considerable resources of the Service are engaged in that. Now . . ."

She blurted, "It was a folly sending him in the first place."

"This is not a kindergarten, Miss Duggan. The Service is an active arm in the defense of this country. If the risks are too great for individuals, then they are at all times entitled to transfer wherever they wish."

She might have slapped his face. There was a haggardness at his eyes. There was a thinness at his lips.

"We have been through the disks from Mr. Furniss's personal computer, and we can find no record of an individual with whom we believe Mr. Furniss to be associated. To maintain private files is in breach of all standing instructions. It is a sufficient misdemeanor to have you summarily dismissed. Do you hear me, Miss Duggan?"

She nodded.

"Miss Duggan, who is Charlie Eshraq?"

She told him.

It is the age of light-speed communications, but the tit pushers and the button thumpers still rule.

The information was first gathered by the Anti-Terrorist squad. They in their turn fed the information into the central computer of Criminal Records. A lead from Criminal Records, and that same information was passed to the National Drugs Intelligence Unit. For further details the National Drugs Intelligence Unit punched into the jointly operated CEDRIC computer.

What followed started the sprint down the corridors, the raw excitement.

She was jolted out of her sleep by the ringing of her telephone.

He wasn't going to wake. An earthquake wouldn't have moved him. The curtains were still open, but the darkness had come down outside, and she could see the rain pelting the window-panes. The telephone was on his side, but he wasn't going to pick it up. Ann leaned across him. Her breast, out of her slip, was crushed into his face, and he didn't stir. She wriggled, she kissed her man. He looked ten years younger, at peace. She reached for the telephone.

Softly, "Yes?"

"David?"

"This is Ann Park."

"Bill Parrish—could I speak to him?"

She looked down. She saw the calm in his sleep, and she saw the livid bruise on his forehead.

"He came home injured. . . . Why wasn't I told?"

"Because I'm not a nanny, Mrs. Park. Please get him to the phone."

"Damn you, he's asleep."

"Tickle his toes, whatever you do. Wake him up."

"Mr. Parrish, have you any idea what life is like for me because you can't manage your bloody office for ten minutes without my David?"

"I went to your wedding, and I'm not daft . . . just wake him up."

"He's exhausted and he's hurt, and he needs the rest."

"Don't accuse me, young lady, of not caring. Have you forgotten Aberystwyth . . . ?"

She would never forget Aberystwyth. They hadn't been married then. A stakeout on the Welsh coast, waiting for a yacht to come in from the Mediterranean and drop a load off on a beach. A ruined cottage had been the base camp for the

April team, and David was the new boy, just selected, and the wedding had been postponed until
after the knock. Bill Parrish had broken every
rule in the C & E's book. Parrish had told his
Keeper to get his fiancée up to a campsite four
miles from the cottage, and he'd made damned
sure that David slipped away to the tent where his
Ann was every single night. She had cooked their
supper over a Calor gas burner, cuddled him and
the rest in her sleeping bag, and sent him back to
the stakeout each dawn. It had been heaven for
her, and Bill Parrish had fixed it, and it had never
happened again.

"He wouldn't do it now," she said, "Why can't
you get someone else?"

"We're all in the same boat, and it's the way we
work, and if we don't work like that then the job
doesn't get done."

"Oh boy, have I heard that before."

"Do me a favor, wake him up."

Her voice was breaking. She was across David
and she could hear the constant rhythm of his
breathing. "You're destroying us, you're breaking
us apart."

"He'll be collected in half an hour. Tell him
there's movement on the target."

She put the phone down. She woke him. She
saw the flare in his eyes when she told him what

Parrish had said. She watched him dress fast. She fed him some scrambled egg and toast in the kitchen, and all the time he was looking out of the window, waiting for a car's headlamps. When she saw the lights she could have cried. She cleared away the plate. She heard the doorbell. He grabbed for his anorak, shrugged into it, opened the door.

Ann still wore her slip. She stood in the kitchen, and she could see through to the front door. There was a girl standing there. A boyish, stocky girl, with her hair cut short, and a windbreaker like a sleeping bag. She saw her husband go out.

They walked across to the car. She could see them. When the taillights had gone, then Ann Park cried.

Token talked, Keeper listened.

"It's the oldest one I know. There was a notepad beside the telephone in Shabro's flat. The Anti-Terrorist people had a look at it, and there was an indent. A name and a number. They checked, there's quite a bit on the name at Criminal Records, all drugs-related, so they fed it over to CEDRIC. He's hot. He's been busted for possession and went inside, but that was years back. More important, just a couple of years ago he was in the slammer and went to the Bailey. He should have got a Fifteen for dealing, but the bastard had a nobble. Four of the jurors came out for him. The trial had cost nearly a million, had run for four months. Public Prosecutions didn't go back for another bite. His name was written on the notepad in Shabro's house. It's Shabro's writing. The top note wasn't in Shabro's pockets. If that doesn't add up to Tango One finding himself a dealer in lieu of Manvers, I'll do a streak round the Lane. Cheer up, David, it's going to work out. We've got taps on him, and we've got surveillance on him. . . . Your Missus, David, what was up with her?"

Two guards carried Mattie back up the two flights from the cellar.

He was not unconscious—that had been before, many times. He was conscious and the water dripped from his head. To himself, he was now detached from the pain in his feet, and he was aware of what went on around him. He could hear no traffic in the street outside. He thought that it must be very late in the night. He had no sense of how many hours he had been in the basement, nor could he remember how many times he had lost consciousness, and how many times he had been dunked in the zinc bathtub.

He thought that he was still in control of himself. He could understand that there was no longer any more point in them beating him because the pain had begun to cancel itself out. He was carried because he could not stand on his feet. His head was sagging, and he could see his feet. His shoes were gone. His feet were grotesque, bloody and swollen. He could not count how many times in that long day they had thrashed the soles of his feet with the heavy electrical flex, and how many times he had lapsed, thank the Good Lord, into unconsciousness.

They took him into his room, and they let him fall from their arms and onto his bed. He lay on his bed, and the pain came out of the numbness of his feet. The pain came like maggots tunneling from rotting meat. The pain spread from the soft ripped flesh at the soles of his feet and into his ankles, and into his shins and calves, and into his thighs, and into his guts.

It was just their beginning.

Through the long day, into the long night, the investigator had not asked Mattie a single question. Softening him. Beating him and hurting him. Just the start, unless he would scream for the pain to stop. The questions would follow when they thought it opportune, when they judged it best to peel from his mind the names held there.

The pain throbbed in him, welled in him. He lay on the bed and he writhed to escape from the pain,

Chapter ✣ 11

"*H*ow are we this morning, Mr. Furniss?"

Nothing to say. Mattie took in the greater heat in the airless cellar.

"The doctor came, yes?"

Nothing to say. It was a ritual. Of course the investigator knew that the doctor had been to examine him, because he had sent the doctor. The doctor had been sent to make certain that no serious damage had been done to the prisoner. A slob of a man, the doctor, and his eyes had never met Mattie's because the bastard had betrayed his oath. The doctor had glanced at the feet, taken the pulse, above all checked that his heart would last, stretched up the eyelids to see the pupils, and

✣ 293 ✣

checked with a stethoscope for Mattie's breathing pattern.

"How are your feet, Mr. Furniss?"

Nothing to say. He could stand, just. He had leaned on the shoulders of the guards who had brought him down, but his feet could take some weight.

"Please, Mr. Furniss, sit down."

He sat, and the pain sang into his legs as the weight came off the feet.

"Mr. Furniss, it has been broadcast on the World Service of the BBC that Dr. Matthew Owens, an archaeologist, is missing in Turkey . . ." The smile was winter water. The voice was powder-snow soft. "They are trying to protect you, and they cannot. Do you understand that, Mr. Furniss?"

Nothing to say.

"They cannot protect you."

Stating the bloody obvious, dear sir. Tell me something I don't know. . . . Through all his mind was the memory of the pain, and the memory of the dying that seemed to come each time he had lapsed toward unconsciousness. That was yesterday. The art of resistance to interrogation, as taught by Professor Furniss, was to take it one day at a time, one step at a time. Yesterday had been endured, survived . . . but they had not questioned him. Yesterday was gone, so forget yesterday's pain. Yesterday's pain was what they wanted Mattie to remember. The "old school" had been put through the full works on the Resistance to Interrogation courses at the fort—the old school in the Service reckoned that they were a tougher breed than the new intake—resist at all costs, never crack, hang on to the bitter bloody end, and some fearful disasters there had been on simulated interrogation sessions. Queen and Country, that's what the old school believed in.

If he cut the pain from his memory, then the mind was voided, then filled with other matter. The other matter was the names. He tried to find the guards beyond the brilliance of the light in his eyes.

"What were you doing in Van, Mr. Furniss?"

"I've told you repeatedly, I was visiting the fortress of Sardur the Second."

"That is particularly idiotic, Mr. Furniss."

"I cannot help the truth."

"It is idiotic, Mr. Furniss, because you deny reality. Reality is this cellar, reality is the power at my disposal. Yesterday was amusement, Mr. Furniss, today is the beginning of reality. If you go on with this fabrication, then it will go badly for you, Mr. Furniss."

Stick to the cover, cling to the cover at all costs.

"A long time ago, yes, it is possible that you saw me in Tehran. I've been out of that sort of thing for years. I am an academic now. I am an authority on the Urartian civilization."

"That is your sole interest."

"The Urartians, yes."

"In Turkey?"

"The Urartian civilization was based in northeastern Turkey and across the frontier of modern Iran as far as the western shore of Lake Urmia. That was the scope . . ."

"Did the Urartians, Mr. Furniss, travel to Dubai, Abu Dhabi, Bahrain? Is it necessary for an academic, an authority in this rather limited field, to be escorted around the Gulf by the various Station Officers of the Secret Intelligence Service?"

The light was in his face. The guards were behind him. He could just make out the rhythm of their breathing. They would have been told to be still, to offer to the prisoner no distraction from the questions of the investigator.

"I am an academic."

"I think not, Mr. Furniss. I think you are Dolphin. Desk Head for Iran at Century House in London. You were a regular soldier and posted to Iran to liaise over arms sales to the former regime. You were the Station Officer in Tehran from

1975 to 1978. In 1982 and 1983 you were the senior Station Officer in Bahrain with responsibility only for Iranian affairs. In 1986 you spent four months in Ankara. You were promoted to Desk Head on January first, 1986. You are a senior intelligence officer, Mr. Furniss. Understand me, I do not want to hear any more about your hobby. One day, perhaps, I shall have the pleasure of reading your published work. For today we shall put away hobbies, Mr. Furniss, and just talk about what you were doing on this journey around our borders."

The names were in his head, swirling. He was a man under water and trying to hold his breath, and his breath was the names. In time, as night follows day, the lungs would force out the breath, the pain would spit out the names. Even the old school knew that. It was a question, simply, of how many nights. How many days. The agents should have been warned by now. . . . But was it known who held him? Would Century flush out its best men before they had confirmation that Mattie was in Iran?

What would he have done himself, in their place? He thought of the complications of the structure for getting the necessary signals inside Iran. He knew how complicated it was, he had set the system up. Far more complex than bringing the agents out to the prearranged rendezvous meetings that he had just had. Oh, a lifetime of complications if the agents were to be aborted, and no going back. London would not be hurrying to destroy its network. He swept the names from his mind. He lifted his head. There was escape from the white, bright light only in the face of the investigator.

"It is quite scandalous that an innocent scholar . . ."

The investigator gestured with his arm. The guards came forward, ripped Mattie up from his chair.

Charlie made his call. The same telephone box, after the same night's sleep under a cardboard blanket.

After the call, after he had helped the dossers pile away the packing cases, he went to the left luggage inside the ticket hall of the underground station, and he took out his rucksack.

They had a fine view of the Greek's house.

Parrish had smoothed it. Keeper reckoned that Parrish was gold-plated when it came down to sweet talking for window space. It was a great window. The early summer foliage was not yet thick enough on the trees to obstruct the vision across the garden and across the road and across the Greek's garden and onto the front porch of his house.

It was an old Victorian house that Parrish had fixed, weathered brick three stories high with an ivy creeper thick enough to have held the walls together. They had chosen the top floor for the camera position and from there their sight line went well clear of the high paling fence opposite. Keeper and Token knew her life history by now. She came upstairs on the hour, every hour, with a pot of tea and biscuits. She was a widow. Her late husband had been a brigadier general. She had lived alone in the house for nineteen years, and every year she resisted another try by the developers to put a check in her hand—this year it was for three quarters of a million pounds—so that they could bulldoze her property and replace it with a block of flats. She didn't think her cats would want to move. She had no love for her neighbor across the road. His dogs were a threat to her cats. Anything that threatened the owner of the dogs was fine by this lady. From the upper window they could see the dogs. Dobermans, lean and restless, wandering, and cocking their legs against the wheels of the midnight blue Jaguar outside the front porch. She was an artful old girl, the general's widow. Keeper had seen her giving them both the coy look, and checking the ring on his finger, and observing that Token's finger was bare.

He was comfortable with Token. She let him talk about Colombia, about targeting the problem at its source. There had been other cars come and go at the house across the road. They had photographed all the movements, but they hadn't seen the Greek. They had the mug shots done by the plods when he was last in custody. It was a hell of a house that the bastard lived in. Half an acre, heated swimming pool, hard tennis court, five, maybe six bedrooms.

The general's widow was telling them that when her husband had first purchased The Briars they had been able to look across fields, real countryside . . .

The radio crackled to life.

"April One to April Five, April One to April Five . . ."

"April Five, come in April One . . ."

"Tango One has been on the telephone to your location. Text of call coming. . . . Tango One: It's Charlie here. . . . Your location: Same place as yesterday, same pickup. Bring it all. . . . Tango One: Right . . . Did you get that, April Five?"

"April Five to April One. Received, understood, out."

His head shook, and his knees.

Token said, "Keeper is back from the dead."

"What's Keeper mean?" the general's widow asked.

"It's a very solid person, Ma'am, and very vulnerable." Token smiled.

"Those brutes got out once, they killed one of my cats. They tore Disraeli to shreds."

"George, a word in your ear."

The Secretary of State for Defense paused in the corridor outside the Cabinet room.

"The distributor. A strange thing has happened and I may need your help."

"What on earth do you mean?"

"Customs and Excise have a suspect. He has a vague profile. They are trying to get into that profile, and they reckon that a chap called Matthew Furniss, listed as FCO but in reality, SIS, could help them. The spooks won't wear it. Mr. Furniss is being kept under wraps. The Customs investigation officers can't get at him." The look of pure rage on George's face was worth all the humiliations of the past weeks. As he slipped into the doorway, he said, "Just thought you'd like to know."

Parrish sat hunched forward at the console on the top floor of the Lane, coordinating a raft of radio signals competing for attention. This was big enough for the investigation of which Harlech was case officer to be sidelined, and for Corinthian's to be relegated out of sight. Big enough to soak up all of April's resources.

Parrish to Keeper: "April Five, just keep remembering that your single responsibility is Tango One. Our brothers look after every other Tango but Tango One."

Harlech to Corinthian: "April Seven to April Eleven . . . Hey, ugly nose, this is just fantastic, this is just brilliant. What they're doing is this. They've Tango One in the white van and there's another van about fifty yards behind, that's the green one. They're taking Tango One's stuff from the white to the green, that must be where they're running the spot checks. You got me? They're doing it all on site. The Jag's parked between the two, the Jag Tango is in the white van with Tango One. This has to be Christmas. It's the best I've ever seen."

Keeper to Token: "April Five to April Nine. Try another walk past. You got the canvassing board. Do another rundown, those houses you missed out the first time. I want to know if the Tango One van has the engine running. I have to know when those wheels are about to go."

Corinthian to Keeper: "April Eleven to April Five. Just to keep your knickers dry, Keeper, this is the layout. Tango One is in the white van, plus the Greek. The stuff is taken from the white van to the green van, probably running the checks on it. The guy who takes it to the green van then comes back empty and reports through the rear doors. Dangerous-looking creep in blue overalls. So, the stuff is in the green van. The green van is for the plods. Are you clear, April Five?"

Parrish talking to all April call signs: "Keep it going, very cool, very calm. Any bugger shows out, he's in uniform for the rest of his natural. Tango One is to run. . . . That is confirmed. Tango One will run. We are concerned only with Tango One."

A quiet road running beside the brick perimeter wall of Richmond Park. Two vans parked in the road, and a Jaguar car separating them, and a girl calling at the houses on the park side and asking questions on the doorsteps about which washing powder the occupants used. A 500mm lens in an upper room 175 yards north of the green van. Three more cars parked in the road, two of them facing the direction that the white van would come if it didn't do a three-point.

"This is great stuff . . ."

"I watched it packed myself."

"And there's more . . . ?" The Greek could not hide the greed.

"I'll be coming back with more, a couple of months," Charlie said.

The hand of the Greek rested lightly on Charlie's arm. "You get lifted and you talk and you get the knife, wherever. You won't know how to hide."

Charlie said, "My friend, you get lifted and you talk and you get the bullet, your head blown. Take it as a promise, I'll find you." Charlie flicked his fingers through the wads of 20 pound notes. They went into his rucksack.

There was a handshake, of sorts.

"You be careful there, when you go back."

"Watch yourself across the road," Charlie said.

There was a flash of light as the van door opened. The Greek gave him his mirthless, twisted smile and stooped out.

As the van pulled away Charlie heard the big thunder cough of the Jaguar's engine.

In a side street in Hammersmith, near the river, a police Land-Rover rammed the white van, front off-side wing, crashed it and jammed the driver's door tight.

In Shepherds Bush, detectives of the Drugs Squad boxed the green van.

An hour later, across the city in the Essex suburb of Chigwell, the Greek had been back in his house three minutes. A police marksman put down his cup of tea in the house opposite, asked the general's widow please to stand well back, and shot both dobermans clean through the heart, four seconds between shots. The marksman spoke briefly into his radio and shut the window, and was very much surprised to be kissed, just under his ear, by the old lady. They were still at the window when a Land-Rover with a ramming guard attached drove fast into the high wooden gates, smashing them. A few seconds later the pseudo-Georgian front door splintered open at the second massive blow of a policeman's sledgehammer.

On the underground, starting at Wimbledon station, Keeper and Token and Harlech tracked their Tango One, and above them, through the traffic, Corinthian drove as if his life depended on it to stay in touch.

He was dropped with his bodyguard, as always, at the door of the Cabinet Office, and he walked through that building and down steps, and then through the deep corridor linking the Cabinet Office to Downing Street. At the final door, the security check, before entry to Downing Street, he was greeted like an old friend by the armed policeman. He had known that policeman since forever. God alone knew how the man had wangled the posting, but he seemed never to have been more than one hundred yards from Whitehall all his working life. Always the sort of greeting that put him in a better mind frame.

His bodyguard peeled away from him. He'd be in the waiting room, and he'd be brought a cup of coffee by one of those haughty, leggy kids who hit the word processors down the corridor. A good life his bodyguard had, nearly as cushy as the policeman's on the tunnel door. The Director General was shown into the Prime Minister's office.

For a moment he wondered whether a previous meeting had overrun. He nodded coolly to the Secretary of State for Defense. They'd met a few times, but the Secretary of State was too flashy by half for his taste.

"Thank you for coming so promptly, Director General."

As if he had the choice.

"It is much appreciated. You know each other? Yes. I am sorry to say that a most serious complaint has been brought to me by my colleague."

He couldn't help but notice the unease of the Prime Minister, nor the hostility of the Secretary of State.

"I'm sorry to hear that, Prime Minister."

"George's daughter, Lucy, died a short time ago following a narcotics accident . . ."

The Director General stared back. He read the newspapers. The girl was an addict.

". . . An investigation is in process by the police and Customs and Excise to try to identify the importer of the narcotics concerned . . ."

And then he saw what was coming.

". . . Their very strenuous work, as I gather, leads them to a foreign national currently holding a Stateless Person's document which was issued on the guarantee of good character provided by a member of the Service. Customs and Excise quite properly wish to interview that member of the Service, but the Service has pulled down the shutters."

Had the Prime Minister been told who it was? Couldn't have been. Would surely have made the connection.

"It's outrageous," the Secretary of State chimed.

"I think we can get this sorted out quite quickly, don't you, Director General? Before it gets out of hand."

No, obviously hadn't a clue. "In front of a third party, Prime Minister, I am not free to discuss this matter."

"You damn well will." The Secretary of State's voice rose and his jowls were purple.

The Director General looked the man up and down. He'd learned that from his classics master at Marlborough, a cutting stare from ankle to Adam's apple. "I am answerable to the Prime Minister, sir, and to the Foreign Secretary. Matters affecting the Service are beyond the remit of Defense."

"Just let's have this crystal clear. You are saying that the importing of heroin is a matter which affects the Service. Is that it? What the devil is the Service coming to, I should like to know. Are you importing heroin, Director General? Is that it? Is it your Secret Service that I must hold responsible for the death of my only child?"

"George, I believe that's enough."

"No, Prime Minister, it most assuredly is not enough. I demand that the Director General produce this Matthew Furniss, and straight away, and stop wasting valuable police time, Customs people's time, or tell us without all this waffle about matters affecting the Service why he won't."

"We all know how precious is police time,

George. I don't think you, of anyone, need labor that, but did you say Matthew Furniss? Was that the name?"

"Yes, Prime Minister. That is the Service man's name. The Home Secretary tells me that the importer is an Iranian called Charles Eshraq."

"Well, Director General, what will you say to all this?" And there seemed to have evaporated from the Prime Minister the anxiety he had detected earlier.

"I would say this, Prime Minister. I might in different circumstances simply explain to you in what way the Service is affected and in what million-to-one chance lies its connection to the death through narcotics addiction of the Secretary of State's daughter. But I have just observed the hysterical speculations and accusations of a man with whom, unless ordered to do so, I shall share not one iota of information relating to this case or any other. Furthermore it is quite outrageous that a dedicated public servant should be vilified when, as the Prime Minister well knows, he is in no position to defend his good name."

"I'll see you broken."

"Your privilege, sir, to try."

"Prime Minister, are you going to tolerate that impertinence?"

"I hope, Prime Minister, that I may count upon your support."

A reeded and hesitant voice. "I am going to think about it."

There were many thoughts cavorting through the Director General's mind as he marched back through the tunnel. He thought of Mattie Furniss, prisoner, facing torture. He thought of three quarters of an hour with Miss Duggan, a woman whose loyalty he could only admire, and two glasses of barley water to keep her talking, and the story of Charlie Eshraq. He thought of a girl hanged from a crane. And he thought of the value that Eshraq could be to the Service. So long as he wasn't named by Furniss under torture. So long as he wasn't caught by Customs and Excise first.

"April Five to April One, April Five to April One."

"April One, come in April Five."

"Just a sitrep, Bill. He's in the pub, apparently killing time. He's had one half-pint in front of him for an hour, not had anything since we last called you. What did the boss say?"

"Had his arm twisted half out of its socket, that's what ACIO said. Sold him my line, a good line and I say it myself, we want to see where Tango One leads us, clean up the whole network.

Bossman'd be happier if he was in cuffs, but he can stand it because we've the stuff."

"How much was it?"

"Around seven kilos, that's one hell of a load, Keeper. You know what? It's the same markings on the packets as Manvers's load. That sweetened the boss's pill."

"That's the bastard, isn't it, not knowing."

The Deputy Director General sat in the easy chair. "The more noise we make, then the worse it can be for him. I mean, we can hardly ask the Swedes to trot round to the Foreign Ministry and ask the night duty chappy if they're interrogating a British Desk Head who we have reason to believe they've kidnapped across an international frontier. . . . No, we've got to sweat on it, and you've to make a decision."

"Aborting the agents? I'll decide in the morning."

"You owe it to them, to give them time to abort. Field agents are brave people. If they're lifted they will be lucky to be hanged."

The Director General seemed to miss his stride. His eyes closed as if he were in pain.

"Didn't you know that, when you took the job?"

"I'll decide in the morning."

"We may have hours, hours, Director General.

Mattie is going to be having their names tortured out of him, he's going to be hung up by the finger-nails until the names come tumbling out, willy-nilly. It is only a question of when, not a question of if or if not."

"In the morning, I'll make that decision. . . . Poor old Mattie."

All day he had been suspended from the wall hook. He had read about it often enough. Every-one who studied the affairs of Iran knew of this method of extracting confessions. He thought it must be a day, but he had gone insensible three times. He had no track of time. The pain in his back, his shoulders, his ribs, was more sharp than had been the pain in the soles of his feet. It was a pain as if he were snapping, as if he were the dry kindling that he put across his thigh at Bi-bury. His left arm was above his left shoulder and then twisted down toward the small of his back. His right arm was below the shoulder and then turned up to meet his left arm. His wrists were tied with leather thongs, knotted tight. The thongs were on the wall hook, looped over the car-cass hook. Only the toes of his feet were able to touch the floor. When the strength of his toes col-lapsed and he sagged down, then the pain was ex-cruciating in his shoulders and his ribs burst. It had been better at first. His feet, swollen, bruised, had been able to take most of his weight. Through the day, however long the day had been, the strength had seeped from his feet. The pressure had built up on the contortion of his arms. He had gone three times, sunk into the foul-smelling heat, unconscious. They hadn't taken him down. They had just thrown water into his face. No respite from the hook on the wall. Ever-increasing pain that hacked into his back and his shoulders and his ribs . . . God . . . God . . . couldn't know how his muscles, how his body, survived the weight, or his mind the pain.

"Mr. Furniss, what is the point of your obstinacy? For what?"

Answer in not less than 750 words. Bloody good question.

"Mr. Furniss, the most resolute of the fighters among the 'hypocrites,' the MKO, they appear on television and they denounce to the world all of their former comrades, all of their former activities. How does that happen, Mr. Furniss?"

"I haven't the least idea. . . . It's not the sort of thing . . . an archaeologist would . . . know about." He heard the scratchy hoarseness of his voice.

"The bravest of the 'hypocrites' betray their comrades and their ideals because of pain, Mr. Furniss."

He had seen the photographs. He knew what they did to their enemies. He had seen videotapes of the confessions. Raven-robed women, track-suited men, sitting on a dias and lit by the cameras in a gymnasium at the Evin jail, and competing with each other to slag off their comrades and their cause, and still not escaping the firing squad or the hangman. It hurt him to talk. Getting air down into his lungs so that he could speak brought more pain stabs in his back and shoulders and ribs.

He mouthed the words. No voice in his throat, only the twist of his lips. He was an academic, and his research was concerned with the Turkish city of Van.

He remembered one lecturer at the fort. He had been an elderly man and his back was bent as though he suffered from curvature of the spine, and the fingernails had never grown back over the sheer pink pastel skin. He had talked in a thick, proud, central European accent, guttural. There had been brave pride in the speaker's eyes, and above a faded and shined suit he wore the collar of a Lutheran pastor. They had been told that the speaker had spent the last two years of the Second World War in Dachau. He talked faith, he talked about his God, he talked about prayer and of the strength that his religion had been to him. Mattie

was not a regular churchgoer, not in the way that
Harriet was. When he was in church he bent his
knee with the rest of the congregation, and he
sang in a good voice, but he would not have called
himself close to his God. What a wonderful arm
faith had given that speaker in the dreadfulness
of Dachau. Mattie was alone, as the speaker had
been alone in his Dachau cell, as the disciples had
been alone in the face of persecution. Mattie
would have said that his religion was based on a
knowledge of what was right, what was wrong,
and he would have said that he was afraid of death
because he did not believe himself yet ready to
face his Maker. He wished that he could pray. He
could not pray because the pain diverted his mind.
He wondered how that speaker had prayed while
the fingernails were ripped off, while his spine was
damaged.

"Mr. Furniss, you are a gentleman. This should
not be happening to you, Mr. Furniss. This is the
treatment that is proper for the 'hypocrite' scum.
It does not have to happen for you, Mr. Furniss.
Help me, help yourself. Why were you traveling?
Who were you meeting? So very simple, Mr.
Furniss."

In truth, Mattie did not think that at that moment he could have spoken the names. The names
were gone. There was only pain in his mind. The

light was in his face. The pain soared when he
tried to turn his head away from the light and
away from the face of the investigator. The investigator sat on a stool not more than four feet from
Mattie's cracked, dry lips. He thought the pain
was good. He thought that the pain squeezed out
of his mind the names of his agents. He could
smell the cigarettes of the guards. They seemed
to smoke continuously.

Abruptly the investigator flicked his fingers. He
slid off his stool, and went to the table and began
to push his notepads into his case.

To Mattie, the expression of the investigator
was neither that of annoyance nor was it of pleasure. A job of work done.

"Mr. Furniss, there is tomorrow, and after tomorrow there is another day, and after that day
there is another. Each day is worse for you. For
obstinacy you will pay a high price."

"No, Mother, there is no crisis, it's just that Mattie is a little overdue. . . . I am not prepared to discuss Mattie's work with you, Mother. . . . There
is no need for you to come, Mother. You cannot
come anyway because you would be missing your
bridge on Friday. I am perfectly all right,
Mother. . . . I'm sorry, but I really am much too
busy to have you come here. If there was some-

thing wrong then I would have the girls here. The girls are not here. . . . Mother, I really do not want to have you come to stay. . . . Will you listen to me, I don't want you here, I don't want anyone here. . . . I am not crying, Mother, I am just trying to get on with my life."

She put the telephone down.

She thought that she had been miserably rude. She turned back to the minutes of the previous evening's meeting of the Conservation Society.

She tried not to think where he was, how he was, her Mattie.

At Century they would not be expecting a fuss from Harriet Furniss. It would have been, she thought, in Mattie's file that his wife was psychologically sound. It would have been noted that her two children had been born in Tehran because she hadn't thought it necessary to come home for the births, and there had never been trouble from her when they were in the Gulf, nor when they were in Ankara on short stay. It would have been entered in the file that she was a good sort, and did well on the embassy circuit, the right stuff to be a Desk Head's consort.

Even so, to go these last days without a call from anyone at Century was very, very hard.

"April One to April Five, April One to April
Five . . ."

"April Five to April One . . ."

"OK, Keeper, your location. . . . The occupier is
listed as Mr. Brian Venables, Christ knows what
Tango One is there for . . . Venables works, middle
rank, for Thames Water."

"Understood."

"When do you want relief?"

"Bill, I'm going nowhere . . . don't argue, Bill,
you'll have to burn me off him . . . In my locker,
Bill, there's a battery razor and some socks, I
wouldn't mind them."

"What about the others?"

"We'll want backup at dawn. We're all
staying. . . . Bill, Token says that in her locker she
has a change of kit in a green plastic bag."

"Sweet dreams, champions. April One to April
Five, out."

They lifted off. It was a French helicopter, and
new, and mounts had been welded on at the open
doorways to take heavy machine guns. To avoid
ground-to-air missiles from their enemy the helicopter pilot flew low over the rear area of the battlefield. It was a killing zone to the east of the Iraqi
town of Basra, much fought over. The Mullah,
strapped in his canvas seat, his back against the
hull, was a young man in anguish. There had been
that morning, as the red sun had slipped above
the flat horizon, an artillery barrage. Some of the
worst of the casualties were on the deck of the helicopter, their stretchers against his feet, and medical orderlies holding drips, but the casualties
were only those who had been hit close to the landing zone, the fortunate few. When he twisted his
head the Mullah could see through the dust-
smeared portholes of the helicopter, and when he
looked straight ahead he could see past the torso
of the machine gunner in the open doorway. They
hugged the flat and featureless ground. He saw
the old trench lines that had been disputed four,
five, six years before, where that dawn's shells had
burst. He saw the angular dead, and he saw the
stricken faces of the wounded and he saw the
stretcher parties running toward them. He could
see the tanks hull down, sheltered in revetments,

that would stay hull down until there were spare parts.

Nothing grew upon this battlefield. Where there had been fields there were now just the patterns of the armor tracks. Where there had been trees there were now only the shell-broken stumps. Where there had been marsh weed there was now only a yellow mat because the weed had been sprayed with herbicides to kill potential cover for any enemy. The helicopter scurried over a rear camp, tents and bombproof bunkers, and it flew sufficiently low for the Mullah to see the faces of the troops who squatted on the ground and stared up. They were the same faces that he had seen farther forward at the front the night before. The sullen gaze that had greeted his speech of exhortation. Pressed troops, afraid to ask with their voices, bold enough to demand with their eyes; where is the air support, where are the tank parts, where is the victory, when is the end?

That same morning he had sat in judgment of fifteen recruits who had held back in the last assault on enemy lines. Young men, eyes downcast, denounced in monotone by their officers and sentenced by the Mullah to field execution. There could be no tolerating cowardice.

The Mullah had won his spurs in the service of the Imam as one of the investigators of the coup attempted by air force officers of the Nouzeh barracks at Hamadan. He had seen the tears and the pleading of the pilots, and he had not been diverted.

He had achieved good results, satisfactory enough results for him to be chosen above many to unravel the plot woven around the Great Satan's attempt to fly a commando force into the country for the release of prisoners from the Nest of Spies. So many traitors to be found, and he had found so many. He had found those who would have driven the lorries, and those who would have made the air base available, and those who had switched off the defensive radar. For himself, he thought the plan of the Great Satan was an absurd plan, bound to fail.

The Mullah was a devotee of the Revolution, a child of the ferocity of the Revolution. He knew no other way.

When they were out of range of the Iraqi ground-to-air missiles, the helicopter climbed. It would fly first to a field hospital. After that, with two further stops for refueling, the helicopter would fly on to Tabriz. At the front, close to the artillery exchanges, he had slept badly. On the way to Tabriz he dozed fitfully, and the straggling thoughts in his mind were of a man known as Dolphin.

Brian Venables was late leaving home. He was late because the guest had been in the bathroom when it should have been clear for him, and he was late because his wife had forgotten his breakfast. Too busy scrambling eggs for the guest. And to top it all, the look on his Polly's face across the kitchen table had been shameless, damn near brazen.

Brian Venables had not brought up his daughter to have her bring home a foreigner and then have that foreigner creep in the small hours across the landing into his Polly's room. That was clean out of court, and they would talk it out this evening. Oh yes.

He went down his neat front path to the newly painted wrought-iron gate. The last of the blossom was still on the trees in the road. Once Wellington Street had been a quiet and respectable street, but the riffraff were closing in. He slammed the gate shut behind him.

He walked down the pavement.

He saw the two scruffs inside the car. Brian Venables was a founder member of Neighborhood Watch in his road. Two scruffs sitting in a car and watching the houses. He had listened to every word that the WPC had told them when the Neighborhood Watch had been introduced. They wait for the man to go to work, for the children to go to school, for the wife to go shopping. Well, those two youngsters were in for a shock. He swung on his heel.

They were watching the house. They had seen the man come out onto the pavement, with his raincoat and his briefcase, then stop, turn to go back inside. Corinthian had said that he had probably forgotten his sandwich box. The patrol car came up fast alongside them, from behind.

Park swore softly. There was the rap on the driver's window.

"Driving license . . ."

"Piss off," Corinthian mouthed.

"OK, laddie, out."

Corinthian just reached inside his anorak and lifted clear his Customs and Excise ID card. He held it up to the uniformed constable's face. "Do get lost."

The constable stiffened, full height, full authority of his uniform. "Down at our division, have they been informed you are on our patch?"

"Please, just go back to your canteen," Corinthian said.

The constable tried for a long, hard stare, didn't find it easy, but he went back to his patrol car.

Park had his radio against his mouth. His voice

was terse. "April Five to April Nine and April Seven . . . I don't know how bad it is, we may have shown out, may not. On your bloody toes for Christ's sake. Out."

"What do you reckon?" Corinthian asked.

Keeper was thinking what Bill Parrish would have to say to his little Keeper if they were blown by the plods. He wasn't liking what he was thinking.

Charlie came down the stairs.

He had heard the telephone ring while he was packing the rucksack. He felt pretty good. Not having slept too well, that didn't matter. She was a great girl, and her mum was good, and the breakfast had been brilliant. Not as brilliant as Polly. Polly was marvelous, and her father was a pig. He hesitated at the bottom of the stairs because he'd thought Polly's father had left, and now he could hear his voice on the telephone, ending a conversation.

He heard Polly's mother querying Polly's father. He put down the rucksack and listened.

Polly's father said, "No, the police were not complaining, and they had no cause to complain. That's what they're there for, that's what crime prevention is all about. Two men sitting in a car watching our street, that certainly entitles me to know what is going on. They have our street under surveillance, that's what the police said, the Health and Social Security have our street under surveillance, looking for those loafers who work on the black, cleaning windows and such, and then draw unemployment. That's what the police said. I'm off, then. And I trust that your gentleman friend will be gone by this evening."

Charlie beamed at Polly's father as they passed in the hall. He thought the man was pretty shaken when he knew he'd been overheard. The door banged. Polly's mother, starting to wash up, said, "That's quite ridiculous. You can't get a window cleaner round here for love nor money."

The smile was gone from Charlie's face. Polly's father had said surveillance. He felt he had been kicked in the stomach.

She came into the hall and she had a happy light in her face. He felt the shiver in his legs and the sweat on his stomach. Surveillance. He heard the clatter of the dishes.

"What's at the back?"

"The garden and the garage."

"And there's another road?"

"Has to be another road, dumb head, or there wouldn't be a garage—why do you want to know?"

She was owed it and she wouldn't get it, an explanation. He carried the rucksack into the kitchen. Formally, because that was the way he had been taught as a child, he thanked Polly's mother for her hospitality. He opened the kitchen door and walked through into the garden.

She followed him.

She caught him down by the small vegetable patch, her father's joy.

"Are they watching for you, Charlie?"

"It doesn't help you to know."

"It is for you. Why, Charlie?"

"It's a long story, and there isn't enough time."

He should have been gone. If they were watching the front, then they might have the back covered.

She had hold of his hand. "What have you done wrong?"

"Nothing, everything."

"Mr. Shabro told me what had been done to your family. He said that you weren't capable of friendship."

Gently, he took away his hand from her. "Perhaps one night we'll go dancing, dance till it's morning. You have to believe that I'd like that."

"Is that a lie, Charlie?"

"No, it's not . . . sweet Polly, the more you tell someone the more you involve someone, the more you involve them then the more you open them to hurt . . . it's best left unsaid."

"Will I see you again?"

Charlie caressed her cheek. "We'll dance all night. Promised."

"Am I not old enough to know? Is that it?" A bitterness, a choke, in her voice.

"It would hurt you to know."

He kissed her.

He felt the sweetness of her.

Perhaps one night they would go dancing . . .

He ran out of the back of the garden.

There was a grim satisfaction in it for Keeper. They'd all sweated, each of them on the track that had lost the Tango, then found him again. Token had done well when he'd come out of the garage and gone fast to the right and then turned in mid-stride. Token had done well to keep walking and go straight past him. Token said she'd been close enough to rub the sleepy dust out of the Tango's eye and she'd said that she found him quite dishy. Harlech had done well, because the Tango had climbed on a bus, and then hopped off at the lights and doubled back. Harlech had done a terrific job because he'd been fast enough on the radio for the car to pick the Tango up. Corinthian had tracked the Tango down onto the underground, and stayed with him for the train jump, predictable but tricky. Then Token's turn again, in her reversible anorak with headscarf and the glasses with no power in the lenses. Between them they'd held on to him, all the way to King's Cross main line station.

It was Keeper's opinion that the Tango was trying what he thought were good evasion tactics, and Keeper reckoned he was a rank amateur, good instinct and poor training, but he wasn't complaining.

He sat on the InterCity. He could see the back of the Tango's head. Harlech was way down the carriage and he would be able to see the top of the Tango's forehead, and Token was in the carriage behind Keeper, and Corinthian was in the carriage ahead. Going very smooth, hammering at a hundred miles an hour plus on the rails heading north.

David reckoned that the Tango might have nodded off, his pillow the rucksack which had to hold the best part of a quarter of a million pounds in cash. Unless Mr. Venables had it, and that didn't seem likely, not if he was tipping off the constabulary. Better get Statesman in to give the gnomes the once over after dark.

Mattie Furniss knew it was late at night.

It seemed an age since they had carried away

the tray on which his supper plate had been, and the glass of water.

They came for him when he was lying on his bed, when he had taken off his trousers, and he had pulled the blanket over his body to hide his nakedness from the peephole. His underpants were hanging over the bottom of the bed frame to dry.

It had been a hideous day. He had been waiting for the rattle of the door, and the sight of the men come to take him down to the cellar. There had been only the tray with his food in the early morning, and the tray for his food in the early evening. He had heard a car come in what he had judged to be the middle of the day, and he had heard voices outside, and he thought that he had heard the voice of the investigator, but they had not come for him.

He could walk, just about, on his own. The soles of his feet were heavily swollen, but he had learned a rolling gait that would take him over a short distance. He was hunched from the strain that had been put on his shoulders.

When at last they came, they had not allowed him time to put on his trousers, nor the pants, nor his socks. Between his guards, Mattie Furniss went down the stairs. He wore only his shirt. He was hobbling and bent. He was beyond reach of help, he was going toward pain.

Down the stairs and into the hallway, and his instinctive turn was to the left, toward the doorway to the cellar. He was pulled to the right.

He stumbled and fell. They let him go down, and his knees felt the coolness of the tiled floor. They jerked him up and onto his feet and the pain shivered through him.

They took him through a kitchen. There were moths arcing around the light bulb that had no shade. There were two large metal pots on an electric cooker and on the table there were plates laid out with salads at the side. He saw the food that was unlike anything that was brought on the trays to his prison room. He was frog-marched through the kitchen and out into the glare of the lights in what he thought must be the yard at the back of the house.

The light came from the headlamps of a Mercedes. The lights threw a bright wash across the yard and against the wall of concrete blocks. He thought the height of the wall was a foot or so above the height of his own head had he been standing erect and not been bent by the pain in his shoulders and ribs. That, too, was instinctive, that he checked the height of the wall. Many scenes now, all fast in his mind. He saw the pockmarks where bullets had struck the wall, and the holes were in a group that was only three, four feet across. He saw the guard who cradled a rifle, probably a Soviet AK-74, across his elbow. He saw the investigator standing with his hands deep in the pockets of his trousers. He saw a young cleric with the turban of brilliant white and the camel hair cape and the thin-rimmed spectacles.

It was done as if it were a routine in which the only character who didn't know his part was Mattie. And he was learning, so fast. No talk. The sounds of the engine of the Mercedes idling and of the scrape of Mattie's feet across the hard earth yard. The feet scraped because he was losing the power to walk, going jelly in the legs. Across the yard to the place in the wall with the bullet holes.

They had to drag him.

The use was gone from his legs. Thinking of Harriet who was his wife. Thinking of the cottage that was his home. Wanting to plead, and wanting to cry, and the voices strangled in his throat. Against the wall the guards loosed his arms. He collapsed. The dirt was on his knees, and on his arms and on his chest. Death was groveling in the dirt yard of a villa on the outskirts of Tabriz. Death was choking in the night air, beyond the reach of help. Death was feeling the slackening of the gut muscles. . . . Death was the metallic

crack as a Soviet rifle was cocked. There was a
hand in his hair and his head was wrenched upward and his body weight was taken so that he
was left in a kneeling position and the cold damp
dirt of the yard cloyed on his privates. Too frightened to pray, like that Lutheran pastor would
have prayed. Thinking of all those who were too
far from him to help him, but closer than the God
he hadn't troubled to know. Thinking of the men
at Century and Flossie Duggan. Thinking of Harriet alone in the cottage at Bibury where the
spring was over and the summer was coming, and
of Will, who would be coming soon to cut the grass
around the apple trees. Thinking of the agents in
Tehran and Tabriz and the harbormaster's office
in Bandar Abbas. Thinking of Charlie, who should
have been his son. They would all see the morning, they would all know the freshness of another
day. The morning, and another day, they were beyond his reach.

Against the back of his neck, where his hair
thinned out, was the pressure of the barrel of the
rifle. There was a pain prick from the foresight.

No questions.

No demand for names.

He opened his eyes. He saw the face of the investigator and the face of the cleric, expressionless.

He was shaking, and as his neck rolled so the muzzle of the weapon followed.

There was the firing click.

His ears exploded. His stomach failed.

He rolled, fell, collapsed.

He was on the dirt in the yard, and his mouth gaped and bit at the filth.

Mattie heard the low chuckle of the investigator. His eyes opened. He gazed into the cleric's face. He saw a silently mirthless smile.

He was pulled to his feet. His urine had run down the length of his thighs and had stained the dirt. He couldn't speak, couldn't help himself up. He made no attempt to cover himself as they took him back into the kitchen and past the cooker where a meal was in preparation, and up the stairs, and back to his prison room.

He was their toy.

On his bed he wept. The names were in his mind. In his mind were the names of the agents and the name of Charlie Eshraq.

Mattie could recognize it all, the shredding of his will to fight.

From his room he could see the west face of the clock. Big Ben showing a couple of minutes past midnight. He had slept on the decision, and he had killed a whole day on the decision. He had taken advice, but the decision was his. He could keep his options open no longer.

He went down to the thirteenth floor.

He didn't knock, he went straight into the room. A very strange noise in the room stopped him in his tracks. Past midnight in central London and the sounds were of the countryside at dawn. They'd put old Henry Carter on night duty. Finding a job for Henry in the twilight of his service at Century was putting him on night duty in the room used by the Crisis Management Committee. There was a camp bed over by the window. The man wore long combination underpants and a woolen vest with short sleeves and buttons at the throat. Typical of Whitehall, typical of government service, that a Crisis Management Committee should wind up once it was past midnight as a solitary individual, past retirement if he wasn't mistaken, sitting in ancient underclothes, and listening to God knew what. . . . The man was quick off the bed, and was straight into his suit trousers, and was hooking on the braces over his vest. Didn't bother with his shirt. There was an expensive radio on the floor and a cassette was playing through it. A sharp note on the track among what, to the Director General, was a clatter of noise, and he saw the attention of Henry Carter waver, then disappear. A moment of bliss on his face. He switched off the machine.

"Sorry, sir, bless you for your patience . . . *phylloscopus inornatus,* that's the yellow-browed warbler, a little beauty. I did the tape in Norfolk last weekend. I thought I had her, never can be sure. Very intense, very penetrating call. Did you hear it, sir? Just off to Siberia for the summer, remarkable little lady. . . . Apologies, you didn't come in here to listen to a yellow-browed warbler."

The Director General handed over a single sheet of paper, in his own hand, his own signature. Carter read it. He hadn't his close work glasses on and he had to hold his spectacles away from his face to get a clear focus.

"You'll not mind me saying it, sir, but it's a wee bit late."

"You don't have a drink in here, do you?"

Henry took a bottle of Scotch from a cupboard, and two glasses, and he poured two liberal scoops.

The Director General drank deep.

"I know we've warned them, sir, but we've taken an awful time to tell them to run."

"Big step, Carter, dismantling a network. A bigger step when that network is down to three agents and will take years to rebuild."

"I just pray to God they've got time."

"Furniss, he's trained to withstand pressure."

"Interesting usage, pressure . . . sir."

"For Christ's sake, we are talking about the dismantling of a network."

"No, sir, if you'll excuse me, we are talking about pressure."

"He's been trained. . . . Please, I'll have the other half."

The glass was taken, filled, handed back.

"Oh yes, sir, he's been trained. He was very good at the fort. One of the best lecturers they've had there. But my experience is that training and the real thing are wholly different."

The Director General shuddered. His hands were tight on the glass.

"How long can he hold out, that's what I need to be sure of."

"He's a man I've been proud to know for more than twenty years, but if he's in Iran it's asking rather a lot of him that he hold out this long."

The Director General headed for the lift and his car home. He left Henry Carter to the business of sending the messages that would instruct the three agents to take flight.

Chapter ✤ 13

"**I** am Matthew . . .
Furniss. I am . . . the Iran Desk . . . Head at Century House."

It was said. . . . It was as if they were all exhausted, as if a birth had taken place and Mattie was the mother and the investigator was the midwife and the confession was the child.

He could see into the investigator's face, and there was running sweat on the man's face and red blotches from his exertion, and the breath came hard to the investigator. Mattie lay strapped on the bed. He could see into the face of the investigator as the man reeled away, as if he'd run more distance than he could cope with, and the heavy-duty flex sagged from the man's hand. He could not take any more of the heavy-duty flex on the soles of his feet. The pain ran up from his feet and into his knees and into his thighs and up into his stomach, in his stomach the pain spread out and burst into every particle of him. The pain was in his mind, and his mind could take nothing more.

It was done.

"Matthew Furniss."

It was as if they had all been on a great journey together. There was Mattie who had endured, he no longer knew how many days, there were the guards who had started the day playing football with him, blindfolded, punching and kicking him from one to the other and heaving him against the damp scrape of the cellar walls, there was the investigator who sweated because of the force he had used to beat the soles of Mattie's feet. All on a great journey together, and the guards and the investigator had broken Mattie, and Mattie was strapped to the bed and needing to talk to save himself from the pain.

The investigator gripped the side of his table for support, then steadied himself and breathed in a gulp of the cellar's foul, hot air. All the body smells were trapped in the cellar. He levered himself along the side of the table and threw the switch on the tape recorder.

That morning had been different, as if everything else that had gone before had been child's play. No breakfast brought down to the cellar while it was still dark outside, a long age hanging from the wall hook until the pain in his shoulders had given way to agony, then the football, then the beating with the heavy-duty flex. As if they were now bored with him, as if they had other business to be about and could spare Mattie no more time.

So simple to speak the words. The hammering of new pain had ceased, and the tape recorder was turning, and the investigator was sitting at the table, and the guards had pulled back to the wall and there was the rank sweet smoke of their cigarettes.

At that moment there was no thought in the mind of Mattie Furniss other than the killing of the rising pain. The pain stayed where it was. The guards came from behind and they unstrapped the thongs that held down his legs and his wrists. They let him lie free on the bed.

He must be a pitiful sight. Not Mattie Furniss at all. He had not washed, not after having been brought back from the yard the previous evening. His hair was unkempt and filthy, his lips were parched gray and cracked, his eyes were big and staring and racing. They had broken him. He curled his knees to his chest and tried to control the pain that was all over his body. Broken, but free from the beating.

"Well done, Mr. Furniss. That was the hardest, Mr. Furniss, and the worst is now past."

Mattie talked about Century.

He could see from the eyes of the man that little that he said was not previously known. He spoke in a slow wheezing monotone. There was no character, no wit, he was a tour guide at the end of a long season. The investigator had pulled up his chair close to Mattie, and he was hunched forward so that his face dominated Mattie. Sometimes the investigator repeated what Mattie had said as if that way he ensured that the microphone picked up the words with greater clarity. The investigator took no notes, to have written on a notepad would have deflected the concentration that now settled over Mattie. He talked about the budget that was given to Iran Desk, and he talked about the resources that could be made available to Iran Desk from the Station Officers in Ankara and Baghdad and Dubai and Abu Dhabi and Bahrain.

All the old loyalties, all he stood for, beaten from him.

He heard the drone of his own voice . . . he'd done them well. He'd stayed silent longer than they could have counted on. There was nothing that he should be ashamed of. He'd given them time to save the field men.

He was given a glass of water. He held it in his two hands, and the water slopped down his shirt-front when he tried to drink, and his lips were rigid like plastic sheeting . . . he'd won them time. They should be thankful for what that precious time had cost him.

Mattie gave the name. ". . . His business is on Bazar e Abbas Abad."

He could see him clearly. He was hugely fat, sat on a reinforced chair in the back office behind a cave of merchandise and held court over cigars and coffee. He was a connoisseur of carpets and a collector of gossip, and he was a field agent of Century from far back. Mattie had known the merchant for twenty years, and it was Mattie's joke each time they met that he couldn't get his arms round his old friend when they hugged a greeting. There was gossip to be had from the merchant about the rivalries of the army colonels, about the interfactional fighting among the Mullahs, about the industrialists squabbling for foreign exchange with which to buy overseas plants. Every time they met then Mattie laughed, and sometimes the choicest of the gossip, if it were of matters sexual, could even bring a smile to those witheringly dull fellows from the Agency across the ocean. He had known the merchant since he had been a liaison officer in Tehran, and there was a rug in front of the fire in the cottage at Bibury that had cost him an arm and a leg, and the last time he had been seriously angry with Harriet had been when she had put a wet pine log on that fire that had spat a knot onto the rug. Mattie named the merchant, and they brought a damp towel to put across the soles of his feet to quiet the anger of the pain.

Another name. ". . . he works in the harbor-master's office at Bandar Abbas."

When he was Station Officer in Tehran he had once made the long road journey south, and he had been sure that he had thrown off the tail of the SAVAK agents that was supposed to be with him, and he had gone to the home of the official from the harbormaster's office. The man had been recruited by a previous Station Officer, and until the Revolution had been of minimal importance, and maintained only because he did not want money. He was pure gold now, a field agent in the office which observed the comings and goings of merchant shipping in and out of the country's chief port. He had gone to the man's small brick house, he had sweated and sat on a floor rug and wondered why the ventilation chimney seemed so inadequate in the blasting Gulf heat. On that oc-

casion, after the wife had scurried in with a tray
and glasses holding diluted lime juice and scurried out, the official had told Mattie that he was
a democrat, and therefore opposed to the regime
of the Shah of Shahs. The Revolution had come,
the official had found no democracy from the clerics, he had stayed on the list of active agents and
he had begun to grow in importance. A small,
frightened man, who believed that the work he
carried out for Mattie was a short step in the long
road to bring parliamentary rule to his country.
A sandwich with sweet cheese was brought for the
prisoner.

Another name given. "... he runs a repair workshop in Tabriz for lorries, and he also has con-
tracts to keep the Revolutionary Guards' vehicles
on the road."

A basic and human individual, a man who
might have been in Mattie's eyes almost a European. The engineer was the sort of fellow who was
always popular, perpetually in demand, and he
worked all the hours that his God gave him. The
engineer had been recruited in Turkey. A good
and active Station Officer, long before this academic boy in the job now, had sought him out in
a café and talked to him when he was over for the
collection of a broken-down lorry that would need
a new gear box. That Station Officer had been

lucky. The son of the engineer's close friend had been shot in the old jail in Tabriz after a cursory trial by the Komiteh. The engineer had been ready for recruitment. The engineer's pay went into an account at the Etibank in Van, and it was Mattie's business to know that the credit mounted and was never reduced. Perhaps there was a day on some far horizon in his mind when the engineer would drive out his truck, with his family hidden among a cargo. It was useful, the information provided by the engineer. In any time that approached normality it would have been second grade, but they were not normal times, and Iran Desk were pretty damn thankful to have anything coming out of Iran. Mattie had been given a glass of water and a damp towel again soothed the soles of his feet.

It was a good hotel. Charlie could sleep on the pavements with the dossers when he had to, not for the sake of it. The room was sixty-six and a half pounds a night and the best that Leeds could provide. He locked the door behind him. He went along the landing, he was carrying his rucksack by the straps, the two straps twisted around his wrist. He wore his cleanest slacks, a clean shirt and a navy blazer.

There was a man at the end of the corridor, in

jeans and a sweat shirt, polishing hard at the muzzle of a fire hose. He didn't look at Charlie and went on with his polishing. Pretty damn obvious . . . Charlie understood. . . . What could be so compelling about getting a shine onto a fire hose nozzle? A lift was waiting for him.

He came out into the hotel lobby. Too crowded for him to spot the watchers, and he wasn't hanging around to search them out. He knew what he was at. He strode across the lobby, not looking right and not looking left, went as though he belonged and hadn't a care in the world. He pushed his way through the revolving doors, then hesitated. It was colder up in the north than in London. There were taxis waiting in line, engines off. He paused on the pavement.

He moved sharply. He ducked back through the swing doors and across the lobby to the staircase.

He went up the stairs three at a time. Six flights to climb. He went up the stairs like there was no tomorrow, and took the last flight that was to the roof, and he put his shoulder against the stiffness of the fire escape door.

He stepped out onto the flat roof. He skirted the air-conditioning machinery. He had no interest in a fine view over factories or the brick terraces or the munificence of the Victorian civic buildings and churches.

He went to the edge of the roof. He looked down onto the street below. He could see the line of parked taxis. His eyes roved. He saw a green sedan that was behind the taxis. He could see that there were two people in the front seats, and there was the exhaust showing that the engine was idling. He saw that the man who had been polishing the nozzle of the fire hose was now across the street, and his lips were moving and there was no one close enough to hear him.

In his bath, Charlie had remembered that he was a friend of Mr. Furniss.

He was going to piss on them.

"Where the hell is he?"

"Went back up the fire stairs."

"I know he went up the bloody stairs—where did he go?"

"He was coming out and he just turned around."

"I've got eyes myself—where is he now?"

Harlech was across the road from the front of the hotel. Corinthian was stranded in the hotel lobby.

Token was round the back. "Not a whistle of him here."

There was the local joker in the Sierra, to drive. Keeper thought he was going to be a disaster because he was VAT, and VAT investigators were the pits. When the Head Office came up from the big city they had to put up with whatever they could get, and they needed a local man for the driving. The VAT man said, "Not a bad start of the day."

The repartee insult was rising in Keeper. The interruption, the insult never spoken.

Corinthian into Keeper's earpiece: "April Eleven to April Five, our Tango One is in the lobby, heading for the front door . . . going through the front door, you should be picking him up . . ."

"Your lucky day," the VAT man said.

Keeper saw Charlie come through the swing doors. He felt the relief jar through him. He saw the target walk toward the first taxi on the line holding the rucksack. It had been Keeper's opinion that Tango One was a rank amateur, but he didn't know why the target had gone back into the hotel, and he didn't know what he had done there, and he didn't know whether they had all shown out, and he was no longer sure how amateur the target was.

They followed the taxi out of the line. He told the VAT man that he didn't need a running commentary on the splendors of Leeds, thank you, and he had to shout at the joker to let Token through with the backup car, and neither Token nor Harlech acknowledged them as they went by and took up prime station behind the taxi. They had the message too.

Perhaps the target was not such a rank amateur after all.

Herbert Stone was used to dealing with middle trade businessmen and government representatives. The boy fitted no pattern that he was used to. Middle trade businessmen came to him from Hamburg or Rotterdam or Barcelona because he had earned a reputation for discretion and efficiency, for putting paperwork into place with speed. Government representatives arrived at his office, once a vicarage, because they depended on his discretion in placing hardware in the hands of people they could not acknowledge.

He dealt with corporations and institutions, not with bearded young men who wore yellow socks, and who sauntered in with rucksacks, for heaven's sake. And the kid seemed relaxed, as if it were the most normal thing in life to take an InterCity north and then come and chat about taking delivery of armor-piercing hardware.

Herbert Stone followed the principles of the Shavian Andrew Undershaft—he would do business with anyone, offer a realistic price, not trouble himself with principles or politics . . . and the

young man had given Mattie Furniss's name, and
Furniss's office had confirmed the connection.
Century put quite a bit of business this way, matters too delicate for public knowledge. There had
not been as many Belfast-produced Blowpipe
shoulder-fired ground-to-air missiles in the mountain valleys of Afghanistan as there had been
California-built Stingers, but the British had been
there, their warheads had joined the fireworks,
and Stone had been the conduit used by Century
to get the missiles into the hands of the *Mo-
jahedin,* never mind that they generally made a
hash of them.

He would be wary, cautious, but never dismis-
sive.

In a neat hand, in pencil, he wrote down the details of Charlie Eshraq's order. It was a pleasant,
airy office. There was no illustration of any matter
military on the walls, just watercolor originals of
the Yorkshire Dales. He might have been noting
the necessary information prior to the issuing of
a personal accident policy.

"If I'm to help you, and I'm not at this stage saying that I can, if I'm to help you then there has
to be a degree of frankness between us . . ."

"Yes."

"If you lie to me then I might just lie to you.
Your problem, you have to trust me. . . ."

"But I am recommended by Mr. Furniss, that's your guarantee . . ."

True, that was on the youngster's side, and a surety for him too. "What country do you mean to operate in—where will the weaponry be used?"

"Iran."

No whistle in the teeth, no pursing of the lips. "And the delivery point?"

"Past Turkish Customs, I collect in Turkey."

"What targets for armor-piercing?"

"First target is an armored Mercedes, six hundred series. After that I do not at the moment know."

"Not all to be fired in one engagement?"

Charlie paused, considered. "Each one different. Perhaps more vehicles, not tanks, perhaps buildings."

The scratching of Stone's pencil. "I see."

"So, what should I have?"

For the first time Stone was shaken. A small, puzzled frown escaped him. "You don't know what you want?"

"I'm not a soldier, what should I have?"

Everyone who came and sat in Stone's office knew what they wanted, problem was could they get it. They wanted howitzers, or 81mm mortars, they wanted white phosphorous shells, or ground-to-air, they wanted attack helicopters, or a Claymore system of ground defense. None of them, his clients, ever asked his advice on what they should have.

"Do you have *any* military experience, Mr. Esh-raq?"

"None."

The pencil stopped, hovered . . . but it was none of his business. "Light anti-tank weapon. It's called LAW eighty. How many are we talking about?"

Charlie said, "Three, maybe four."

Stone looked up from his notes. "I see. We are talking about a relatively, ah, small order."

"Yes."

There was a crocodile of barges going down the Thames, and seagulls hovering in chaos over the cargo.

The Deputy Director General was concise. "You won't know this man, this Stone, but he's used by us. He's an arms dealer, reliable sort of fellow. Right now Charlie Eshraq is sitting in his office and trying to place an order for a handful of LAW eighty missiles."

"I was never in the forces, what do they do?"

They bust tanks. . . . Stone rang through two or three days ago to check on Furniss's reference. Miss Duggan told me this and I asked Stone to ring me as soon as Eshraq appeared. He's trying to buy these missiles to take back with him into Iran. Does he get them, or not?"

The seagulls swirled in aerial combat over the barges. "It would be an illegal exportation, no doubt."

"Yes, but we're not squeamish. Presumably he brought back heroin in order to pay for these weapons, as soon as he has the weapons he'll be going back inside."

"Shows extraordinary courage." The Director General had a son at university, studying philosophy, and allergic to the lawn mower. "I like young people with purpose and guts."

"That's Eshraq—in full."

"Give them to him. Give him this anti-tank whatever . . ."

The Deputy Director General grimaced. "Quite, but it ignores the problem."

"What problem?"

"The problem of Mattie Furniss. The problem of Mattie talking, spilling under torture what he knows about his agents and about his young protégé. Got me?"

The Director General swung away from the window, swiveled his chair.

"I tell you what I think . . . I think Mattie is a very experienced and dedicated officer. I think he's of the old school. I think he'd go to his grave rather than betray his network."

The Deputy Director General murmured, "That's just not realistic, sir. I am afraid all we know today about interrogation techniques tells us that he will, inevitably, brave as he unquestionably is, talk. Would it help you to meet with our own interrogators, have them to tell you what, exactly, is being done to Mattie?"

"It would not. . . . It is simply that I have a greater faith in the resilience of an old dog. And furthermore, you stand there lecturing me as though you know for certain that Furniss is in an Iranian torture chamber. Well, you don't. We don't. We haven't the least idea where he is. He may have been kidnapped by Turkish thugs who haven't the slightest notion who he is. He may be with some free-lance outfit who simply want to ransom him. Tell me, if you would, how long it has generally taken for any of the extremist sects in Beirut to announce the capture of hostages. They're onto a telephone to Reuter before you can count to ten, or there is no word for months. There is no pattern about which we can be definite. So we'll just play it my way, if you don't mind."

"So, what is your instruction?"

The Director General said, "Eshraq is to have his missiles. He is to be encouraged to return to

Iran. Give him any help he needs, without tripping over the Customs people, if you can."

The Deputy Director General, swearing silently, flushed at the cheeks, went back to his office and spoke to Herbert Stone.

Parrish pounded down the fifth floor corridor of the Lane. Those who saw him, through open office doors, and those who flattened themselves against the corridor walls to give him room, wondered whether he'd got the trots or whether he'd heard the four-minute warning. He charged into the ACIO's office, and the ACIO had an audit team with him, and none of the audit team complained, just packed their briefcases and left. The door closed behind Bill Parrish. He didn't wait to collect his thoughts, gather in his breath.

"Just had Park on, from Leeds, right? Park is with Eshraq, right? Eshraq is currently sitting in the office of one Herbert Stone. Mr. Stone sells weapons. Eshraq is buying weapons. That's the strength of it. He's using heroin money to buy weapons. . . . This is going too far. Eshraq's run enough, it's time to knock the bugger over."

The ACIO rang through to the CIO and while he was talking Parrish loosened his tie and thought he was too old for this sort of caper, far too bloody old.

The voice was in her ear.

"I'm terribly sorry, Mrs. Furniss, I really am sorry, but I just cannot talk about it on the telephone. It's an open line, you see. They haven't been in touch with you? It's a scandal. I know I shouldn't say this, Mrs. Furniss, but the day of the gentleman is past here. . . . Mrs. Furniss, please don't ever say to anyone that I spoke to you. . . . They don't know what to do. They know that Mr. Furniss was kidnapped in Turkey, they believe that he was then taken into Iran. After that they don't know anything. They've set up a committee to watch developments, but they've staffed it with fools, people like that old idiot Carter. I mean, Mrs. Furniss, those sort of people are not competent enough. I was taken up to see the Director General. He had me in his office. He is not a gentleman, Mrs. Furniss, I hold him responsible. What he was interested in was all I knew about Charlie. You see, Mr. Furniss kept all his files on Charlie in his personal safe, didn't let them go down to Library, and didn't let me put them on any computer roll which anyone else could plug into. They were very concerned about Charlie. To tell you the truth, Mrs. Furniss, they seemed more concerned about Charlie than they were about Mr. Furniss. Mrs. Furniss, I don't know what it is, his trouble, but Charlie is in some sort of trouble, very deep, I'd swear on that. It's disgraceful, Mrs. Furniss, them not being in touch with you every day, should be in touch with you two or three times a day. I have to ring off, good-bye, Mrs. Furniss. Mr. Furniss has a great many friends here and they are all thinking of you. Good-bye."

She was grateful to kind Miss Duggan. When she was a child, before she had been sent away to school, her parents had employed a Flossie Duggan as a nanny, a nice, soft woman with a big bosom and a well of loyalty. Mattie used to say that, at Century, life would not be worth living if he didn't have Flossie Duggan to take care of him.

Harriet Furniss would not have called herself a Service wife, rather described herself as a Service widow. The Service had no room for wives. In more than twenty years, since Mattie had come out of the Coldstreams and joined the Service, she had never set foot inside Century. How could she have done? She had never even been allowed to drive to the corner on the Embankment and wait to collect him after work. She had never been to a social function that involved Century people. The only person that she knew at Century was Flossie Duggan, because Flossie would once or twice a year come down to Bibury and type up a report over a weekend if it had to be on the DG's desk or the DDG's desk first thing on a Monday morning. The life of the Service was a closed book to her. Little boys playing secretive games. But dangerous games. So hideously dangerous that Mattie was a prisoner in Iran . . . and she had good memories of Iran. She remembered when they had been young and together there, when she had been the young mother of two small girls, the swimming trips to the Caspian in the summer and the skiing trips to the Elborz in the winter, when the future was stable and set to last for a millennium. It had been a lovely country, kind and welcoming and comfortable. Infuriating, too, because it had aped Europe and of course she couldn't get a plumber or an electrician, never for love and rarely for money. Endless dinners by candlelight, because as night followed day it was inevitable her social calendar would be dogged by power failures.

She looked out into her garden. It was time to strip the wallflowers from the beds, but the rain was beating on the windowpanes. She loved her garden in summer. . . . She could picture Mattie pacing the lawn and then coming inside to tell her, bluff and still because he could never handle matters that were emotional, that Juliette Eshraq had been hanged from a crane in a square in Tabriz. She would never forget that, how he had walked backward and forward past the lupins and pinks and stocks before he had come inside to tell her of the execution of the girl she had known as a cheeky and darling child perched on her knee.

And what could Miss Duggan have meant about Charlie being in trouble and why did the Service know anything about Charlie? He was bound to call when he came back from his trip overseas. She would get him down to the cottage and ask him. Straight out. She wasn't going to let Charlie get himself mixed up with Century. That would be unbearable.

She thought of her man. Darling Mattie, everybody's friend, her husband.

Later, she would go down to the post office for some stamps, and if she were asked then she would put on a smile and say that Mattie was fine, just abroad for a few days, and before she went to the post office there were more circulars to send about the footpath.

She was a Service widow, and she would be good at it. Mattie would expect that.

Herbert Stone had the brochure on the desk in front of him.

"It's just what you want, Mr. Eshraq, and it's the best of British technology. Very much up to date, only been in service with our own forces for a few months. 'Provides an exceptional hit and kill capability for its size and weight . . . outstanding accuracy against both fixed and moving targets is achieved using a built-in spotting rifle . . . high technology warhead provides excellent kill probabilities from all angles of attack . . . not complicated to teach . . . zero maintenance.' Sounds pretty good, and it is. It'll get through six hundred fifty millimeters of armor, it has an effective range of five hundred meters, and the whole thing weighs only ten kilos. The beauty of LAW eighty, Mr. Eshraq, is in the spotting rifle, you fire a tracer round, you get a hit, you depress the main firing button and away you go. If this is designed to take out a main battle tank then it goes without saying, Mr. Eshraq, that it will make a frightful mess of an armored Mercedes."

"What is it going to cost me?"

"Let's have a drink . . . you'd like a drink, Mr. Eshraq?"

"What will it cost?"

"Expensive."

"How much?"

"Right, Mr. Eshraq, no drink, just the figures. We're talking about a round half dozen, correct?"

"No, four."

Herbert Stone's voice did not waver. There was

no apology. "I'm quoting you fifty thousand pounds for four . . ."

"What does that include?"

Herbert Stone had seen that the young man hadn't blinked, hadn't gagged. "Each missile would have cost the army two thousand pounds, that's for ordinary bulk dealing. You are not ordinary and you are not bulk, and if I had not just spoken to a colleague of Mr. Furniss you and I would not be dealing at all. You have a good friend, young man, but even with friends there are complications. You don't want all the seamy details, do you? You just want delivery through Customs at Istanbul. For that money you get four missiles. Don't worry yourself with the details, Mr. Eshraq."

"Four missiles at fifty thousand pounds?"

"Right," said Stone and made a swift note.

Charlie bent over, and he lifted his rucksack onto his knee. He delved into it. He laid on the edge of the desk a dirty shirt, and two pairs of dirty socks, and then his washing bag. From the bottom of the rucksack he drew out a plastic bag. He pushed the washing bag and the socks and the dirty shirt to one side, and from the plastic bag he took the first wad of notes, wrapped by an elastic band. Other wads followed. A less-experienced businessman might have shown surprise, but

Stone had the first wad in his hand and was counting. Twenty-pound notes, one hundred notes in each wad. The heaps of notes moved from the side of the desk where Charlie sat with his laundry across to Stone's side. Twenty-five wads of notes on the desk top, and Charlie lifted the bag back into the bottom of his rucksack, and covered it with his clothes and his washing bag.

"That's it, thank you." The money was shoveled, fast, into Stone's safe.

"Mr. Stone, what are the complications that cost so much extra, please?"

It was a reasonable question, and that was how Stone treated it. "You're better off without details, Mr. Eshraq, details tend to get messy in the wrong hands. . . . I have to have a cut. They have to come off the tail of a truck, and someone has to put them on a truck, and someone has to make the paperwork right, and someone has to find a bit of room on a lorry, one or two palms to be crossed at frontiers on the way to Turkey, and someone has to make sure Istanbul doesn't look that closely at what's coming through. There are quite a lot of people who would go to prison for quite a long time, that adds up to the difference, as you think of it, above two thousand pounds per weapon."

Charlie said, "In that price, in the load, I'd like

there to be included three wholesale cartons of bath soap, the best there is, whatever Mrs. Stone would recommend. Can you manage that?"

"Yes, I believe we can manage that."

"I'll give you my number in London. You'll call as soon as you are ready?" Charlie's eyes narrowed. "If they were tampered with, if they didn't work . . ."

"I think we can let Mr. Furniss be our mutual surety, don't you, Mr. Eshraq?"

Park said, "If we don't get into Columbia and start to hit the bastards in their own backyard, then we're going to lose. It's the Americans who are at the sharp end at the moment, but our turn's coming. We won't avoid the really big cocaine traffic if we don't act much more positively. The demand's here, for the lunchtime snort, and that demand'll grow in London just as it's grown in New York. Do you know that there's a guy in Medellin, that's in Colombia, who has a fortune estimated at two billion dollars? That's cocaine money. We have to go in, get stuck in on the ground. We can't just be sitting at Southampton and Dover and Heathrow."

The VAT investigator chewed gum and said, "Myself, I never reckoned to change the world between nine and five, five days a week."

"We have to beat the power of these bastards. Did you know that there was a Justice Minister of Columbia, and when he quit he was given the job of Ambassador to Hungary—and he was shot there, in Hungary. That's the power of the bastards, that's what's got to be beaten."

"Good luck." The VAT investigator took the gum from his mouth, put it in the ashtray. "So, you're off to Bogotá?"

"If I can get there."

"Me, I'm looking forward to staying in Leeds and sorting out the fiddles of Mr. Gupta and the corner shop."

Park said, "Haven't you ever wanted to do anything that mattered?"

"Smart talk. Makes a change. We don't get much smart talk up here."

"Terrorism, that's crap compared with the drugs threat, and that's not recognized . . ."

"Are you married?"

"What of it?"

The VAT man settled comfortably in his seat and peeled another strip of gum. He said airily, "Your good lady, is she going to Bogotá?"

He didn't answer. Park had the camera at the window. He photographed Charlie leaving through the front door, and when he had the photographs then he was on the radio and alerting his team. Corinthian passed them, on foot, and in the mirror he saw Harlech and Token in the backup motor.

Tango One was walking back toward the center of the city, and the rucksack was trailing from his hand, and the tail was on him.

David Park had them all keyed.

They couldn't let the target run much more, not now that he was into weaponry, and too damn right he was going to get himself to Bogotá when this target was knocked. Been right to let him run up to now, but all changed once he'd started talking hardware. Too damn right he didn't know if Ann would be with him.

"You asked to be kept informed," the ACIO said. "So I am informing you that it is our intention to arrest Eshraq."

"When will this be?"

"Tomorrow at four A.M."

The Home Secretary lowered his eyes. "You could do me a favor."

"What sort of favor, sir?"

"You could allow me to consult."

"*Consult,* Home Secretary? The case is two thousand percent rock solid."

"No, no. I don't mean on a point of law. You've run a splendid show. I've nothing but admiration for the way it's been handled. No, it's not that. It's . . . it's well, frankly, it's odd, but it's turned political and I need to consult upward."

"There's nothing odd about that, sir. It started out political. 'Turn the country upside down, chaps, bring in the pusher, bring in the dealer, spare no expense, bring the distributor to book, scrap every other investigation'—and we did— and I rather think my job was on the line if we didn't. Well, Home Secretary, we did. We've got him, this heroin importer, this degenerate killer, the man who carried in the stuff which Miss Lucy Barnes killed herself with—or are the political fortunes of Mr. Barnes so wonderfully on the wane that heroin has been struck from the political agenda?"

"Commissioner, I am totally sympathetic to your point of view, believe me."

"I'll believe you, Home Secretary, if, and only if, you fight our corner. You've got, well, I am in danger of revising that, because you are a politician and *you* have nothing—the country you are elected to serve has got a dedicated, a passionately dedicated Investigation Division. They earn peanuts, they work twice as hard as you do. They get no perks, hardly any holidays, and they deliver. They deliver and you want to consult."

"I take in what you say."

The ACIO took out his small notepad. He wrote down his home telephone number. "Four A.M., sir. You can reach me at home this evening. But we'll be rooting for you, sir. Don't let us down."

It was a slow process, getting the messages to the field agents. Some messages could be sent over coded inserts into broadcasts of the BBC's World Service, but an order to close shop, abandon ship, must be delivered by hand. Terence Snow was to send a low-level but reliable man to Tabriz. The Station Officer in Bahrain had to find someone to fly to Tehran. The Station Officer, in Abu Dhabi had to find a dhow owner to ferry the message across the treacherous Gulf waters to Bandar Abbas. Of course, it would have been quicker to have enlisted the help of the Agency, but then it would also have had to be explained that Mr. Matthew Furniss, Desk Head (Iran), had been lost. And that was news that Century was unwilling to share with the Americans, a matter of dirty linen made public.

Charlie slept in his hotel, the plastic bag under his pillow.

The green Ford Sierra was outside the hotel. The VAT investigator had gone home, and Keeper was asleep across the backseat with the Vodaphone cradled in his arms. Harlech and Corinthian and Token had the room across the corridor from the target, and would be on two-hour shifts watching the door.

Keeper was well asleep when the Vodaphone warbled in his ear.

"That you, Keeper?"

"Bill? Yes, it's me."

"Are you sitting comfortably? No knock tomorrow . . . got that? No lift in the morning . . ."

"For Christ's sake, Bill . . ."

"I said, no knock tomorrow."

"Why not?"

"David, the tablets just come flying off the mountain, and I pass on the messages."

"I don't fucking believe it. What more do they want?"

"What they do not want is for the target to be lifted."

"I hear you."

"You cuddled up with Token?"

"I am bloody not."

"Good thing . . . do us all a favor, give your missus a bell, will you? I gave her my promise that you'd be back for the dance. Sweet dreams, Keeper . . . just ring your missus in the morning, and you do not lift the target."

The boot went in, and the fist.

There was a hand snaking into Mattie's hair in order to pull up his head, so that it was easier to punch him, kick him, so that it was harder for him to protect himself.

He was trying to tell them the name, but his lungs were emptied by the beatings into his stomach pit, and he had not the breath to shout the name. His throat was too raw to speak the name. If he told them the name then the beating and the kicking would stop.

The man was too good to have been fobbed off with three names. Mattie had known why the beating had started again. He had shown the flicker of success. He thought he had won small victories with three names. The investigator had read him. Buying off the pain of a beating with three names. But three names was the sliding slope. It was what Mattie would have taught at the fort—once the names start then the walls come tumbling in. He had no more defense. He had used all the tricks that he knew of. The last trick had been the feigning of unconsciousness, and the cigarette end, lit, on the skin under his armpit, tender, had blown away the deceit in a scream of pain.

He knelt on the floor. His arms hung at his side. There was the taste of blood in his mouth, and there was a tooth socket for his tongue to rest in. He hated the men that he had named. The pain and the shame had been brought down on him because he had known their names. The fist in his hair held his head upright, and they punched and slapped his face, and they buffeted the bridge of his nose so that there were tears in his eyes, and they kicked his stomach and his groin. For Mattie, the only way of ending the pain was to surrender the name. He had thought he could satisfy them with three names, and he had failed.

His arms flailed around him, as if he tried to drive them back. If he did not drive them back, away from him, then he could not draw the breath into his lungs and the saliva down into his throat, and he could not name the name. He did not see the flick finger gesture of the investigator. He was not aware that the hand was no longer in his hair, and that his body had buckled. He saw only the investigator's face.

His chest heaved. The breath flooded into his body.

"You killed his sister."

"Did I, Mr. Furniss?"

"You tortured her, you killed her."

"Who did I torture, who did I kill?"

"His sister . . . he's going to get you for his sister."

❖ 370 ❖

"Where is he going to come from, to get to me?"

"Coming from UK, coming through Turkey, coming through the Dogubeyezit frontier post."

"How is he going to get to me, for what I did to his sister?"

"Armor-piercing missile, for you and the Mullah who sentenced his sister."

"Who is the Mullah who sentenced his sister?"

"I don't know."

"How will he come here, to get to me?"

"Papers, papers of the *pasdaran.*"

"Where do the papers come from?"

"Istanbul."

"Where in Istanbul?"

"From a hairdressing shop, in the Aksaray district, it is just to the right of the Mirelaon church. It is the only hairdresser there."

"When is he coming, with his papers from the hairdressing shop?"

"Very soon."

"Would he be known to me, my hopeful assassin?"

"You knew his sister, you tortured her. There were two Guards that took her to the execution, he shot them in Tehran. The executioner of Tabriz, he blew him up, bomb on a car roof. You'll know him."

"Mr. Furniss, what is his name?"

He knelt at the feet of the investigator. His head was bowed down to his knees. From his clothes there was the smell of vomit, in his nose was the smell.

"God forgive me . . ."

"What is his name?"

"Harriet . . . please, Harriet, forgive me."

"His name, Mr. Furniss?"

"Charlie, you can't know what they've done to me . . . the pain, Charlie . . ."

"The name?"

"He's coming to get to you, for what you did to his sister. He's Charlie. His name is Charlie Eshraq."

"We'll get the doctor to you. . . . Thank you, Mr. Furniss."

Chapter 14

It was morning. There was enough of a knife line of light at the edge of the plywood over the window to tell Mattie that it was morning, another day. He rolled a little on the bed and his knees were hunched against his stomach as if he still needed to protect himself from the boots and the fists. He could feel the tightness of the bandages around his feet, and there was the irritation of the stitch that the doctor had put into his lower lip. At first he was too frightened to move, because he believed that any movement, any slight movement, would hurt him. With the movements of his muscles and his limbs he was like a man walking in a darkened room, hesitating and testing. He went from his side to his back, and he lay on his back and looked at the ceiling light. The ceiling light was always brilliant, bright enough for him to have to sleep with the blanket pulled over his head. From his back he maneuvered himself across to his other side. All of his concentration, his determination, had gone into those movements. He had managed the movements. . . . He rolled back until his spine was against the mattress. He gazed at the light bulb that was recessed into the ceiling, and that threw a trellis of faint shadows through the mesh that protected it. He closed his eyes. Not bloody much to show for it, a couple of bandages and a single stitch and aches all over his body . . . not bloody much for cracking, for talking. His eyes were squeezed shut. He tried to shut out all that was around him.

Pretty damn easily he'd talked.

More easily than he'd have believed.

Less hurt than he'd have thought possible.

He could move from his side to his back and to his other side and onto his stomach. The pain was . . . to have cracked and not been hurt, that was agony. What had he said? A hazed memory. The memory was of the face of the investigator, and with the eyes of the investigator seeming to plead with him for the telling of it. The memory was of the hair-covered hands of one guard, and

the nicotine stains of another guard's fingers, and
of the stale sweat smell of their fatigues, and of
the rough dirt of their bootcaps. What had he
said? There were sounds in his mind. The sounds
were of his own voice speaking names. Good
names, the names of old friends . . . God, the
shame of it . . . God, the bloody disgrace of it . . .
It was faint, he could not be sure that he heard
the voice. The voice seemed to say the name of
Charlie Eshraq. Couldn't be certain, but the voice
among the confusion seemed to be the voice of
Mattie Furniss.

"His name is Charlie Eshraq."

No, no, couldn't be certain, and the memory was
misted.

"His name is Charlie Eshraq."

For years in the Service he had used them. They
were almost friends to him, almost family, and
he'd named them . . . and they hadn't even hurt
him so that it lasted. He had his fingernails and
a back he could straighten. He had not been hurt
as the Gestapo jailers had hurt that Lutheran pastor who had come to the fort and talked of his
faith. Shame and disgrace and failure. . . . He
rolled off the bed. Gently, as if he were frightened,
he lowered his feet to the tile floor. He put the
weight of his body on his feet. It was as if he
wanted to feel pain, as if the pain in his feet would

justify his having talked. Of course there was pain, but not enough pain. The pain was sustainable when he put his weight onto the soles of his feet. They wouldn't understand in Century. They had a routine in Century for those who came back—if he ever came back—those who'd talked under interrogation. A debrief and a good-bye. No one wanted to know about a man who had talked. All the successes forgotten. And the irony was that it had been Mattie who had contradicted the embassy's reports in the late seventies, Mattie who had said the Peacock throne was on shifting sand and would sink. Good reporting, and all for nothing. A debrief for damage limitation and then a good-bye that was cold and without emotion.

He heard an engine revving outside. He struggled to get up from the bed and he pressed his ear against the plywood at the window. The engine dulled the voices, but he recognized the voice of the investigator. There was a place in hell for that man. Mattie Furniss would never forget the voice of the investigator. Then the scrape of the tires on chip stones and the squealing of a gate. Mattie understood. The investigator would be setting up the surveillance on the field agents. He would return. Mattie tried to calculate how long it would have taken to abort the field agents. He knew the system because he had drawn it up himself. He couldn't keep track of the days anymore, should have done, should have scratched a marking for each day on the wall beside his bed. He didn't know whether he'd given them enough time. What he'd been through, that would be a suite at the Ritz compared with what the field agents would suffer in the interrogation rooms at Evin.

Mattie would have whetted the appetite of the investigator, he knew that. He'd be back. They would strip him and gut him of all he knew, and then they would kill him. Stood to reason, they would take their fill of him, and they would dispose of him. They would take him through the kitchen and across the yard, and they would put him against the concrete-block wall where the other poor bastards had been put.

In his life he had never known such agony of failure.

If he didn't make it back ... in time, they'd hear at Century that their man had cracked. Just as the Agency had heard that Bill Buckley, good guy and brave guy, had cracked. The bastards had tortured Buckley and then they sent the tapes of Buckley screaming to Langley. The shit pigs had made sport with Bill Buckley's pain.

He went to the wash basin and he ran the tap, and when the water came it did not matter to Mattie that it was foul-tasting and ditchwater brown.

While the water still dripped from his beard growth he sat on his bed. He waited for them to bring him his breakfast. He would watch each movement of the guards when they brought him his breakfast.

Past six, and Charlie sang in his shower. He felt good. He knew what was the source of his soaring spirits. It was his meeting with Mr. Stone, gunrunner By Appointment. Stone had taken Charlie's money, and would deliver, because Charlie was the friend of Mr. Furniss. He began to realize that the friendship of Mr. Furniss was a protective shield to him.

He dressed and packed his rucksack.

He came out of his room quickly. He walked on the corridor carpet on the balls of his feet, and he went quietly, and he could hear the scramble of movement behind the door across the corridor, and he heard the static and the squeal of a radio hurriedly activated. He ran down the fire stairs.

In the lobby he went briskly to the swing doors. He drifted into the street.

Charlie turned, and he went past the line of taxis. At the end of the line was the green Sierra.

The call on the radio, fed into his earpiece, had battered Keeper awake.

Still in the back of the car. He was wrenching the sleep out of his eyes and shaking his head clear. Harlech telling him that Tango One had come out of his room. Corinthian telling him that Tango One had crossed the lobby.

He sat upright. He saw Tango One coming down the line of taxis, and behind Tango One was Corinthian spilling out through the swing doors, and then behind Corinthian was Token, fumbling to get her blouse into her jeans. Why the hell was Token tucking her blouse in? Why the hell did it ever get untucked when she was mounting night surveillance in a hotel room with Harlech? Harlech would be at the back, in the car park, getting the backup onto the street. Of course Token had to sleep, like he'd slept, silly thought, and fast because the target was closing on his car, striding up past the taxis. It happened, it wasn't desirable, but it sometimes happened, that a target would walk right past the surveillance position, within spitting distance. The routine was to look away, get your face out of his field of vision. Make it look like there was nothing there out of the ordinary.

This was just about the closest that he had been to Tango One, just closer than the one-way window at Heathrow. He turned away. He had yesterday's newspaper in his hands, and his head was away from the pavement, and his body was low in the backseat. All standard procedure.

The car lurched.

The front of the car bucked down.

His eyes opened. Keeper's eyes coming half out of his head. He gazed through the front windshield at the back of Tango One.

Tango One sat on the hood of the green Sierra, and his feet swung close to the nearside front wheel and he was grinning as he looked down and through the windshield. The fucking Tango was sitting on the hood of Keeper's car . . . no standard procedure for that one. Keeper looked into the amused face. Past Tango One he could see Token stop dead in her tracks, and Corinthian behind her.

"Excuse me." He wound down the rear window. "Would you mind getting off my car."

He heard the voice that mimicked his accent. "Excuse me . . . excuse me, would you mind getting off my back."

All the training said that in a show-out the surveillance team backed off, and fast. Keeper couldn't back off. He was half lying in the back of his car, and the target was comfortable on the hood.

Token was twenty yards from the car, and hesitating, and not knowing what was expected of her, and Harlech had stalled his engine and there was a frustrated horn hammering behind him, and Corinthian was cutting through the traffic to get to the far side of the road, which was right. A bitter, raw anger in Keeper.

"Would you mind getting off my car, please."

Again the mimicking of his voice, but this time shouted, "April Five to April One, April Five to April One . . . for fuck's sake come in, please. What a funny little name, April Five."

"Get off."

"Get off my back."

The words were clear in Keeper's memory. There was room for discretion when there had not been an order. But there had been an order. "You do not, repeat not, pull in Tango One." Bill had not said, "You do not, repeat not, put your fist in the target's grin." He climbed out of the car. He felt awkward, stiff, from sleeping in the backseat, and out with him came an empty soft drink can that clattered into the gutter beside him.

"Get the hell off my car, Eshraq."

"Didn't you hear me, April Five? Get off my back."

"I'm going to stay on your back until they close the door on you."

"I don't think so, April Five."

"I'll put you off my car."

"Try."

"Don't think, Eshraq, that Furniss can protect you."

And Charlie Eshraq laughed at him, the flash of wide white teeth.

"Out of your depth, April Five. Heh, April Five, can you swim?"

And he was left. He stood beside the car, and he had to put his hand on the roof of the car to steady himself, and it was not the tiredness that had weakened his legs. He was trembling with rage.

They went through the routine. They watched the target in his seat throughout the journey, as if they hadn't shown out, as if he hadn't sat on the hood of the case officer's car, as if they knew what they were doing, as if it hadn't been the biggest foul-up any of them could remember.

No one actually asked Keeper what had been said at the green Sierra sedan, because none of them dared. The April team went back to London and half a dozen rows in front of them Charlie Eshraq slept.

Keeper went forward, matching the motion of the train. He caught at the seat heads to balance himself.

His hand brushed the ear of Charlie Eshraq

when he went past that seat, and he saw the annoyance curl on the man's face. Didn't give a damn. He was whistling, cheerful.

He went to the buffet. Twelve cans of Newcastle Brown, four whiskey miniatures, eight packets of crisps, eight packets of roasted peanuts.

He spilled them down onto the table. Harlech looked like he couldn't remember when Keeper had last volunteered his shout, Corinthian looked like it was Christmas morning, Token was grinning.

He sang. Big voice, might have had a trace of baritone, but he didn't know about such things . . .

> *Eshraq has only got one ball,*
> *His dad had two but they were very small,*
> *Khomeini has something similar,*
> *But the Shah had no balls at all . . .*

Heads turned. Businessmen dropping their pocket calculators and their financial reports, and Eshraq twisting his head to look back at them. "One more time," Keeper shouted.

> *Charlie has only got one ball,*
> *His dad had two but they were very small,*
> *Khomeini has something similar,*
> *But the Shah had no balls at all . . .*

And into the decibel joke competition. Loudest laughter wins. Token's was filthy, Harlech's was rugby, Corinthian's was subtle, which meant he couldn't win, Keeper's was Irish. Filth rules. A miniature emptied into Token's second can. They were all laughing, all rating it a hell of a good morning, and Token had her arm looped up and over David's shoulder and she tousled the hair at the back of his neck.

"Well done, big boy."

He looked forward to what he could see of the shoulder six rows in front of him. He looked past the dark suits and the starched shirts and the disapproval.

"Just to let him know that I'll take his legs off at the knees."

"Go home, David."

"I will go home when I know what is happening."

"What makes you think that I know what's happening?"

"That's not an answer, Bill, and you know it."

"It's the answer you'll have to make do with."

"We could have knocked him and you blocked it."

"I told you, David, it was up the mountain from me."

The frustration showed. Park thwacked his right fist into the palm of his left hand. Parrish didn't look as though he were impressed. It was the first time that Park had ever shouted at Bill Parrish, because Parrish was a cuddly old sponge, and shouting at him was blowing bubbles out of the window. Too nice a man to shout at.

"For fuck's sake, Bill, we are talking about a heroin trafficker. We are talking about a heroin distributor. We are talking about a joker who is walking away from major dealing. Since when did that sort of track get a block on it?"

"The instructions to me, the instructions that I passed on to you, were that Eshraq should not be lifted."

"It's criminal, Bill, and you know it."

"Me, I know nothing, and I do what I am told. You should do what you're told and go home."

David Park went to the door. He turned, he spat, "And I thought this was supposed to be a serious outfit, not a comic strip . . ."

"Don't give me that shit, Keeper."

"And I'd have thought you'd have honored your promise."

"Listen . . . don't pull the old holy number with me . . . listen. The ACIO went to see the Home Secretary last night, said we were ready for a lift. The Home Secretary called him in his beauty sleep. I shouldn't be telling you, but the Home Secretary gave the instruction, that's how high it came from. You want to know what's happening, I want to know what's happening. What I know is that on the top floor the ACIO and the CIO are not available to me. I will be told what is happening when they are ready to tell me, and you will be told when I am ready to tell you. . . . So do me a favor and bugger off home. . . . Did you ring your missus?"

"He's just a filthy little trafficker . . ."

"I hear he saw you off."

"What the hell . . . ?"

"Merely making an observation. . . . Did you ring your missus?"

"He's a cocky little swine."

"And you showed out to him—so go home and take your missus out and buy her a pretty dancing frock."

"Are you going to let them walk right over you?"

"That's a slogan, and that's not worthy of you . . . just go home."

A few minutes later, from his window, Bill Parrish saw David Park on the street below, walking through the traffic like it wasn't there. He thought that he might have destroyed one of his best young men, and he hadn't known how to stem the rot. He called up on the radio. He was told that Tango One was back at his flat. He had two of the April team on the flat, but the soul had gone out of the surveillance and the investigation, and the bugger of it was that no one had felt it necessary to tell Parrish why the block had gone down. Why take it seriously . . . it was only heroin, it was only kids' lives being chucked on the garbage heap, it was only evil bastards getting rich off misery. Why worry? Only bloody fools would worry. Bloody old fools like Parrish, and bloody young fools like Park. He knew that Park hadn't taken any leave for two years, and he hadn't put in for holiday time for the coming summer. He might just book a couple of weeks for the two of them on the Algarve, and handcuff Keeper to his Ann and kick him onto the plane. Could be sentimental, Bill Parrish, when he wanted to be. It was a crying shame, that couple was. Another day . . . of course, there would be another day.

One step at a time, sweet Jesus. It was the favorite hymn of Bill Parrish, who was a rare Christian once a year, late at night and Christmas Eve. One step at a time, sweet Jesus, the hymn that he liked to hear on the radio when he was in his car. One step at a time . . . and he ought to teach the words to Park, if the youngster hadn't gotten himself run over crossing Holborn and not looking. He

rang the ACIO's extension, and was told he was
in a meeting. He rang the Bossman's extension,
and was told he was in conference. One step at a
time, sweet Jesus . . . it was only heroin.

He sat on the floor of his prison room beside the
door. He had worked out the angles of vision from
the peephole in the door, and he believed that
where he sat he was hidden if his guards checked
at the peephole before entering. He sat on the
floor in his underpants and his vest and his socks.
He had used the pillow on his bed and his rolled
up shirt and his bunched together trousers to
make a shape under the blanket. He always slept
with the blanket over his head, to shut out the
ceiling light. He had put his shoes at the end of
the bed and half covered them with the blanket.
A long time he had listened at the door before
making the preparations, long enough to satisfy
himself that he was not watched.

They had shamed Mattie Furniss, humiliated
him. To break that shame he would kill. He would
try, damned hard, to kill.

Eventually the Mullah remembered Juliette Eshraq. Not well, of course, but he remembered her.

He had to remember her. If he had not remembered her then he would have been the only living

being among close to two thousand present at the hanging who had forgotten Juliette Eshraq. The investigator thought it a great spur to memory, his information that the brother of Juliette Eshraq was coming to Iran with an armor-piercing missile on his shoulder, and revenge in his mind.

"But you are assured, Excellency, of my best endeavors. It is in my interests, also, that the brother of Juliette Eshraq be found. If he is not found then it is me that he will come for, after he has gone to you."

When he left the Mullah, now very clear in his recollection of Juliette Eshraq who had smiled at the crowd who had come to see her lifted high on the crane's arm, he went to his own office in the capital and there he made the arrangements for the watching of an official in the harbormaster's office at Bandar Abbas, and of a merchant in carpets, and of an engineer who repaired broken lorries.

It would be late in the evening before he could catch a military flight back from Tehran to Tabriz.

Go for it, that was the Major's oft-repeated injunction at the fort. Go for it.

"You go for it, gentlemen, because if you're going to be all namby-pamby then you'll fail, and

after you've failed then you'll wish to Christ that
you'd never tried. If you like living then you go
for it, because if you don't go for it then you won't
be living."

Mattie sat on the floor behind the door and he
gazed at his made-up bed, and he listened for the
footfall of the guards bringing him his evening
food.

The Major was from Hereford. The Major had
grown tired of lying on his belly in ditches in
Northern Ireland and branched into consultancy,
which paid better and which was safer. It was said
of the Major that he had once spent two clear
weeks living rough on the fringe of the Creggan
Estate in Derry, and that was not a friendly place.
The Major advised multinational companies in
the security of their overseas executives, and he
came down to the fort to let the Service know the
current thinking on Escape and Evasion. He said
that a prisoner must look for the opportunity of
escape from the moment of capture. He said that
it didn't matter how often the circumstances of
imprisonment changed, the captive must be prepared to rip up his plan and start again. And there
was another story about the Major. A new high-
security jail in Worcestershire, and the first con-
victs due to arrive on a Monday morning. The Friday before there had been an escape prevention

drill. The Major had been the guinea pig, and he'd been out by the evening; problem was, the Major said he'd been paid to get out, not to tell how he'd done it. Never did tell them. . . . Mattie thought of the Major and scratched his memory for every last nugget of what he had been told.

There were low voices on the stairs, and the soft shuffle of sandals.

The bolt was withdrawn, the key was in the door.

Chapter ❖ 15

*T*here was the numbing shock spreading from the heel of his hand. And the body was at his feet.

There was his food tray on the table.

Go for it . . .

Mattie went. Fast and cold, just as the Major had told them. He went out through the heavy door. He went straight at the second guard standing back from the doorway. He saw the surprise wheeling across the face of the second guard, and Mattie's hands were at his throat and his knee rose sharply with all the force Mattie had into the man's groin. No going back because the body of the guard who had carried the food tray was on the tiled floor behind him. The second guard crumpled to his knees. Mattie let go of his throat and brought his knee swinging back into the man's face. His head flew back, struck the wall. One more jerk with the knee to the head now slumped against the wall, and he was almost gone. Mattie dragged him into the prison room and then his hands were closing on the man's throat. The guard picked feebly at Mattie's wrists, and his eyes bulged, and his tongue arced, and his voice choked, and his breath died. The Major had always said it would be easy, if they went for it. Nothing easier than chopping the heel of the hand onto the nape of a man's neck. Nothing simpler than locking the fingers around a man's throat, and taking the pressure onto his windpipe, so that it sealed. His fingers were a tourniquet, and the voice and the breath and the life of the second guard were dying. He felt no fear. He felt only a determination to carry out all that he had been told. The second guard was sinking to the tiled floor, and all the time he looked up and into the face of his killer. Wrong place, dear boy, to come looking for mercy. It had been the second guard who had always smoked and seemed so casual and so indifferent when the real pain was being worked into Mattie's body down in the cellar. Never any mercy in the cellar from you, dear boy. The second guard had his hands on Mattie's wrists, and the stupid, pathetic creature had not had the wit to let go of the hands and to go for the pistol in the holster at his belt. Bad mistake, dear boy. Mattie heard the last choke shudder, and his fingers on the second guard's throat had the weight of the man's corpse.

He dragged the body of the second guard across the tiles and toward the bed.

A hell of a weight, and the tiredness was flooding into Mattie. With his foot he pushed them both under the iron-framed bed.

He took the tunic and plimsoll shoes off the bigger of the two guards. The man was taller than Mattie and had bigger feet, and his plimsolls went onto Mattie's feet over the bandages, and he took the holster belt, and when he had retrieved his own trousers from under the blanket, then he threaded the belt through the loops and put on the tunic. He had the pistol. He checked the breach and the magazine. It was East bloc manufacture and it was a hell of a time since he had last seen a pistol made in Czechoslovakia. He took bread from the food tray, forced it into his trouser pocket along with a chicken piece and a fistful of rice.

Mattie stepped out onto the landing.

He listened. There was a radio playing. He recognized a news bulletin on the radio, the Tehran

Home Service, and he could hear low voices. There was no other way. The way out was down the stairs. The pistol stayed in his holster. If he had taken it out then he would have had to spend time learning its mechanisms, he had not that time. The Major had always said that the initial movement was what gave you the chance of escape. He went down the stairs. He stopped at the bottom of the stairs. It was a good house for him. The house had concrete floors under the tiles, and a concrete staircase. No sound as he came down the stairs. The hallway ran the length of the villa, from the front door, and into the kitchen at the back. He paused again, he kept himself flat against the hall wall. Ridiculous, but he was actually listening to the news broadcast, something about the price of long-grained rice. Come on, Mattie, get on with it. He saw the poster of Khomeini in front of him, across the width of the hallway, taped to the wall. . . . Up yours, dear boy. . . . The voices that he heard were low, relaxed, and came with the radio from behind a nearly closed door that was opposite to him. The Major had said that the guards who most mattered were the guards that had never been seen by the prisoner. There could be guards outside. Mattie had to accept that there might be guards outside the villa and that he had no idea of their positioning. He was listening, but his ears were filled with the radio broadcast, and the words of the men inside the room. He pushed himself away from the wall and walked past the door, trying to make himself upright. He should have brought the tray, either as disguise or something to throw. He undid the catch on the holster, put one hand on the butt of the pistol and went into the kitchen. No one there. They had already eaten. His own food would have been the last to be prepared. The sink was stacked with plates and with cooking dishes. They'd come soon, perhaps when the radio broadcast was over. They'd wash the dishes and then they'd wonder where were the two guards who had taken the food tray to the prisoner.

Mattie told himself that he was going for the wall in the backyard, he was going and he wasn't stopping. If they were going to stop him then they were going to have to shoot him.

The kitchen was behind him. He had passed through the door and he would have been silhouetted in the doorway. He didn't know a way of going through a doorway, from a lit room and out into darkness, without throwing shadows.

The backyard, beyond the kitchen, was the only area outside the villa that he had seen, and he knew there was a high wall. If there was one guard outside then the likelihood was that he would be at the front, by the gate, but that was the area of chance.

He went on tiptoe across the yard. He had never heard a dog, and he didn't think there was a dog there. The Major had said that dogs were the nightmare of the escaper, but he hadn't heard a dog, not a guard dog nor a pet dog. He went for the wall. He went for the wall where there were the bullet marks in the concrete blocks. If they caught him, if they brought him back, then it would be at the wall that his life would end. He reached up. The palms of his hands and his fingers could just reach the top of the wall.

A terrible pain when he pulled himself up. In his shoulders and his upper back and down to the cage of his ribs. The hurt was from the times that he had been on the hook in the cellar. He struggled to get his feet off the ground, and he scrambled with his knees to give him purchase up the wall. There was a moment when he had his head and his shoulders above the summit of the wall, and then he was balancing on his chest and the pain was excruciating. He could see into a street, and he could see low bungalows.

There were the headlights of an approaching car. The lights played on the center of the road and lit up the walls of the buildings, and the lights were rushing closer to the wall of the villa, surging toward Mattie who was high on the wall and working to swing his legs onto the top of the concrete blocks.

Behind him, through the open kitchen door, came the signature music of the end of the news broadcast. He knew the music because most days at Century he listened to the recording picked up at Caversham. He thought that if he fell back from the wall then he would never find the strength again that had carried him to the top of the wall, and the music at the end of the broadcast told him there would in a few moments be guards in the kitchen. He had his elbows over the top of the wall, and he ducked his head as low as was possible, and his legs dangled, and the blood and the pain roared in his feet. He waited for the lights to pass, and it seemed to him impossible that the lights would not search him out for the driver. So bloody long. He seemed to hear the shouting in the kitchen, and the stampeding of feet, and he seemed to feel the hands grabbing at his knees and at his ankles and dragging him down.

The lights passed.

Quiet behind him, gray shadow ahead of him.

He heaved himself up and onto the wall. He levered one leg across. He rolled, he slid and fell.

Mattie tumbled eight feet from the top of the

wall and down onto the weed verge at the side of the road, and he was winded.

Go for it. It would have taken more than the breath being knocked from his lungs to hold him. He was up and he ran.

He did not know where he was running. Distance was the name of the game. He hobbled down the street, away from the prison gate. Mattie ran for survival and running was risk. He did not know whether there was a curfew in Tabriz, and if there was a curfew then at what time it started. He didn't know where in the city he had been held. He only thought he was in Tabriz.

He ran until the stitch cut into his belly lining. When he saw a café, benches outside, chairs and plastic-topped tables inside, he had slowed and crossed to the far side of the road. Where there was a shadow he tried to find it, and he had to skin his eyes to peer ahead of him, hard because his head was shaking from the exertion of running, because it would be fatal to be running and not looking and to barge into a patrol of the Revolutionary Guards.

He ran for a full five minutes. He was fifty-two years old, and he thought that he had run a mile. He had run on back streets, and he had heard laughter and shouting from inside small homes, and he had heard the voice of a radio announcer reciting verses from the Koran.

When he rested, when his legs and his wind had died, he crouched in a concrete storm drain.

Grab any luck that begs to be taken, the Major had said at the fort. Luck is earned. Luck doesn't show itself that often, and if it's not grabbed then it's gone. He thought of Harriet, and he thought of his girls. The first time this day that he thought of his women tribe at home. They would have expected it of him, and it's for you, my darling, that I run. No other beacon for Mattie.

A car pulled up in the street, ten paces from him. The driver took a parcel from the backseat of the car and carried it into a house. The engine was left running.

The driver made a gift of a car to Mattie.

Out of the storm drain, into the car. At first very gently away, hardly changing the beat of the motor. And once round the first corner, then he really went at it. He had not driven so fast since the year before he was married, since he had owned the Austin Healey Sprite. No sports car, this, but the bloody thing went, and he drove like there was no tomorrow, and probably there wasn't. He drove away out of the town, until he was surrounded by darkness, and then he stopped and axed the lights. He found a map in the glove compartment.

He was, by his best calculation, between 150 and 200 miles from the Turkish frontier, and by the grace of God, the stars were clear and bright and he was on the northwest edge of the town that he thought must be Tabriz.

The three guards who had been in the house placed the blame in entirety on those two men who had taken no precautions to defend themselves. . . . The investigator would have done the same in their position, in his position he would do the same.

The investigator was told that there had been a period of fifteen minutes between the time that the food had been carried upstairs, and the discovery of two comrades, dead in the prisoner's cell.

Furniss had a start. More important was the fear of the guards who had survived. While they had searched the villa a full hour had passed, and only then had they summoned an ambulance. The police had not yet been informed, neither had the army, neither had the headquarters of the Islamic Revolutionary Guards. They had waited for the investigator to return.

It crossed his mind that he could do worse himself than make tracks for the Turkish frontier.

But there was too much blood on his hands for him to be welcomed into asylum by the Western agencies.

It was like a wound to him, the escape of Matthew Furniss. He had the names of three agents, and the name of an infiltrator, nothing more. He had no detail yet on the running of Century's Iran Desk, on the collaboration between Century and Langley, on the gathering of intelligence from the British listening posts on the frontiers and the American satellites. He should have had hard information on the passing of information from the Americans and the British to Baghdad, and on the battle engagement instructions to Royal Navy warships on the Armilla patrol. He had taken so little, and he had promised so much to the Mullah, and the Mullah would, no doubt, have repeated these promises to his own patrons. Well, he would start again when Furniss was recaptured, as he must be. No one would shelter an English spy in Tabriz. Deep in his gut was the tremor of insecurity, the ripple of the sensation of his own vulnerability.

When he had pieced together the story, he had himself driven to the IRG headquarters in the center of the city. He gave the commander photographs of Matthew Furniss. He described what he knew him to be wearing when he escaped from the jail, warned him that Furniss was armed with a pistol.

He wrote out the messages to be sent by radio.

He sent a terse report to the Mullah in Tehran.

He sent a description of Matthew Furniss to the Army Command of the northwest region.

There was no choice but to broadcast his failure over the airwaves.

Mattie had driven out on the Marand road. He had the map, and he reckoned the petrol tank had a minimum of a hundred miles, perhaps more. He would draw attention to himself if he speeded, and if he dawdled then he faced the greater risk of being trapped inside the gun net when the alarm was raised. He took the wide bridge across the Meydan Chay. He rattled past factories that had been idle for years now that the war had soaked the resources of the nation; huge unlit ghost buildings. Just after the road crossed the old railway track that had once carried passengers and exports into the Soviet Union, he swung left off the main road. Any time on the main road had been risk, and he was sure that at Marand, the high oasis town, and at Khvoy, which was a center of agricultural production, there would be roadblocks. The roadblocks would not necessarily be for him, but he could not afford to be stopped when he had no papers for the car, and no papers for himself.

The road that he chose was metaled for a dozen miles, then petered out into dirt and stone. The car took a hammering but he would not have need of it for long.

When he was high above the northern shore of Lake Urmia, when he could see the lights of the villages where before the Revolution a good wine had been produced, he saw the roadblock ahead.

Mattie recognized the block because on the road in front there was a line of taillights, red, queueing, and he could see a torch being waved. There was a queue. It must be half a mile ahead of him. He was slowing, going down through his gears. He killed his lights . . . he pulled up to a halt. He had used his luck to make good ground away from Tabriz. . . . No choice now. It was time to walk. No way of knowing whether this was a block in position to halt him, or just there for routine. He swung the wheel hard to turn in the road.

He hadn't reckoned they would have read the manuals. He hadn't rated that there would be a guard stumbling up from the tree thicket at the side of the road, probably been dozing, probably awakened by the scrape of the tires on the gravel-hard shoulder of the tarmac road. He switched his headlights back on and saw the guard lumbering into the center of the road. The lights blinded the guard. The guard was old, and under his forage cap there were locks of silvered hair and his beard was down to his throat; he seemed to wave at Mattie while the car was twenty yards from him, only realized at the last moment, in time to raise his rifle, aim the barrel into the heart of the light. Mattie drove straight at the guard.

He felt the shudder blow of the impact. He felt the heave of the bouncing wheels. For what felt many seconds Mattie's heart stopped. He drove, every second expecting a machine gun to sweep his life away. No, that was absurd. Not on this back road. And the odds were that the old man was alone. Should have stayed where he was, fired first, no questions. Perhaps the old man had children or grandchildren who had run from the guards. Past the next corner he saw a track into the trees. He turned onto it and followed it far enough to be hidden from the road and pulled the wheel hard to the left and sank the car into scrub. Out, Mattie, out. He was drained. He would gladly rest in this wood. *Out,* Mattie, the guard's in the road. Right, Major, be right with you.

Mattie took the pistol and the map and got out. He let the dark flood into his eyes. He searched in the car and then in the trunk, but there was nothing he could use. He thought of Harriet's trunk, first-aid kit, blanket, shovel. . . . Mattie, get on with it. Coming, Major, just checking.

There was no sign of lights approaching. He walked cautiously toward the dark shadow in the road. The body was still. He suppressed a little jolt of regret for the old man who had not stayed in hiding and shot him as he turned. It's all right, Major, Mattie's not going soft on you. This was a good guard. He may be a dead guard, but he did me a favor. Costly favor, oh yes. And he hauled the body into the trees. Five yards in, rest a minute, ten yards in. Fifteen will do.

He found the rifle. The bolt mechanism was crushed. And there were no rounds in the magazine, and not one in the spout. He carried the rifle to where the guard lay. Poor defenseless old man. If he'd had a round, you stupid cunt, Furniss, you'd be dead. Now, get the hell out of here.

His stomach was empty, he had not yet touched the bread and the chicken and the rice squashed into his pocket, damp on his thigh. On his feet were plimsoll shoes. The mountains were ahead of him, dark against the night sky. He reckoned he had four or five hours of darkness left to him. He walked out of the treeline, took his bearings from the stars and began to climb.

She had had the family row, and forgotten it.

Her case was at the foot of the bed, and her dress was on the floor. Polly didn't care that she had stormed out of the house with her father shouting and her mother crying, and she didn't care that the dress that had cost her £199.95 was crumpled on the floor.

His head was across her stomach, and his beard tickled at her skin, and her fingers played patterns across his shoulders. He had loved her and he'd slept, and he had given her the best evening she had ever had before he took her to his flat. He was a dream when he danced. Polly had never learned to dance, not properly, not until that night when she had been shown the magic of the tango and the rumba. She knew a bit of quick-step and she could waltz if she wasn't watched too closely. She hadn't known that she could dance as she had danced with Charlie. And the meal had been amazing, and the drink had only been champagne, and his attention had been total.

She had forgotten the family row. She had forgotten what Mr. Shabro had told her. Must have been jealous, the old goat . . .

"Have you traced it?" Corinthian asked of his radio.

The reply was in his ear. "As far as we can go . . .

but there's a problem. Vehicle registration say they are not permitted to give out any details on ownership of that registration. . . . That's all."

"So, what do we do?"

"Try pretending it isn't there."

"That's daft."

"And that's the best you're getting."

He shivered. He hadn't the engine running so there was no heating. In the passenger seat Token was asleep, and she'd forgotten herself, or she was so hellish tired, because she had let her head slide down onto his shoulder. But he didn't rate his chances. He didn't rate them because all the skirt seemed to want to talk about was goddamn almighty Keeper. In the considered view of Peter Foster, codename Corinthian, Keeper was not long of their world, stood to reason. He could not be long with them because the guy was too intense, too tied down by all the shit about winning the narcowar in Bogotá, in the Golden Crescent, that sort of shit. Keeper might be the best they had, but it couldn't last. The guy ran too hard. Himself, he paced himself, he wasn't in a hurry, he did his job and he clocked up the overtime, and he thought that he might just grow old in Customs and Excise. Keeper wouldn't. . . . Keeper was a shooting star, bloody brilliant, and then gone.

It didn't bother Corinthian that the light was

going out of the investigation, had been on the slide ever since the order had come through from the Lane that Tango One was not to be knocked. No one from Parrish downward seemed to know what the fuck was going on, and the target was cocky enough to have gone back to his address like there had never been a problem, like importing heroin and being under ID surveillance didn't spoil his day one bit. Great-looking fanny he'd with him, and a great-looking bill he'd have run up at the swish joint he'd taken her. The light had gone so far down the hill, over the other side, that Keeper had gone home, been sent home, and they weren't told when he'd be back.

She started. She awoke, and then she realized where her head was, and he gave her the evil eye, and she gave him the daggers. She straightened in her seat.

"Bugger . . . I was just about to rape you," he said.

"Oh, do piss off."

"Quite the lady."

"Is it still there?" She turned to look back down the street at the other car. "What's the news on it?"

"No news is permitted on that registration."

She shook her head, tried to get the sleep out

of her eyes. "What does that mean when it's at home?"

"It's what they tell you when the vehicle is used by either the Security Service or the Secret Intelligence Service. What confuses me is, are they watching the target, or are they watching us?"

The radio messages, relayed from Tehran, went to military and IRG bases on the western side of Lake Urmia, and to the north. But this was wild and mountain country, an area through which a fugitive could with luck pass undetected and over which no security screen could guarantee success. The lake lies as a huge natural barrier between the Iranian hinterland and the mountain ranges that peak at the Turkish frontier.

The messages were in simple codes. It was not possible to send complicated enciphering to outposts such as Mahabad and Oshnoviyeh and Reza'iyeh and Dilman and Khvoy.

The messages were plucked from the airwaves by antennae at the Government Communications Headquarters outpost at Dhekelia on the island of Cyprus.

He was south of Dilman, too far south to see the lights of the town. Ahead of him were the mountains. His sights were set on Mer Dag, immediately across the border, his 12,600-foot beacon. He had long ago wolfed down the food that he had taken from the prison. Now he was famished. His shoes were disintegrating. He had torn off the sleeves of his shirt, and the sleeves were now bound around the plimsoll shoes to hold them together. He had walked through two complete nights, and when the sun was high, when the lake shore was at siesta, he had walked in the haze heat. All through the daylight hours he could see the summit point of Mer Dag. It was his target. . . .There was the ache of hunger in his stomach, there was a numbed death in the muscles of his legs, there was throbbing pain behind his forehead. Stick to the goat tracks, Mattie, and find water. Very well, Major. He would find water. The mountain summit floated in the moonlight ahead of him. He thought that it was too late now to fail.

The Director General was taking breakfast at his desk, his appetite sharpened by the brisk walk over Hungerford bridge.

The door flew open. The coffee slurped over the rim of his cup.

To the Director General, Henry Carter was a most incredible sight. He wore no tie or jacket, no shoes even. Henry Carter had barged into his office, practically brought the door in with him, and now stood panting, obviously unshaven, in front of the desk. The Director General could see the top of the man's vest at his open shirtfront.

"He's on the run, sir . . . splendid, isn't it? . . . Dolphin's running."

It was the third consecutive day that Park had been at home, and all of them weekdays. Ann was dressing for work, and late. She hadn't an idea why he had stayed at home, and since he was as tight as a soup tin, she didn't dare ask. He had begun redecorating their spare bedroom—God alone knew why, they weren't awash with overnight visitors. They hardly had any visitors. She thought it was a peace move on his part, and in the evenings she had cooked his meals and tried to remember what he liked, and she'd ironed his shirts, and she'd hidden her feelings in concentration on one television program after the other.

She had known there was a target, and he had told her that the target was not to be arrested. She didn't know any more than that. And, small mercies, not a squeak about Colombia.

He was still in bed.

They had a sort of routine in bed. She went to bed earlier than he, and she'd pretend that she was asleep when he came in. And he pretended that he acknowledged that she was asleep. The pretense worked until he was asleep, and he wasn't ever long going. She thought that she had never seen him so deeply exhausted. When he was asleep she'd lie half the night on her back with her eyes open, and she could have screamed . . .

He was still in bed and she was dressing in front of the wardrobe. She hadn't shown it to him yet. The dress had cost her what she earned in a week. It was black, full skirt, bare back, a halter at the neck. The dress was as bold as anything she had bought since they had been married.

It was an impulse.

She took the dress from the wardrobe. She held it against her body. She saw that he was watching her.

"For the dance, David. . . . Is it OK?"

He said, "It's super."

"You mean that, really mean it?"

A quiet voice, as if the strength had been taken from him. "It's a terrific dress, I really mean that."

"I hoped you'd like it."

"You'll look wonderful."

"We are going, aren't we?"

"Sure, we're going."

"You want to go, don't you?"

"I want to go, I've joined their club."

"David, I'm trying, no riddles, what club?"

He struggled to sit upright in the bed. "The club all the others are in. The club that's worrying about the pension scheme. The club that's ratty about annual leave and days in lieu of bank holidays. The club that's serving out time. The club that's given up. I've joined their club, Ann. Entry to the club is when you don't fucking care that a heroin trafficker is running round central London like he owns the fucking place. . . . Yes, we're going. We're going to have a hell of an evening. . . . Ann, that dress, it's really brilliant."

She went on with her dressing. "Things will get better. You'll see." And she blew him a kiss as she hurried to be at work.

Mattie had walked until he could not put one leg in front of the other.

He had crawled until he no longer knew where he was going, where he was. The sun beat down on him. He had no food and he had no water. The track was of hot, sharp rock, and he had no more strength and he could not walk on rock and the plimsolls were ripped from his feet. He lay on the path.

Don't panic, Major, just getting the old head down. Just leave me in peace. I'll be better when it's cooler.

For a moment Harriet had forgotten her husband. She put down the telephone. He was a sweet man who lived out on the Cirencester road from Bibury, and one of the few people that she knew who lived in the community for seven days in each week, didn't just commute down at weekends. He had some pull, and he could get things done. He had rung to say that the farmer was bending, and was going to agree to roll a strip across the middle of the plowed field so that the right of way was intact. It was a little triumph for all of them who had contested the plowing up of the track. Actually there was no good reason why the old route should not have been redrawn round the outside of the field, but that would have surrendered the principle. The principle said that the footpath ran across the middle of the field, and it had run there for more than a century, and the principle said that if only one person a year wanted to walk that path then the route should stay unplowed. She reveled in her small triumph. Mattie would have enjoyed . . .

If Mattie had been there, then he would have enjoyed her moment.

So many times they had been separated, and she had never felt such loneliness.

She seemed to shake herself. It was a gesture

that was all her own, as if she were shrugging away dust from her shoulders, as if she were hardening her resolve.

She hadn't even told the girls.

The phone rang. The bell was in the hall, recessed into a rafter, and the ringing burst throughout the whole cottage. It was a loud bell so that it could be heard if she and Mattie were out in the garden.

Each time the telephone rang, she expected the worst. There was a couple in Bibury who had lost an only son, a paratrooper, at Goose Green five years ago and in the final push on the Argentine machine gun nests. They'd sent an officer down from the depot to break the news. She didn't think they'd send anyone down from Century immediately, but she had supposed that the Director General would at least speak to her on the telephone.

She had shaken herself. She was prepared.

"Mrs. Furniss?"

She recognized the voice. "It is . . ."

"Flossie Duggan, Mrs. Furniss, from Mr. Furniss's office. . . . I've only a moment. Have you heard anything?"

"I have not."

"Dreadful, they are. . . . Mrs. Furniss, there's some wonderful news. Well, it's nearly wonderful. Old Carter, that idiot, he told me. He's escaped.

Mr. Furniss, I mean. He'd been night watch in the Committee's room, and he was so up in the air that he went into the DG's office without his shoes on. Apparently he doesn't wear his shoes at night when he's on duty. . . ."

"How extraordinary."

"Indeed, that's rather the tenor of things here nowadays. Oh dear . . . sorry, sorry . . . what'll you be thinking of me. What I meant to say was, yes, that he's escaped, Mrs. Furniss. He's on the run, that's what Carter went to tell the DG. It's been picked up by the monitoring people abroad, they listen to everything, they've heard the messages on the radios inside Iran. Mr. Furniss has escaped. They're all searching for him of course but the main thing is, he's free."

"But he's still inside?"

"But he's not in his prison, Mrs. Furniss. That's wonderful news, isn't it?"

"Miss Duggan, you are very kind to call. I am so grateful. What would we do without you?"

Harriet put down the telephone.

She closed the front door behind her. She didn't remember to lock the front door, nor to take with her a raincoat. She walked down to the church, old and lichen-coated stone.

He came out of his stupor because a boot was in his rib cage and was pushing him over from his stomach to his back. The boot was in his ribs as if he were a dog, dead in the road. Mattie saw the gallery of faces above him. They were all young faces, except for one. The one face was cold, without sympathy. A tribesman's face, heavily bearded, and the man wore the loose shirt and the all-embracing leather waistcoat and the baggy trousers of the Kurdish mountain people. There was an ancient Lee Enfield on his shoulder. The look on his face seemed to say that if the body had not been on the path, in the way, it would have been ignored. Eight young faces. They were all boys, early twenties, late teens. They gazed down on him. They carried packs on their backs, or there were sports bags in their hands. He lay on his back, then struggled to push himself upright. He understood. Mattie knew who had found him. A young smooth hand ducked down and pulled the pistol from his waist. He did not try to stop it. Because he knew who had found him he had no fear of them, not even of the tribesman who would have been their guide on the last stage toward the frontier.

Mattie spoke in Farsi.

Would they have the kindness, in the name of humanity, to take him with them?

Would they help him because he had no footwear?

Would they share food with him, because it was more than two days since he had last eaten?

They were nice enough, the boys, they were tense as if it were an adventure, but they welcomed Mattie among them, and the guide just spat and grunted in the Kurdish patois that Mattie had never mastered. The guide now had the pistol.

Mattie was given bread and sweet cheese, and he was allowed to sip from a water bottle before the impatience of the guide overwhelmed the anxious care of the boys. Two of them helped him to his feet and supported him, his arm across their shoulders. Damn good kids. And heavy going for the kids, with Mattie as their burden, and the track was wild, difficult, damn bloody awful. He saw butterflies, beautiful and vivid, beside the path, on flowers that he did not know from England. He saw high above them the winter snow that was still not melted. They passed through thick forest that had taken root where there seemed to be only rock and no soil. They went down into gullies and waded through ice-cold torrents, and they climbed razor rocks out of the gullies. Mattie was no skeleton. They were struggling, all of them, and particularly those two who supported Mattie. The guide didn't help them. The guide was always ahead, scouting the route, sometimes whistling for them to come forward faster. Without them he would have been finished. Probably would have frozen to death, carrion for beasts of the mountain.

They wanted to know who he was, of course, and at first he had made a joke of it and told them that he was in Iran to sell tickets for the World Cup finals, and then he had said, quietly and between the spurts of pain when his feet hit the rocks on the track, that he was like them, that he was a refugee from the regime. Some of them spoke English, some came from the sort of household in Tehran where English could be taught with discretion. They were dodging the draft. He knew that long before they told him. They were the kids from rich families who couldn't bear to give their offspring up to the butchery in the trenches outside Basra. They'd have paid through the nose for the guide, and some would have more money in belts around their waists for after they had an entry visa to California or Paris from Turkey. They'd learn, Mattie thought. They'd join the wretched flotsam in the refugee camps, and they'd learn the hard way that Turkey didn't want them, that America and France didn't want them. One thing was pretty damn certain in Mattie's mind.

The two boys who had manhandled him up the
rock slope, levered him down the track, carried
him across the fast streams—he'd do his utter-
most to get them visas into the United Kingdom.
They told him, those who carried him, that they
were going to make for Hakkari, that they had
heard there was a refugee center at Hakkari ad-
ministered by the United Nations. They said that
once they had reached the camp there they could
send telegrams to relatives who were already living in the United States. They thought that their
relatives would be able to fix the visas. Had their
friend ever been to America?

They came to a ridge. The snow-peaked summit
of Mer Dag was away to their right. The guide had
stopped, was crouched down. They struggled the
last paces to reach him, and Mattie had swung his
arms off the shoulders of the two boys.

The sun was crisp in an azure sky above them.

The bandages, mud-brown, trailed from Mattie's feet. No pain now in his feet.

The guide pointed below.

There was a path snaking down from the ridge
and in the far distance was the sprawl of a small
town, and running farther away from the town
was a twisting road. It was Turkey.

And the guide was gone. He gave them no farewells. There was no hugging, no slapping of hands

on the back of the guide. He was just gone, loping away down the path that they had just climbed. Mattie felt the moistness in his eyes. He had taken his luck, and he was within sight of home. The tears came, rolled on his bearded cheeks. And around him the elation bubbled.

"Wait, wait . . . wait . . ." His arms were around the shoulders of two of the boys and they had his weight between them. He spoke slowly, so that he could be translated by those who understood him. Too important, he didn't trust himself in Farsi. "How are you going from here?"

"We are going down the hill."

"We are going to the refugee center."

Mattie said, "You must, you must absolutely go down the hill by night."

"We have nothing to be worried of, Mister."

Mattie said, "You must wait until nightfall." He tried to summon his authority.

"And you?"

"Different, I'll get down on my own . . . now be good lads." Mattie said.

"Mister, you cannot even walk."

"I'll roll down if I have to, but you should go by night. Let me go ahead and prepare the people on the other side to expect you—their army patrols."

They were all giggling at him, and they were no longer listening to him. They were the children

that he knew so well from his own house, and from
the homes of every one of his contemporaries, children who thought their parents were half-witted.
He was hoisted up.

"I really do urge you . . ." But they had no patience for him. They were too happy. They went
down the slope. The wind cut at their clothes,
deadened their ears. The pain welled in his legs,
but he shrugged away the hands that offered to
help him. He had started on his own and he would
damn well finish on his own. There you are,
Major, we made it and we will have a long night's
carousing over this adventure, you and I. They
were coming down the slope fast. Darling, he
thought he heard Harriet cry out. Darling. They
were strung out in a line.

"Dur . . ."

The shout in the clear air.

Mattie saw them.

"Dur . . ."

He thought they were paratroops. Toughened,
hard men. Weapons that were aimed as if their
use were second nature. He saw five at first, block-
ing the track down the slope. He knew a little
Turkish, and the word to halt would have been
clear enough if he had known nothing. He didn't
have to be a linguist. There were more of the patrol at the flanks now. Guns covering them. Mat-

tie raised his hands. His hands were high above his head. His mind was clear. There might be officials of the United Nations at Hakkari, but there would be no officials of the United Nations High Commission for Refugees on the upper slopes of Mer Dag. He looked for the officer.

He pushed his way past a rifle barrel. He had the authority now. He was filthy and he could barely hobble without support, but he had been commissioned in the Coldstream Guards, and for a few weeks in his life he had been a junior commander of the Sovereign's guard at Buckingham Palace. He knew how to deal with soldiers.

He saw the tabs on the officer's shoulder, the Americanstyle bars. He would understand English if it were spoken slowly and loudly.

"Good afternoon, Lieutenant. My name is Furniss. I am an official of the government of Great Britain. I am in flight from Iran, and I ask for your help. Should you wish to confirm my identity then you should radio back to your headquarters and tell them to contact my embassy in Ankara, Mr. Snow . . ."

He was waved forward. He was trying to walk upright, with dignity. He thought the officer had a good bearing, might have been on a NATO exchange course. He passed each of the young men, the draft dodgers, the refugees, the flotsam.

"Now, most important, any help that you can afford these boys, Lieutenant, my government will be grateful for it. Without their assistance I would not have been able to cross your frontier. I ask you to treat them with compassion."

The officer looked through him. He gave orders, sharp and clear commands. A corporal was at Mattie's arm, and leading him farther down the slope. When he looked back he saw that the boys had been corralled by rifle barrels and were sitting hunched on the track. Mattie was taken forward, whether he wanted to go or not. At the edge of the track, Mattie stopped. He resisted the tug of the corporal's hand on his sleeve.

"What are you going to do with them?"

The officer gestured, in annoyance, to his corporal. Mattie was forced off the track and into thorn scrub. He had been taken from sight. He sat on the earth, and his head was buried between his knees.

He saw the officer take from his belt a Very pistol. He saw the burst of color high above him. Afterward he heard the officer shouting on the radio.

It might have been fifteen minutes later, it might have been half an hour, it might have been his lifetime, and between the foliage and sprigs of the thorn Mattie saw the patrol of Revolutionary Guards approach carefully down the slope. The refugees were prisoners, they were given into the custody of their own people. They didn't struggle, no one broke away and ran. They went meekly.

"They are scum," the Lieutenant said. "And they bring into my country drugs and crime."

"They saved my life, goddammit," Mattie said.

"You could have gone back with them."

He had not argued. He had not jeopardized his own safety. He thought that it would be a long time before he forgot the laughter of the boys at the warnings of an old man, and he thought that the Major would have wondered what all the fuss was about.

An hour later the radio crackled to life. Orders from headquarters. The biggest man in the patrol, a giant of a man, lifted Mattie onto his shoulders and tucked Mattie's thighs over his arms, and carried him like a child under the sinking sun, away down the slopes of the Mer Dag.

Chapter ❖ 16

$\mathcal{H}$oughton did the opening, not that successfully, and the first cork careered into the ceiling of the Director General's office and chipped the plasterwork.

Champagne, and a good vintage, the PA had been sent out with a wad of notes from the Director General's wallet. Must have run all the way back with it.

The occasion called for the best.

"I said he'd surprise us all . . . not quite true, I said he'd surprise a lot of people. I had faith in him. Always the way, yes? Just when life seems darkest the sun blesses us. I tell you what— Furniss is a real hero. You can have your soldiers doing daft things and getting medals for what they've achieved in the heat of battle, no harm in that, but Furniss has done it on his own. Can you just imagine how the chaps are going to be feeling back in Tehran, all of those unshaven baskets? They'll be slitting each other's throats. . . . A toast to Mattie Furniss. . . . I'll bet he feels like a million dollars right now."

The Deputy Director General muttered, "He hasn't been on a fun run, Director General."

Ben Houghton said, "I can't get a link through to him. We expect that the Turkish military will have taken him down to Yuksekova, they've a base there. Crisis Management have been trying to patch through a line, but they can't make it through. Pretty soon now he'll be airlifted to Ankara."

The Director General beamed. "There's a hand that I am much looking forward to shaking."

"The debrief comes first," the Deputy Director General said. "He'll be sanitized until his debrief is complete, that's the way things are done."

"So when do I get to congratulate him?"

"When he's debriefed, and after the debrief there'll be the inquest."

"You are one hell of a killjoy, you know that. You're a real damp rag."

"It's no more or less than Mattie would expect. We debrief him on what's happened, who held

him, and then we hold the inquest as to how he
was in a position that left him so vulnerable. Mattie'll know the form. My view, he's likely to be
scarred for rather a long time, that's just my personal opinion."

"He's done bloody well."

"Of course he has."

"And I'll not have him harassed."

"No question of him being harassed, Director
General, just debriefed."

The Deputy Director General proffered his glass
to young Houghton. He refilled his own glass, and
then the Director General's and the DDG had the
last of the bottle. If the Director General ever
stumbled under a number nineteen omnibus, and
the Deputy Director General moved into his office, that young man would be out on his neck,
damn fast.

The DDG knew the answer, but he still asked
the question. "Have we spoken to Mrs. Furniss?"

Ben Houghton said, "She's been out ever since
the news came through, no answer on either of
her phones. She hasn't been forgotten."

"Well done, Furniss. This calls for a second bottle, I think, Ben. Damned shame that we aborted
the network, but at least we can move Eshraq."

The Deputy Director General frowned, then the
smile caught his face. "Forgive me, I may have

sounded churlish. . . . Good old Mattie . . . he's been terrific. I don't think it would be out of order for you to meet him off the plane if that's what you'd like . . . Director General. Again, forgive me, but I want you to understand that labeling Furniss a hero may well, will almost certainly, be somewhat misplaced. He will have talked, and this whole expedition has cost us a network. Realistically it all adds up to Dunkirk, not to the Normandy landings."

"I'm wagering that he'll have surprised you."

"Also, we may not have aborted our people in time. I can show you the photographs from Kermanshah when the MKO moved out and the Mullahs came back in, if you would like to see them. The hangings were photographed. Mattie getting himself captured was only one inevitable step away from a death sentence for our field agents, even, you may console yourself, if the signals to bring them out had been sent without delay."

"They may well come out, and Mattie may well not have talked, in which case perhaps, who knows, they can go back in again."

"We're not talking about Bond or Biggles, Director General, we are talking about one man against a very sophisticated team of torturers. We are talking about a regime that will do unspeakable things to their own people, and who won't have cared a toss what is done to a foreigner."

The Director General said, "I am at a loss to know what you want."

"I would want to know whether Eshraq is compromised before we let him go back."

"My money is on Mattie, and I'll drink to him."

And among the three of them they killed the second bottle.

It might have been the sense of guilt that had dogged the Station Officer ever since he had left Mattie Furniss unprotected in Van, but he most certainly made wheels turn now. From the moment that the Military Attaché at the embassy had passed on the news of the refugee Furniss falling into the hands of a patrol near the border in Hakkari province, Terence Snow had wheedled facilities from his contacts. An official in the National Intelligence Agency had earned a handsome gift.

Mattie sat beside the road.

He had a paratrooper's smock draped over his shoulders, and a medic had cleaned his feet and then bandaged them, and a colonel had loaned him a stick to help himself along.

The road was the airstrip. It ran along a shallow valley between Yuksekova and Semdinli. The road was widened and reinforced and provided a facility for fixed wing to land in all weathers, night and day, and had been built to further military operations against guerrillas of the Kurdish Workers' party.

There were lights laid out, fired by portable generators, and the area where Mattie sat was illuminated by the headlights of military jeeps and trucks. He sat on an old ammunition box. He was a source of interest to the soldiers, they were crowded behind his back, silent and watchful. They gazed at him with a fascination because they knew that he was an Englishman, and they knew that he had walked out of Iran, and they knew from the medic that the soles of his feet were cut and horribly swollen from beatings. He had lost that sense of exhilaration that had gripped him when he had stood on the ridge looking down into Turkey. He was overcome with exhaustion. Of course he was. He could still see in his mind the picture, cruelly sharp, of the Revolutionary Guards coming down the slope and the boys being escorted at gunpoint up the slope. And there was Charlie, and there were his agents. He wanted only to sleep, and he declined food. The last food he had eaten, before the ridge, had been the boy's food freely shared with him.

The Hercules C-130 came down onto the road,

a noisy and jolting landing, and the reverse thrust was on from the moment the wheels touched. The aircraft taxied toward the knot of soldiers, and when it turned Mattie had to shield his face from the flying grit thrown up from the hard shoulder by the four sets of propellers. The pilot kept the engines idling while Mattie was helped up the rear loading ramp. It was only when the aircrew had fastened his seatbelt for him that he realized that he had forgotten to thank the paratroop officers for their hospitality. He waved as the loading ramp was raised, but he couldn't tell whether they would have seen. On full power the Hercules lifted off, then banked heavily to avoid a shoulder of the Samdi Dag, then climbed for cruising altitude. They were three hours in the air. He was offered orange juice from a paper carton and a boiled sweet to help his ears during the descent to Ankara, otherwise the aircrew ignored him. They were taking him back from a nightmare, returning him to the world that he knew.

They were on a military airfield. They were parked beside an executive eight-seat jet. On the jet were the roundels of red and white and blue.

The Station Officer made no secret of his emotion. He hugged Mattie.

"God, Mr. Furniss, you've done magnificently well . . . and the Director General said for me to tell you . . ." He recited, "Warmest personal congratulations on your epic triumph."

"Very decent of him."

"You came through, Mr. Furniss, I can't tell you how pleased I am, how proud I am to know you."

"Steady, Terence."

"You're a hero, Mr. Furniss."

"Is that what they think?"

"Of course. They had the whole army out trying to catch you and you got clean through them. You beat the bastards."

"Yes. . . . What about my agents?"

"All I know is that the abort signals were sent."

"But are they out?"

"That I don't know. I'm very sorry, Mr. Furniss, but I've been ordered not to attempt any sort of debrief on you. That's the usual form, I suppose."

Snow took Mattie's arm and led him to the steps of the executive jet, and a nurse came down them and took over and grabbed firmly at his arm and hoisted him on board, and when he ducked into the interior there was an RAF corporal to salute him, and through the open door of the cockpit he saw the pilot leaning sideways so that he could wink at Mattie, and give him the thumbs-up. He was strapped into a seat, back to the driver, always the way of RAF flights, and Snow was opposite him, and the nurse was peeling off the bandages from his feet, even before they took off, and there was a look on her face that suggested that no one could be trusted with medical hygiene but herself. The plane had come from Cyprus, from the Sovereign Base at Akrotiri. They roared away into the night, lifted sharply, as if the pilot would have preferred to be at the controls of a Tornado strike plane.

Terence Snow kept his silence. That was the way of things when a Service man came back from captivity. Nothing should interfere with the debrief, standard operating procedure. When the nurse had unwound the bandages of the Turkish army medic, when she had examined the puffed, welted soles of Mattie's feet, then he saw the frown settle on her already stern forehead, and he saw the Station Officer wince. The nurse took off his shirt, tugged it off him, and her lips pursed when she saw the bruising at the base of his shoulders. The swollen feet and the bruised shoulders brought a gentleness to the nurse's fingers, and a gaze of youthful worship from the boy. He could have wiped the gentleness out of her fingers, and the adulation from his eyes. He could have told them that he was a fraud. He could have shouted inside that small aircraft cabin, going home at 550 surface miles per hour, that the Service's hero had cracked and talked.

They put down at the Royal Air Force base at
Brize Norton in the small hours of the morning.

He was helped down from the aircraft and into
a waiting ambulance, a lone vehicle on the huge
airfield. He was driven to the base hospital.

The Director General was waiting for him, and
his hand was pumped.

"Bloody good show, Furniss. Welcome home.
It's a red letter day for all of us."

They ran an electrocardiogram test. They asked
him for a urine sample and then put him in the
lavatory, where there was a bag under the seat because they required his stool to check for typhoid
or dysentery. They X-rayed his feet and his chest
and his shoulders. They did blood tests on him for
signs of vitamin deficiency. They were brisk and
methodical and quick, and Mattie saw that the
form they filled in with the results of the examination and the tests was blank at the top, at the
space provided for the patient's name. Over the
new bandages on his feet they gently fitted plastic
slippers, and they told him he should see his den-
tist within the next week.

The Director General was waiting for him in
the reception area. He beamed at him. Mattie
grinned back, ruefully, like a man embarrassed
by all the attention.

"Well, Furniss, I don't know what the devil

you've been up to since we last saw you. I expect it will make a superlative story and one which the Prime Minister will not want to see published, dear me, no, but you'll dine with us when you're up to snuff, I do look forward to that. Messages of deep esteem from Downing Street. Should have said so at once. And Mrs. Furniss. I expect you'd like to put through a call before you leave here. Snow, arrange that will you? Then you'll be off to Albury for a day or so, Furniss, just to get it all off your chest, but you know all about that."

"My field agents . . . ?"

"Steady down, old chap. You worry about yourself, leave the others to us. Carter's coming down, he'll tell you what you need to know about your agents. It's been a wonderful show, Furniss. I said you would surprise us all. But I mustn't keep you from the telephone. . . . Well done, Furniss, first class. The Service is very proud."

From the road outside they could hear the telephone ringing.

The telephone had rung three times while Parrish and Park had sat in the car.

It was ringing again as the woman drove past them and then swung sharply to pull into the drive at the side of the cottage.

And as soon as she had her door open she was

hearing the telephone ringing, because she was out of her car like a rabbit, and she hadn't bothered to close the car door, and she'd left her keys in the front door.

Park started to move, but Parrish's hand rested lightly on his arm.

"Give her a moment."

It had been Parrish's initiative, the drive to Bibury. No warning, just pitching up at Park's address, waiting for Ann to leave, then coming to the door. Park had already started on the spare-bedroom ceiling, and he hadn't been given time to clean the paint off his fingers.

"We'll just give her time to answer. I'm out of line, but I might just be past caring. It's all too ambiguous for a simple soul like me. I have a direct order that Tango One is not to be lifted, and yet I am ordered to maintain a low-level surveillance on him—I don't know what that adds to. . . . I am told that we will get no help in locating Mr. Matthew Furniss but the ACIO is not telling me that I cannot approach Furniss. If it adds up to anything it is that on the top floor of the Lane they haven't a clue what we're supposed to be doing. I'm pushing my luck, David, because I don't appreciate being pissed on. So, if I get my wrist slapped, and you get your butt kicked, then it's all in a good cause. . . . Come on."

They stepped from the car.

"I'll do the talking," Parrish said. "You can give her the keys."

He smiled, a real hangman's smile. He reached for his wallet in his inside pocket. When he knocked on the door he had the wallet open so that his identification card was visible.

She came to the door.

She was radiant.

Park handed her the keys, and Parrish showed the ID and she grinned at the keys, like a small girl.

"Mrs. Furniss?"

"Thrilling, isn't it? Do come in. It's quite wonderful. I suppose they sent you down when I wasn't answering the phone. I've been at my elder daughter's. . . . You've come all the way from Century, a wasted journey? You'll have a cup of coffee before you go, of course you will. I suppose really I should be opening the champagne, the DG said that he opened champagne last night. He said the whole Service was proud of Mattie, that's a splendid thing to have said of your husband . . ."

"When will Mr. Furniss be home?"

"You will have coffee, I'm so excited, do come inside . . ." She had stepped aside, then stopped, spun. "You should know when he's coming home."

Parrish asked calmly, "Did you look at my ID?"

"You're from Century, yes?"

"Customs and Excise, ma'am, Investigation Division."

Her voice whispered, "Not Century?"

"My name is William Parrish, and I am investigating heroin trafficking from Iran. My colleague here is Mr. Park."

Her hand was across her mouth. "I thought you were from my husband's office." She stiffened. "What did you say you want?"

"I'd like to know when I can interview your husband."

"What about?"

"In connection with a guarantee given by your husband to a man now under investigation."

She barred their path. "We don't know anyone like that."

"Your husband knows a Charles Eshraq, Mrs. Furniss. It's about Eshraq, and your husband standing guarantee to him that we've called."

She stared up from her eyeline that was level with the knot of Parrish's tie. "Have you been through Century?"

"I don't have to go through anyone, Mrs. Furniss."

"Do you know who my husband is?"

Park could have smiled. Parrish wasn't smiling.

He would be later, right now he had his undertaker's calm.

"Your husband is the guarantor of a heroin trafficker, Mrs. Furniss."

"My husband is a senior civil servant."

"And I serve my country too, Mrs. Furniss, by fighting the importers of heroin. I don't know what threat your husband safeguards us from, but where I work the threat of heroin coming into the UK is taken pretty seriously."

She was shrill. "You come here, you barge into my house, you make preposterous allegations about a boy who is virtually a son to us, on the morning that my husband has just returned home after breaking out of an Iranian torture jail."

"So he's not here at present?"

"No, he isn't here. I should think he will be in the hospital for a long time. But if he were here, Mr. Parrish, you would be terribly sorry you had had the disgraceful manners to break into this house. . . ."

Parrish said, "Maybe it's not the best time . . ."

She went to the hall table. She picked up the telephone. She dialed fast.

Her voice was clear, brittle. "This is Harriet Furniss, Matthew Furniss's wife. I want to speak to the Director General . . ."

Park said, "Come on, you disgraceful person, time we barged out."

They left her. When they were at the gate they heard her voice rise in anguished complaint. They reached the car.

"Shall I serve my country and drive?"

"I tell you what, Keeper, that wasn't one of my happiest initiatives, but we did shake the nest."

He had spoken to the Prime Minister, and the Prime Minister had asked after Mattie Furniss and said he must be a quite remarkable man, and the DG bathed in reflected glory. He looked forward rather keenly to the first of the debrief papers that would be coming through in a couple of days, and he would certainly send a digest across to Downing Street. Now he was making a tour, being seen, as he put it to Houghton.

They were in that section of the third floor occupied by Assistance (photographic) when he was passed a telephone by Ben Houghton. For a moment he was puzzled. He had spoken to the woman at breakfast time.

He listened.

"No, no, Mrs. Furniss, you were quite right to reach me . . . intolerable behavior. Rest assured, Mrs. Furniss, you won't be troubled again."

The four wooden packing cases and the two cardboard boxes were the first items to be loaded into the container. The lorry had backed into Herbert Stone's driveway. He gave the driver a manifest for the packing cases that listed machine parts for agricultural equipment. Later the container would be filled with more machine parts for tractors and refrigeration units. The haulage company was a regular carrier of machine parts to Turkey.

When the lorry had left he went inside his house, and into the quiet of his work room. He telephoned the number Charlie Eshraq had left him and told him that the soap was on its way, and he gave him the name of a contact, and where he should go and when.

"I tell you, Bill, it wasn't sensible behavior."

"If you want London to become like Amsterdam, Chief, then sensible behavior would be the order of the day."

"And I don't want a press office handout."

"My guys have worked their balls off, we just don't like to see it go down the plughole."

Parrish had been at the Lane for one and a half years longer than the Chief Investigation Officer, and for two and a half years longer than the

ACIO. He rarely spoke his mind. When he did he could get away with murder.

The ACIO said, "If you'd come to us first, Bill, cleared it with us . . ."

"You wouldn't have let me go."

The CIO was hunched forward in his chair, elbows on his desk. "There's another way of looking at it, Bill. We are stretched so damn thin that in effect we are a fraud. We intercept a minute proportion of what's brought in. I know that, you know that. . . . When you are losing the battle, as we are, then we need friends where friends matter . . ."

"You have to go for the throats of the bastards and hang on."

"It's a great world that you live in, Bill, and it's not a world I see much of across this desk."

"So, who are the friends we need?"

"They're the high and the mighty . . . and right now they're peeved with you."

"I just gave the nest a little shake."

"Very self-indulgent of you, Bill, and no help to me, because I am summoned to a meeting this afternoon with the faceless wonders at Century House. What do I tell them, Bill?"

"To get fucked."

"But my world isn't your world, more's the pity, and I'm looking for friends. . . . I have one man

in Karachi, one DLO on his ownsome, and when
he goes up to the northwest frontier, who escorts
him? The spook escorts him and drives the Land-
Rover. Why does my DLO ride in the spook's
Land-Rover? He rides in it because I don't have
the funds to provide a Land-Rover of our own. I
have one DLO in Cyprus, and how does one man
get to know what's coming out of Jounieh, how
does he know what's sailing from any Lebanese
port? Cyprus is awash with spooks. . . . I am trying
to cultivate friends, Bill, not shake the nest and
telling them to get fucked."

"I promised Park, and he's the best I have, that
I wouldn't let your friends the faceless wonders
stand in our way."

"Then you opened your big mouth too wide. Tell
us about your Keeper, Bill. We begin to hear quite
a lot about Master Park. Is he ready for a move
upward, do you think?"

"We're going to have a celebrity on our hands,"
the Director General mused.

"How so?"

"I anticipate great mileage out of Furniss.
They'll want him at Langley. The Germans'll
want him, and I dare say even the French will recognize that they could learn a thing or two."

The Deputy Director General said coolly, "I'd

put that out of your mind for a start. If I were in this office, I would make double damn certain that no one outside this building gets to know that we allowed a Desk Head to plod about on a hostile frontier without a semblance of security. It'll get out sooner or later, of course. As like as not Tehran will be drafting a press release even as we sit here: 'Why We Let British Spy Go,' and, by the way, not a few people will be wondering already."

The Director General scowled. "I don't mind telling you that I told Furniss that the whole Service was proud of him."

"Not clever . . . I'm going to run a fine-tooth comb over Terence Snow. The report on how Mattie came to get himself kidnapped is pretty conclusive. Indeed, I doubt that he has any sort of future here. He'll have to go back to Ankara in the short term. There may just be a way he can be useful to us in the short term."

"You're a hard man."

"I am what the job requires."

The snort of the Director General, "And Furniss, has he a future?"

"Very probably not, I am afraid."

The Deputy Director General reported that a man had been sent down to Bibury with the instruction to break the bones of any Customs Investigation creature who came within a hundred yards of the Furniss cottage, and he said that he would be at the Director General's side at the meeting with the Customs hierarchy.

"What sort of people will they be?"

"I expect you'll be able to charm them, Director General. Think of them as glorified traffic wardens."

He had no doubt that his life depended upon the success with which he stood his ground against the inquisition of the clerics.

Ranged on the far side of the table to him were four of them. They were the power and the glory of the Revolution of today, and once he would have called them fanatics and bigots. They were the ones who had been to *maktab* where the Mullahs taught the Koran to boys aged four, and then they had become the *talabeh,* who were the seekers after truth as handed down from the wisdom of the Ayatollahs. They had taken child brides because it stated in the book that a girl should not experience her first bleeding at her parents' home. They had spent time in the holy city of Qom. It was the failure of the SAVAK that these creatures still existed. They were his masters. He claimed that he had already bled the British spymaster dry before his escape. He told them of the young Eshraq, and they were quiet as he explained the mission of Eshraq, heading back toward Iran, and they heard of the precautions that were in hand to prevent the traitor crossing over the frontier with armor-piercing missiles. He said that Eshraq's first target was the Mullah who sat immediately in front of him. He saw the way that the others turned sharply to the one among them who had been singled for attack, and he told them that he, himself, was the target that would follow.

For more than an hour and a half he defended himself, and at the end he told them of his arrangements to prevent Eshraq crossing the border.

It was implicit in his argument that if he were removed, if he were sent to Evin, then the shield in front of his masters would have been dismantled.

The life of Charlie Eshraq would safeguard the investigator's life. Nothing more, nothing less.

He had flown back to Tehran from the Gulf that morning to resume work at the new power station to the west of the city.

He browsed in the bazaar. He was on the Bazar e Abbas Abad, among the carpet shops.

He paused. He could not linger for more than a few seconds. In front of him were the heavy steel shutters, and fastening them to the concrete paving was a powerful padlock. His eye caught that of the man who stood in front of the next cavern of carpets, open—and the man ducked back into his shop. There was no sign, no explanation of why this one business should be shut. If there had been illness, if there had been bereavement, then he would have expected an explanation from the merchant's neighbor.

He walked on. He walked into the warmth of the sunlight beyond the bazaar's alleys. He took a taxi back to his hotel, and in his basin he burned the message that he had been paid to carry.

Henry was late getting down to Albury.

Everyone who knew Henry Carter, which wasn't many, had told him that he should dump the Morris 1000 Estate on the nearest corporation tip and failing that at the side of any road, and buy something reliable. Trouble again with the carburetor.

He was late getting down to Albury, and Mattie had already arrived, and the men who had brought him from Brize Norton were fretting to be on their way. He ignored the show of annoyance as he struggled through the front door with his bag and his Wellington boots and two weatherproof coats, binoculars, camera with a long lens, and tape recorder. Typical of the sort of youngster they recruited into the Service now, neither of them offered to help, and they scarcely bothered to report that Mattie was in one piece, sound asleep now, before they were off.

There weren't many of them, the old brigade, left at Century these days, and it was obvious that the Director General would have wanted one of the long servers to be down at Albury to take Mattie's debrief. He would not have called himself a friend of Mattie Furniss, rather a colleague.

He looked back through the front door. He had heard the call. He was festooned with his gear. He saw the bird. *Picus Viridis.* The green woodpecker was halfway up a dead elm across the lawn. There would be gaps in the debrief for him to set his camera on a tripod, and to rig his microphone. He went inside. It would be something of a reunion for him, coming back to the country house in the woodland of the Surrey hills. Mrs. Ferguson greeted him. She was rather a dear woman, the housekeeper, and there had been a time when he had actually thought of making a proposal of marriage to her, but that was quite a long time ago and he had been at the house for weeks on end. It was her cooking that had settled it. It was awful. She pecked his cheek. He saw George behind her, hovering at the kitchen door. George touched his cap. He wore a cap always now, since the baldness had set in, wore it even in the house. A loyal fellow, George, but lazy, and why not, with so little to do. Through the kitchen he could see that the outside door was closed, and the door shook and there was a ferocious scratching from the far side of it.

"Am I not to be greeted by old 'Rotten'?"

George grinned. "Your gentleman doesn't like dogs, and he certainly doesn't like Rottweilers."

Not many did. Henry had a fear of some men, and of most women, but of no animal, not even an animal that weighed more than a hundred pounds and was famously unpredictable.

"Then make sure the brute's kept clear of him."

He had to smile. . . . Wouldn't do for Mattie Furniss to have fought his way out of an Iranian prison only to find himself savaged by the safe house Rottweiler. He looked around him. He could see the glimmer of fresh paint on the woodwork and the carpet in the hall had been cleaned. Things were looking up.

"Where is he?"

"He's just come down. Been asleep ever since he got here. He's in the library."

He left George to carry the bag and his kit upstairs. He hoped that he would have his usual room, the one that overlooked the vegetable garden where the songbirds gathered to feed off the groundsel and dandelion seeds.

He walked through to the library. His steps echoed on the bare board floor. It had been a bare board floor since the pipes had burst in the freeze of three winters before and the carpets had been ruined and not replaced. He opened the door. He was almost obsequious. He went on tiptoe into the room. To call the room the library was somewhat overstating the case. Of course, there were books on the shelves, but not many, and few of them would have held anyone's interest. The books had been a job lot when a local house had been cleared out on the death of a maiden lady without surviving relations.

Mattie was in a chair by the empty hearth.

"Please, don't get up, Mattie."

"Must have just nodded off."

"You deserve a very long rest. . . . I mean, what a change . . . where were you, Mattie, twenty-four hours ago?"

"Walking out of Iran, I suppose. It's pretty strange."

"You've spoken to Mrs. Furniss?"

"Had a few words with her, thank you. Woke her up at first light, poor thing, but she was in good form. . . . Flapping a bit, but don't they all?"

"There's grand news through from the medics. A very good bill of health, no bugs."

"I just feel a bit shaken."

Henry looked into Mattie's face. The man was completely shattered.

"I'll tell you something for nothing, Mattie. . . . In twenty years' time, when the DG's been forgotten, when no one at Century will know my name, they'll still talk about 'Dolphin's run.' Dolphin's run out of Iran is going to go into the history of the Service."

"That's very decent of you, Henry."

"Don't thank me, you did it. The fact is that the Service is buzzing with collective pride. You have given us all, down to the tea ladies, one hell of a lift."

He saw Mattie drop his eyes. Perhaps, he had been over the top, but he knew the psychology of the debrief, and the psychology said that an agent back from abroad, where he'd had a rough time, needed praise, reassurance. A colleague of Henry's, with a brood of children, had once likened the trauma of return to a woman's postnatal depression. Henry couldn't comment on that, but he thought he knew what the colleague had meant. He had told the Deputy Director General when he had been given his marching orders, before finding that his carburetor was playing up, that he would take it gently. It would have been scandalous to have taken it otherwise, after a man had been tortured and broken . . . oh yes, the DDG had been most sure that Mattie would have been broken.

"Thanks, Henry."

"Well, you know the form. We'll hammer through this over the next few days, and then we'll get you back home. What you've been through is going to be the basis of study and teaching, no doubt, at the fort for the next decade. . . . Shall we get down to things sometime this evening? Mattie, we're all very, very excited by what you achieved."

"I think I'd like to be outside for a bit. Can't walk too comfortably just yet, perhaps I'll sit in the garden. Can you keep that ghastly dog at bay?"

"By all means. I'll ask George to put him in the kennel. And I'll see if Mrs. Ferguson can find us something rather special to drink this evening. I don't think we can hold out much hope for the meal itself."

Chapter ✤ 17

A good early start, because Henry Carter thought that Mattie would feel stronger at the beginning of the day. They ate breakfast of tepid scrambled eggs and cold toast. They discussed the possible makeup of the team for the first test. They had a chuckle over the new switch in the Socialists' defense policy. Henry told Mattie about Stephen Dugdale from Library who had been laid low last week with thrombosis. It was a good room, the old dining room, fine sideboards, and a glasses cabinet, and a carving table, and the main table could have seated twelve in comfort. The worst thing about eating in the dining room and at the big table, in Carter's opinion, was that Mrs. Ferguson having polished the table then insisted that it be covered with a sea of clear polythene.

"Shall we make a start then, Mattie?"

"Why not?"

He settled in the chair by the fireplace. Across the hearth rug from him Carter was fiddling with a cassette player. It was the sort of cassette player that Harriet had bought the girls when they were teenagers. He saw the spools begin to move on the cassette player. He could see the investigator, he could see the cellar walls, he could see the bed and the leather thongs, he could see the hooks on the wall, he could see the length of electrical flex wire . . .

"How long is this going to take?"

"Hard to say, Mattie. Depends on what you've got to tell me. My immediate target is to get home."

"Goes without saying. . . . Where shall we begin? Shall we start in Van?"

Mattie told the tape recorder everything about the way the attack on his car had been carried out. He felt uncomfortable describing his carelessness. Henry looked rather schoolmarmish but didn't interrupt. Mattie's account was perfectly lucid. He seemed to Henry to take pleasure in the clarity of the narrative, in the orderly compilation of details that would one day be of value at the fort. At eleven Mrs. Ferguson knocked and came in with coffee and a packet of chocolate digestives. Mattie stood at the window until Henry said, "This house they drove you to?"

"I was blindfolded when we got there, I didn't see it. When I went out of it then it was dark."

"Tell me what you can about the house."

"They didn't take me on a tour, they weren't trying to sell it me."

He saw the puzzle at Henry's forehead. Stupid thing to have said. . . .

"Is there a problem, Mattie?"

"I'm sorry—of course, there's a problem. You are asking me to recall a house where I was tortured, where others have been put to death."

"We'll just take it slowly, that way it won't be so painful. You've nothing to be ashamed of, Mattie."

"Ashamed?" He spoke in Henry's soft voice. He rolled the word. "Ashamed?" Mattie spat the word back at him.

The conciliatory raising of the hands. "Don't misunderstand me, Mattie."

"Why should I be ashamed?"

"Well, we've been working on the assumption . . ."

"What assumption?"

"We had to assume that you had been taken by agents of the Iranian regime, and that of course you would be interrogated, and in due course that you would be, well, broken or killed. . . . That was a reasonable assumption, Mattie."

"Reasonable?"

"You'd have made the same assumption, Mattie, of course you would."

"And at what stage did you decide that Mattie Furniss would have been broken?"

Henry squirmed. "I don't know anything about pain."

"How could you?"

"Myself, I wouldn't have lasted a day, perhaps not even a morning. I think just the knowledge of what was going to be done to me would have been enough to tip me into the confessional. You shouldn't feel bad about it, Mattie."

"So, I was written off?"

"Not by the Director General. I am afraid almost everyone else did."

"Most touching faith you had in me. And did you shake the dust off my obituary? Had you booked St. Martin's for a memorial? Tell me, Henry, who was going to give the address?"

"Come on, Mattie, this isn't like you. You've been on this side of the fence. You know what the form is."

"It's just abominable, Henry, to realize that Century believes a senior officer of the Service will cave in at the end of the first day, like some damn Girl Guide—I'm flattered . . ."

"We made our assumption, we aborted the field agents."

A sharpness in Mattie's voice, "They're out?"

"We aborted them, they're not out yet."

Mattie sat upright in his chair, his chest heaved. There were still the pain pangs deep in his chest. "You assumed that I would be broken within twenty-four hours, can I assume that you aborted as soon as I went missing? How can it be that two weeks later the agents are not out?"

"It was felt, I believe, that aborting a very precious network was a big step, takes years to rebuild. It took them a little time to get to the sticking point. Part of it was that the DG convinced himself that you would never talk. All sorts of waffle about Furniss of the old school. Frankly, I don't think he knows the first thing about interrogation. Anyway wiser heads prevailed, as they say, and the messages were sent, but the agents are not yet out . . ."

"Christ . . ."

Mattie stood. Dreadful pain in his face. Pain from his feet that were bandaged and inside bedroom slippers that would otherwise have been three sizes too large.

"It wasn't easy, knowing nothing, hearing nothing."

A cold whip in Mattie's voice. "I clung on, I went through hell—yes, hell, Henry, and at Century you couldn't get your fucking act together . . . it makes me sick to think of it."

"I have the impression that there was more interest, more interest even than in the safety of the field agents, in whether Eshraq was compromised . . ."

Mattie swung his shoulders. His eyes fixed on Henry. "What do you know about Eshraq?"

"That he is of very considerable importance."

"While I was away my safe was rifled, yes?"

"Rifled? No, Mattie, that is unreasonable. Of course we went through your safe. We had to know about Eshraq. . . ." Henry paused. The silence weighed. He looked up at Mattie. There was the attempt at kindness, and understanding, and friendship. "I gather that Charlie Eshraq is not just important for this potential in the field, but also that he is very close to your family."

"So my safe was gutted."

"Mattie, please . . . we had to know everything about the boy, and now we have to know whether he is compromised."

"So you burrow about in my private files and you find that he is close to my family, is that it?"

"That's right."

"Here you assumed that I would talk to my torturers about a young man who is like a son to me?"

"I'm sorry, Mattie, that has been our assumption."

"Your assumption, but not the Director General's?"

"Correct."

"But all the rest of you?"

"The Director General said he thought that you would go to the grave before you named names."

"You, Henry, what do you think?"

"I've seen the medical reports. I know the extent of your injuries. I have an idea of what was done to you. To have escaped after all that argues a phenomenal constitution, phenomenal courage."

"I killed three men getting away. I broke the neck of one, I strangled one, I drove one down."

"If there were doubters, Mattie, they will obviously keep their doubts to themselves. I didn't know that, of course, and I am horrified to hear it. One has no idea what one may be capable of *in extremis*."

"Am I capable of betraying Charlie, that's what you are asking yourself."

"To me, Mattie, God's truth, you are one of the finest men that I have known in my lifetime with the Service, but no one, no one in the world, is capable of withstanding torture indefinitely. You know that and nobody in the Service is holding it against you. Everyone thinks it was wrong to send you—my God, I hope the DG doesn't listen to this tape—and, well, to tell you the truth, quite a few people think you were a fair old chump to be gallivanting about on your own near the border. That's what comes of being an archaeologist, I suppose."

Mattie smiled at the irony. He walked to the window. He did not need to hold on to the chair backs. He walked as if there were no pain in his feet, as if he could straighten his back and there were no pain in his chest. He stared out. There was a brisk sunshine lighting the lawn.

"I may have named the field agents, I can't be certain. There were times that I was unconscious, I might have been delirious. There were times when I thought I was dead and certainly prayed I would be. But that was, oh Christ, after days of agony. If the agents were not aborted immediately then I won't accept the blame for that. . . ."

"And Eshraq, did you name Eshraq?"

The dog was barking in the kitchen, frustrated

at being denied the run of the house. Mattie turned, stared levelly across the hearth rug at Henry.

"No, Henry, I couldn't have done that. I'd much sooner be dead than have done that."

"Mattie, truly, I take my hat off to you."

The lorry began the journey from the north of England to the port of Dover midday Saturday, and observed strictly the speed limits set for it. The driver would not approach the Customs checks at Dover until the evening of the following day. Lorry movement through the port of Dover was always heaviest on a Sunday night, when the drivers were jockeying to get a good start on the Monday morning on the through routes across Europe. The volume of traffic on the Sunday night sailings dictated that the Customs checks on outgoing cargo were lightest. And the early summer was a good time, also, for the sale of machine parts. The ferries' vehicle decks would be jammed with both commercial and holiday traffic. The chances of the lorry's cargo being searched, of the containers being stripped out right down to the four wooden packing cases, were very slight. The haulage company also took care to check whether there was any form of tail on the consignment. The lorry had been followed away from the ware-

house at the loading depot by a car that checked
to see whether it was under surveillance. The car
varied the distance between itself and the lorry;
at times it was a mile back, and then it would
speed up and catch the lorry. The purpose of this
was to pass the cars traveling in the wake of the
lorry, and to look for the telltale evidence of men
using radios in the cars, or vehicles that were too
long in the slow lanes.

It was a wasted exercise.

The Investigation Division had no tail on the
lorry.

Not yet six o'clock and she had already had her
bath. She was at her dressing table. She could
hear him in the next room, working at the final
touches. It was the trip out with Bill Parrish that
had set him behind. He hadn't told her where they
had gone, and she hadn't asked. He might not
have told her where he'd been, what he'd done,
with Bill Parrish, but at least when he had returned he had peeled out of his work clothes and
put on the old jeans and the sweat shirt and
headed back to his decorating. He was pretty
quiet, had been ever since he'd come back from
the north of England, and she was almost sorry
for him. More vulnerable than she'd ever known
him. She thought he must have been wanting to

please her, because he had set out to decorate the spare bedroom. Not that David would ever have admitted to a living soul, let alone his wife, that his case was up the river and no punt. She didn't care what he said. She'd liked coming home from work and finding the flat smelling of paint and wallpaper paste, it was a big change in her experience, that her husband had gone down to the DIY and had managed the best part of a week without referring to Bogotá or the Medellin cartel.

"Who am I going to meet there?" she called out.

"A gang of complete morons."

She yelled, and she was laughing, "Will it all be shop talk?"

"Absolutely. Blokes all up at the bar, wives sitting down by the band."

"You'll dance with me?"

"Then you'd better wear boots."

He came into the bedroom. She could scent the paint on his hands that were on her shoulders. Christ, and she wanted them to be happy. Why couldn't they be happy? In the mirror, his face looked as though the light had gone from him. Her David, the Lane's Keeper, so crushed. It was a fast thought, she wondered if she didn't prefer him when he was bloody minded and confident and putting the world into its proper order.

He bent and he kissed her neck, and he was hesitant. She took his hands from her shoulders and she put them inside her dressing gown, and she held them tight against her.

"I love you, and I'm just going to dance with you."

She felt his body shaking against her back and the trembling of his hands.

Past six o'clock, and a Saturday evening, and the magistrate sat at his bench in a yellow pullover, and his check trousers were hidden under the desk top.

The convening of the court on that day of the week, and at that time of day, guaranteed that the public gallery and the press seats would be empty.

Parrish, in his work suit, stood in the witness box.

"I understand you correctly, Mr. Parrish? You have no objection to bail?"

Boot-faced, boot-voiced. "No objection, sir."

"In spite of the nature of the charges?"

"I have no objections to bail, sir."

"And the application for the return of the passport?"

"I have no objection to the passport being returned, sir."

"You have no fear of the defendant going abroad and not surrendering his bail?"

"No fears, sir."

"What sort of figure of bail are you suggesting, Mr. Parrish?"

"Two sureties, sir. Two thousand pounds each would be my suggestion, sir."

The magistrate shook his head. It was as though he had now seen everything, heard everything. Day in and day out the police sniped at the magistrates for their willingness to grant bail. There could be many reasons and he was not going to waste time speculating on them. If that's what the Investigation Division wanted, that's what they wanted. What he wanted was to get back to the golf club. He granted bail on two sureties of two thousand pounds.

The flight had been delayed, technical problems. The problems were resolved a few minutes after Leroy Winston Manvers and his common-law wife and children boarded the British Airways 747 to Jamaica.

When he'd seen the bird up, then Bill Parrish drove home to change for the dance.

The detective thought that Darren Cole was very pale, and his fingers were nicotine-stained because that was the only fix he was getting on remand.

He resented being pulled from home on a Saturday evening and told to drive halfway across the county. He wasn't in the mood for hanging about.

"You're coming out, Darren. Tomorrow morning, eight o'clock, you're walking out. The charges against you will not be pressed, but they will be held in reserve. The charges can be reactivated if you should be so silly as to open your dumb little mouth to any scribbler, anyone else for that matter. I wouldn't come home if I were you. You should stay away from my patch. There are people who know that you grassed and if they know where to find you then they will most certainly come looking. Take the wife and the kids and take a very long bus ride, Darren, and stay safe. Have you got me, young 'un?"

The detective left the necessary paperwork with the Assistant Governor. He could be phlegmatic. He reckoned that letting out young Darren Cole would save three, four days of court time. He was not concerned with the morality of letting out a proven narcotics pusher. If his Chief Constable could cope with the morality then there was no way that a detective was going to get out his worry beads.

He would have liked to know why Cole was being given the heave, but he doubted if he ever would.

"Who was it, George?"

Libby Barnes called from her dressing room. She sat in front of the mirror in her underclothes and housecoat, and she worked with the brush at applying the eye shadow.

"It was Piper Mother."

"On a Saturday evening? Is it something serious?"

"Called about Lucy. . . . I'm not supposed to tell you this, but you've the right to know. I've lost, dear. I wouldn't want you to think that I lost without a fight, but I've lost, and that's the long and the short of it."

The photograph was in front of his wife, at the right side of the dressing-table mirror. A photograph of when Lucy was sixteen, and sweet. A happy teenager in a Corfu café. The photograph had been taken the last time they had been together as a family, before Lucy had started her problem.

"What do you mean, you lost?"

"The boy who pushed to Lucy has been freed from remand in prison. He will not go to trial. The man who supplied the pusher will also not face charges and has been allowed to leave the country. The importer of those drugs, who has been under intense Customs and Excise investigation, will not be arrested . . ."

"And you've swallowed that?"

"Not lying down. . . . It's for the best, Libby. A trial would have been awful, three trials would have been quite hideous . . . all those bloody journalists at the front door . . . perhaps it's best to forget."

Libby Barnes whispered, "And best for your career."

She held the photograph tight against her chest and her tears made a mockery of the work at her eyes.

"Piper Mother did say that, yes."

Charlie watched her go, and he was left on the pavement where the streets merged into Piccadilly. He watched her through the traffic and he saw the hips swing, and he saw that her shoulders were well back, and once he saw her shake the long hair free of her collar and the hair tossed and caught in the last of the sun.

First he lost her behind a bus that was caught at the lights, and then she was gone. She had been carrying her bag loosely against her knee. She was going home with her new dress, because Polly Venables and Charlie Eshraq were going nowhere. She'd go back to Mahmood Shabro on Monday morning, and she'd try to forget Charlie

Eshraq because he had told her that he was going back to Iran.

He turned. The other girl was still close to him. She was leaning against the shop doorway, and she wasn't even bothering to pretend. The car was behind her. All the time that he had been walking with Polly, the girl had been close to him, and the car had been hugging the curb. She was a dumpy little thing, and he thought they must have cut her hair with garden clippers, and he didn't understand why she wore an anorak when it was almost summer.

He walked up to her.

"I'm going to have a drink, April lady. Would you join me?"

Token snarled back at him. "Piss off."

The truck driver was Turkish and he drove his Daf vehicle with the choke out so that the engine seemed to race, as if on its last legs. He maneuvered into the narrow cul-de-sac and then killed the engine in front of the battered sheet-metal gates. When the engine was off, when he could look around him, there came to him the curious quiet of the repair yard. From his cab he could see over the wall and into the yard. No work there, no activity. He had been told they worked late into the evening.

There was a child watching him from against the wall, chewing at an apple.

The Turk called to the child. He asked where was the engineer.

The child scowled at him. The child shouted back the one word.

"Pasdaran."

Choke in, the engine running smoothly, the driver backed his truck out of the cul-de-sac. He drove at speed out of Tabriz, chewing and chewing and eventually swallowing the message that had been taped against the skin of his belly.

She had heard of all of them, heard their names, but she had never before been able to put faces to the names.

She knew them by their actual names and by their codenames too, because sometimes David referred to them at home by one and sometimes by the other.

If she had been honest, and she might be honest later when they were home, and that depended on how much she had drunk, then she might have said that she didn't think that much of them. There wasn't much that was special about any of them. On Ann's table were some of the names she knew best. There was dear old Bill, unusually quiet, and his wife who had not yet closed her mouth. There was Peter Foster, whose collar was too tight, and whose wife hadn't stopped talking about the standard of teaching at infant and primary school level since they sat down. There was Duggie Williams, who was Harlech, and he was in a foul mood because, according to David, he had been stood up. Mrs. Parrish was talking about the holiday they were going to take in Lanzarote. Bill wasn't saying much, and looked as though he had had a death in the family, and Foster seemed as if he might choke. But she rather liked Harlech. She thought that Harlech might just be the pick of them, and she thought that the girl who had stood him up must be just a bit dumb. The music had started, the band had begun, but the floor was still empty, and there was no way she would get David onto his feet before there was quite a throng. The glasses were filling the table. The raffle tickets had been round, and they would be drawn, and then there would be the buffet supper, and after that she might get David onto the floor.

Duggie Williams brought her a drink and changed places with Maureen Foster to sit next to her.

"You must be half bored out of your knickers."

"I beg your pardon."

"How did Keeper get you to come along?"

"It was I that said we were coming."

"You must be off your pretty head."

"Perhaps I just wanted to have a look at you all."

"Then it's a bloody miracle you haven't run away already . . . I'm Harlech."

"I know. I'm Ann."

Bill had started talking. Ann couldn't hear what he was saying, but David was leaning away from her to listen.

"We're not in the best of form."

She said drily, "I gathered."

"We've lost a nice juicy one."

"He told me a bit."

"We got fucked up—excuse me—your man, trouble with him is that he cares."

"Don't you?"

He had strong eyes. When she looked at Harlech then it was into his eyes. She had nowhere else to look. It was only from the side of her eye that she saw Bill's empty chair.

"Not a lot bothers me, that's because of where I used to work. I used to be at Heathrow . . . ."

"So was David."

". . . He was front of house . . . me, I was backstage. I was on the stuffers and swallowers drill. You know what that is? 'Course, you don't. Nobody tells a nice girl about swallowers and stuffers. . . . I used to be on the duty that checks

the daily in from Lagos—I never found anything
else that the Nigerians were good at, but, Christ,
they can stuff and swallow. Do you want to know
all this? You do? Well, the women stuff the scag
up their fannies, and the men stuff it up their
arses, and they both swallow it. Are you with me?
They put it in condoms and they stuff it up and
they swallow it down. We have a special block for
the suspects, and that's where I used to work before I came to ID. We shove them in a cell, and
we sit and watch them, and we feed them on good
old baked beans, and we wait. God, do we wait. . . .
Has to go through, law of nature. Everything has
to come out except from where the women stuff
theirs, but that's a job for the ladies. You have to
be like a hawk, watching them, and every time
they go in then it's out with the plastic bag and
on with the rubber gloves and time for a good old
search around. They train by swallowing grapes,
and they dip the condoms in syrup so they travel
more comfortably, and they use something called
Lomotil, because that's a binder. You know, once
we had a flight in from Lagos and we pulled in
thirteen, and we had every bog in action that we
could lay our hands on. We were swamped, and
just as well, because half of them were positive.
When you've sat, hours and hours, watching guys

of great sensitivity an engineer from Tabriz and a carpet merchant from Tehran.

He had a tail on an official of the harbor-master's office in Bandar Abbas, to see where the man would run, what else could be trawled.

He had the plan in his mind of the show trial at which confessions would be made. Confessions, their extraction and their presentation in court, were the great pride of the investigator. A confession was the closing of a book, it was the finishing of the weaving of a carpet, it was orderliness. The confessions of the engineer and the carpet merchant were near to being in place, and that of the official in the harbormaster's office would follow when he was ready to receive it.

Oh that evening, late, in the office of the Mullah, he reported on all these matters, and he received permission to continue the surveillance in Bandar Abbas. Later, sipping freshly pressed fruit juice, he talked of Charlie Eshraq. He was very frank, he kept back nothing.

"Mattie, I don't want to go on about this, not all night, but you are quite sure?"

"I'm getting very tired, Henry."

"The investigator was a professional, yes?"

"Old SAVAK man, knew what he was at."

"And it went on being pretty violent?"

"Henry, if you knew how ridiculous you sounded . . . 'pretty violent' for Christ's sake. If you've got any heavy-duty flex in the garage here we'll see, if you like, if we can elaborate the distinctions. Violent, pretty violent, or we'll try twelve hours of continuous violence and see what that becomes. Or haven't we been through this all before . . ."

"Yes, Mattie, yes, we have. . . . It's so important that we are absolutely clear on this. Your investigator is a SAVAK man, the worst of the breed, and violence was used against you, quite horrifying violence, on and on. . . ."

"How many times do you have to be told, Henry? I did not name Charlie Eshraq."

"Easy, old chap."

"It is not easy to break out of Iran and then to come home to an inquisition."

"Quite right, point taken. Mattie, there were times that you fainted, other times when you were semiconscious. When you were really groggy, could you have named him then?"

The room was shadowed and dingy. The light came from a ceiling triple, but one of the bulbs had popped early in the evening and George had stated that he had no replacements and would not be able to buy more bulbs until Monday. The furniture was old but lacking in quality, a Sotheby's man wouldn't have given the room a second glance, not as good a room as the dining room.

"When you're in a place like that, Henry, you cling to anything that's sacred. You hold on to your family, to your Service, your country, your God if you have one. Any damned thing that is important in your life you hold on to. When the pain's so bloody awful, the only things you can hold to are the kernels of your life. You have that feeling that if you broke, you would be giving them all that is sacred to you."

"I just have to be sure, that I understand you."

And it was such a damn shame. . . . He thought that old Henry, tatty old Henry Carter, who wouldn't have known a thumb screw from a bottle opener, might just be a better interrogator than the investigator in Tabriz.

Park drove, and Parrish was beside him with the directions written on a sheet of paper. He'd asked where they were going, and Bill had said that the building was called Century House. He'd asked why they were going there, and Bill said it was because the Chief had told him to present himself with Keeper in tow. No point in any more questions, because Bill hadn't any more answers.

They came down the Albert Embankment, and

the tower blocks loomed against the night skyline.
There was only one block alive with light.

Parrish waved for Park to pull into the forecourt. The Chief Investigation Officer was on the
steps, and looking at his watch, and the ACIO was
beside him, and then coming forward to organize
the parking space. They climbed from the car, and
Park locked the doors. They walked toward the
main entrance. He saw a small brass plate for
Century House.

The Chief Investigation Officer nodded curtly at
Parrish then moved to stand in front of Park.

"Inside, your opinion isn't wanted, you just listen."

They were offered drinks, and on behalf of all
of them the Chief declined.

Not an evening for social pleasantries, Park
thought, just an evening for learning the realities
of power.

He stood in front of the desk and the Chief Investigation Officer was beside him, and the ACIO
was on the other side and a half-pace behind, and
Parrish was out in the secretary's office with a
young twerp watching over him. Parrish hadn't
even made it inside. The lesson was delivered by
two men. One sat in an armchair, and did the talking, and was called DDG, and the other sat on the
front of the desk. The one in the armchair drawled

and the one on the desk, with his socks held up by suspenders, had a voice that was silk and honey. He heard it from the armchair.

"You don't have a right to the detail, Park, but I will tell you what I can, and you should understand that everything I propose has been considered and approved by your immediate supervisors. . . . In your work for Customs and Excise Investigation Division, you are a signatory to the Official Secrets Act. That signature of yours is an obligation to lifelong confidentiality, whatever recent events may have suggested to the contrary. What you hear in this room is covered by the act. Between your superiors and ourselves, Park, there is a deal. You are being volunteered . . ."

"That's nice. What have I done to deserve this?"

"Just button it, Park," the Chief said, side of mouth.

". . . Charlie Eshraq runs heroin. He is also a field agent of some value to the Service. Mr. Matthew Furniss is one of the finest professional officers to have been reared by this Service in the last two decades. That's all fact. Eshraq, for reasons that are not your business, is about to return to Iran and he will be taking across the frontier a certain amount of hardware, purchased, as I am sure you will have deduced, with the proceeds of

the sale of his last load of heroin. He is going back
into Iran, and he will be staying there. He will be
told tomorrow that should he renege on an agree-
ment with us, should he ever return to the United
Kingdom, then he will face prosecution on the
basis of the evidence that you and your colleagues
have collected against him.

"You will join Eshraq on Monday, you will ac-
company him to Turkey, and you will satisfy yourself and your superiors that he has indeed
traveled back into Iran. Following your return to
the UK, it has been decided by your superiors that
you will then be posted as DLO to Bogotá in Colombia. I can assure you that it will be my intention to make certain that you have there the full
cooperation of Service personnel in that region.
That's the deal."

"All neatly wrapped up between you, no loose
ends. And if I tell you that it stinks, that I don't
believe it? He doesn't belong to your outfit and if
he does I'd like to know what's the point of my
going to Bogotá if you lot are running the stuff in
the back door from Iran?"

"Watch it, Park."

"No, Chief, I won't. . . . Just to get Mr. Furniss's
young friend off the hook and just to get me out
of the way. That's it, isn't it?"

"Quite right, Park, we may just have to get you

out of the way. Do you remember a Leroy Winston
Manvers. An early morning interrogation, un-
supervised, quite outside the book . . . ? You do?
I gather the file isn't closed yet, some ugly first
shots across the Division's bows from his solicitor.
Isn't that so, Chief?"

"I think you're shit, sir."

"Five years' imprisonment, minimum. You
could bet money that we'd know the judge. For the
beating of a helpless black prisoner, it could be a
bit more than five. Good night, Park. You'll enjoy
Bogotá. It's full of your type. Good night, gentlemen."

Park went for the door.

If he had looked into the face of the Chief Investigation Officer then he might just have put his
fist into the man's teeth, and if he had looked at
the ACIO then he might just have kneed the bugger.

"By the by, Park, a little note of warning . . ."
The voice drawled behind him, an incoming tide
over shingle. "Don't play any clever games with
Eshraq, I think he'd give you more of a run for
your money than Manvers did."

The dog slept in a wicker basket beside the Aga
in the kitchen, on its back with its legs in the air,

and wheezed like a drayman. The sound of snoring filled the night quiet of the house. He thought that a burglar would have to have kicked over the kitchen table to have woken the brute. But it was not the Rottweiler's growled breathing that kept Henry Carter awake. He would have been asleep by now, well asleep because it had been a hard enough day and rounded off with a good malt, if it had not been for the nagging worry.

The descriptions of the torture had been so wretchedly vivid. The telling of the brutality had been so cruelly sharp. Never, not ever, would Henry have accused Mattie of telling "war stories." Nothing was volunteered, everything had to be chiseled for, but in his own laconic way Mattie had transported Henry into a world that was deeply, desperately frightening.

He understood why he had been chosen for the debrief.

Quite impossible that the Director General would have permitted any of those aggressive youngsters that now seemed to fill the building to be let loose on a man of Mattie's stature. Perhaps the Director General had been wrong. Perhaps one of the young men, brash and cocksure, would have been better able to understand how Mattie had survived the pain, had survived and kept Eshraq's name safe.

God forbid that he should be selling Mattie short, but Henry, coward that he was and without shame of it, could not understand it.

Chapter ❧ 18

SUNDAY MORNING, and the light catching the east side of the Lane. Empty streets around the building, no rubbish wagons, no commuters, no office workers. The buses were few and far between, there were taxis cruising without hope.

The bin beside Park's desk was half filled with cardboard drinking beakers. He had long before exhausted the dispenser, which would not be filled again until early on the Monday, and he had been reduced to making his own coffee, no milk left over the weekend. Stiff black coffee to sustain him.

Some of it he had read before, but through the night he had punched up onto his console screen

everything that the ID's computer had to offer on
Turkey and Iran. That was his way. And a hell of
an amount there was. . . . And he read again what
little had been fed into CEDRIC on Charlie Eshraq. It was his way to arm himself with information, and it was also his way to dig himself a pit
when circumstances seemed about to crush him.
He couldn't have gone home, not after the visit to
Century. Better to get himself back to the Lane,
and to get his head in front of the screen. He'd
been alone until dawn, until Token had shown.
She'd shown, and then she'd gone heaven knew
where and come back with bacon rolls.

She sat at the desk opposite him. He was latch-
ing the plastic sheet over the console.

"I spoke to Bill last night, when he'd got home."

"Did you now?"

"He said you'd had a pretty rotten evening."

"And he was right."

"He said that Duggie took your wife home."

"I asked him to."

"He said that you might be in need of looking
after."

She didn't wear makeup, and she hadn't
combed her short hair, and her anorak was slung
on the hook on the wall between the windows that
looked down onto New Fetter Lane. She wore a
sweat shirt that was tight over her radio transmit-

ter. He thought that he knew what she was saying, what Parrish had said to her.

"Have you finished?"

"I've finished with the computer, I don't know what else I've finished with."

"Another day, another dime, David."

"You know what . . . ? Last night they walked all over us. We were the little chappies who had stepped out of their depth, and we were being told how to behave, and the Chief took it . . . I still feel sick."

"Like I said, another day. Do you want to come home with me?"

"What for?"

"Don't be a cretin . . ."

"I'm going home, got to change."

"Might be best to give home a miss."

She was the girl he ought to have married, that's what he thought. He knew why she offered her place, her bed. He knew why she was on offer, if she had spoken to Bill Parrish on the phone.

"Thanks," he said.

He came round the desk and when she stood he put his arms around her shoulders and he kissed her forehead. It was a soft kiss, as if she were his sister, as if she could only ever be a friend.

"Don't let the bastards hurt you, David."

He slung his suit jacket over his shoulder. Still

in the buttonhole was the red rose that Ann had said he should wear for the dance. He walked out on Token, who would have taken him home to her bed. He started up the car. It was a fast drive through the desert that was the city and it took him little more than an hour to reach home, and he'd bought flowers at a railway station stall.

She'd left the lights on.

The lights were on in the hall and in the bedroom and in the bathroom.

She had left the wardrobe door open, and inside the wardrobe there was a chasm, her dresses gone. The bed wasn't made, and the envelope was on the pillow, the pillow, for God's sake.

He went into the bathroom because he thought that he was going to throw up, and her dressing gown was on the bathmat and her bath towel, and beside her bath towel was his.

Perhaps that was the way it always was, that a marriage ended. The flowers were in the kitchen sink and he didn't know how to make a display of them.

There was a light knock at the door. Mrs. Ferguson, beckoning Carter out. He went, and smiled an apology at Mattie.

If there was a way back then Mattie did not know it. He paced in the room. He faced the alternatives, and his future. There was no going back. To go back, to admit the lie, that was resignation. He was a member of the Service, and if the lie were admitted then he would be out of the Service.

"Sorry, Mattie, so sorry to have abandoned you. The telephone is one of the great tyrannies of modern life. Things are a little more confused. Our message to our man in Tehran, the message for him to abort, it didn't get through."

"Why not?"

"Seems that our man had disappeared, couldn't be traced. That's a shame."

A long sad silence in the room. And Henry's eyes never left Mattie's face. He walked across the carpet and he stood in front of Mattie.

"What I've always heard, and you know that I've no personal experience, when you start talking under pressure then you cannot ration yourself. If you start then you have to finish," he said.

The explosion. "Damn you, how many times do I have to tell you?"

"I think we'll have a walk down to the pub, you'd like that, wouldn't you, Mattie? I'll ask George to tether the hound."

The message was very faint.

The message from the shortwave transmitter, that was in itself hardly larger than a cornflakes packet, was carried the ninety miles from Bandar Abbas, across the shipping lanes of the Straits of Hormuz to the listening antennae on the summit of the Jebal Harim in Oman.

Only the height of the Jebal Harim, 6,867 feet above sea level, enabled the message to be monitored. It was known by the Service that the transmitter could reach the antennae with short messages, and it had been given to the official who worked in the harbormaster's office for use only in emergency.

He knew his situation was critical, he knew he was being watched.

He sent the one short message.

He was a man filled with fear that spilled toward terror. And that afternoon he prayed to his God that he could have the protection of Mr. Matthew Furniss, and the colleagues of Mr. Furniss.

Park was waved forward by the Military Police corporal. There was no salute. A Ford Escort didn't warrant a salute from a corporal who was losing Sunday at home. Park drove forward, bumping over the rutted dirt track, and he parked beside the Suzuki jeep. On the far side of the jeep was a black Rover, newly registered, and the driver was quietly polishing the paintwork and minding his own business. Park had changed at

home. After he had tidied the bathroom and made
the bed that Harlech had been in, then he had
stripped off his suit and put the rose from his buttonhole in water, and put on jeans and a sweater.

He walked toward Charlie Eshraq. Eshraq
stood with the man, the supercilious and drawling
creep who had lectured Park at Century.

He walked toward them, and their conversation
didn't hesitate.

". . . So, that's it?"

"That is it, Mr. Eshraq. Mr. Park will accom-
pany you to the border. You will not attempt to
impede his job. You don't fool with him and he has
been told not to play silly buggers with you. Got
it?"

"And I get the weapons?"

"Mr. Eshraq, if you were not getting the weapons then this afternoon's exercise would be somewhat pointless."

"I don't get to see Mr. Furniss?"

"You will be handled from Ankara, good chap
there."

"Why do I not see Mr. Furniss?"

"Because from inside Iran you will need to deal
with someone else. All that will be explained to
you once you are in Turkey. Good luck, we'll be
rooting for you."

The driver had finished his polishing, and had

started up the Rover. There were no farewells. The car drove away.

In the cause of duty . . . Park walked to Charlie Eshraq.

"I'm David Park."

"No, you're not, you're April Five, but you may call me Charlie."

"I'll call you any name I want to. . . . Probably, like me, you reckon this setup stinks."

Eshraq was Tango One, trafficker in heroin, always would be. There was no handshake. Charlie turned his back on him and walked away toward the army Land-Rover. Park followed, and behind him the Military Police corporal reckoned that it was safe to light a cigarette. There was an officer standing beside the Land-Rover, and squatting on the low seats in the back were two sergeants. David saw the olive-painted case lying on the floor between their feet.

The officer said, "Which of you is it? I was told the instruction was for one."

"For me," Charlie said.

The officer looked him up, down. "The LAW eighty is pretty straightforward."

"Oh, that's good, you'll be able to manage the tutorial."

Park thought the officer might have cracked Charlie. He heard the sergeants laugh aloud.

They went out onto the range. The officer led. They'd given Charlie a tube to carry, and the sergeants each carried one. They seemed to walk a hell of a distance, past red flags, past warning signs, until they came to a place where the heather ground sloped away. There were tank tracks, and ahead of them was the burned, black hull of an armored personnel carrier.

"Where are you going to use this, young man?"

"Is that your business?"

"Don't fuck me about, Mr. Eshraq. . . . On where you are going to use it depends my briefing. Are you going to use it in a battlefield condition? Are you going to use it over open ground? Are you going to use it in an urban environment? You don't have to tell me, but if you don't then you are wasting my time and you are wasting your time. Got me?" The officer smiled. He reckoned he had the upper hand.

"The first one will be fired on a street in Tehran. That's in Iran."

And the smile died on the officer's face.

"All I can say is that I am not totally confident at the moment," Henry said. It was the scrambled phone. "He's peculiarly aggressive when I attempt to pin down detail. . . . Yes, it bothers me very much that I may be selling him short. . . . I suppose we just have to soldier on. Thank you."

It was quiet in the house. They had indeed been to the pub, but that had not been a good idea, because the two pints of ale and Mrs. Ferguson's lunch had given Mattie the excuse to retire to his room for a siesta. And it was Sunday afternoon, and the Director General was in the country, and the Duty Desk weren't quite sure where the Deputy Director General was, and the man who had taken the call from Carter was only a minion and Carter was a tedious fusser, and Mattie Furniss was a hero. Nothing would happen, not until Monday morning.

He crouched. His left knee was bent forward, his right knee was on the ground.

There were the steel gates ahead of him.

There was the derelict house behind him.

The oleanders were in flower and gave him cover, and he had elevation from the ruined and overgrown gardens and he could see over the wall that fronted the derelict house and he could see across the road and to the high sheeting of the security gates. There was a cramp settling in his legs, but he did not respond to it, and he struggled to hold the tube steady on his shoulder. The tube was well balanced and its weight of eighteen pounds kept it firmly in place on his collarbone. His left hand gripped tight at the cradle under the tube, holding it, and the index finger of his right hand was on the smooth plastic of the trigger and the thumb of his right hand was against the switch that would change the firing mechanism from the spotting round to the main projectile. His right eye was locked onto the sight and in the center of his vision were the steel gates to the Mullah's home. He knew that the Mullah was coming because he had heard the revving of the engine of the big Mercedes. The traffic in the road was continuous and the Mercedes would have to stop before it could nose out.

So hard to be still, because the adrenaline flowed, and the thrill of revenge stampeded in him. The gates opened. He saw two guards running forward and across the pavement, and they were gesturing for the traffic to stop, and the whistles in their mouths were raucous. The snout of the Mercedes poked through the gates. He had a clear view of the radiator grille and the front windshield. The head-on target was not the best, side shot was better, but the side shot would be against an accelerating target . . . even better would have been the magnet bomb that Mr. Furniss had given him, and the motorcycle, and the chance to see the face of the Mullah as he

pulled away, as the pig knew that he rode underneath death—not possible, not with the escort car
behind. . . . He could not see the Mullah, he would
be in the back, and through the sight he could only
see the radiator and the windshield and the face
of the driver and the face of the guard who sat beside the driver. A boy pedaled past on his bicycle,
and was not intimidated by the whistles and the
shouts and the flailed hand weapons of the guards
who were on the road, and the driver waited for
the boy on the bicycle to clear the path ahead. The
spotter rifle first. The flash of the red tracer round
running flat, and the impact against the join of
the hood of the Mercedes and the windshield, and
the windshield had a clouded mark at the base,
nearly dead center. Thumb to the switch, push the
switch. The finger back to the trigger. Holding the
tube steady, ducking it back into the line of sight
because the kick of the tracer round had lifted
the aim fractionally. Squeezing a second time on
the trigger . . . and the blast, and the recoil, and
the white heat flash roaring behind him, behind
his crouched shoulder. A shudder of light that
moved from the muzzle of the tube at a speed of
235 meters in a second, and the range was less
than forty meters. The explosion on the front of
the Mercedes, the copper slug of the warhead
driven into the body of the car, and the debris

scabs following it, and the car rocked back, and lifted, and the first flicker of fire. . . . What he had waited for. The car burned, and the road was in confusion.

"Move yourself, Eshraq."

The shout in his ear, and his hands still clasped the tube, and the voice was faint because his ears thundered from the firing.

"Get yourself bloody moving."

And the officer was dragging at his collar, and snatching the tube from his grip.

"You don't stand around to watch, you move as if all the demons in hell are on your tail, and about half of them will be."

The officer had flung the tube aside, and Charlie was on his feet. He saw for one last time that the smoke billowed from the armored personnel carrier target. He ran. He was bent low, and he ran for more than one hundred yards up the shallow slope of the hill and away from the officer and the sergeants and the three discarded tubes and the target. He ran until he reached Park.

At his own pace the officer walked to him.

"That wasn't bad, Eshraq."

He was panting. The excitement throbbed in him. "Thank you."

"Don't thank me, it's your skin that's on offer. You have to move faster in the moment after firing. You do not hang about to congratulate yourself on being a clever kid. You fire, you drop the tube, you move out. You were wearing ear protectors, no one else in the target zone will be and they will be disorientated for a few seconds. You have to make use of those seconds."

"Yes, understood."

"You won't have realized it, time goes pretty fast, but you were four seconds and the rest between the rifle aiming round and the missile discharge. Too long. The target today was stationary, that's kids' play."

"Inside an armored Mercedes . . . ?"

"I'd rather not be the passenger. The LAW eighty is designed to take out main battle tanks up to five hundred meters. No car, whatever the small arms protection, has a chance. Don't lose any sleep over that. Are you happy?"

"I will remember your kindness."

"Just give my love to the Ayatollah . . ."

Charlie laughed, and he waved. He walked away and Park followed him. He thought Park was like the Labrador dog that Mrs. Furniss had owned when the girls were still at school, and which had been detested by Mr. Furniss. He thought the officer was great, because there was no bullshit about the man and he had given him the depth of his experience, and freely. He reached the jeep.

"I am going back to London, are you coming with me?"

"Those are my instructions, that I stay with you, but I've my own car."

He heard the tang of dislike in the brittle voice. "Then you can follow me."

"I'll do that."

"I'm going to my flat."

"I know where your flat is."

"I'm going to my flat and I am going to take a shower, and then I am going out to dinner. I am going to have a very good meal. Perhaps, you would care to join me?"

He saw the snarl on Park's face, his face was almost amusing. "I'll eat with you because I have to be with you, and I'll pay my own share. So we understand each other—I don't want to be with you, but those are my orders. I'll tell you where I'd like to be with you. I would like to be sitting alongside the dock in Number Two, Central Criminal Court, and I'd like to be there when a judge puts you away for fifteen years."

Charlie grinned. "Perhaps you'll win some other ones."

He had stayed in his room all afternoon, and when Henry had come to the door and knocked and told him that supper was ready he had said that he had no appetite and that he would skip the meal. It had been late when he had come down. He had been driven downstairs by his growing loneliness that had become keener as the light fell over the trees in the garden.

They were in the drawing room. For that time of year it was unusual for it to have been so cold, and Mattie stayed close to the fireplace, which was idiotic since there was no fire, but he felt the chill of his loneliness and he could not shrug the warmth back to his mind. Henry wasn't communicative. It was as though he were watching the clock, had decided that Sunday evening was his free time and that the debrief would continue in the morning. Henry had brought him a whiskey, sat him in a chair with back editions of the *Illustrated London News* and *Country Life*, and returned to the study of a brochure advertising holidays for ornithologists. He craved to ask the question, but Henry was far from him, lost in the Danube's marshes. He held the drink. He hadn't spoken to Harriet, not since the phone call that was their reunion, three quick minutes, and stiff lips, and both too gushing because they were too old and too regimented to have cried down the lines, and he wouldn't speak to her again, not until this was over. Harriet would have known what he should do. And equally certainly Henry would turn down any request that he can her. Oh yes, he'd do it politely, but he'd do it. Carter had a calculator out, and must have been adding up the damage because just after he had made the final punch a frown plowed his high forehead. Mattie saw that Henry did nothing by accident. He also realized that for all his seniority at Century, here he was subordinate. Old Henry Carter, Century's vacuum cleaner for gathering up the odds and sods of administration, was running the show, and had determined that Mattie Furniss would be left through that evening to sweat.

Henry smiled. Melting butter. A wrinkled choirboy's smile, such innocence.

"Too damned expensive for me. It'll be the Fens again."

Mattie blurted, "Eshraq, Charlie Eshraq . . . he was due to go back inside. Did he go?"

Henry's eyebrow lifted. Deliberately he put down the calculator and closed the brochure. "Any day now, going in the next few days. . . . I must say, it sounds as if he's taken on more than he can possibly chew."

Mattie thought a knife could have been sharpened on Henry's voice.

"He's a fine young man."

"They're all fine young men, Mattie, our field agents. But that'll keep till the morning."

The Director of the Revolutionary Center for Volunteers for Martyrdom was still in his office because on many evenings the office doubled as his bedroom. He was in an easy chair and reading a manual of the U.S. Marine Corps on base security procedures, and he was happy in the discovery that they had learned nothing, the authors of this study.

They took coffee, thick and bitter, and with it was served orange juice. They were two men of cultures that were chasms apart. The Director had spent six years in the Qezel-Hesar jail in the times of the Shah of Shahs, and he had spent six years in exile in Iraq and France. If a young Mullah who was a rising star had not offered the investigator his protection, then, in great probability, the Director would have used the pistol, holstered and hanging from a hook behind his door, on the back of the neck of the onetime SAVAK man.

The investigator spoke of a watch that was now maintained on a barber's shop in the Aksaray district of Istanbul. He told of a man who would come to the shop. At the back of the shop, Charlie Eshraq, the son of the late Colonel Hassan Eshraq, would collect forged papers that he would use when he came back into Iran. He asked a great favor of the Director. He said that he would have this Eshraq under surveillance from the moment that he left the shop. His request was for a small force of men who would be in position on the frontier to intercept Eshraq at whatever crossing point he used. Would he come over at a crossing point? Of course—and the investigator had researched the matter—because of the weight of the armor-piercing missiles he was known to be bringing and their packaging he would have to come by road. He asked for the service as if he were a humble creature at the feet of a great man.

He asked for nothing. The Director would be most pleased to make such a squad available, in the name of the Imam.

The Director said, "Consider the words of the martyred Ayatollah Sadeq Khalkhali: 'Those who are against killing have no place in Islam. Faith requires the shedding of blood, we are there to perform our duty. . . .' He was a great man."

And a great butcher, and a hanging judge without equal. His patron, the Mullah that he served, was but a boy in comparison with Khalkhali, the unlamented protector of the Revolution.

"A great man, who spoke words of great wisdom," the investigator said. And he asked the second favor. He asked that after Charlie Eshraq had collected his papers from the barber's shop, that the shop be destroyed by explosives. Profusely, he thanked the Director for his cooperation.

It was necessary for him, business completed, to stay another hour in the company of the Director. The Director was pleased to report the details of the killing in London of Jamil Shabro, traitor to the Imam, traitor to his faith, and guilty of waging war against Allah.

When they parted, in the quiet of the dark, on the steps outside the old University, their cheeks brushed each other's lips.

If the restaurant had been half empty, and not full, then Park would have sat at a separate table. There was only their reserved table, so he had to sit with Eshraq if he wanted to eat. And he did want to eat.

Eshraq made conversation, as if they were strangers who had crossed paths in a strange city and needed company. And he ate like he was starting a hunger strike in the morning. He ate *fettucine* for starters, main course bowl, and he followed with the *fegato,* and took the lion's share of the vegetables they should have shared, and he finished with strawberries and then coffee and a large Armagnac to rinse down the Valpolicella of which he had drunk two thirds of the bottle. Park hadn't talked much, and the first real exchange was when he had insisted on halving the bill when it came. He took his time, Eshraq, but he pocketed the money, and he paid the whole bill with an American Express card.

Park said, "But you won't be here, not when they bill you."

"Present from America."

"That's dishonest."

"Why don't you call the head waiter?" The mocking in the eyes.

"And you eat like a pig."

Eshraq leaned forward and he looked into Park's face. "Do you think where I am going that I will be eating a meal like this, do you think so? And you know what is the penalty for drinking wine and for drinking brandy, do you know?"

"I don't know, and I don't care."

"I could be flogged."

"Best thing for you."

"You are a generous member of the human race."

There was a hesitation, and Park asked, "When you get there, what do you do?"

"I build a life for myself."

"Where do you live?"

"Sometimes rough and sometimes in safe houses, at first."

"How long does it last?"

"How long is a piece of string, April Five?"

"I don't care, it's nothing to me, but it's suicide."

"What did your man offer you, many years ago? He offered you blood and sweat and tears, and he offered you victory."

He couldn't find the words. The words seemed to mean nothing. The face loomed ahead of him, and there was the chatter and the life of the restaurant around them, and the flapping of the kitchen doors, and laughter. "And you're not coming back. There's no coming back, is there? It's all one way, isn't it? You're going back, and you're staying there. Is that right?"

"You said that you didn't care, that it was nothing to you, but I have no intention of dying."

The bill came back, with his plastic. He put his tip on the table, between his coffee cup and the brandy glass, everything that Park had given him.

At the door, Eshraq kissed the waitress on the mouth, and he bowed to the applause of the other customers. Park followed him out. Eshraq was on the pavement and flexing himself, as if he were breathing in the London street air, as if he were trying to keep a part of it for himself, for always.

Park walked alongside him, back toward Eshraq's place. He followed the big bounding strides. There was an excitement about the man. Everything before was windup, tomorrow was real. They reached the entrance to the flats.

"Eshraq, I just want to tell you something."

"What?" Charlie turned. "What do you want to tell me, April Five?"

It had been going through Park's mind most of the time at the restaurant. He waited while an old lady walked her dog between them, waited until the dog had cocked its leg against a railing and was then dragged away.

"I just want you to know that we will follow you anywhere you go, except Iran. If you come out of Iran then we'll know, and that goes for the rest of your life. We'll circulate you, Eshraq, they'll hear about you in Paris, Bonn, Rome, Washington, they'll know you're a trafficker in drugs. If you come out of Iran, if you pitch up at any airport, then I'll hear, I'll get the call. You want to play games with us, just try us. That's the truth, Eshraq, and don't ever forget it."

Charlie smiled. He fished his keys from his pocket.

"You're welcome to sleep on the floor."

"I prefer my car."

"Are you married?"

"What's that to you?"

"Just assumed you hadn't a home to go to."

"My instructions are to stay close to you until you go over the border."

"I asked if you were married."

"I was."

"What broke it?"

"If it's any of your business . . . you broke it."

The Director General was at the Joint Intelligence Committee, the Deputy Director General was on his way back from the country. Of all the many hundreds who worked on the nineteen floors and the basement at Century they were the only two who had an overall picture of Furniss's case. Both would be at their desks by the late morning of Monday, neither was available for the fast reaction that was needed to coordinate a jumble of information originating from differing sources. There was Carter's call from Albury on Sunday that had been logged by the Duty Officer. There was the monitoring of a shortwave radio message in Oman that required immediate response. There was a report, brought by a Turkish lorry driver to Dogubeyezit, and from there telephoned to Ankara. Related matters, but early on that Monday morning, as the building strove without enthusiasm to throw off lethargy, those matters remained unrelated. The transcript of Henry Carter's message was passed to the Director General's PA. The shortwave radio message ended on the desk of a man with the title of Special Services (Armed Forces) Liaison. The communication from Ankara lay in the In tray of the Desk Head (Near East).

Later, a subcommittee would be set up to examine means of ensuring that all crucial intelligence was distributed at once to the desks that were available to deal with it. There had been subcommittees with that brief as long as the old hands could remember.

Faced with the absence of the Director General and his deputy, the SS(AF)L officer took a car across the Thames to the Ministry of Defense, to ask a rare favor of old Navy chums.

They went on the morning flight.

Charlie's ticket was one-way, Park's a return. They flew tourist class. They didn't have to talk on the flight because Charlie slept. Park couldn't sleep, not with the stiffness settling in after a cramped night in the back of the Escort. He was grateful that Eshraq slept, because he'd had his bellyful of small talk.

It had started with a police phone tap on a dealer, but Parrish didn't tell them that, nor did he tell April team that there had been all but blood on the carpet when the NDIU had passed it from police control to ID. His style was matter-of-fact. He showed no signs of having had about the worst weekend he could remember since joining Customs and Excise. It would have been a passable weekend if his wife hadn't pitched in with her opinions, and her report. . . . He told it as he knew it. The dealer's supplier was a Turk who operated out of the port of Izmir. The scag would be Iranian and across the land border and into Turkey, and then overland to Izmir. He had the name of the ship out of Izmir, and its route was via Naples. It was known that Naples, information provided by the Drugs Enforcement Agency, was a pickup point for a consignment of Italian pinewood furniture. The assumption was that the scag would be coming into Southampton Docks all tucked up with the table legs. April would be there in force. He would be there himself, along with Harlech and Corinthian and Token and the new kid from Felixstowe who had joined them that day and who hadn't yet a codename which meant that they'd call him Extra, and there would be backup from Southampton ID. Parrish said that it was good they had the dealer spoken for, and the supplier, but that they wanted the distributor. He reckoned the distributor would show at Southampton. They'd be going down that morning, and he didn't know when they'd be back, so they'd better have their clean socks with them. There were the jokes about the cars from the depot being clapped out, and the Vodaphones not working, all the usual crap. . . . He was pretty pleased that they'd another investigation to latch on to so soon, and better still to get them out of London. Those of April who were not going to Southampton would be for the delights of Bethnal Green, chez the dealer, and for the banks where he had his accounts. The ship was coming in that night, was already down the Channel with a Brixham pilot on board, so could they get their backsides off their seats, please.

He'd finished. His finger snaked out, pointed to Duggie Williams. He gestured toward the inner office, and headed there.

He sat at the desk. He let Harlech stand. He'd get it off his chest. He thought April was the best team in the Lane, and he was damned if he'd see it broken.

"Saturday night, Duggie, that was insufferable."

"She asked for it."

"You only had to take her home, drop her."

"How did you know?"

"I know, but if I hadn't known, I'd have read it all over your face."

"She was ready for it."

"She was the wife of your colleague."

"I didn't start the dumping."

"He's your brother-in-arms, for heaven's sake."

"He's a prig and a bore and he doesn't keep his missus happy. Sorry, Bill, no apologies."

"If I catch you round there again . . ."

"You going to sit on the doorstep?"

". . . you're back in uniform."

"She was the unhappiest woman I've ever poked, and she's a good kid. And where is our brother-in-arms?"

"Don't know. Don't know where he is, what he's got himself into. . . . Lose yourself."

"The DG rang, Mattie, he's just back from the Joint Intelligence session. He wanted you to know that your praises were sung to the roof."

"Thank you, much appreciated."

"And I'm to tell you that you're being put up for a gong."

"I thought those sort of things were supposed to be a surprise."

"Be the Order of the British Empire, Mattie. I expect the DG wanted to cheer you a bit."

"Why, Henry, do I need cheering?"

"Your agent in Tabriz . . . Revolutionary Guards beat us to him."

"And what exactly are you implying?"

"Which comes on top of your man in Tehran, also not reached, also gone absent, although we don't know for certain that he was arrested. We do know it of the man in Tabriz."

"I'll tell you what I think. I think that I was compromised from the time that I landed in the Gulf. I think that I was trailed right the way across the Gulf, right the way to Ankara and on to Van. I think I was set up from the start. . . . What's happened to my man in Bandar Abbas?"

"Making a run for it tonight. Navy are going to try and pick him up at sea. I think that's rather dodgy. He knows they are watching him."

"I told you. I gave their names. Looking back on it, on the moment that I knew, knew absolutely that my cover was a farce, was when the investigator asked me what I had been doing all round the Gulf. He practically gave me the addresses I had been at, starting in Bahrain. I wish you'd get someone onto this at once, see just who is in and out of that Service wing. But yes, what must have been two weeks later, I did give their names. But what I can't get over is the utter uselessness—it makes me sick to think of it—of day upon day of torture while the Service twiddles its thumbs and now you come moping in here and say alas, we've lost another agent. Lost, for God's sake, Henry, not lost, thrown away."

Henry said, "I'm on your side, Mattie, and was from the very start. No professional would have let it happen. I've told you that. But I'd like to leave the jail now, come back to it later, and we'll certainly do as you say about the Bahrain station. I want to talk this afternoon about the actual escape. . . ."

They sat either side of the unlit fire, and Henry was mother and poured the tea.

Chapter ❖ 19

*C*arter wriggled in his shirt. He had not brought enough shirts to last him and he had had to entrust his dirty ones to Mrs. Ferguson, and the woman used too much starch. The shirt was uncomfortable against his skin. Worse, the summer had come at last and even with the lounge curtains half drawn the room still sweltered, and Henry boiled unhappily in his three-piece suit and stiff shirt.

"Your investigator, Mattie, your torturer, what was he looking for in general?"

"They wanted to know why I was in the region, what was my brief."

"And what did you tell them?"

"I told them that I was an archaeologist."

"Of course."

"You stick to your cover story, it's all you have to hang on to."

"And you're not believed?"

"Right, I'm not believed, but you have to stick to your cover, whatever the holes are in it. And I was never going to be believed. The interrogator was an old SAVAK hand and he had met me years ago in Tehran. He knew exactly who I was. Called me Furniss the first time I was sat down in front of him. They caught a BBC bulletin saying that Dr. Owens was missing. He made fun of that."

"On that day you still hadn't abandoned your cover?"

"Do you understand anything? You are alone, you are beyond help. If you give up your cover story then you are finished."

"They wanted to know your mission in the region, and what else were they fishing for?"

"Names of agents."

"They knew you were in the region, and they knew your identity. . . . What did they know of the identity of the agents?"

"They didn't have the names."

"Did they have anything on them?"

"If they did they didn't give me any hint of it."

Henry said quietly, "You gave them what they wanted, but not the name of Charlie Eshraq."

He saw the head go down. He did not know how long it would take. It might take the rest of the day, and it might take the rest of the week. But Mattie had dropped his head.

"How many sessions, Mattie?"

"Plenty."

"Torture sessions, Mattie, how many?"

"Six, seven—they were whole days."

"Whole days of torture, and in essence the questions were the same?"

"What I was doing in the region, and the names of the agents."

"I'm very admiring of you, Mattie, that you were tortured day after day, that the questions were over such a small area range, and that you held the cover story so long, very admiring. Did you consider, Mattie, telling them a little about Charlie Eshraq?"

"Of course you consider it."

"Because the pain is so great?"

"I hoped the names of the field agents would be enough."

"You'll have to talk me through this. . . . You are in great pain. You are the subject of the most vicious and degrading treatment. The questions are asked again and again because they don't believe you have named all the agents. . . . What do you say?"

"You stay with your story."

"Damn difficult, Mattie."

"You have no choice."

"Through the kickings, beatings, faintings—through a mock execution?"

Henry made a note on the pad that rested on his knee. He saw that Mattie watched him. He saw the trickle of relief on the man's face. Of course he was relieved. He saw his inquisitor make a note on his pad and he would have assumed that Carter made the note because he was satisfied with the answer. And the assumption was incorrect. Henry noted on his pad that he must ring Century for more clothes for Mattie. There was always a stock of clothes held there for visitors. There was a wardrobe full of slacks and jackets and jerseys and shirts and underwear and socks, assorted styles and shapes. Even shoes. Mattie would need more clothes because he was trapped in a lie, and the debrief would go on until the lie was disowned.

"I think you are a very gentle man, Mattie."

"What does that mean?"

"I think that you care about people over whom you exercise control."

"I hope I do."

There was a sad smile on Carter's face. He would have been deeply and sincerely upset to have had Mattie believe that he took pleasure from his work.

"Mattie, when you left the kids on the mountain, the kids who lifted you up when you were finished, shared their food with you, and so on, that must have hurt."

"Obviously."

"Super kids, weren't they? Great kids, and they helped you when you were at your weakest."

Mattie shouted, "What did you want me to do?"

"You didn't argue their case. You told me that. You walked away from them and you sorted yourself out with the officer."

"I did try. But it's true I didn't upset the applecart as far as to get pushed back up the hill myself. My first priority, my duty as I saw it, was to get myself back to London."

"That's a very heavy cross, that sort of duty . . ."

"You weren't there, Henry bloody Carter . . . you weren't there, you can never know."

The sun played on the windows and the distortions of the old glass were highlighted, and the brilliance of the rare sunshine showed up the dirt dust on the panes. If George, if the handyman, were to hold his job, then it was about time the idle wretch started to get round the windows with a bucket of warm water and a pocket full of rags. Carter said, "My assessment, Mattie, and this is not meant as a criticism, is that you were looking to save yourself. . . . Hear me out. . . . Saving yourself was pretty important to you. Saving yourself was more important to you than speaking up for those kids who had carried you to the border."

The hoarse rasp in Mattie's voice. "One minute you want me to hang on long enough in the victim's chair and get every bone in my body broken, fingernails tugged out, all that, and the next minute you want me to have got myself booted back across the border."

"I want to know what you would have done to save yourself from the pain of torture."

"Why don't you refresh your memory with a glance at my medical report? Or would you like me to take my socks off?"

"I need to know if you named Eshraq to save yourself from the pain of torture."

"I might have named them all the minute the interrogation began."

"No call for that, Mattie . . ." There was a grimace from Carter, as if he had been personally wounded. ". . . When I was down here, must have been a couple of years back, there was an old croquet set in the cellar. I've told that lazy blighter to mow a bit of the lawn. Would you fancy a game of croquet, Mattie, after we've had our lunch? . . . To save yourself, your own admission, you let

those kids be herded to a firing party. What would
you have done to save yourself from the pain of
torture?"

"I've told you."

"Of course . . . Eshraq's going back over, very
soon."

They went to their lunch, and through the open
windows there was the coughing drone of the old
cylinder mower out on the lawn, and the pandemonium of the dog at George's heels.

The route of the lorry had been through Calais,
Munich, Salzburg, Belgrade, and then the poor
roads of Bulgaria. Nineteen hundred miles in all,
and a run of ninety hours. Sometimes the driver
worried about the tachograph, sometimes his em-
ployer took care of his lorries and paid him extra
money for hammering across Europe. There was
the potential that the tachograph would be examined at a border post, but that potential was slight,
and the driver, with extra funding, could live with
that slight potential. The driver was skilled at ne-
gotiating the overland Customs point at Aziziye.
It had been his habit for years to telephone ahead
from Bulgaria to his friend at the Customs at Aziziye, to warn of his arrival. The driver called the
Customs officer his friend, to his face, but in fact
had similar friends at most of the entry points to

European countries where he might be ending his journey and requiring Customs clearance. The bribe that was given to the Customs officer at Aziziye was not so much to prevent search of the containers on the lorry and its trailer, more to ensure a smooth passage for the cargo. A present, a gift, for the Customs officer was an essential part of any swift movement of goods. His vehicle was well known at the Aziziye crossing point. There was no reason for him to attract attention, and with the gift to his friend he ensured speed. It was a healthy arrangement, and paid for on this occasion by a carton of Marlboro cigarettes, a Seiko watch, and an envelope of U.S. dollar bills.

The lorry traveled through. The seals of the containers had been legally broken. He had his manifest list signed, stamped.

The driver was free to drop off at an assembly of addresses the contents of his containers. He had brought into Turkey, quite illicitly and quite easily, four LAW 80 armor-piercing missiles, and he carried in his wallet a passport-sized photograph of the man to whom he would deliver four wooden crates, and he'd get a holiday with the wife and the kids in Majorca on the bonus he was promised for the successful shipment of the particular cargo that was stowed at the bulkhead of the container that was immediately behind the driver's cab.

A piece of cake, the Customs point at Aziziye. The lorry headed for Istanbul.

The envelope contained a dog-eared and well-scuffed Shenass-Nameh recognition paper, and a certificate of military discharge following injury, and a driver's license for a commercial vehicle. Included also in the envelope was a letter of authentication from a factory in Yazd that produced precision ball bearings and would therefore be classified as important to the war effort. And there were bank notes, *rials*.

As he took each item out of the envelope, Charlie held it against the light that hung down from the ceiling of the room at the back of the barber's shop. He looked for the signs of overwriting and overstamping. It was right that he should check carefully. His life depended on them. He paid cash, he paid in sterling, £20 notes. He thought that the forger could have bought a half of the Aksaray district with what he made in documentation provided for the refugee exiles. He thought that he was a case of interest to the forger, because the forger had told him, not the time before, but the time before that, had confided in Charlie, that he was the only customer who looked for documentation to go back inside Iran. The barber's shop was in the center of the Aksaray district that was the Little Iran of Istanbul. To the room at the back of the shop there came, by appointment, a stream of men and women seeking the precious papers that were required for them if a new life were to be born out of exile. And he charged . . . He charged what he thought he could get, and those from whom he could get nothing received nothing from him. For a Turkish passport he charged $500, and this was the bottom of his range and full of risk to the bearer because the number would not tally with any of the records maintained on the Interior Ministry computer. For a British or a Federal German passport, with entry visa, he would expect to relieve his customer of $10,000. Most expensive, top of his range, was the American passport, with multiple-entry visa, and there were very few customers who had managed to secrete that sort of cash, $25,000 in used notes. Sometimes, but only occasionally, the forger took diamonds in lieu of cash, but he was loathe to do that because he had no knowledge of precious stones and then he must go and put himself at the mercy of the young Jew in the covered bazaar that was a thousand meters away down Yeniceriler Caddesi—and he might be cheated. With fast and busy fingers he counted the cash. When they shook hands, when Charlie had pocketed the brown envelope, when the forger had locked away the money, then Charlie noticed the tic flicker on the right upper eyelid of the forger. Charlie did not consider that the tic flicker might have been caused by fear, apprehension; he thought the twitching came from an overindulgence in close and painstaking work.

Charlie Eshraq walked out into the sunshine.

He looked up the street for his shadow. He saw Park. He was at least 150 yards up the street. Charlie was about to wave a curt acknowledgement when he saw the shadow turn away from him.

He had first seen the tail in the Aksaray district, where the walls were covered with posters that rubbished Khomeini, where the kids gathered to plot crimes that would bring them the money to get out of Turkey and onward into Europe. He had first seen the tail when Eshraq had come out of the doorway of the barber's shop and started to walk toward him. He wasn't sure whether there were two cars, but he was certain that there was one car. There were three men, on the hoof. There was the man in the forecourt of the café who stood and then came after Eshraq as soon as he emerged into the sunshine; he was a tail because he left three quarters of a glass of cola undrunk. There was a man who had been leaning against a telephone pole and who had been busy cleaning his nails, and his nails didn't seem to matter once Eshraq was out. There was a third man, and when the car had pulled level with him, then he had spoken quickly into the lowered front passenger window.

He knew a tail when it was in front of him.

He'd thought that the tail was good in Istanbul. He'd thought the tail was better in Ankara. He didn't doubt that the tail had been in place from the time they had walked out of the terminal of the Esenboga airport, but he hadn't picked it up until Eshraq had gone park walking with the young man who called himself Terence. In the park, the Genclik Park, with the lakes and the artificial islands and the cafés, he had kept himself back and he had watched Eshraq and his contact from more than a quarter of a mile. Three men again, but different from those who had done the footslog in Istanbul.

He could have rung Bill Parrish, and he didn't. He could have called up the ACIO, and he didn't. They had passed him on from the Lane. They would be into the priority of Harlech's case, and sifting everything else that had taken backseat to the Eshraq investigation. They wouldn't have wanted to have known that there was a tail on Eshraq.

He acknowledged that the tails were in place. He allowed them to stay in place.

A man who wore a new black leather jacket, and who had a trimmed goat's beard, he saw him in the Genclik Park and he saw him at the airport when he and Eshraq boarded for Van.

There was no communication between them. There was no bond in formation. Eshraq was moving to the frontier and Park was his shadow. They hardly spoke. When they spoke it was commonplace and factual. They spoke about where Eshraq was going, how long he would be there, where he would be going afterward. That didn't bother Park, and it seemed to him that it didn't concern Eshraq. No need for it to have concerned either of them. They were the subjects of a deal.

And if Eshraq had a tail on him, had had a tail ever since he had walked clear of the barber's shop in the Aksaray district of Istanbul, then that was his worry, not Park's.

4984I/TL/7 6 87.

To: TURKDESK, CENTURY   CC IRANDESK, DDG.

From: ANKARASTATION

MESSAGE: CE Vanward, in company of Park. Transshipment from UK complete, no hitch, and now in transit Vanward. Have fully briefed up, beefed up, CE on communications procedures, and

agreed that most epistles will be hand carried out by courier. CE in good humor, good morale. Eye stressed need for detail in material rather than frequency. My opinion, eye think they have major handful tripping over their frontier. Eye didn't meet Park. CE ignores him, says he is harmless. In answer your query—TURKDESK CENTURY 6 6 87—CE says Park is no problem, but frightened of being away from home without his Mum, exclaimer . . . CE will cross 9 6 87, using Dogubeyezit checkpoint. CE has necessary papers to drive commercial vehicle inside, will be carrying hardware via commercial van, and supply of electrical flex as per your suggestion. Upsummer: No problems, looks good, more follows.
MESSAGE ENDS.

"You off then, Henry? That'll be a break."

"I'll be in London, Mattie, reporting back."

"I won't be sorry, Henry, if they slap your wrist."

"Probably will, won't be for the first time. . . . What I was saying, it's not quite a matter of bolting the stable door after the horse has gone. There's still one horse in the stable. Eshraq is in the stable, not for much longer, but he's there right now. Are you quite sure there is nothing you wish to add to what you have already told me?"

"Quite sure."

"When I get back, if there's still enough light, we might get the mallets out again, very soothing is croquet. Do you think we should have a nightcap, one for the stairs? . . ."

Boghammer Bill was a blip, lime-shaded, on the emerald wash of the screen.

The operator, the egghead of the radar room crew, had identified the blip, and called over the 2 i/c to watch its progress.

The crew of the Type 22 guided missile frigate were on defense watch. They were dripping sweat, those in the radar room, those on the bridge, those manning the 20mm rapid-fire close engagement guns. The middle of the night, and the temperature close to 95 degrees Fahrenheit, and all crew members swaddled in the white gown action suits and hooded.

The technician knew that it was Boghammer Bill from the speed of the blip on the screen. It was a Swedish-built patrol boat and the fastest craft in the Gulf.

The Type 22 would not hang about, not in the waters where it was now cruising, maintaining radio silence and blacked out, just outside the Iranian twelve-mile limit, for any more minutes than were essential. The 2 i/c thought the world was getting dangerously daft. There was a bright moon, high in a clear sky, and there was no wind. It was a ridiculous night to be stooging just off the limit without identification or prior warning. They were east of the Iranian island of Larak and west of the small fishing harbor of Minab, far too bloody many sea miles from their regular station, on escort duty in the Straits of Hormuz. The 2 i/c knew the mission, but he didn't know his skipper's Rules of Engagement orders if they came under Iranian fire. They had been watching the dhow on the screen for more than half an hour, and they could picture the fishing craft chugging on a small engine away from Minab. The 2 i/c knew it was the dhow they were to rendezvous with because its course was directly toward the longitude/latitude reference that he had been given, and there were no other crawling blips on the screen. It was now seven minutes since the patrol boat had speared onto the screen, going fast out of Bandar Abbas, powered by engines that could attain in excess of 50 knots. Staccato reports from the 2 i/c to the bridge, gestures that were self-evident from the technician to the 2 i/c. The dhow was on course for the rendezvous, and Boghammer Bill was on course to intercept the dhow some four miles short of the rendezvous. No hiding place, not on a clear night.

When he was home on leave, when he was in Plymouth, the 2 i/c's idea of relaxation was to get himself up to one of the Devon water supply reservoirs and to put a small roach onto a damn great treble hook and let it flutter underneath a big bobbing float until it attracted the attention of a pike. Of course, the 2 i/c never saw the pike actually close on the tethered roach, couldn't see under the murk of the reservoir surface, but he imagined it. He told himself that the pike didn't stalk its dinner, it charged it. He thought of Boghammer Bill as the pike, he thought that some poor creature on the dhow was the roach bait. He watched the blips closing, he watched the racing speed of the blip that was Boghammer Bill. The blips closed, merged.

He had waited in his office at the Ministry building.

He had waited for the final message to be telexed to the communications rooms in the basement.

In place were the arrest at sea of the official who worked in the harbormaster's office at Bandar Abbas. In place were three teams of men from the Revolutionary Center for Volunteers for Martyrdom, settled into a Guards Corps barracks at Maku that was close to the main overland crossing point from Turkey. In place were three men who had tracked Eshraq from the airfield at Van to Dogubeyezit.

There was one aspect of the situation that still puzzled the investigator as he cleared his desk, shoveled the maps and the briefing notes into his case. Furniss had named Charlie Eshraq, and yet Eshraq was in Dogubeyezit. Eshraq was in the Ararat Hotel in Dogubeyezit. Why was he not warned off?

At this time, he did not concern himself with the man who had accompanied Eshraq from Istanbul to Ankara to Van to Dogubeyezit. Time enough for that, but later.

His car waited. At the military airfield, an aircraft waited.

He was a coming man. When he had Eshraq at the border he would be a man who had arrived. . . . If Eshraq came to the border. Very confusing.

He had started early, certainly before Mattie Furniss was on the move. He had gone to his flat, one bedroom and a large living room and all the usuals, which was plenty for him, fixed rent, too, and they couldn't get him out, to collect his post.

He sat on the bench in front of the spinning soapy window. He had raised a few eyebrows. There weren't many who came to the launderette and stuffed into the cavern an armful of clean, ironed shirts. He'd paid for a double rinse, which he thought would be sufficient to sort out the starch once and for all. He gazed at the maelstrom in front of him. He was a regular and sometimes there were people there who knew him and talked to him. Quite a little social club on a Thursday evening.

He doubted there was a man or woman in the building who would want to hear what he had to say. Certainly not the Director General, who was giving him fifteen minutes. And it was bad news for him that the DDG was on his way that morning to Washington.

When his shirts were washed, rinsed and dried, he folded them carefully and carried them back to his flat and gave them a quick iron.

His car was on a good parking place, too good to lose, and so he took a bus from Putney Bridge along the river route to Century.

No one loved the bearer of evil tidings. But what choice did he have? He believed that Mattie was lying.

The dog was chained to the leg of the one solid garden seat. Mattie strode behind the mower. He had George at the wheelbarrow for the cuttings. He made neat lines.

He knew where Henry Carter had gone. Poor old Henry, and not half as clever as he'd thought, he had seen to it that the telephone in the hall was removed, but he had forgotten the telephone in Mrs. Ferguson's bedroom.

He did the croquet lawn, close cut. He assumed that George was prepared to be outside with him, ferrying the cuttings to the compost heap, because George had been instructed to mind him.

His name is Charlie Eshraq . . .

Mattie mowed, pure straight stripes, and he scrubbed from his mind the echo of his own words.

". . . But he has told you nothing . . ."

"That is quite correct, sir, he has admitted absolutely nothing."

The Director General's smile was withering, "But you don't believe him."

"I wish I could, sir, and I cannot."

"But you have no evidence to substantiate your distrust?"

"I have the conviction that a man who is driven by days of torture to name his field agents is not going to be allowed to stop there."

"But why do you think he didn't make his escape before giving Eshraq's name?"

"Ah yes. That, sir, is a hunch."

"And you are prepared to damn a man because of your hunch."

"On the basis of what I might rephrase as a lifetime of listening to debriefs, sir, I would simply avoid sending this young man into Iran until we are certain. No one has explained to me the reason for the haste."

"There are all sorts of things that you don't know, Carter."

There was a light knock. Houghton walked in like a man who has been told that his banker has defaulted. He didn't seem to notice Henry Carter. He laid a single sheet of paper on the Director General's desk. There was the moment of quiet while the Director General ferreted in his breast pocket for his reading glasses.

"From our naval friends in the Gulf. You'd better hear what it says, Carter. It's timed at 0700. Message: No, repeat no, rendezvous. Subject craft intercepted by Iran Navy Boghammer missile boat. Believed all crew of subject craft taken on board before subject craft sunk. Boghammer returned to base, Bandar Abbas. We resuming escort duty . . . Message ends."

The Director General placed the sheet of paper back onto his desk. He removed his reading glasses.

"What would Furniss say?"

"Mattie would say that he had been through a hell that neither you nor I can comprehend in order that we would have had the time to get those three men clear. Mattie would say that our lack of resolution condemned our network to death."

"He admits the names came from him?"

"Yes, but only after withstanding what I reckon to be anywhere between five and seven days of torture."

"If he admits that, why then can he not admit to naming Eshraq?"

"Pride." Carter spoke the word as if it were an obscenity, as if he should now go and wash out his mouth with soap.

"What in God's name has pride got to do with it?"

"Eshraq is more or less part of his family. He cannot bring himself to admit that to save himself from pain he would betray his family."

"Are you really telling me, Carter, that Furniss would sacrifice Eshraq for his pride?"

"Just my opinion, yes."

The Director General went to his safe. He obscured the combination from Henry Carter's view. He played the numbers, he opened the safe. He took out a file. The file was old, worn. The writing on the outer flap was faint, faded. "Since he was taken I've been looking into Furniss's history. I've come across nothing that indicated any vestige of vanity. I have found only a man of outstanding loyalty and steadiness. Did you know that he was in Cyprus during the emergency, in the Guards with a platoon, very young? Did you know that? I'm not surprised, because I gather that period is not on his general biography. He was on a search mission on the Troodos slopes. Some idiot decided that the brushwood should be fired so that an EOKA gang would be smoked out and driven toward the positions where Furniss's unit were waiting for them. The wind got up. The fire ran out of control. Furniss's platoon was surrounded by a wall of fire. The report I've read is from his company commander, who watched it all through field glasses. Furniss held his men together, kept them calm, waited until their clothes were damn near burned off their bodies. He waited until he saw a break in the fire wall, and he led his guardsmen through it. And all this time the platoon was under enemy fire, they lost six men. I haven't come across anyone in Century who knows that story. Obviously Furniss has never mentioned it. Does that strike you, Carter, as symptomatic of a vain or proud man?"

Carter smiled, tired, wearied. "That was about winning, sir, this is about losing."

"Well, tell me. What do you want?"

"I need some help with Furniss, sir. If you will be good enough to authorize it."

He had the number of the lorry and he had photographed the driver—that would wait, that was other business. Park looked down from the hotel room into the backyard. He saw the driver and Eshraq transfer the crates, one at a time, and heavy, from the lorry to the tail doors of the transit.

The evening was closing on Dogubeyezit.

Chapter ✛ 20

The car crunched on the drive, scattered the gravel.

Mattie heard it and he saw Henry's flickering eyebrow register the arrival of the car. Mattie coughed, as if he tried to draw attention to himself and away from the car that arrived at the country house at past ten in the evening, and Carter wasn't having it, Carter was listening for the car, and for the slammed door, and for the suburban chime on the bell in the porch. Mattie did not know what was to happen, only that something was to happen. He knew that something was to happen because Henry had been back four hours from London, and had not said what had happened in London, and had said precious little about anything else. Mattie understood. Henry's silence through the evening was because he was waiting, and now the waiting was over.

To Mattie it was absurd, the pallid smile of apology as Henry let himself out of the drawing room. He thought that it was possibly the end of the road for them both and he reckoned that he had Henry's measure. Another night, another day survived, and he would be on his way to Bibury, and back to his desk at Century.

Of course, Mattie had not asked what Henry had been up to in London. To have asked would have been weakness. Weakness was no longer a part of Mattie's world. Weakness was the villa at Tabriz and the hook on the wall and the electrical flex and the firearm that was not loaded, and that was all behind him. Weakness was scrubbed away by the trek across the mountains to the slopes of Mer Dag. On that evening, after the long silences over supper, there was a part of Mattie's mind that could no longer remember with any clarity much of the days and nights in the villa. If he had tried, and there was no damn way that he was going to try, then he might have been able to recall fragments, moments. No damn way that he was going to try ... *His name is Charlie Eshraq* ... No damn way at all.

The door opened.

Henry stood aside, made room.

The man was sturdy. The hair on his head was close cut, barely tolerating a parting. He wore a suit that was perhaps slightly too small and which therefore highlighted the muscle growth of the shoulders. His face was clean-shaven bar the stub brush moustache.

Mattie couldn't help himself. "Good God, Major, this is a surprise. Grand to see you . . ."

"I hear we've a little problem, Mr. Furniss," the man said.

The moonlight was silver on the snow peak of Ararat. When he tilted his head, dropped his gaze, then he could see the outline shadow of the transit. The heavy gates of the hotel's yard were padlocked for the night. The lorry and its driver were long gone, they would be in Erzerum tonight, he'd heard that said when he had watched from the window and seen Eshraq pay the driver off, seen him pay him off with the money that had once belonged to a Greek. Christ, and that was simple, watching the house of a Greek, with Token in tow, and doing the things that came easy to him. Nothing came easy for Park in a shared hotel room in Dogubeyezit.

Eshraq was sitting behind him, on the bed that he had chosen.

Eshraq had taken the bed farther from the door.

Eshraq ignored Park. He had laid out on the bed a series of large-scale maps of northern Iran.

Eshraq hadn't spoken for more than an hour, and Park had stood by the window for all of that time, and stared over the unmoving, unchanging vista that ran toward the distant summit of Ararat.

"Get up."

The voice rattled in Mattie's ears. There was no place of safety.

"Get up, Mr. Furniss."

But there had never been a place of safety. No safety here, no safety in the cellar of the villa in Tabriz. They merged. There was the carpet of the lounge, and the tiled floor of the cellar. There were the pictures on the wall of the lounge, and there was the hook on the wall of the cellar. There were the armchairs with the faded floral covers, and there was the iron bed frame with the straps and the stinking blanket. There was the rasp of the Major's voice, and there was the hushed clip of the investigator's voice.

The hands reached down for him.

"I said, Mr. Furniss, to get up."

The hands were at the collar of Mattie's jacket, and grasping at the shoulders of his shirt, and the jacket was too loose and did not make a good fit and was climbing up his arms and over the back of his head, and the shirt was too tight and could not be fastened at the collar and was ripping. He didn't help. He lay as lead weight.

He was pulled upright, but when the grip weakened, because his jacket was coming off him and the shirt was too torn to hold, then Mattie collapsed back onto the carpet.

He was lifted again, and the Major was panting, just as they had panted in the cellar. He was lifted to his feet, and he was held, and he was shaken, as if he were a rug. He was thrown backward. His arms were flailing and found nothing to catch, and he cracked down onto the carpet, and the back of his head hammered the floor. He gazed up. Henry stood in front of the fireplace, looking away, as if he wanted no part of this.

Mattie no longer knew how long it had been since the Major had first slapped his face. Out of the blue. A question, a deflecting answer, and the slap homing onto his cheek. The smarting at his eyes, the reddening of his cheek. But the slap across the face had been only the start.

He had been slapped, he had been kicked, he had been punched. It was not vicious, the pain was not inflicted on him for the sake of it. The pain was a humiliation and a progression. They did not want to inflict pain on him, they only wanted him to talk. The blows were harder, the kicks fiercer. They wanted to do it with the minimum . . . the bastards.

He lay on the carpet.

Mattie let his head roll to the side.

Oh, yes, Mattie had learned from the cellar in Tabriz. Kids' play this, after the cellar and the hook on the wall and the electrical flex and the unloaded weapon. He looked at Henry, and Henry had his hand over his face. Mattie let his head sag. He lay still.

He heard Carter's voice, the whinny of apprehension. "They said that he wasn't to be abused."

"He's only faking. Do you want an answer or do you not want an answer?"

"For Christ's sake, it's Mattie Furniss. . . . I want the answer, of course I want the answer, but I'll be minced if he's hurt."

"So, what's at stake, Mr. Carter?"

"A mission—God, what a mess—the life of an agent is at stake."

He was splayed out on the carpet, and he was trying to control his breathing, as a man would breathe when he was unconscious, slow and steady. The blow came between his legs. He had no warning of the kick. He cried out, and he heaved his knees into his stomach, and he rolled on the carpet, and his hands were over his groin. His eyes were squeezed shut, watering.

"Good God, Major . . ." The tremor in Carter's voice.

"He was faking, told you." And the Major had dropped down beside Mattie. Mattie felt his head lifted. He opened his eyes. He saw the Major's face a few inches from his own.

His name is Charlie Eshraq.

"Mr. Furniss, don't be a silly chap. What did you tell them?"

The merging of the face of the Major and the face of the investigator. Christ, they must think he was pretty piss poor. They were the same face, they were the same voice. Mattie Furniss did not talk, Mattie Furniss was Desk Head (Iran). And he had the second chance. He had lost the first chance, talked, cracked, broken. But he had the second chance. The pain was through his stomach, and the retching was writhing in his throat. He had the second chance.

"My name is Owens. I am an academic. A scholar of the Urartian civilization."

And he was sliding, slipping, and the blackness was closing around him.

Charlie lay on his bed. The light was off. He was close to the window and the moon silver filtered the cotton curtains. He knew that Park was awake. Park's breathing told him that he was still awake. He was packed, he was ready. He was going at the dawn. At the foot of the bed, beside the soap box, his rucksack was filled, and in the yard outside the transit was loaded with drums of electrical flex for industrial use, and under the drums were three wooden packing crates. He was going in the morning, and Park hadn't spoken since the light in the hotel room had been turned off. There was the bleat of animals in the night air, the call of the goats and the cry of the sheep, there was once the wail of a *jandarma* siren, there was the drone of the hotel's generator, there was the whirring flight of a mosquito. He was Charlie Eshraq. He was twenty-two years old. He was the man with the mission and with the target. He was not afraid of death, not his own and not the death of his enemies. . . . And why couldn't the bastard talk to him? Why in hell's name not? In the moon darkness, in the hotel room, he wanted to talk. If he had been with the dossers under the arches of Charing Cross station then he would have had someone to talk to. He was going back inside. He knew how to fire the weapon, and he knew the faces of his targets, and he knew the routes that

town. They stood my sister on a table and they put a rope around her neck. There were many hundreds of people there to watch her die, David. I am told by people who were there that when my sister stood upon the table and looked down onto the people who had come to watch her die that she smiled at them. She made the smile of a girl who was not yet a woman. It was talked about for many weeks afterward, the way that my sister smiled. . . . They kicked her off the table and they hoisted the crane up. That was how she died. They tell me that she died in great pain, that she did not die easily. There were two men who held her on the table as the executioner put the rope around her neck. I killed them as I killed the executioner. If it had been your wife, David, and not my sister, would you not have wanted money for weapons?"

"Running heroin is wrong, for me that's the beginning and the middle and the end of it."

"Because you have no love?"

"Because I have no love for people who run heroin."

"Your father is alive?"

"My father is alive."

"Do you love your father?"

"I want to go to sleep."

"Is it shaming to say that you love your father?"

"My feelings for my father, that's not your concern."

"My father was in the jail at Evin. He was a soldier. He was not a policeman, he was not in the SAVAK, he never commanded troops who were used to put down the revolt of the masses. He was an enemy of no man, and he was my father. I know about my sister, David, her last hours, and I know also something of the last hours of my father. I know that he was taken from his cell at dawn one morning out into the killing yard at Evin. He was tied to a stake in the yard, and shot there. When that has happened to your father, and your uncle has been butchered, is it wrong to want weapons?"

"You can talk all night, Eshraq. Me, I'll be sleeping."

He heard the heaving of the bed. He saw the shadow of Park's body toss as the back was turned to him.

He thought that by the next nightfall he would be far inside. He thought that at the next dusk he would be approaching the stone hovel of Majid Nazeri on the frost cold slopes of Iri Dagh. He would be where there were eagles, and where there were wolf packs, and where as the light came or as the light went there was the chance of seeing the fleeting passage of a leopard. Per-

haps that was his world. Perhaps he did not belong, never had belonged, in the world of David
Park.

"David, may I ask you a favor?"

"I doubt you'll get it, what?"

"That you take back a letter for me."

"Just a letter?"

"To a very fine man, a very kind man, a man
who knew about love."

There was the grated concession. "I'll take it."

Charlie crawled from his bed, and he went to
his rucksack and took out the envelope. The envelope had been bent while it had been lying among
his clothes and his map charts in the rucksack. He
laid the envelope on the table beside Park's bed.

He stood at the window. Carefully, slowly, he
edged aside the curtain. He looked down at the
transit. He saw the jutting nose of a Mercedes car,
and he saw the white light flash. He felt the thunder roar in his ears, and he felt the hot heat back
draft of the LAW 80.

"You should try to find love, David. Without
love then life is empty."

He had waited all evening for a call to be routed
through to the nineteenth floor.

His chauffeur was in the car park below. Houghton was yawning.

The Director General dialed the number, and they were a long time answering.

"Carter—is that you, Carter? Have you any idea of the time? It is past midnight, I have been waiting for two and a quarter hours for your call. What has Furniss said?"

The voice was faint, tinny. The scrambler connection had that effect. And the scrambler could not disguise the hesitancy of the faraway metallic voice.

"He hasn't said anything."

"Then you've a problem, Carter, by Christ you have."

"I'm aware of the problem, sir."

"My advice to you, Carter, is that you have one hour . . . I want to speak to Furniss."

He heard the telephone put down, clumsily. He heard the tramp of departing footsteps. He waited. What was the bloody man at? He didn't know how he would ever again face Furniss. He heard the footsteps returning.

"Not possible at the moment, sir, to speak to Mattie."

"Carter, understand me . . . understand your position. I'll see you gutted if harm has come to Furniss, if you turn out to be wrong. I'll have you skinned. You have one hour."

He thought that he had betrayed Furniss. He

felt deep shame. He strode out of his office, and he had no word for his personal assistant who padded behind him. He thought that he had betrayed a very good man.

The Station Officer could no longer stay awake.

On a pad beside the telephone in the bedroom was written the code of Dogubeyezit and the number of the Ararat hotel. The call from London, if it came, would be in clear. There was no difficulty in that. The codeword for a halt, a postponement, had been agreed via the teleprinter in his office before he had shut up shop for the evening. In an ideal world he should not have been snuggling against his wife's back, in his own bed, he should have been close to that wretched frontier, up in northeastern Anatolia. He should have been hugging the Iranian border, not his wife's slim back. No question of him being there. The frontier was out of bounds, the border was closed territory after the lifting of the Desk Head (Iran). He had not been told the reason that there might, possibly but not probably, be a hold put on Eshraq's movement. He had no need to know why there might conceivably be a hold. . . . If there were a hold then he would communicate it. He drifted toward sleep. He had rather enjoyed the company of the young man who had come to the park in Ankara.

A bit wild, of course. Any man going inside Iran with LAW 80's was entitled to be a bit bloody-minded. But they had thrashed out their lines of communication. Not that he would last. Not possible that he would survive.

"Terrence, is that phone going to ring tonight? There'll be murder if it does."

"Don't know, love, I really don't know."

They had not slept. They had lain on sleeping bags on the concrete floor inside the inner hall of the Guards' barracks at Maku. The investigator was among the last to push himself back up to his feet. There were some among them who prayed, and some who worked with clean cloths at the firing mechanisms of their automatic rifles. The investigator wandered out of the inner hall in search of the latrine, and after the latrine he would be in search of the communications room and news from the men who watched a hotel across the border. It was sensible of him to leave the inner hall-way for the latrine and the communications room. If he had stayed then it would have been re-marked that he had not prayed. It was hard for him to pray because the words of the Koran held no place in his mind. He had no time that early morning because his mind was filled with the vision of armor-piercing missiles and a transit van

and the man who had been named by Matthew
Furniss.

He would enjoy his meetings with Mr. Eshraq.
He thought that he might enjoy conversing with
Charlie Eshraq more than he had enjoyed talking
to Matthew Furniss.

The clock was striking in the hall.

And the dog was restless, and sometimes there
was the heavy scratching at the kitchen door, and
sometimes there was the clamor of the animal
shaking the big link chain on its throat. The dog
wouldn't sleep, not while there were still people
moving in the house and voices.

Mattie heard the clock.

The light was in his eyes. He was on the sofa
and they had stripped his shoes off and they had
heaved his feet, too, onto the sofa. His tie was off,
and the shirt buttons were undone down to his
navel. He could see nothing but the light. The
light was directed from a few feet so that it shone
directly into his face.

It was a long time since they had hit him, kicked
him, but the light was in his face and the Major
was behind him and holding his head so that he
could not look away from the light, and the bastard Henry fucking Carter was behind the light.

Questions . . . the soft and gentle drip of ques-

tions. Always the questions, and so bloody tired . . .
so hellishly tired. And the hands were on his head,
and the light was in his eyes, and the questions
dripped at his mind.

"Past all our bedtimes, Mattie. Just what you
told them . . . ?"

"A young man's life, Mattie, that's what we're
talking about. So, what did you tell them . . . ?"

"Nobody's going to blame you, Mattie, not if you
come clean. What did you tell them . . . ?"

"All that barbarian stuff, that's over, Mattie, no
more call for that, and you're with friends now.
What did you tell them . . . ?"

Too tired to think, and too tired to speak, and
his eyes burned in the light.

"I don't remember. I really don't remember."

"Got to remember, Mattie, because there is a
life hanging on you remembering what you told
them . . ."

Park watched the peace of Charlie Eshraq's sleep.

He wondered how it would be, to live with love.
He was alone and he was without love. He was
without Parrish, and Token, and Harlech, and Corinthian. He was without Ann. He was away from
what he knew. What he knew was behind him,
back at the Lane. What he knew had been

stripped from him on the nineteenth floor of the Century House.

He did not know how to find love.

He thought that going to Bogotá was a journey to escape from love . . .

There was the sharp bleep of the alarm on Eshraq's wrist. He watched as Eshraq stirred, then shook himself. Eshraq was rubbing hard at his eyes, and then sliding from his bed and going to the window. The curtain was dragged back.

There was a gray wash of early light in the room. Eshraq stretched.

"Pretty good morning to be starting a journey."

There was a glass of Scotch and water beside him. The Major sat on the sofa beside him. Henry was at the window. He had his ear cocked and he stared outside, and probably he was listening to the first shouted songs of the blackbirds.

It was the third Scotch that had been given to Mattie, and each had less water than before.

The Major had his arm, shirt-sleeved, loosely around Mattie's shoulder.

The Major smiled into Mattie's face.

"You know where you're going, Mattie, in a few hours? You know where you'll be by lunchtime? Do you know, Mattie?"

The slurred response. "I want to see a doctor,

I want to go to bed and sleep, and then I want to go home."

"A magistrate's court, Mattie."

"Bollocks."

"The charge will be conspiracy to import heroin."

"Don't be so fucking silly, Major. It's too late at night for games."

"Charlie ran heroin. Heroin subsidized him. You ran Charlie. You're going down, old boy, going down for a long time."

And the arm was round his shoulder, and Mattie was trying to push himself up from the sofa and away from the calm of the voice in his ear, and he hadn't a prayer, hadn't the strength.

"Nothing to do with me."

"Fifteen years you'll get. Very hard years, Mattie."

"Not me."

"You'll be in with the queers and the con artists and the GBH lads, in with them for fifteen years. It's all sewn up, Mattie. How's Mrs. Furniss going to cope with that? Is she going to traipse up to the Scrubs every first Tuesday in the month? And your daughters. I doubt they'll come more than once or twice."

"I don't know anything about heroin, nothing, not at all."

"Ask the magistrate to believe you, Mattie. . . . Ask him to believe that you didn't know how Charlie Eshraq, more or less a son to you, funded himself . . . and ask Mrs. Furniss to believe that you didn't know. It'll break her, Mattie, you being inside. Think on it."

"It's just not true."

"She won't have a friend in the world. Have to sell up at Bibury, of course. Couldn't face the neighbors, could she? Your neighbors'll be a bit foul, Mattie, the jokers in your cell, they have their pride and heroin they don't like."

"It's a lie, I know nothing about heroin."

"It's all been a lie, Mattie. It starts with the lie that you didn't name Charlie Eshraq. . . . Did Eshraq fuck your daughters?"

The pause, the silence. Henry had turned, Henry looked at his watch, grimaced. The Major nodded, like he thought that he was nearly dry, close to home.

"Mattie, Charlie Eshraq was running heroin out of Iran when he was fucking your daughters. Do you reckon heroin came with the service, Mattie?"

"It's not, tell me that's not true."

There was the first shrill call of the birds.

"It's what I hear."

"God . . ."

"Pushed heroin to your daughters, Eshraq did."

"The truth . . .?"

"It's you I want the truth from."

"Charlie gave that filthy stuff to my girls?"

"You've just had bad luck, Mattie, a long run of terrible luck."

There were tears running down Mattie's cheeks, and the hands that held the glass shook. The Major had raised his head and Henry could see his eyebrows aloft.

Carter said, from the window, "You named him, Mattie?"

"It wasn't my fault."

"No, Mattie, it wasn't. And nobody will hold it against you."

Henry came to the sofa. He had his notepad in his hand. He wrote a single sentence and he put a pencil in Mattie's hand, and he watched the scrawled signature made. He buffeted off the hall table on his way to the telephone and there was pandemonium in the kitchen.

The Major was at the door of the lounge, on his way out. It did not seem necessary for them to shake hands. Henry went back into the lounge. He went to Mattie. He took his arm and hoisted him, unsteady, to his feet.

"Can I go home?"

"I think that's a good idea . . . I'll drive you myself."

"Tell me that it wasn't true."

"Of course not, Mattie. It was an unforgivable
trick. I am so very sorry."

Dawn was coming, and at first sight the day
looked promising.

Chapter ❖ 21

$\mathcal{H}$e was looking down from the window and into the yard.

There was a kid, ten or eleven years old, scrubbing at the windshield, and Eshraq was hunched down by the front radiator screen and he already had the Turkish registration off and he was holding the Iranian plate in place while he screwed it tight. There were lights in the kitchens that backed on to the yard, and they threw shadows into the yard.

He was dressed and he was shaved when the telephone bell rang in the room. He was zipping shut his bag, and he had his passport and his wallet on the bed beside him, and the ticket for the flight back to Istanbul. The telephone in the room had not rung since they had arrived in Dogu-beyezit.

Below him, Eshraq had the front plate secure, and was moving to the rear of the transit. He was moving easily and casual in old jeans and trainer shoes and a service blue cotton shirt. And the telephone was still ringing.

He picked it up. He heard the clicking of big-distance connections. He heard a small voice and far away.

"Is that room twelve?"

"This is room twelve."

"Is that David Park?"

"Park speaking."

"I want to speak to Charlie."

"He's not here."

"Bugger . . . I've been cut off twice on your switchboard. Can you get him?"

"Take me a bit of time."

"And we'll get cut again, God. Name's Terence, I met him in Ankara."

He remembered the Genclik park. He had been four hundred yards back, and Eshraq and the man had walked, and there had been a tail. He remembered it very clearly. He could picture Terence. Terence was pale-skinned, almost anemic, with fair hair and a missing chin, and he looked to have come from a good school.

"If you give me the message I'll pass it."

"You can reach him?"

"If you give me the message I can reach him."

"The telephones in this country are bloody awful. . . . You guarantee he gets my message?"

"I'll pass it."

"This is an open line."

"That's stating the obvious."

"He's not to go. . . . That is a categorical instruction from my people. He is not to approach the border. He is compromised, can't say more than that. He is to return to Ankara. Do you understand the message?"

"Understood."

"Most grateful to you."

"For nothing."

"I might see you in Ankara—and many thanks for your help."

He replaced the telephone. He went back to the window. The rear plate was in place and the kid was scrubbing dust off the transit's headlights. There had been the tail in Istanbul, and the tail in Ankara. He assumed they had been better in Dogubeyezit, because he had not been certain of the men on the tail, not certain as he had been in Aksaray and the Genclik park. He was a long time at the window. There were many images in the mind of David Park. There was, in his mind,

Leroy Winston Manvers back in the corner of the cell, and he was at safe haven in Jamaica. There was the wife of Matthew Furniss at the door of a cottage in the country, and her husband was the guarantor of a heroin trafficker, and he was on safe wicket back in the United Kingdom. There was Charlie Eshraq sitting on the hood of a Sierra sedan and mocking him, and he was on safe passage out. There were images of Ann and wet towels on the bathroom floor, and images of the supercilious creature who had done the big put-down at Foreign and Commonwealth, and images of Bill Parrish stuck in an anteroom outside the office of the power and the glory at Century. He knew what was right and he knew what was wrong. He had to know. Right and wrong were the core of his life. He moved around the room. He checked each drawer of the chest and each shelf of the cupboard, and he frisked the bathroom. He made sure that they had left nothing behind. He slung on his jacket and put his passport and his airline ticket into the inner pocket with his wallet, and he threw his grip bag over his shoulder.

You will satisfy yourself that he has indeed traveled back into Iran.

At the reception desk he paid for the room. They had made out a joint bill, and he paid it. He folded the receipt carefully and put it into his wallet. He didn't give the porter a tip, because he couldn't claim on tips, and anyway he preferred to carry his own bag. He put his bag in the small hire car, locked it away from sight. He went back inside the hotel and took a side door beside the staircase, and then the corridor that led into the yard at the back. The tail doors of the transit were open and David could see the drums of electrical flex piled to the roof and stacked tight.

"What kept you?"

He started. He hadn't seen Eshraq at the front of the transit, he'd lost him. He was looking at the drums and he was wondering how successfully they hid the wooden crates.

"Just clearing up the room."

"Did I hear our phone go?"

"Front desk, confirming we were leaving today. Probably thought you were running out on them."

He saw the big smile on Eshraq's face. "I suppose you paid."

"Yes, I paid."

He saw the big smile and the big buoyancy of young Eshraq. Park didn't smile, himself, often, and it was rarer for him to know happiness. And Eshraq was smiling and he looked as though he had found true happiness.

And the big smile split.

"You hate me—yes?"

"Time you went for the border."

"Your problem, you're too serious."

"Because I've a plane to catch."

"And you'll do my letter?"

"It'll be posted."

"What I'm doing—don't you think it's worth doing?"

"Thinking about you makes me tired."

"Don't I get a good-bye and a kiss."

"Good luck, Charlie, brilliant luck."

He said that he would see Eshraq in front of the hotel. He walked back through, and out of the front doors. As he pushed them open he heard the farewell greeting from the reception clerk, and he didn't turn. He unlocked the car, and when he was inside he wound down the windows to dissipate the heat. Keys into the ignition. It was slow starting, he thought that the plugs needed cleaning. There was the blast of the horn behind him. The transit came past him. He didn't think that he would see Eshraq's face again. He thought that the last that he would see of Charlie Eshraq was a grin and a wave.

He pulled out into the traffic. By the time that he had found a space there were two lorries between himself and the transit. A wide and straight and potholed bone shaker of a road. Two lorries ahead of him he could see the transit. He drove slowly. As far as he could see ahead there was the column of commercial vehicles heading for the Customs post.

Mattie stood in the hallway.

He could hear their voices. It was typical of Harriet that she should have walked back to the front gate with Henry Carter. She had that inbred politeness, it was a part of her.

Sweet scents in his nostrils. He could smell the polish on the walnut hall table. He could smell the cut chrysanthemums that were in the vase on the shelf of the window beside the front door. Sweet sounds in his ears. He could hear the passage of the honey-searching bees in the foxgloves that lined the path between the house and the front gate, and he could hear the whine of the flies against the panes, and he could hear the purring of his cat as it brushed against his legs.

The car left.

She came back inside. She closed the front door. She latched the door and made him safe from all that had happened to him. She came to stand against him and her arms were loosely around his waist. She kissed his cheek.

"You need a jolly good shave, Mattie."

"I expect I do."

"What a dear man, that Carter."

"I suppose he is."

"He spoke so well of you, how you'd come through it all."

"Did he, darling?"

"And he said that you needed looking after. What would you like most, Mattie, most and first?"

"I'd like to sit outside in the garden, and I'd like *The Times*, and I'd like a mug of coffee with hot milk."

"He said it was pretty rotten where you'd been."

"We'll talk about it, but not yet."

"He said they're all talking about it at Century, your escape. . . . Such a nice man, he said they were all talking about what they call 'Dolphin's Run.' "

"I'll go and sit in the garden."

The sun was hardly up. There was still dew on the grass. He heard the first tractor of the day moving off to cut silage.

The road was quite straight and it ran bisecting a wide green valley. To his left was Ararat, magnificent in the sunlight. To his right was the lower summit of Tenduruk Dag. There were grazing sheep alongside the road, and when they were clear of the town they passed the folly palace of Ishak Pasha. He glanced at it. The building was above the road, dominating. He had read in the guidebook that a Kurdish chieftain in the last century had wanted the finest palace in the wide world, and he had an Armenian architect design it and build it. And when it was completed then the chieftain had had the Armenian architect's hands cut off, so that he could never design another that was as fine. . . . Rough old world, Mr. Armenian architect . . . Rough old world, Mr. Charlie Eshraq.

Far ahead, where the haze of the shimmered heat had begun to settle, he could see the flat-roofed buildings of the Turkish Customs post, and he could just make out the blood-red of the Turkish flag.

Among the fields stretching to the foothills of Ararat that was to his left and Tenduruk Dag that was to his right, he could see the brilliant scarlet oases of poppies. Where the poppy flowers were, that was a good place for the burying of Charlie Eshraq.

He eased down through the gears.

The Turkish Customs post was one old building of two stories and a sprawl of newer, more temporary buildings. A wind lifted the flag. There were troops there, pretty lackadaisical bunch, too, and there was a Customs official in the center of the road who seemed to stop, briefly, each lorry, speak to the driver, then wave it on. On the other side of the road was the queue of vehicles traveling the other way, coming out from Iran, stopped and waiting for clearance. No delays for the lorries going into Iran. The transit was two lorry lengths ahead of him. And the going was slower. One hand on the wheel, and his thumb was inches from the horn. One hand on the gear stick, and his fingers were inches from the arm that could have flashed his lights.

The transit was stationary.

The Customs official was walking down the length of a lorry and trailer, and heading for the cab of the transit. Park watched. It was what they had sent him to do. He watched the Customs official peer into the driver's window, then nod his head, then step back, then cheerfully wave the transit forward.

The lorries in front of him nudged forward. Park swung his wheel. He drove off the metaled surface and onto the stone grit of the hard shoulder.

He walked away from his car. He walked toward the buildings and the soldiers who were already seeking what shade was offered. His shirt stuck to his back, there was the shiver in his legs as he walked. He took as his place the flagpole. The wind pushed his hair across his face.

He estimated that the Iranian flag and the Iranian buildings were five hundred meters down the road. He thought that the border was at a point that was halfway between the two where a small stream crossed under the road through culvert tunnels. The road fell on its way to the tunnels, then climbed on a gradual gradient toward the Iranian buildings and the Iranian flag.

The transit was slipping away down the slope, going steadily for the dip where the culverts were set under the road. The wind in his hair, the sun in his eyes, the roar of the heavy engines in his ears.

A young officer, regular army, had strolled to stand beside him, would have seen a foreigner at the post, and wondered, been interested. There were binoculars hanging loosely at his neck. Park didn't ask. A fast, sharp smile, his finger pointing to the binoculars. He knew nothing of the Turkish, nothing of their generosity. His gesture was enough. He had the binoculars in his hand.

The transit was climbing up the slope from the stream. His vision roved ahead.

He saw the buildings of the Customs post, and huge on the wall facing the oncoming road was the image of the Imam.

Past the buildings, uniformed and armed men held back a line of lorries from further movement toward Turkey. From a side door in the largest of the buildings he saw three men duck out and run, crouching and doubled, to take up positions behind parked cars. On the far side of the road, the far side to the buildings, was a heap of sandbags, inexpertly stacked and no more than waist height. With the glasses, through the power of the binoculars, he saw the sun flash on belted ammunition. There was a man standing beside the building closest to the roadway. He wore sandals and old jeans and his shirttails weren't tucked in. He was not a young man. He was talking into a personal radio.

The transit was into Iran, heading up the shallow slope of the road.

There was the crash of the gunfire.

He started up. He clasped his hands to halt the shaking.

"It's all right, dear, just the Pottinger boy. . . . I don't mind him shooting pigeons, and I suppose I can't object at carrion crows, but I do think that killing rooks is the limit. I hope that you'll have a word with his father. . . . Here's your coffee. Mattie, darling, you look frozen. I'll get you a warmer sweater, and when you've had your coffee, you're coming straight in."

The sun was sharp on his forehead. There was the distortion of the binoculars and from the heat on the ground, but he could see well enough.

The road was clear ahead and in front of the transit, and a man in dun uniform had emerged from the ditch that ran alongside the road as soon as the transit had passed him and he was waving down the following lorry. There was a moment, as the transit came to an easy and unhurried stop beside the building, that it was the only vehicle within one hundred yards in front or behind.

Quick, fast movements. The van surrounded. He saw the men who ran forward toward the back of the van, and he saw their weapons raised to their shoulders and aimed at the transit. Carried on the wind, must have been a megaphone, he heard a shouted order. They were closing on the cab. He saw the door of the cab open. He saw the barrel shape, the tube shape, jutting out from the opened door.

There was the fire squirt.

There was the following thunder hammer of the recoil of the LAW 80.

Smoke and fire, and the building ravaged, and toy doll figures laid out in crazy posture under the galloping spread of black smoke and brilliant flames of the fire.

He saw the transit burst forward. He wondered when in hell Charlie had taken the launcher from the crates in the back of the transit. . . . He had seen the flash of the brass cartridge cases. He knew where it would come from. He knew where the stopping fire would come from.

He thought the van might have made twenty-five yards. It was lurching forward, as if the driver were trying to hit the higher gears too fast. The transit might have made twenty-five yards when the machine gun behind the sandbags opened fire, belting the transit. The van swerved, he saw that, he followed the swerve through the glasses. The van straightened. He was cold. He was not willing the escape of the van, nor was he cheering for the death of the van. He was the witness and he was watching. The transit had swerved and it had straightened and it had swerved again. It was across the road. It was against the pole that carried the telephone line from the Customs post back into the interior. The hammer of the drum, the belt of the machine gun, and the target was stationary, crippled. There was a shouting in his ear. It was the Turkish soldier, insistent but courteous. He held out his hand for his binoculars.

There was little more for him to see. There was

the bright orange glow of the ultimate explosion. He watched a dream's destruction. He thanked the officer, who was lost in concentration on the scene unfolding across the valley, and he turned and walked back toward his car. He thought that if he hurried he would still be in time to catch the flight from Van. He turned only once. When he had opened the door of the hire car he looked behind him. The sun was a high white orb, its brilliance shed by the rising pillar of smoke. Park drove away. He drove back along the straight road to Dogubeyezit, and past the sheep flocks, and past the shrill patches of scarlet. A job done, a man going home.

Chapter ❖ 22

She was first out of the chapel and Belinda and Jane were close at her back. She had dressed rather boldly and that had been her decision and without the prompting of the girls. She wore a suit of navy and a matching straw hat with a crimson ribbon. Perhaps the girls would not have approved. She had worn the same suit and hat only once before, nearly two years ago, and then she had sat in the gallery and looked down onto the investiture room. She had watched with pride as Mattie had gone forward to receive from his sovereign the medal of the Order of the British Empire. She thought it right, on this autumn morning, when the leaves cascaded across the road from the plane trees in the park, to wear

the same clothes as on that day. Mattie would
have approved, and he would have liked the way
that she held herself.

She took her place a few yards from the doorway and there was a fine spit of rain at her back,
and behind her the traffic streamed on Birdcage
Walk. The girls were on either side of her. They
were sentries positioned to protect their mother.
Not that Harriet Furniss was in need of protection. There would be no choke in her voice, no
smear on her cheek. She had been a Service wife,
and now she was a Service widow. She understood
very clearly what was expected of her.

She thought that the Director General had
aged, that his retirement had not given him a new
lease of life. His morning coat seemed too large
and his throat had thinned.

"It was kind of you to come."

It was he who had insisted on Mattie's immediate retirement.

"To pay my respects to a very gallant gentleman, Mrs. Furniss."

She knew that he had resigned from the Service
on the day the report of the internal inquiry had
reached Downing Street.

"You're looking well."

"Good of you to say so. . . . I've a little to occupy

me. . . . I shall remember your husband with nothing but admiration."

It gave her strength to see his fumbling walk toward the parade ground, the man who had sent her Mattie to his doom.

She had made it clear that she had wanted none of them to make the journey from London for the funeral. The funeral, three weeks earlier, had been family and in Bibury, she had insisted on that. Two hard years they had been, from the time that he had come home to her to the time of death and release from his personal agony. Two wretchedly hard years they had been as the will to survive had ebbed from Mattie. The new Director General stood in front of her. His face was a little puffed as though he ate too much too often at lunchtime.

"Most fittingly done, Mrs. Furniss."

"It was as Mattie would have wanted, I think."

"We miss him very much at Century."

"As he missed being there, desperately."

"They still talk about his run, it was a magnificent memory for us all. He's not forgotten."

"I expect that Iran Desk is substantially changed."

"Well, yes, very changed. Now that we have the embassy back in Tehran we are much more efficient."

"I think Mattie understood."

"Should you have any problem . . . well, you wouldn't hesitate, I hope."

"Mattie would never have left us in difficulties."

The new Director General nodded. She thought that she would have gone on the streets, put her daughters into a workshop, before she would have gone back to the Century to plead hardship. All so different now. In the last months of his life Mattie had fumed at the exchange of diplomats, the reopening of relations with the Islamic Republic of Iran. They had angered him, insulted him. She had seen those wounds on his body, she had forced herself to look at them when he was bathing and pretended that she saw nothing, and she had raged in her mind each time she saw our people and their people shaking hands on the television screen. She had no line into Century for gossip because Flossie Duggan had gone the same week that her Mattie had been brought back to her, nor did she want a line. The wind caught at her hair and she pushed it decisively back. There was a surge of men past her, faces that she did not know. She imagined them to be from the Century desks, and from the administrative departments, and few caught her eye, most avoided her gaze. Henry Carter stood in front of her, and he held a trilby across his chest. It was Henry Carter who had come down to Bibury a week after he had first brought Mattie home and who had gone out into the garden with him to report that Charlie had been killed on the Iranian border. And Mattie had never spoken the name of Charlie Eshraq, would never even let the girls refer to him, from that day to the day of his slipping, passing, going.

"So good to see you, Henry. Are you still . . . ?"

"Alas, Mrs. Furniss, no longer. I have a part-time job with the Royal Society for the Protection of Birds, the mail-order section. I get the tea towels out, and the nesting boxes."

"Was anything achieved, Henry, that spring, by any of you?"

"Desperate question, Mrs. Furniss. My opinion, it's better to believe that so much mayhem led to something positive, don't you think?"

And he was gone, before she could press him. He almost ran. They were almost all gone from the church now, and the music had stopped. There was a middle-aged man standing a few feet in front of her, making no move to come toward her. He wore an old raincoat that was too small for him and that was gathered in tight lines across his stomach, and the half-moon of his hair blew untidily in the wind. He met her gaze, he stared back at her. He was an intruder, she was sure of that, but she could not place him. She straightened her back.

"Do I know you?"

"I'm Bill Parrish."

"Have we met?"

"I came once to your house, a bit more than two years ago."

"You'll have to excuse me, I don't recall the occasion . . ."

"I'm fulfilling a promise to a friend, Mrs. Furniss. He's abroad and can't be here. Me being here is closing a file, you might say that it's shutting up shop. A very nice service, Mrs. Furniss."

She watched them all go. The old Director General was waving down a taxi, flourishing his umbrella at the driver. The new Director General was climbing into the black limousine. Henry Carter was arguing down the street with a traffic warden across the hood of an old car. Bill Parrish was striding purposefully toward Whitehall. She let the girls link their arms through her elbows. Had anything been achieved? Was there something positive? She hated them all, every last one of them who were now hurrying away to escape from the contact with the life and death of Mattie Furniss.

GERALD SEYMOUR is the author of eleven novels, including HARRY'S GAME, IN HONOR BOUND, and AN EYE FOR AN EYE. Formerly a television news reporter, the author lives with his family in the West Country of England.